GREAT GERMAN

SHORT NOVELS

AND STORIES

EDITED BY

BENNETT A. CERF

MODERN LIBRARY · NEW YORK

830
C

Random House IS THE PUBLISHER OF

THE MODERN LIBRARY

BENNETT A. CERF · DONALD S. KLOPFER · ROBERT K. HAAS

Manufactured in the United States of America

Printed by Parkway Printing Company   Bound by H. Wolff

CONTENTS

The Fifteen Stories in this volume are arranged in chronological order of the Authors' births.

———

v

CONTENTS

INTRODUCTORY NOTE

THE knowledge that this anthology would have to be limited to some 600 pages by the practical considerations that govern the manufacture of a Modern Library book, plus the fact that the German idea of a "short story" differs by some thousands of words from our own, made the ultimate selection of stories an unusually difficult task.

The result seems to me to have been well worth the trouble. The greater part of the volume is devoted to contemporary writers. The inclusion of "The Sorrows of Werther," "Amok," and "Death in Venice," meant that a dozen shorter tales by writers whose names are hall-marks in German literature had to be discarded. The purist, too, may cavil at the inclusion of Gottfried Keller and Arthur Schnitzler, who, though their medium was the German language, were not actually Germans themselves. And yet, the reader who goes through this collection from beginning to end will be able to form an impression of the whole of German literature that is comprehensive and sound. The profound sentimentality of the German soul finds its fullest expression in Goethe's "Werther," in Storm's "Immensee," in Zweig's "Amok." The century-old folk-lore of the German peasant is represented in the famous little stories by the Brothers Grimm, in "Krakatuk," and in Heine's "Gods in Exile." The sobering German sense of order and morality motivates the Schiller story and Hauptmann's "Flagman Thiel." And although the lighter touch is not too conspicuous in German literature, the inclusion of "Saint Vitalis" and Schnitzler's "Fate of the Baron," which, despite its dramatic conclusion, is told with a verve and spirit that is so very foreign to many of the other stories in this volume, serve to round out the picture.

The reader who is inclined to protest at the omission of many famous names from this collection must be reminded, too, that some of the most illustrious German authors chose other mediums than the novelette or short story, and could not, therefore, be included here.

I must say a few words about the editing of this anthology. It was entrusted originally to a gentleman who once enjoyed a considerable reputation in this town as a publisher and editor. He expressed confidence in his ability to prepare the book, and a contract was duly signed, so long ago, it seems to me, that goats were still roaming around empty lots on Park Avenue when the details were settled. At long last, a manuscript appeared, though a new generation of German authors had flowered in the interim. I was thoroughly dissatisfied with the job. Of the ten stories that this painstaking editor had managed to gather in all these years, I liked only six well enough to publish, and exercising that prerogative which is one of the few privileges still left to the publisher in these harrowing days, I threw the others into the wastebasket, and set about compiling an anthology of my own.

Six of the fifteen stories in this volume, in other words, were chosen originally by another person, but several of the six obviously would have to be included by anybody who was attempting to collect a volume of representative German stories, and I cheerfully assume the responsibility for the entire table of contents. I publish the book under my own name with the deep conviction that its literary quality will bear comparison with the finest and most famous works in the Modern Library series. That some thousands of Modern Library readers will dispute my choices in no uncertain terms, I know, from previous experience, to be a certainty. This time I shall look forward to the letters of protest with even more than the usual excitement.

I should like to conclude this note with a line of public

thanks to Mr. Alfred A. Knopf for his permission to include in this anthology so lengthy and well known a story as Thomas Mann's "Death in Venice"—a story so important to the collection, from my point of view, that I seriously believe we would have abandoned the entire project if the permission to reprint it had been denied us.

BENNETT A. CERF.

NEW YORK,
February, 1933.

THE SORROWS OF WERTHER

By Johann Wolfgang von Goethe *

Book I

May 4.

How happy I am that I am gone! My dear friend, what
a thing is the heart of man! To leave you, from whom I
have been inseparable, whom I love so dearly, and yet to
feel happy! I know you will forgive me. Have not other
attachments been specially appointed by fate to torment a
head like mine? Poor Leonora! and yet I was not to blame.
Was it my fault, that, whilst the peculiar charms of her
sister afforded me an agreeable entertainment, a passion
for me was engendered in her feeble heart? And yet am I
wholly blameless? Did I not encourage her emotions? Did
I not feel charmed at those truly genuine expressions of
nature, which, though but little mirthful in reality, so often
amused us? Did I not—but oh! what is man, that he dares
so to accuse himself? My dear friend, I promise you I will
improve; I will no longer, as has ever been my habit, continue to ruminate on every petty vexation which fortune may
dispense; I will enjoy the present, and the past shall be for
me the past. No doubt you are right, my best of friends,
there would be far less suffering amongst mankind, if men
—and God knows why they are so fashioned—did not employ their imaginations so assiduously in recalling the memory of past sorrow, instead of bearing their present lot with
equanimity.

* Translated by Orson Falk. Copyright, 1933, by the Modern
Library, Inc.

Be kind enough to inform my mother that I shall attend to her business to the best of my ability, and shall give her the earliest information about it. I have seen my aunt, and find that she is very far from being the disagreeable person our friends allege her to be. She is a lively, cheerful woman, with the best of hearts. I explained to her my mother's wrongs with regard to that part of her portion which has been withheld from her. She told me the motives and reasons of her own conduct, and the terms on which she is willing to give up the whole, and to do more than we have asked. In short, I cannot write further upon this subject at present; only assure my mother that all will go on well. And I have again observed, my dear friend, in this trifling affair, that misunderstandings and neglect occasion more mischief in the world than even malice and wickedness. At all events, the two latter are of less frequent occurrence.

In other respects I am very well off here. Solitude in this terrestrial paradise is a genial balm to my mind, and the young spring cheers with its bounteous promises my oftentimes misgiving heart. Every tree, every bush, is full of flowers; and one might wish himself transformed into a butterfly, to float about in this ocean of perfume, and find his whole existence in it.

The town itself is disagreeable; but then, all around, you find an inexpressible beauty of Nature. This induced the late Count M—— to lay out a garden on one of the sloping hills which here intersect each other with the most charming variety, and form the most lovely valleys. The garden is simple; and it is easy to perceive, even upon your first entrance, that the plan was not designed by a scientific gardener, but by a man who wished to give himself up here to the enjoyment of his own sensitive heart. Many a tear have I already shed to the memory of its departed master in a summer-house which is now reduced to ruins, but was his favorite resort, and now is mine. I shall soon be master of the place. The gardener has become attached to me within the last few days, and he will lose nothing thereby.

May 10.

A wonderful serenity has taken possession of my entire soul, like these sweet mornings of spring which I enjoy with my whole heart. I am alone, and feel the charm of existence in this spot, which was created for the bliss of souls like mine. I am so happy, my dear friend, so absorbed in the exquisite sense of mere tranquil existence, that I neglect my talents. I should be incapable of drawing a single stroke at the present moment; and yet I feel that I never was a greater artist than now. When, while the lovely valley teems with vapor around me, and the meridian sun strikes the upper surface of the impenetrable foliage of my trees, and but a few stray gleams steal into the inner sanctuary, I throw myself down among the tall grass by the trickling stream; and as I lie close to the earth, a thousand unknown plants are noticed by me: when I hear the buzz of the little world among the stalks, and grow familiar with the countless indescribable forms of the insects and flies, then I feel the presence of the Almighty who formed us in his own image, and the breath of that universal love which bears and sustains us, as it floats around us in an eternity of bliss; and then, my friend, when darkness overspreads my eyes, and heaven and earth seem to dwell in my soul and absorb its power, like the form of a beloved mistress,—then I often think with longing, Oh, would I could describe these conceptions, could impress upon paper all that is living so full and warm within me, that it might be the mirror of my soul, as my soul is the mirror of the infinite God! O my friend— but it is too much for my strength—I sink under the weight of the splendor of these visions!

May 12.

I know not whether some deceitful spirits haunt this spot, or whether it be the warm, celestial fancy in my own heart which makes everything around me seem like paradise. In front of the house is a fountain,—a fountain to which I am bound by a charm like Melusina and her sisters. Descending a gentle slope, you come to an arch, where, some twenty steps lower down, water of the clearest crystal gushes from the marble rock. The narrow wall which encloses it above, the tall trees which encircle the spot, and the coolness of the place itself,—everything imparts a pleasant but sublime impression. Not a day passes on which I do not spend an hour there. The young maidens come from the town to fetch water,—innocent and necessary employment, and formerly the occupation of the daughters of kings. As I take my rest there, the idea of the old patriarchal life is awakened around me. I see them, our old ancestors, how they formed their friendships and contracted alliances at the fountain-side; and I feel how fountains and streams were guarded by beneficent spirits. He who is a stranger to these sensations has never really enjoyed a cool repose at the side of a fountain after the fatigue of a weary summer day.

May 13.

You ask if you shall send me books. My dear friend, I beseech you, for the love of God, relieve me from such a yoke! I need no more to be guided, agitated, heated. My heart ferments sufficiently of itself. I want strains to lull me, and I find them to perfection in my Homer. Often do I strive to alloy the burning fever of my blood; and you have never witnessed anything so unsteady, so uncertain, as my heart. But need I confess this to you, my dear friend, who have so often endured the anguish of witnessing my sudden transitions from sorrow to immoderate joy, and from sweet melancholy to violent passions? I treat my poor heart like a sick child, and gratify its every fancy. Do not mention this again: there are people who would censure me for it.

May 15.

The common people of the place know me already, and love me, particularly the children. When at first I associated with them, and inquired in a friendly tone about their various trifles, some fancied that I wished to ridicule them, and turned from me in exceeding ill-humor. I did not allow that circumstance to grieve me: I only felt most keenly what I have often before observed. Persons who can claim a certain rank keep themselves coldly aloof from the common people, as though they feared to lose their importance by the contact; whilst wanton idlers, and such as are prone to bad joking, affect to descend to their level, only to make the poor people feel their impertinence all the more keenly.

I know very well that we are not all equal, nor can be so; but it is my opinion that he who avoids the common people, in order not to lose their respect, is as much to blame as a coward who hides himself from his enemy because he fears defeat.

The other day I went to the fountain, and found a young servant-girl, who had set her pitcher on the lowest step, and looked round to see if one of her companions was approaching to place it on her head. I ran down, and looked at her. "Shall I help you, pretty lass?" said I. She blushed deeply. "Oh, sir!" she exclaimed. "No ceremony!" I replied. She adjusted her head-gear, and I helped her. She thanked me, and ascended the steps.

May 17.

I have made all sorts of acquaintances, but have as yet found no society. I know not what attraction I possess for the people, so many of them like me, and attach themselves to me; and then I feel sorry when the road we pursue together goes only a short distance. If you inquire what the people are like here, I must answer, "The same as everywhere." The human race is but a monotonous affair. Most of them labor the greater part of their time for mere subsistence; and the scanty portion of freedom which remains to them so troubles them that they use every exertion to get rid of it. Oh, the destiny of man!

But they are a right good sort of people. If I occasionally forget myself, and take part in the innocent pleasures which are not yet forbidden to the peasantry, and enjoy myself,

for instance, with genuine freedom and sincerity, round a
well-covered table, or arrange an excursion or a dance
opportunely, and so forth, all this produces a good effect
upon my disposition; only I must forget that there lie dormant within me so many other qualities which molder use-
lessly, and which I am obliged to keep carefully concealed.
Ah! this thought affects my spirits fearfully. And yet to be
misunderstood is the fate of the like of us.

Alas, that the friend of my youth is gone! Alas, that I
ever knew her! I might say to myself, "You are a dreamer
to seek what is not to be found here below." But she has
been mine. I have possessed that heart, that noble soul, in
whose presence I seemed to be more than I really was, because I was all that I could be. Good heavens! did then a
single power of my soul remain unexercised? In her presence could I not display, to its full extent, that mysterious
feeling with which my heart embraces Nature? Was not our
intercourse a perpetual web of the finest emotions, of the
keenest wit, the varieties of which, even in their very eccen-
tricity, bore the stamp of genius? Alas! the few years by
which she was my senior brought her to the grave before me.
Never can I forget her firm mind or her heavenly patience.

A few days ago I met a certain young V——, a frank,
open fellow, with a most pleasing countenance. He has just
left the university, does not deem himself over-wise, but
believes he knows more than other people. He has worked
hard, as I can perceive from many circumstances and, in
short, possesses a large stock of information. When he
heard that I am drawing a good deal, and that I know Greek
(two wonderful things for this part of the country), he
came to see me, and displayed his whole store of learning,
from Batteaux to Wood, from De Piles to Winkelmann:
he assured me he had read through the first part of Sultzer's
theory, and also possessed a manuscript of Heyne's work
on the study of the antique. I allowed it all to pass.

I have become acquainted, also, with a very worthy person, the district judge, a frank and open-hearted man. I am

told it is a most delightful thing to see him in the midst of
his children, of whom he has nine. His eldest daughter especially is highly spoken of. He has invited me to go and see
him, and I intend to do so on the first opportunity. He lives
at one of the royal hunting-lodges, which can be reached
from here in an hour and a half by walking, and which he
obtained leave to inhabit after the loss of his wife, as it is
so painful to him to reside in town and at the court.

There have also come in my way a few other originals
of a questionable sort, who are in all respects undesirable,
and most intolerable in their demonstrations of friendship.
Good-by. This letter will please you; it is quite historical.

May 22.

That the life of man is but a dream, many a man has surmised heretofore; and I, too, am everywhere pursued by this
feeling. When I consider the narrow limits within which our
active and inquiring faculties are confined; when I see how
all our energies are wasted in providing for mere necessities,
which again have no further end than to prolong a wretched
existence; and then that all our satisfaction concerning certain subjects of investigation ends in nothing better than a
passive resignation, whilst we amuse ourselves painting our
prison-walls with bright figures and brilliant landscapes,—
when I consider all this, Wilhelm, I am silent. I examine my
own being, and find there a world, but a world rather of
imagination and dim desires, than of distinctness and living
power. Then everything swims before my senses, and I
smile and dream while pursuing my way through the world.

All learned professors and doctors are agreed that children do not comprehend the cause of their desires; but that
the grown-ups should wander about this earth like children,
without knowing whence they come, or whither they go,
influenced as little by fixed motives, but guided like them by
biscuits, sugar-plums, and the rod,—this is what nobody is
willing to acknowledge; and yet I think it is palpable.

I know what you will say in reply; for I am ready to admit

that they are happiest, who, like children, amuse themselves with their playthings, dress and undress their dolls, and attentively watch the cupboard, where mamma has locked up her sweet things, and, when at last they get a delicious morsel, eat it greedily, and exclaim, "More!" These are certainly happy beings; but others also are objects of envy, who dignify their paltry employments, and sometimes even their passions, with pompous titles, representing them to mankind as gigantic achievements performed for their welfare and glory. But the man who humbly acknowledges the vanity of all this, who observes with what pleasure the thriving citizen converts his little garden into a paradise, and how patiently even the poor man pursues his weary way under his burden, and how all wish equally to behold the light of the sun a little longer,—yes, such a man is at peace, and creates his own world within himself; and he is also happy, because he is a man. And then, however limited his sphere, he still preserves in his bosom the sweet feeling of liberty, and knows that he can quit his prison whenever he likes.

May 26.

You know of old my ways of settling anywhere, of selecting a little cottage in some cozy spot, and of putting up in it with every inconvenience. Here, too, I have discovered such a snug, comfortable place, which possesses peculiar charms for me.

About a league from the town is a place called Walheim.* It is delightfully situated on the side of a hill; and by proceeding along one of the footpaths which lead out of the village, you can have a view of the whole valley. A good old woman lives there, who keeps a small inn. She sells wine, beer, and coffee, and is cheerful and pleasant notwithstanding her age. The chief charm of this spot consists in two linden-trees, spreading their enormous branches over the

* The reader need not take the trouble to look for the place thus designated. We have found it necessary to change the names given in the original.

little green before the church, which is entirely surrounded by peasants' cottages, barns, and homesteads. I have seldom seen a place so retired and peaceable; and there often have my table and chair brought out from the little inn, and drink my coffee there, and read my Homer. Accident brought me to the spot one fine afternoon, and I found it perfectly deserted. Everybody was in the fields except a little boy about four years of age, who was sitting on the ground, and held between his knees a child about six months old; he pressed it to his bosom with both arms, which thus formed a sort of armchair; and notwithstanding the liveliness which sparkled in its black eyes, it remained perfectly still. The sight charmed me. I sat down upon a plow opposite, and sketched with great delight this little picture of brotherly tenderness. I added the neighboring hedge, the barn-door, and some broken cart-wheels, just as they happened to lie; and I found in about an hour that I had made a very correct and interesting drawing, without putting in the slightest thing of my own. This confirmed me in my resolution of adhering, for the future, entirely to Nature. She alone is inexhaustible, and capable of forming the greatest masters. Much may be alleged in favor of rules; as much may be likewise advanced in favor of the laws of society; an artist formed upon them will never produce anything absolutely bad or disgusting; as a man who observes the laws and obeys decorum can never be an absolutely intolerable neighbor nor a decided villain: but yet, say what you will of rules, they destroy the genuine feeling of Nature, as well as its true expression. Do not tell me "that this is too hard, that they only restrain and prune superfluous branches, etc." My good friend, I will illustrate this by an analogy. These things resemble love. A warm-hearted youth becomes strongly attached to a maiden: he spends every hour of the day in her company, wears out his health, and lavishes his fortune, to afford continual proof that he is wholly devoted to her. Then comes a man of the world, a man of place and respectability, and addresses him thus: "My good young friend, love is natural; but you must love within bounds. Divide your time: devote a portion to business, and give the hours of recreation to your mistress. Calculate your fortune; and out of the superfluity you may make her a present, only not too often,—on her birthday, and such occasions." Pursuing this advice, he may become a useful member of society, and I should advise every prince to give him an appointment; but it is all up with his love, and with his genius if he be an artist. O my friend! why is it that the torrent of genius so seldom bursts forth, so seldom rolls in full-flowing stream, overwhelming your astounded soul? Because, on either side of this stream, cold and respectable persons have taken up their abodes, and, forsooth, their summer-houses and tulip-beds would suffer from the torrent; wherefore they dig trenches, and raise embankments betimes, in order to avert the impending danger.

May 27.

I find I have fallen into raptures, declamation, and similes, and have forgotten, in consequence, to tell you what became of the children. Absorbed in my artistic contemplations, which I briefly described in my letter of yesterday, I continued sitting on the plow for two hours. Towards evening a young woman, with a basket on her arm, came running towards the children, who had not moved all that time. She exclaimed from a distance, "You are a good boy, Philip!" She gave me greeting: I returned it, rose, and approached her. I inquired if she were the mother of those pretty children. "Yes," she said; and, giving the eldest a piece of bread, she took the little one in her arms and kissed it with a mother's tenderness. "I left my child in Philip's care," she said, "whilst I went into the town with my eldest boy to buy some wheaten bread, some sugar, and an earthen pot." I saw the various articles in the basket, from which the cover had fallen. "I shall make some broth to-night for my little Hans (which was the name of the youngest) : that wild fellow, the big one, broke my pot yesterday, whilst he was scrambling with Philip for what remained of the contents." I inquired for the eldest; and she had scarcely time to tell me that he was driving a couple of geese home from the meadow, when he ran up and handed Philip an osier-twig. I talked a little longer with the woman, and found that she was the daughter of the schoolmaster, and that her husband was gone on a journey into Switzerland for some money a relation had left him. "They wanted to cheat him," she said, "and would not answer his letters; so he is gone there himself. I hope he has met with no accident, as I have heard nothing of him since his departure." I left the woman with regret, giving each of the children a kreutzer, with an additional one for the youngest, to buy some wheaten bread for his broth when she went to town next; and so we parted.

I assure you, my dear friend, when my thoughts are all in tumult, the sight of such a creature as this tranquillizes my disturbed mind. She moves in a happy thoughtlessness within the confined circle of her existence; she supplies her wants from day to day; and when she sees the leaves fall, they raise no other idea in her mind than that winter is approaching.

Since that time I have gone out there frequently. The children have become quite familiar with me; and each gets a lump of sugar when I drink my coffee, and they share my milk and bread and butter in the evening. They always receive their kreutzer on Sundays, for the good woman has orders to give it to them when I do not go there after evening service.

They are quite at home with me, tell me everything; and I am particularly amused with observing their tempers, and the simplicity of their behavior, when some of the other village children are assembled with them.

It has given me a deal of trouble to satisfy the anxiety of the mother, lest (as she says) "they should inconvenience the gentleman."

May 30.

What I have lately said of painting is equally true with respect to poetry. It is only necessary for us to know what is really excellent, and venture to give it expression; and that is saying much in few words. To-day I have had a scene which, if literally related, would make the most beautiful idyl in the world. But why should I talk of poetry and scenes and idyls? Can we never take pleasure in Nature without having recourse to art?

If you expect anything grand or magnificent from this introduction, you will be sadly mistaken. It relates merely to a peasant-lad, who has excited in me the warmest interest. As usual, I shall tell my story badly; and you, as usual, will think me extravagant. It is Walheim once more—always Walheim—which produces these wonderful phenomena.

A party had assembled outside the house under the linden-trees, to drink coffee. The company did not exactly please me; and, under one pretext or another, I lingered behind.

A peasant came from an adjoining house, and set to work arranging some part of the same plow which I had lately sketched. His appearance pleased me; and I spoke to him, inquired about his circumstances, made his acquaintance, and as is my wont with persons of that class, was soon admitted into his confidence. He said he was in the service of a young widow, who set great store by him. He spoke so much of his mistress, and praised her so extravagantly, that I could soon see he was desperately in love with her. "She is no longer young," he said; "and she was treated so badly by her former husband that she does not mean to marry again." From his account it was so evident what incomparable charms she possessed for him, and how ardently he wished she would select him to extinguish the recollection of her first husband's misconduct, that I should have to repeat his own words in order to describe the depth of the poor fellow's attachment, truth, and devotion. It would, in fact, require the gifts of a great poet to convey the expression of his features, the harmony of his voice, and the heavenly fire of his eye. No words can portray the tenderness of his every movement and of every feature; no effort of mine could do justice to the scene. His alarm lest I should misconceive his position with regard to his mistress, or question the propriety of her conduct, touched me particularly. The charming manner with which he described her form and person, which, without possessing the graces of youth, won and attached him to her, is inexpressible, and must be left to the imagination. I have never in my life witnessed or fancied or conceived the possibility of such intense devotion, such ardent affections, united with so much purity. Do not blame me if I say that the recollection of this innocence and truth is deeply impressed upon my very soul; that this picture of fidelity and tenderness haunts me everywhere: and that my own heart, as though enkindled by the flame, glows and burns within me.

I mean now to try and see her as soon as I can: or perhaps, on second thoughts, I had better not; it is better I should behold her through the eyes of her lover. To my sight, perhaps, she would not appear as she now stands before me; and why should I destroy so sweet a picture?

June 16.

"Why do I not write to you?" You lay claim to learning, and ask such a question. You should have guessed that I am well—that is to say—in a word, I have made an acquaintance who has won my heart: I have—I know not.

To give you a regular account of the manner in which I have become acquainted with the most amiable of women would be a difficult task. I am a happy and contented mortal, but a poor historian.

An angel! Nonsense! Everybody so describes his mistress; and yet I find it impossible to tell you how perfect she is, or why she is so perfect: suffice it to say she has captivated all my senses.

So much simplicity with so much understanding—so mild,

and yet so resolute—a mind so placid, and a life so active.

But all this is ugly balderdash, which expresses not a single character nor feature. Some other time—but no, not some other time, now, this very instant, will I tell you all about it. Now or never. Well, between ourselves, since I commenced my letter, I have been three times on the point of throwing down my pen, of ordering my horse, and riding out. And yet I vowed this morning that I would not ride to-day, and yet every moment I am rushing to the window to see how high the sun is.

.   .   .   .   .

I could not restrain myself—go to her I must. I have just returned, Wilhelm; and whilst I am taking supper, I will write to you. What a delight it was for my soul to see her in the midst of her dear, beautiful children,—eight brothers and sisters!

But if I proceed thus, you will be no wiser at the end of my letter than you were at the beginning. Attend, then, and I will compel myself to give you the details.

I mentioned to you the other day that I had become acquainted with S——, the district judge, and that he had invited me to go and visit him in his retirement, or rather in his little kingdom. But I neglected going, and perhaps should never have gone, if chance had not discovered to me the treasure which lay concealed in that retired spot. Some of our young people had proposed giving a ball in the country, at which I consented to be present. I offered my hand for the evening to a pretty and agreeable, but rather commonplace, sort of girl from the immediate neighborhood; and it was agreed that I should engage a carriage, and call upon Charlotte, with my partner and her aunt, to convey them to the ball. My companion informed me, as we drove along through the park to the hunting-lodge, that I should make the acquaintance of a very charming young lady. "Take care," added the aunt, "that you do not lose your heart." "Why?" said I. "Because she is already engaged to a very worthy man," she replied, "who is gone to settle his affairs upon the death of his father, and will succeed to a very considerable inheritance." This information possessed no interest for me. When we arrived at the gate, the sun was setting behind the tops of the mountains. The atmosphere was heavy; and the ladies expressed their fears of an approaching storm, as masses of low black clouds were gathering in the horizon. I relieved their anxieties by pretending to be weather-wise, although I myself had some apprehensions lest our pleasure should be interrupted.

I alighted; and a maid came to the door, and requested us to wait a moment for her mistress. I walked across the court to a well-built house, and, ascending the flight of steps in front, opened the door, and saw before me the most charming spectacle I had ever witnessed. Six children, from eleven to two years old, were running about the hall, and surrounding a lady of middle height, with a lovely figure, dressed in a robe of simple white, trimmed with pink ribbons. She was holding a rye loaf in her hand, and was cutting slices for the little ones all round, in proportion to their age and appetite. She performed her task in a graceful and affectionate manner; each claimant awaiting his turn with outstretched hands, and boisterously shouting his thanks. Some of them ran away at once, to enjoy their evening meal; whilst others, of a gentler disposition, retired to the courtyard to see the strangers, and to survey the carriage in which their Charlotte was to drive away. "Pray forgive me for giving you the trouble to come for me, and for keeping the ladies waiting: but dressing and arranging some household duties before I leave, had made me forget my children's supper; and they do not like to take it from any one but me." I uttered some indifferent compliment: but my whole soul was absorbed by her air, her voice, her manner; and I had scarcely recovered myself when she ran into her room to fetch her gloves and fan. The young ones threw inquiring glances at me from a distance; whilst I approached the youngest, a most delicious little creature. He drew back;

and Charlotte, entering at the very moment, said, "Louis, shake hands with your cousin." The little fellow obeyed willingly; and I could not resist giving him a hearty kiss, notwithstanding his rather dirty face. "Cousin," said I to Charlotte, as I handed her down, "do you think I deserve the happiness of being related to you?" She replied, with a ready smile, "Oh! I have such a number of cousins that I should be sorry if you were the most undeserving of them." In taking leave, she desired her next sister, Sophy, a girl about eleven years old, to take great care of the children, and to say good-by to papa for her when he came home from his ride. She enjoined the little ones to obey their sister Sophy as they would herself, upon which some promised that they would; but a little fair-haired girl, about six years old, looked discontented, and said, "But Sophy is not you, Charlotte; and we like you best." The two eldest boys had clambered up the carriage; and, at my request, she permitted them to accompany us a little way through the forest, upon their promising to sit very still, and hold fast.

We were hardly seated, and the ladies had scarcely exchanged compliments, making the usual remarks upon each other's dress, and upon the company they expected to meet, when Charlotte stopped the carriage, and made her brothers get down. They insisted upon kissing her hands once more; which the eldest did with all the tenderness of a youth of fifteen, but the other in a lighter and more careless manner. She desired them again to give her love to the children, and we drove off.

The aunt inquired of Charlotte whether she had finished the book she had last sent her. "No," said Charlotte; "I did not like it: you can have it again. And the one before was not much better." I was surprised, upon asking the title, to hear that it was ———.* I found penetration and character in

* We feel obliged to suppress the passage in the letter, to prevent any one from feeling aggrieved; although no author need pay much attention to the opinion of a mere girl, or that of an unsteady young man.

everything she said: every expression seemed to brighten her features with new charms, with new rays of genius, which unfolded by degrees, as she felt herself understood.

"When I was younger," she observed, "I loved nothing so much as romances. Nothing could equal my delight, when, on some holiday, I could settle down quietly in a corner, and enter with my whole heart and soul into the joys or sorrows of some fictitious Leonora. I do not deny that they even possess some charms for me yet. But I read so seldom that I prefer books suited exactly to my taste. And I like those authors best whose scenes describe my own situation in life, —and the friends who are about me whose stories touch me with interest, from resembling my own homely existence,— which, without being absolutely paradise, is, on the whole, a source of indescribable happiness."

I endeavored to conceal the emotion which these words occasioned, but it was of slight avail; for when she had expressed so truly her opinion of "The Vicar of Wakefield," and of other works, the names of which I omit,* I could no longer contain myself, but gave full utterance to what I thought of it; and it was not until Charlotte had addressed herself to the other two ladies, that I remembered their presence, and observed them sitting mute with astonishment. The aunt looked at me several times with an air of raillery, which, however, I did not at all mind.

We talked of the pleasures of dancing. "If it is a fault to love it," said Charlotte, "I am ready to confess that I prize it above all other amusements. If anything disturbs me, I go to the piano, play an air to which I have danced, and all goes right again directly."

You, who know me, can fancy how steadfastly I gazed upon her rich dark eyes during these remarks, how my very soul gloated over her warm lips and fresh, glowing cheeks, how I became quite lost in the delightful meaning

* Though the names are omitted, yet the authors mentioned deserve Charlotte's approbation, and will feel it in their hearts when they read this passage. It concerns no other person.

of her words,—so much so, that I scarcely heard the actual
expressions. In short, I alighted from the carriage like a
person in a dream, and was so lost to the dim world around
me that I scarcely heard the music which resounded from
the illuminated ball-room.

The two Messrs. Andran and a certain N. N. (I cannot
trouble myself with the names), who were the aunt's and
Charlotte's partners, received us at the carriage-door, and
took possession of the ladies whilst I followed with mine.

We commenced with a minuet. I led out one lady after
another, and precisely those who were the most disagreeable
could not bring themselves to leave off. Charlotte and her
partner began an English country dance, and you must
imagine my delight when it was their turn to dance the
figure with us. You should see Charlotte dance. She dances
with her whole heart and soul: her figure is all harmony,
elegance, and grace, as if she were conscious of nothing else,
and had no other thought or feeling; and, doubtless, for the
moment every other sensation is extinct.

She was engaged for the second country dance, but promised me the third, and assured me, with the most agreeable
freedom, that she was very fond of waltzing. "It is the
custom here," she said, "for the previous partners to waltz
together; but my partner is an indifferent waltzer, and will
feel delighted if I save him the trouble. Your partner is not
allowed to waltz, and, indeed, is equally incapable: but I
observed during the country dance that you waltz well; so,
if you will waltz with me, I beg you would propose it to my
partner, and I will propose it to yours." We agreed, and it
was arranged that our partners should mutually entertain
each other.

We set off, and at first delighted ourselves with the usual
graceful motions of the arms. With what grace, with what
ease, she moved! When the waltz commenced, and the
dancers whirled round each other in the giddy maze, there
was some confusion, owing to the incapacity of some of the
dancers. We judiciously remained still, allowing the others

to weary themselves; and when the awkward dancers had withdrawn, we joined in, and kept it up famously together with one other couple,—Andran and his partner. Never did I dance more lightly. I felt myself more than mortal, holding this loveliest of creatures in my arms, flying with her as rapidly as the wind, till I lost sight of every other object; and oh, Wilhelm, I vowed at that moment, that a maiden whom I loved, or for whom I felt the slightest attachment, never, never should waltz with any one else but with me, if I went to perdition for it!—you will understand this.

We took a few turns in the room to recover our breath. Charlotte sat down, and felt refreshed by partaking of some oranges which I had secured,—the only ones that had been left; but at every slice which from politeness she offered to her neighbors, I felt as though a dagger went through my heart.

We were the second couple in the third country dance. As we were going down (and Heaven knows with what ecstasy I gazed at her arms and eyes, beaming with the sweetest feeling of pure and genuine enjoyment), we passed a lady whom I had noticed for her charming expression of countenance, although she was no longer young. She looked at Charlotte with a smile, then holding up her finger in a threatening attitude, repeated twice in a very significant tone of voice the name of "Albert."

"Who is Albert," said I to Charlotte, "if it is not impertinent to ask?" She was about to answer, when we were obliged to separate, in order to execute a figure in the dance; and as we crossed over again in front of each other, I perceived she looked somewhat pensive. "Why need I conceal it from you?" she said, as she gave me her hand for the promenade. "Albert is a worthy man, to whom I am engaged." Now, there was nothing new to me in this (for the girls had told me of it on the way); but it was so far new that I had not thought of it in connection with her whom in so short a time I had learned to prize so highly. Enough. I became confused, got out in the figure, and occasioned general confusion; so that it required all Charlotte's presence of mind to set me right by pulling and pushing me into my proper place.

The dance was not yet finished when the lightning which had for some time been seen in the horizon, and which I had asserted to proceed entirely from heat, grew more violent; and the thunder was heard above the music. When any distress or terror surprises us in the midst of our amusements, it naturally makes a deeper impression than at other times, either because the contrast makes us more keenly susceptible, or rather perhaps because our senses are then more open to impressions, and the shock is consequently stronger. To this cause I must ascribe the fright and shrieks of the ladies. One sagaciously sat down in a corner with her back to the window, and held her fingers to her ears; a second knelt down before her, and hid her face in her lap; a third threw herself between them, and embraced her sister with a thousand tears; some insisted on going home; others, unconscious of their actions, wanted sufficient presence of mind to repress the impertinence of their young partners, who sought to direct to themselves those sighs which the lips of our agitated beauties intended for heaven. Some of the gentlemen had gone downstairs to smoke a quiet cigar, and the rest of the company gladly embraced a happy suggestion of the hostess to retire into another room which was provided with shutters and curtains. We had hardly got there, when Charlotte placed the chairs in a circle; and when the company had sat down in compliance with her request, she forthwith proposed a round game.

I noticed some of the company prepare their mouths and draw themselves up at the prospect of some agreeable forfeit. "Let us play at counting," said Charlotte. "Now, pay attention: I shall go round the circle from right to left; and each person is to count, one after the other, the number that comes to him, and must count fast; whoever stops or mistakes is to have a box on the ear, and so on, till we have counted a thousand." It was delightful to see the fun. She went round the circle with upraised arm. "One," said the first; "two," the second; "three," the third; and so on, till Charlotte went faster and faster. One made a mistake, instantly a box on the ear; and amid the laughter that ensued, came another box; and so on, faster and faster. I myself came in for two. I fancied they were harder than the rest, and felt quite delighted. A general laughter and confusion put an end to the game long before we had counted as far as a thousand. The party broke up into little separate knots; the storm had ceased, and I followed Charlotte into the ballroom. On the way she said, "The game banished their fears of the storm." I could make no reply. "I myself," she continued, "was as much frightened as any of them; but by affecting courage, to keep up the spirits of the others, I forgot my apprehensions." We went to the window. It was still thundering at a distance; a soft rain was pouring down over the country, and filled the air around us with delicious odors. Charlotte leaned forward on her arm; her eyes wandered over the scene; she raised them to the sky, and then turned them upon me; they were moistened with tears; she placed her hand on mine and said, "Klopstock!" At once I remembered the magnificent ode which was in her thoughts; I felt oppressed with the weight of my sensations, and sank under them. It was more than I could bear. I bent over her hand, kissed it in a stream of delicious tears, and again looked up to her eyes. Divine Klopstock! why didst thou not see thy apotheosis in those eyes? And thy name, so often profaned, would that I never heard it repeated!

June 19.

I no longer remember where I stopped in my narrative; I only know it was two in the morning when I went to bed; and if you had been with me, that I might have talked instead of writing to you, I should, in all probability, have kept you up till daylight.

I think I have not yet related what happened as we rode home from the ball, nor have I time to tell you now. It was

a most magnificent sunrise; the whole country was refreshed, and the rain fell drop by drop from the trees in the
forest. Our companions were asleep. Charlotte asked me if
I did not wish to sleep also, and begged of me not to make
any ceremony on her account. Looking steadfastly at her, I
answered, "As long as I see those eyes open, there is no fear
of my falling asleep." We both continued awake till we
reached her door. The maid opened it softly, and assured
her, in answer to her inquiries, that her father and the
children were well, and still sleeping. I left her, asking permission to visit her in the course of the day. She consented,
and I went; and since that time sun, moon, and stars may
pursue their course: I know not whether it is day or night;
the whole world is nothing to me.

June 21.

My days are as happy as those reserved by God for his
elect; and whatever be my fate hereafter, I can never say
that I have not tasted joy,—the purest joy of life. You know
Walheim. I am now completely settled there. In that spot I
am only half a league from Charlotte: and there I enjoy
myself, and taste all the pleasures which can fall to the lot
of man.

Little did I imagine, when I selected Walheim for my
pedestrian excursions, that all heaven lay so near it. How
often, in my wanderings from the hillside or from the
meadows across the river, have I beheld this hunting-lodge,
which now contains within it all the joy of my heart!

I have often, my dear Wilhelm, reflected on the eagerness
men feel to wander and make new discoveries, and upon
that secret impulse which afterwards inclines them to return
to their narrow circle, conform to the laws of custom, and
embarrass themselves no longer with what passes around
them.

It is so strange how, when I came here first, and gazed
upon that lovely valley from the hillside, I felt charmed
with the entire scene surrounding me. The little wood oppo-

June 29.

The day before yesterday the physician came from the town to pay a visit to the judge. He found me on the floor playing with Charlotte's children. Some of them were scrambling over me, and others romped with me; and as I caught and tickled them, they made a great noise. The doctor is a formal sort of personage; he adjusts the plaits of his ruffles and continually settles his frill whilst he is talking to you; and he thought my conduct beneath the dignity of a sensible man. I could perceive this by his countenance; but I did not suffer myself to be disturbed. I allowed him to continue his wise conversations, while I rebuilt the children's card-houses for them as fast as they threw them down. He went about the town afterwards, complaining that the judge's children were spoiled enough before, but that now Werther was completely ruining them.

Yes, my dear Wilhelm, nothing on this earth affects my heart so much as children. When I look on at their doings; when I mark in the little creatures the seeds of all those virtues and qualities which they will one day find so indispensable; when I behold in the obstinate all the future firmness and constancy of a noble character, in the capricious that levity and gayety of temper which will carry them lightly over the dangers and troubles of life, their whole nature simple and unpolluted,—then I call to mind the golden words of the Great Teacher of mankind, "Unless ye become like one of these." And now, my friend, these children, who are our equals, whom we ought to consider as models,—we treat them as though they were our subjects. They are allowed no will of their own. And have we, then, none ourselves? Whence comes our exclusive right? Is it because we are older and more experienced? Great God! from the height of thy heaven thou beholdest great children and little children, and no others; and thy Son has long since declared which afford thee greatest pleasure. But they believe in him, and hear him not,—that, too, is an old story;

site,—how delightful to sit under its shade! How view from that point of rock! Then that delightful c hills, and the exquisite valleys at their feet! Could wander and lose myself amongst them! I went, and ret without finding what I wished. Distance, my friend, i futurity. A dim vastness is spread before our souls; the ceptions of our mind are as obscure as those of our vis and we desire earnestly to surrender up our whole be that it may be filled with the complete and perfect bliss one glorious emotion. But alas! when we have attained o object, when the distant *there* becomes the present *here,* is changed; we are as poor and circumscribed as ever, an our souls still languish for unattainable happiness.

So does the restless traveler pant for his native soil, and find in his own cottage, in the arms of his wife, in the affections of his children, and in the labor necessary for their support, that happiness which he had sought in vain through the wide world.

When in the morning at sunrise I go out to Walheim and with my own hands gather in the garden the peas which are to serve for my dinner; when I sit down to shell them, and read my Homer during the intervals, and then, selecting a saucepan from the kitchen, fetch my own butter, put my mess on the fire, cover it up, and sit down to stir it as occasion requires,—I figure to myself the illustrious suitors of Penelope, killing, dressing, and preparing their own oxen and swine. Nothing fills me with a more pure and genuine sense of happiness than those traits of patriarchal life which, thank Heaven! I can imitate without affectation. Happy is it, indeed, for me that my heart is capable of feeling the same simple and innocent pleasure as the peasant whose table is covered with food of his own rearing, and who not only enjoys his meal, but remembers with delight the happy days and sunny mornings when he planted it, the soft evenings when he watered it, and the pleasure he experienced in watching its daily growth.

and they train their children after their own image, etc.

Adieu, Wilhelm. I will not further bewilder myself with this subject.

July 1.

The consolation Charlotte can bring to an invalid I experience from my own heart, which suffers more from her absence than many a poor creature lingering on a bed of sickness. She is gone to spend a few days in the town with a very worthy woman, who is given over by the physicians, and wishes to have Charlotte near her in her last moments. I accompanied her last week on a visit to the vicar of S——, a small village in the mountains, about a league hence. We arrived about four o'clock. Charlotte had taken her little sister with her. When we entered the vicarage court, we found the good old man sitting on a bench before the door, under the shade of two large walnut-trees. At the sight of Charlotte he seemed to gain new life, rose, forgot his stick, and ventured to walk towards her. She ran to him, and made him sit down again; then placing herself by his side, she gave him a number of messages from her father, and then caught up his youngest child,—a dirty, ugly little thing, the joy of his old age,—and kisse it. I wish you could have witnessed her attention to th old man,—how she raised her voice on account of his deafness; how she told him of healthy young people who had been carried off when it was least expected; praised the virtues of Carlsbad, and commended his determination to spend the ensuing summer there; and assured him that he looked better and stronger than he did when she saw him last. I, in the meantime, paid attention to his good lady. The old man seemed quite in spirits; and as I could not help admiring the beauty of the walnut-trees, which formed such an agreeable shade over our heads, he began, though with some little difficulty, to tell us their history. "As to the oldest," said he, "we do not know who planted it,—some say one clergyman, and some another; but the younger one, there behind us, is exactly

the age of my wife,—fifty years old next October. Her
father planted it in the morning, and in the evening she
came into the world. My wife's father was my predecessor
here, and I cannot tell you how fond he was of that tree;
and it is fully as dear to me. Under the shade of that very
tree, upon a log of wood, my wife was seated knitting when
I, a poor student, came into this court for the first time,
just seven and twenty years ago." Charlotte inquired for
his daughter. He said she was gone with Herr Schmidt to
the meadows, and was with the haymakers. The old man
then resumed his story, and told us how his predecessor
had taken a fancy to him, as had his daughter likewise;
and how he had become first his curate, and subsequently
his successor. He had scarcely finished his story when his
daughter returned through the garden, accompanied by the
above-mentioned Herr Schmidt. She welcomed Charlotte
affectionately, and I confess I was much taken with her
appearance. She was a lively-looking, good-humored brunette, quite competent to amuse one for a short time in the
country. Her lover (for such Herr Schmidt evidently appeared to be) was a polite, reserved personage, and would not
join our conversation, notwithstanding all Charlotte's endeavors to draw him out. I was much annoyed at observing,
by his countenance, that his silence did not arise from want
of talent, but from caprice and ill-humor. This subsequently
became very evident, when we set out to take a walk, and
Frederica joining Charlotte, with whom I was talking, the
worthy gentleman's face, which was naturally rather somber, became so dark and angry that Charlotte was obliged
to touch my arm and remind me that I was talking too
much to Frederica. Nothing distresses me more than to see
men torment each other; particularly when in the flower of
their age, in the very season of pleasure, they waste their
few short days of sunshine in quarrels and disputes, and
only perceive their error when it is too late to repair it.
This thought dwelt upon my mind; and in the evening,
when we returned to the vicar's, and were sitting round the

table with our bread and milk, the conversation turned on the joys and sorrows of the world, I could not resist the temptation to inveigh bitterly against ill-humor. "We are apt," said I, "to complain, but with very little cause, that our happy days are few and our evil days many. If our hearts were always disposed to receive the benefits Heaven sends us, we should acquire strength to support evil when it comes." "But," observed the vicar's wife, "we cannot always command our tempers, so much depends upon the constitution; when the body suffers, the mind is ill at ease." "I acknowledge that," I continued; "but we must consider such a disposition in the light of a disease, and inquire whether there is no remedy for it." "I should be glad to hear one," said Charlotte. "At least, I think very much depends upon ourselves; I know it is so with me. When anything annoys me, and disturbs my temper, I hasten into the garden, hum a couple of country dances, and it is all right with me directly." "That is what I meant," I replied. "Ill-humor resembles indolence: it is natural to us; but if once we have courage to exert ourselves, we find our work run fresh from our hands, and we experience in the activity from which we shrank a real enjoyment." Frederica listened very attentively; and the young man objected that we were not masters of ourselves, and still less so of our feelings. "The question is about a disagreeable feeling," I added, "from which every one would willingly escape, but none know their own power without trial. Invalids are glad to consult physicians, and submit to the most scrupulous regimen, the most nauseous medicines, in order to recover their health." I observed that the good old man inclined his head, and exerted himself to hear our discourse; so I raised my voice, and addressed myself directly to him. "We preach against a great many crimes," I observed, "but I never remember a sermon delivered against ill-humor." "That may do very well for your town clergymen," said he; "country people are never ill-humored, though, indeed, it might be useful occasionally,—to my wife, for instance, and the judge." We all laughed, as did he likewise very cordially, till he fell into a fit of coughing, which interrupted our conversation for a time. Herr Schmidt resumed the subject. "You call ill-humor a crime," he remarked, "but I think you use too strong a term." "Not at all," I replied, "if that deserves the name which is so pernicious to ourselves and our neighbors. Is it not enough that we want the power to make one another happy,—must we deprive each other of the pleasure which we can all make for ourselves? Show me the man who has the courage to hide his ill-humor, who bears the whole burden himself without disturbing the peace of those around him. No; ill-humor arises from an inward consciousness of our own want of merit,—from a discontent which ever accompanies that envy which foolish vanity engenders. We see people happy whom we have not made so, and cannot endure the sight." Charlotte looked at me with a smile; she observed the emotion with which I spoke; and a tear in the eyes of Frederica stimulated me to proceed. "Woe unto those," I said, "who use their power over a human heart to destroy the simple pleasures it would naturally enjoy! All the favors, all the attentions, in the world cannot compensate for the loss of that happiness which a cruel tyranny has destroyed." My heart was full as I spoke. A recollection of many things which had happened pressed upon my mind, and filled my eyes with tears. "We should daily repeat to ourselves," I exclaimed, "that we should not interfere with our friends, unless to leave them in possession of their own joys, and increase their happiness by sharing it with them! But when their souls are tormented by a violent passion, or their hearts rent with grief, is it in your power to afford them the slightest consolation?

"And when the last fatal malady seizes the being whose untimely grave you have prepared, when she lies languid and exhausted before you, her dim eyes raised to heaven, and the damp of death upon her pallid brow,—then you stand at her bedside like a condemned criminal, with the bitter feeling that your whole fortune could not save her;

and the agonizing thought wrings you that all your efforts are powerless to impart even a moment's strength to the departing soul, or quicken her with a transitory consolation."

At these words the remembrance of a similar scene at which I had been once present fell with full force upon my heart. I buried my face in my handkerchief, and hastened from the room, and was only recalled to my recollection by Charlotte's voice, who reminded me that it was time to return home. With what tenderness she chid me on the way for the too eager interest I took in everything! She declared it would do me injury, and that I ought to spare myself. Yes, my angel! I will do so for your sake.

July 6.

She is still with her dying friend, and is still the same bright, beautiful creature whose presence softens pain, and sheds happiness around whichever way she turns. She went out yesterday with her little sisters: I knew it, and went to meet them; and we walked together. In about an hour and a half we returned to the town. We stopped at the spring I am so fond of, and which is now a thousand times dearer to me than ever. Charlotte seated herself upon the low wall, and we gathered about her. I looked round, and recalled the time when my heart was unoccupied and free. "Dear fountain," I said, "since that time I have no more come to enjoy cool repose by thy fresh stream; I have passed thee with careless steps, and scarcely bestowed a glance upon thee." I looked down, and observed Charlotte's little sister, Jane, coming up the steps with a glass of water. I turned towards Charlotte, and I felt her influence over me. Jane at the moment approached with the glass. Her sister, Marianne, wished to take it from her. "No!" cried the child, with the sweetest expression of face, "Charlotte must drink first."

The affection and simplicity with which this was uttered so charmed me that I sought to express my feelings by catching up the child and kissing her heartily. She was frightened, and began to cry. "You should not do that," said Charlotte. I felt perplexed. "Come, Jane," she continued, taking her hand and leading her down the steps again, "it is no matter; wash yourself quickly in the fresh water." I stood and watched them; and when I saw the little dear rubbing her cheeks with her wet hands, in full belief that all the impurities contracted from my ugly beard would be washed off by the miraculous water, and how, though Charlotte said it would do, she continued still to wash with all her might, as though she thought too much were better than too little, I assure you, Wilhelm, I never attended a baptism with greater reverence; and when Charlotte came up from the well, I could have prostrated myself as before the prophet of an Eastern nation.

In the evening I could not resist telling the story to a person who, I thought, possessed some natural feeling, because he was a man of understanding. But what a mistake I made! He maintained it was very wrong of Charlotte,— that we should not deceive children,—that such things occasioned countless mistakes and superstitions, from which we were bound to protect the young. It occurred to me, then, that this very man had been baptized only a week before; so I said nothing further, but maintained the justice of my own convictions. We should deal with children as God deals with us,—we are happiest under the influence of innocent delusions.

July 8.

What a child is man that he should be so solicitous about a look! What a child is man! We had been to Walheim: the ladies went in a carriage; but during our walk I thought I saw in Charlotte's dark eyes—I am a fool—but forgive me! you should see them,—those eyes. However, to be brief (for my own eyes are weighed down with sleep), you must know, when the ladies stepped into their carriage again, young W. Seldstadt, Andran, and I were standing about the door. They are a merry set of fellows, and they were

all laughing and joking together. I watched Charlotte's eyes.
They wandered from one to the other; but they did not
light on me,—on me, who stood there motionless, and who
saw nothing but her! My heart bade her a thousand times
adieu, but she noticed me not. The carriage drove off, and
my eyes filled with tears. I looked after her: suddenly I saw
Charlotte's bonnet leaning out of the window, and she turned
to look back,—was it at me? My dear friend, I know not;
and in this uncertainty I find consolation. Perhaps she
turned to look at me. Perhaps! Good-night—what a child
I am!

July 10.

You should see how foolish I look in company when her
name is mentioned, particularly when I am asked plainly
how I like her. How I like her!—I detest the phrase. What
sort of creature must he be who merely liked Charlotte,
whose whole heart and senses were not entirely absorbed
by her? Like her! Some one asked me lately how I liked
Ossian.

July 11.

Madame M—— is very ill. I pray for her recovery, because Charlotte shares my sufferings. I see her occasionally
at my friend's house, and to-day she has told me the strangest circumstance. Old M—— is a covetous, miserly fellow,
who has long worried and annoyed the poor lady sadly; but
she has borne her afflictions patiently. A few days ago, when
the physician informed us that her recovery was hopeless,
she sent for her husband (Charlotte was present), and
addressed him thus: "I have something to confess which
after my decease may occasion trouble and confusion. I
have hitherto conducted your household as frugally and
economically as possible, but you must pardon me for having defrauded you for thirty years. At the commencement
of our married life you allowed a small sum for the wants
of the kitchen and the other household expenses. When our
establishment increased and our property grew larger, I

could not persuade you to increase the weekly allowance in proportion; in short, you know that when our wants were greatest, you required me to supply everything with seven florins a week. I took the money from you without an observation, but made up the weekly deficiency from the money-chest,—as nobody would suspect your wife of robbing the household bank. But I have wasted nothing, and should have been content to meet my eternal Judge without this confession, if she, upon whom the management of your establishment will devolve after my decease, would be free from embarrassment upon your insisting that the allowance made to me, your former wife, was sufficient."

I talked with Charlotte of the inconceivable manner in which men allow themselves to be blinded; how any one could avoid suspecting some deception, when seven florins only were allowed to defray expenses twice as great. But I have myself known people who believed, without any visible astonishment, that their house possessed the prophet's never-failing cruse of oil.

July 13.

No, I am not deceived. In her dark eyes I read a genuine interest in me and in my fortunes. Yes, I feel it; and I may believe my own heart which tells me—dare I say it?—dare I pronounce the divine words?—that she loves me!

That she loves me! How the idea exalts me in my own eyes! And as you can understand my feelings, I may say to you, how I honor myself since she loves me!

Is this presumption, or is it a consciousness of the truth? I do not know a man able to supplant me in the heart of Charlotte; and yet when she speaks of her betrothed with so much warmth and affection, I feel like the soldier who has been stripped of his honors and titles, and deprived of his sword.

July 16.

How my heart beats when by accident I touch her finger, or my feet meet hers under the table! I draw back as if from a furnace; but a secret force impels me forward again, and my senses become disordered. Her innocent, unconscious heart never knows what agony these little familiarities inflict upon me. Sometimes when we are talking she lays her hand upon mine, and in the eagerness of conversation comes closer to me, and her balmy breath reaches my lips,—when I feel as if lightning had struck me, and that I could sink into the earth. And yet, Wilhelm, with all this heavenly confidence,—if I know myself, and should ever dare—you understand me. No, no! my heart is not so corrupt,—it is weak, weak enough—but is not that a degree of corruption?

She is to me a sacred being. All passion is still in her presence; I cannot express my sensations when I am near her. I feel as if my soul beat in every nerve of my body. There is a melody which she plays on the piano with angelic skill,—so simple is it, and yet so spiritual! It is her favorite air; and when she plays the first note, all pain, care, and sorrow disappear from me in a moment.

I believe every word that is said of the magic of ancient music. How her simple song enchants me! Sometimes, when I am ready to commit suicide, she sings that air; and instantly the gloom and madness which hung over me are dispersed, and I breathe freely again.

July 18.

Wilhelm, what is the world to our hearts without love? What is a magic-lantern without light? You have but to kindle the flame within, and the brightest figures shine on the white wall; and if love only show us fleeting shadows, we are yet happy, when, like mere children, we behold them, and are transported with the splendid phantoms. I have not been able to see Charlotte to-day. I was prevented by company from which I could not disengage myself. What was to be done? I sent my servant to her house, that I might at least see somebody to-day who had been near her. Oh, the impatience with which I waited for his return, the joy with

which I welcomed him! I should certainly have caught him
in my arms, and kissed him, if I had not been ashamed.

It is said that the Bonona stone, when placed in the sun,
attracts the rays, and for a time appears luminous in the
dark. So was it with me and this servant. The idea that
Charlotte's eyes had dwelt on his countenance, his cheek,
his very apparel, endeared them all inestimably to me, so that
at the moment I would not have parted from him for a
thousand crowns. His presence made me so happy! Beware
of laughing at me, Wilhelm. Can that be a delusion which
makes us happy?

July 19.

"I shall see her to-day!" I exclaim with delight, when I
rise in the morning, and look out with gladness of heart at
the bright, beautiful sun. "I shall see her to-day!" And then
I have no further wish to form; all, all is included in that
one thought.

July 20.

I cannot assent to your proposal that I should accompany
the ambassador to ——. I do not love subordination; and
we all know that he is a rough, disagreeable person to be
connected with. You say my mother wishes me to be employed. I could not help laughing at that. Am I not sufficiently employed? And is it not in reality the same, whether
I shell peas or count lentils? The world runs on from one
folly to another; and the man who, solely from regard to
the opinion of others, and without any wish or necessity of
his own, toils after gold, honor, or any other phantom, is
no better than a fool.

July 24.

You insist so much on my not neglecting my drawing,
that it would be as well for me to say nothing as to confess
how little I have lately done.

I never felt happier, I never understood Nature better,

even down to the veriest stem or smallest blade of grass; and yet I am unable to express myself : my powers of execution are so weak, everything seems to swim and float before me, so that I cannot make a clear, bold outline. But I fancy I should succeed better if I had some clay or wax to model. I shall try, if this state of mind continues much longer, and will take to modeling, if I only knead dough.

I have commenced Charlotte's portrait three times, and have as often disgraced myself. This is the more annoying, as I was formerly very happy in taking likenesses. I have since sketched her profile, and must content myself with that.

July 25.

Yes, dear Charlotte! I will order and arrange everything. Only give me more commissions, the more the better. One thing, however, I must request : use no more writing-sand with the dear notes you send me. To-day I raised your letter hastily to my lips, and it set my teeth on edge.

July 26.

I have often determined not to see her so frequently. But who could keep such a resolution? Every day I am exposed to the temptation, and promise faithfully that to-morrow I will really stay away; but when to-morrow comes, I find some irresistible reason for seeing her; and before I can account for it, I am with her again. Either she has said on the previous evening, "You will be sure to call to-morrow," —and who could stay away then?—or she gives me some commission, and I find it essential to take her the answer in person; or the day is fine, and I walk to Walheim; and when I am there, it is only half a league farther to her. I am within the charmed atmosphere, and soon find myself at her side. My grandmother used to tell us a story of a mountain of loadstone. When any vessels came near it, they were instantly deprived of their ironwork; the nails flew to the mountain, and the unhappy crew perished amidst the disjointed planks.

July 30.

Albert is arrived, and I must take my departure. Were he the best and noblest of men, and I in every respect his inferior, I could not endure to see him in possession of such a perfect being. Possession!—enough, Wilhelm; her betrothed is here,—a fine, worthy fellow, whom one cannot help liking. Fortunately I was not present at their meeting. It would have broken my heart! And he is so considerate: he has not given Charlotte one kiss in my presence. Heaven reward him for it! I must love him for the respect with which he treats her. He shows a regard for me; but for this I suspect I am more indebted to Charlotte than to his own fancy for me. Women have a delicate tact in such matters, and it should be so. They cannot always succeed in keeping two rivals on terms with each other; but when they do, they are the only gainers.

I cannot help esteeming Albert. The coolness of his temper contrasts strongly with the impetuosity of mine, which I cannot conceal. He has a great deal of feeling, and is fully sensible of the treasure he possesses in Charlotte. He is free from ill-humor, which you know is the fault I detest most.

He regards me as a man of sense; and my attachment to Charlotte, and the interest I take in all that concerns her, augment his triumph and his love. I shall not inquire whether he may not at times tease her with some little jealousies; as I know that, were I in his place, I should not be entirely free from such sensations.

But, be that as it may, my pleasure with Charlotte is over. Call it folly or infatuation, what signifies a name? The thing speaks for itself. Before Albert came, I knew all that I know now. I knew I could make no pretensions to her, nor did I offer any,—that is, as far as it was possible, in the presence of so much loveliness, not to pant for its enjoyment. And now behold me, like a silly fellow, staring with astonishment when another comes in, and deprives me of my love.

I bite my lips, and feel infinite scorn for those who tell me to be resigned, because there is no help for it. Let me escape from the yoke of such silly subterfuges! I ramble through the woods; and when I return to Charlotte, and find Albert sitting by her side in the summer-house in the garden, I am unable to bear it, behave like a fool, and commit a thousand extravagances. "For Heaven's sake," said Charlotte to-day, "let us have no more scenes like those of last night! You terrify me when you are so violent." Between ourselves, I am always away now when he visits her; and I feel delighted when I find her alone.

Aug. 8.

Believe me, dear Wilhelm, I did not allude to you when I spoke so severely of those who advise resignation to inevitable fate. I did not think it possible for you to indulge such a sentiment. But in fact you are right. I only suggest one objection. In this world one is seldom reduced to make a selection between two alternatives. There are as many varieties of conduct and opinion as there are turns of feature between an aquiline nose and a flat one.

You will, therefore, permit me to concede your entire argument, and yet contrive means to escape your dilemma. Your position is this, I hear you say: "Either you have hopes of obtaining Charlotte, or you have none. Well, in the first case, pursue your course, and press on to the fulfillment of your wishes. In the second, be a man, and shake off a miserable passion, which will enervate and destroy you." My dear friend, this is well and easily said.

But would you require a wretched being, whose life is slowly wasting under a lingering disease, to despatch himself at once by the stroke of a dagger? Does not the very disorder which consumes his strength deprive him of the courage to effect his deliverance?

You may answer me, if you please, with a similar analogy:

"Who would not prefer the amputation of an arm to the periling of life by doubt and procrastination?" But I know not if I am right, and let us leave these comparisons.

Enough! There are moments, Wilhelm, when I could rise up and shake it all off, and when, if I only knew where to go, I could fly from this place.

The same Evening.

My diary, which I have for some time neglected, came before me to-day; and I am amazed to see how deliberately I have entangled myself step by step. To have seen my position so clearly, and yet to have acted so like a child! Even still I behold the result plainly, and yet have no thought of acting with greater prudence.

Aug. 10.

If I were not a fool, I could spend the happiest and most delightful life here. So many agreeable circumstances, and of a kind to insure a worthy man's happiness, are seldom united. Alas! I feel it too sensibly,—the heart alone makes our happiness! To be admitted into this most charming family, to be loved by the father as a son, by the children as a father, and by Charlotte!—then the noble Albert, who never disturbs my happiness by any appearance of ill-humor, receiving me with the heartiest affection, and loving me, next to Charlotte, better than all the world! Wilhelm, you would be delighted to hear us in our rambles, and conversations about Charlotte. Nothing in the world can be more absurd than our connection, and yet the thought of it often moves me to tears.

He tells me sometimes of her excellent mother; how, upon her death-bed, she had committed her house and children to Charlotte, and had given Charlotte herself in charge to him; how, since that time, a new spirit had taken possession of her; how, in care and anxiety for their welfare, she became a real mother to them; how every moment of her time was devoted to some labor of love in their behalf,—

and yet her mirth and cheerfulness had never forsaken her. I walk by his side, pluck flowers by the way, arrange them carefully into a nosegay, then fling them into the first stream I pass, and watch them as they float gently away. I forget whether I told you that Albert is to remain here. He has received a government appointment, with a very good salary; and I understand he is in high favor at court. I have met few persons so punctual and methodical in business.

Aug. 12.

Certainly Albert is the best fellow in the world. I had a strange scene with him yesterday. I went to take leave of him; for I took it into my head to spend a few days in these mountains, from where I now write to you. As I was walking up and down his room, my eye fell upon his pistols. "Lend me those pistols," said I, "for my journey." "By all means," he replied, "if you will take the trouble to load them; for they only hang there for form." I took down one of them; and he continued: "Ever since I was near suffering from my extreme caution, I will have nothing to do with such things." I was curious to hear the story. "I was staying," said he, "some three months ago, at a friend's house in the country. I had a brace of pistols with me, unloaded; and I slept without any anxiety. One rainy afternoon I was sitting by myself, doing nothing, when it occurred to me— I do not know how—that the house might be attacked, that we might require the pistols, that we might—in short, you know how we go on fancying, when we have nothing better to do. I gave the pistols to the servant, to clean and load. He was playing with the maid, and trying to frighten her, when the pistol went off—God knows how! the ramrod was in the barrel; and it went straight through her right hand, and shattered the thumb. I had to endure all the lamentation, and to pay the surgeon's bill; so, since that time, I have kept all my weapons unloaded. But, my dear friend, what is the use of prudence? We can never be on our guard against all possible dangers. However,"—now, you must know I can tolerate all men till they come to "however"; for it is self-evident that every universal rule must have its exceptions. But he is so exceedingly accurate that if he only fancies he has said a word too precipitate or too general or only half true, he never ceases to qualify, to modify, and extenuate, till at last he appears to have said nothing at all. Upon this occasion Albert was deeply immersed in his subject: I ceased to listen to him, and became lost in reverie. With a sudden motion I pointed the mouth of the pistol to my forehead, over the right eye. "What do you mean?" cried Albert, turning back the pistol. "It is not loaded," said I. "And even if not," he answered with impatience, "what can you mean? I cannot comprehend how a man can be so mad as to shoot himself; and the bare idea of it shocks me."

"But why should any one," said I, "in speaking of an action, venture to pronounce it mad or wise, or good or bad? What is the meaning of all this? Have you carefully studied the secret motives of our actions? Do you understand—can you explain the causes which occasion them, and make them inevitable? If you can, you will be less hasty with your decision."

"But you will allow," said Albert, "that some actions are criminal, let them spring from whatever motives they may." I granted it, and shrugged my shoulders.

"But still, my good friend," I continued, "there are some exceptions here too. Theft is a crime; but the man who commits it from extreme poverty, with no design but to save his family from perishing, is he an object of pity or of punishment? Who shall throw the first stone at a husband who in the heat of just resentment sacrifices his faithless wife and her perfidious seducer; or at the young maiden who in her weak hour of rapture forgets herself in the impetuous joys of love? Even our laws, cold and cruel as they are, relent in such cases, and withhold their punishment."

"That is quite another thing," said Albert; "because a man under the influence of violent passion loses all power of reflection, and is regarded as intoxicated or insane."

"Oh, you people of sound understandings," I replied, smiling, "are ever ready to exclaim, 'Extravagance, and madness, and intoxication!' You moral men are so calm and so subdued! You abhor the drunken man, and detest the extravagant; you pass by, like the Levite, and thank God, like the Pharisee, that you are not like one of them. I have been more than once intoxicated, my passions have always bordered on extravagance: I am not ashamed to confess it; for I have learned, by my own experience, that all extraordinary men, who have accomplished great and astonishing actions, have ever been decried by the world as drunken or insane. And in private life, too, is it not intolerable that no one can undertake the execution of a noble or generous deed, without giving rise to the exclamation that the doer is intoxicated or mad? Shame upon you, ye sages!"

"This is another of your extravagant humors," said Albert: "you always exaggerate a case, and in this matter you are undoubtedly wrong; for we were speaking of suicide, which you compare with great actions, when it is impossible to regard it as anything but a weakness. It is much easier to die than to bear a life of misery with fortitude."

I was on the point of breaking off the conversation, for nothing puts me so completely out of patience as the utterance of a wretched commonplace when I am talking from my inmost heart. However, I composed myself, for I had often heard the same observation with sufficient vexation; and I answered him, therefore, with a little warmth, "You call this a weakness,—beware of being led astray by appearances. When a nation which has long groaned under the intolerable yoke of a tyrant rises at last and throws off its chains, do you call that weakness? The man who, to rescue his house from the flames, finds his physical strength redoubled, so that he lifts burdens with ease which in the absence of excitement he could scarcely move; he who under the rage of an insult attacks and puts to flight half a score of his enemies,—are such persons to be called weak? My good friend, if resistance be strength, how can the highest degree of resistance be a weakness?"

Albert looked steadfastly at me, and said, "Pray forgive me, but I do not see that the examples you have adduced bear any relation to the question." "Very likely," I answered; "for I have often been told that my style of illustration borders a little on the absurd. But let us see if we cannot place the matter in another point of view, by inquiring what can be a man's state of mind who resolves to free himself from the burden of life,—a burden often so pleasant to bear, —for we cannot otherwise reason fairly upon the subject.

"Human nature," I continued, "has its limits. It is able to endure a certain degree of joy, sorrow, and pain, but becomes annihilated as soon as this measure is exceeded. The question, therefore, is, not whether a man is strong or weak, but whether he is able to endure the measure of his sufferings. The suffering may be moral or physical; and in my opinion it is just as absurd to call a man a coward who destroys himself, as to call a man a coward who dies of a malignant fever."

"Paradox, all paradox!" exclaimed Albert. "Not so paradoxical as you imagine," I replied. "You allow that we designate a disease as mortal when Nature is so severely attacked, and her strength so far exhausted, that she cannot possibly recover her former condition under any change that may take place.

"Now, my good friend, apply this to the mind; observe a man in his natural, isolated condition; consider how ideas work, and how impressions fasten on him, till at length a violent passion seizes him, destroying all his powers of calm reflection, and utterly ruining him.

"It is in vain that a man of sound mind and cool temper understands the condition of such a wretched being, in vain he counsels him. He can no more communicate his own wisdom to him than a healthy man can instill his strength into the invalid by whose bedside he is seated."

Albert thought this too general. I reminded him of a girl

who had drowned herself a short time previously, and I related her history.

She was a good creature, who had grown up in the narrow sphere of household industry and weekly-appointed labor; one who knew no pleasure beyond indulging in a walk on Sundays, arrayed in her best attire, accompanied by her friends, or perhaps joining in the dance now and then at some festival, and chatting away her spare hours with a neighbor, discussing the scandal or the quarrels of the village,—trifles sufficient to occupy her heart. At length the warmth of her nature is influenced by certain new and unknown wishes. Inflamed by the flatteries of men, her former pleasures become by degrees insipid, till at length she meets with a youth to whom she is attracted by an indescribable feeling; upon him she now rests all her hopes; she forgets the world around her; she sees, hears, desires nothing but him, and him only. He alone occupies all her thoughts. Uncorrupted by the idle indulgence of an enervating vanity, her affection moving steadily towards its object, she hopes to become his, and to realize, in an everlasting union with him, all that happiness which she sought, all that bliss for which she longed. His repeated promises confirm her hopes; embraces and endearments, which increase the ardor of her desires, overmaster her soul. She floats in a dim, delusive anticipation of her happiness; and her feelings become excited to their utmost tension. She stretches out her arms finally to embrace the object of all her wishes—and her lover forsakes her. Stunned and bewildered, she stands upon a precipice. All is darkness around her. No prospect, no hope, no consolation,—forsaken by him in whom her existence was centered! She sees nothing of the wide world before her, thinks nothing of the many individuals who might supply the void in her heart; she feels herself deserted, forsaken by the world; and, blinded and impelled by the agony which wrings her soul, she plunges into the deep, to end her sufferings in the broad embrace of death. See here, Albert, the history of thousands; and tell me, is not this a case of physi-

cal infirmity? Nature has no way to escape from the labyrinth: her powers are exhausted; she can contend no longer,
and the poor soul must die.

"Shame upon him who can look on calmly, and exclaim,
'The foolish girl! she should have waited; she should have
allowed time to wear off the impression; her despair would
have been softened, and she would have found another lover
to comfort her.' One might as well say, 'The fool, to die of a
fever! why did he not wait till his strength was restored, till
his blood became calm? All would then have gone well, and
he would have been alive now.' "

Albert, who could not see the justice of the comparison,
offered some further objections, and, amongst others, urged
that I had taken the case of a mere ignorant girl. But how
any man of sense, of more enlarged views and experience,
could be excused, he was unable to comprehend. "My
friend!" I exclaimed, "man is but man; and, whatever be the
extent of his reasoning powers, they are of little avail when
passion rages within, and he feels himself confined by the
narrow limits of Nature. It were better, then— But we will
talk of this some other time," I said, and caught up my hat.
Alas! my heart was full; and we parted without conviction
on either side. How rarely in this world do men understand
each other!

Aug. 15.

There can be no doubt that in this world nothing is so
indispensable as love. I observe that Charlotte could not lose
me without a pang, and the very children have but one wish;
that is, that I should visit them again to-morrow. I went this
afternoon to tune Charlotte's piano. But I could not do it, for
the little ones insisted on my telling them a story; and
Charlotte herself urged me to satisfy them. I waited upon
them at tea, and they are now as fully contented with me as
with Charlotte; and I told them my very best tale of the
princess who was waited upon by dwarfs. I improve myself
by this exercise, and am quite surprised at the impression

my stories create. If I sometimes invent an incident which I forget upon the next narration, they remind me directly that the story was different before; so that I now endeavor to relate with exactness the same anecdote in the same monotonous tone which never changes. I find by this, how much an author injures his works by altering them, even though they be improved in a poetical point of view. The first impression is readily received. We are so constituted that we believe the most incredible things; and, once they are engraved upon the memory, woe to him who would endeavor to efface them.

Aug. 18.

Must it ever be thus,—that the source of our happiness must also be the fountain of our misery? The full and ardent sentiment which animated my heart with the love of Nature, overwhelming me with a torrent of delight, and which brought all paradise before me, has now become an insupportable torment,—a demon which perpetually pursues and harasses me. When in by-gone days I gazed from these rocks upon yonder mountains across the river, and upon the green, flowery valley before me, and saw all Nature budding and bursting around; the hills clothed from foot to peak with tall, thick forest trees; the valleys in all their varied windings, shaded with the loveliest woods; and the soft river gliding along amongst the lisping reeds, mirroring the beautiful clouds which the soft evening breeze wafted across the sky,—when I heard the groves about me melodious with the music of birds, and saw the million swarms of insects dancing in the last golden beams of the sun, whose setting rays awoke the humming beetles from their grassy beds, whilst the subdued tumult around directed my attention to the ground, and I there observed the arid rock compelled to yield nutriment to the dry moss, whilst the heath flourished upon the barren sands below me,—all this displayed to me the inner warmth which animates all nature, and filled and glowed within my heart. I felt myself exalted by this overflowing fullness to the perception of the Godhead, and the glorious forms of an infinite universe became visible to my soul! Stupendous mountains encompassed me, abysses yawned at my feet, and cataracts fell headlong down before me; impetuous rivers rolled through the plain, and rocks and mountains resounded from afar. In the depths of the earth I saw innumerable powers in motion, and multiplying to infinity; whilst upon its surface, and beneath the heavens, there teemed ten thousand varieties of living creatures. Everything around is alive with an infinite number of forms; while mankind fly for security to their petty houses, from the shelter of which they rule in their imaginations over the wide-extended universe. Poor fool! in whose petty estimation all things are little. From the inaccessible mountains, across the desert which no mortal foot has trod, far as the confines of the unknown ocean, breathes the spirit of the eternal Creator; and every atom to which he has given existence finds favor in his sight. Ah, how often at that time has the flight of a bird, soaring above my head, inspired me with the desire of being transported to the shores of the immeasurable waters, there to quaff the pleasures of life from the foaming goblet of the Infinite, and to partake, if but for a moment even, with the confined powers of my soul, the beatitude of that Creator who accomplishes all things in himself, and through himself!

My dear friend, the bare recollection of those hours still consoles me. Even this effort to recall those ineffable sensations, and give them utterance, exalts my soul above itself, and makes me doubly feel the intensity of my present anguish.

It is as if a curtain had been drawn from before my eyes, and, instead of prospects of eternal life, the abyss of an ever-open grave yawned before me. Can we say of anything that it exists when all passes away,—when time, with the speed of a storm, carries all things onward,—and our transitory existence, hurried along by the torrent, is either swallowed up by the waves or dashed against the rocks? There is not a moment but preys upon you, and upon all around you,—not a moment in which you do not yourself become a destroyer. The most innocent walk deprives of life thousands of poor insects: one step destroys the fabric of the industrious ant, and converts a little world into chaos. No: it is not the great and rare calamities of the world, the floods which sweep away whole villages, the earthquakes which swallow up our towns, that affect me. My heart is wasted by the thought of that destructive power which lies concealed in every part of universal Nature. Nature has formed nothing that does not consume itself, and every object near it: so that, surrounded by earth and air and all the active powers, I wander on my way with aching heart; and the universe is to me a fearful monster, forever devouring its own offspring.

Aug. 21.

In vain do I stretch out my arms towards her when I awaken in the morning from my weary slumbers. In vain do I seek for her at night in my bed, when some innocent dream has happily deceived me, and placed her near me in the fields, when I have seized her hand and covered it with countless kisses. And when I feel for her in the half confusion of sleep, with the happy sense that she is near me, tears flow from my oppressed heart; and, bereft of all comfort, I weep over my future woes.

Aug. 22.

What a misfortune, Wilhelm! My active spirits have degenerated into contented indolence. I cannot be idle, and yet I am unable to set to work. I cannot think: I have no longer any feeling for the beauties of Nature, and books are distasteful to me. Once we give ourselves up, we are totally lost. Many a time and oft I wish I were a common laborer; that awakening in the morning, I might have but one prospect, one pursuit, one hope, for the day which has dawned. I often envy Albert when I see him buried in a heap of papers and parchments, and I fancy I should be

happy were I in his place. Often impressed with this feeling, I have been on the point of writing to you and to the
minister, for the appointment at the embassy, which you
think I might obtain. I believe I might procure it. The minister has long shown a regard for me, and has frequently
urged me to seek employment. It is the business of an hour
only. Now and then the fable of the horse recurs to me.
Weary of liberty, he suffered himself to be saddled and
bridled, and was ridden to death for his pains. I know not
what to determine upon. For is not this anxiety for change
the consequence of that restless spirit which would pursue
me equally in every situation of life?

Aug. 28.

If my ills would admit of any cure, they would certainly
be cured here. This is my birthday, and early in the morning I received a packet from Albert. Upon opening it, I
found one of the pink ribbons which Charlotte wore in her
dress the first time I saw her, and which I had several times
asked her to give me. With it were two volumes in duo-
decimo of Wetstein's Homer,—a book I had often wished
for, to save me the inconvenience of carrying the large
Ernestine edition with me upon my walks. You see how
they anticipate my wishes, how well they understand all
those little attentions of friendship, so superior to the costly
presents of the great, which are humiliating. I kissed the
ribbon a thousand times, and in every breath inhaled the
remembrance of those happy and irrevocable days, which
filled me with the keenest joy. Such, Wilhelm, is our fate.
I do not murmur at it: the flowers of life are but visionary.
How many pass away and leave no trace behind; how few
yield any fruit; and the fruit itself, how rarely does it
ripen! And yet there are flowers enough; and is it not
strange, my friend, that we should suffer the little that does
really ripen to rot, decay, and perish unenjoyed? Farewell!
This is a glorious summer. I often climb into the trees in
Charlotte's orchard, and shake down the pears that hang on

the highest branches; she stands below, and catches them as they fall.

Aug. 30.

Unhappy being that I am! Why do I thus deceive myself? What is to come of all this wild, aimless, endless passion? I cannot pray except to her. My imagination sees nothing but her; all surrounding objects are of no account except as they relate to her. In this dreamy state I enjoy many happy hours, till at length I feel compelled to tear myself away from her. Ah, Wilhelm, to what does not my heart often compel me! When I have spent several hours in her company, till I feel completely absorbed by her figure, her grace, the divine expression of her thoughts, my mind becomes gradually excited to the highest excess, my sight grows dim, my hearing confused, my breathing oppressed as if by the hand of a murderer, and my beating heart seeks to obtain relief for my aching senses. I am sometimes unconscious whether I really exist. If in such moments I find no sympathy, and Charlotte does not allow me to enjoy the melancholy consolation of bathing her hand with my tears, I feel compelled to tear myself from her, when I either wander through the country, climb some precipitous cliff, or force a path through the trackless thicket, where I am lacerated and torn by thorns and briers; and thence I find relief. Sometimes I lie stretched on the ground, overcome with fatigue and dying with thirst; sometimes, late in the night, when the moon shines above me, I recline against an aged tree in some sequestered forest to rest my weary limbs, when, exhausted and worn, I sleep till break of day. O Wilhelm! the hermit's cell, his sackcloth, and girdle of thorns would be luxury and indulgence compared with what I suffer. Adieu! I see no end to this wretchedness except the grave.

Sept. 3.

I must away. Thank you, Wilhelm, for determining my wavering purpose. For a whole fortnight I have thought of leaving her. I must away. She has returned to town, and is at the house of a friend. And then, Albert,—yes, I must go.

Sept. 10.

Oh, what a night, Wilhelm! I can henceforth bear anything. I shall never see her again. Oh, why cannot I fall on your neck, and with floods of tears and raptures give utterance to all the passions which distract my heart! Here I sit gasping for breath, and struggling to compose myself. I wait for day, and at sunrise the horses are to be at the door.

And she is sleeping calmly, little suspecting that she has seen me for the last time. I am free. I have had the courage, in an interview of two hours' duration, not to betray my intention. And oh, Wilhelm, what a conversation it was!

Albert had promised to come to Charlotte in the garden immediately after supper. I was upon the terrace under the tall chestnut-trees, and watched the setting sun. I saw him sink for the last time beneath this delightful valley and silent stream. I had often visited the same spot with Charlotte, and witnessed that glorious sight; and now—I was walking up and down the very avenue which was so dear to me. A secret sympathy had frequently drawn me thither before I knew Charlotte; and we were delighted when, in our early acquaintance, we discovered that we each loved the same spot, which is indeed as romantic as any that ever captivated the fancy of an artist.

From beneath the chestnut-trees there is an extensive view. But I remember that I have mentioned all this in a former letter, and have described the tall mass of beech-trees at the end, and how the avenue grows darker and darker as it winds its way among them, till it ends in a gloomy recess, which has all the charm of a mysterious solitude. I still remember the strange feeling of melancholy which came over me the first time I entered that dark retreat, at bright midday. I felt some secret foreboding that it would one day be to me the scene of some happiness or misery.

I had spent half an hour struggling between the contending thoughts of going and returning, when I heard them coming up the terrace. I ran to meet them. I trembled as I took her hand, and kissed it. As we reached the top of the terrace, the moon rose from behind the wooded hill. We conversed on many subjects, and without perceiving it approached the gloomy recess. Charlotte entered, and sat down. Albert seated himself beside her. I did the same, but my agitation did not suffer me to remain long seated. I got up and stood before her, then walked backwards and forwards, and sat down again. I was restless and miserable. Charlotte drew our attention to the beautiful effect of the moonlight, which threw a silver hue over the terrace in front of us beyond the beech-trees. It was a glorious sight, and was rendered more striking by the darkness which surrounded the spot where we were. We remained for some time silent, when Charlotte observed, "Whenever I walk by moonlight, it brings to my remembrance all my beloved and departed friends, and I am filled with thoughts of death and futurity. We shall live again, Werther," she continued, with a firm but feeling voice; "but shall we know one another again? What do you think? What do you say?"

"Charlotte," I said, as I took her hand in mine, and my eyes filled with tears, "we shall see each other again,—here and hereafter we shall meet again." I could say no more. Why, Wilhelm, should she put this question to me just at the moment when the fear of our cruel separation filled my heart?

"And oh, do those departed ones know how we are employed here? Do they know when we are well and happy? Do they know when we recall their memories with the fondest love? In the silent hour of evening the shade of my mother hovers round me; when seated in the midst of my children, I see them assembled near me as they used to assemble near her; and then I raise my anxious eyes to heaven, and wish she could look down upon us, and witness how I fulfill the promise I made to her in her last moments to be a mother to her children. With what emotion do I then exclaim: 'Pardon, dearest of mothers, pardon me, if I do not adequately supply your place! Alas! I do my utmost. They are clothed and fed; and, still better, they are loved and educated. Could you but see, sweet saint, the peace and harmony that dwells amongst us, you would glorify God with the warmest feelings of gratitude, to whom, in your last hour, you addressed such fervent prayers for our happiness.'" Thus did she express herself; but, oh, Wilhelm, who can do justice to her language? How can cold and passionless words convey the heavenly expressions of the spirit? Albert interrupted her gently: "This affects you too deeply, my dear Charlotte. I know your soul dwells on such recollections with intense delight; but I implore—" "Oh, Albert!" she continued, "I am sure you do not forget the evenings when we three used to sit at the little round table, when papa was absent, and the little ones had retired. You often had a good book with you, but seldom read it; the conversation of that noble being was preferable to everything,—that beautiful, bright, gentle, and yet ever-toiling woman. God alone knows how I have supplicated with tears on my nightly couch that I might be like her!"

I threw myself at her feet, and seizing her hand, bedewed it with a thousand tears. "Charlotte," I exclaimed, "God's blessing and your mother's spirit are upon you!" "Oh that you had known her!" she said, with a warm pressure of the hand. "She was worthy of being known to you." I thought I should have fainted. Never had I received praise so flattering. She continued: "And yet she was doomed to die in the flower of her youth, when her youngest child was scarcely six months old. Her illness was but short, but she was calm and resigned; and it was only for her children, especially the youngest, that she felt unhappy. When her end drew nigh, she bade me bring them to her. I obeyed. The younger ones knew nothing of their approaching loss, while the elder ones were quite overcome with grief. They stood around the bed; and she raised her feeble hands to heaven, and prayed over them; then kissing them in turn, she dismissed them, and said to me, 'Be you a mother to them.' I gave her my hand. 'You are promising much, my child,' she said,—'a mother's fondness and a mother's care! I have often witnessed, by your tears of gratitude, that you know what is a mother's tenderness; show it to your brothers and sisters. And be dutiful and faithful to your father as a wife; you will be his comfort.' She inquired for him. He had retired to conceal his intolerable anguish,—he was heart-broken.

"Albert, you were in the room. She heard some one moving; she inquired who it was, and desired you to approach. She surveyed us both with a look of composure and satisfaction, expressive of her conviction that we should be happy,—happy with one another." Albert fell upon her neck, and kissed her, and exclaimed, "We are so, and we shall be so!" Even Albert, generally so tranquil, had quite lost his composure; and I was excited beyond expression.

"And such a being," she continued, "was to leave us, Werther! Great God, must we thus part with everything we hold dear in this world? Nobody felt this more acutely than the children; they cried and lamented for a long time afterwards, complaining that black men had carried away their dear mamma."

Charlotte rose. It aroused me; but I continued sitting, and held her hand. "Let us go," she said; "it grows late." She attempted to withdraw her hand; I held it still. "We shall see each other again," I exclaimed; "we shall recognize each other under every possible change! I am going," I continued, "going willingly; but, should I say forever, perhaps I may not keep my word. Adieu, Charlotte; adieu, Albert. We shall meet again." "Yes; to-morrow, I think," she answered with a smile. To-morrow! how I felt the word! Ah! she little thought, when she drew her hand away from mine. They walked down the avenue. I stood gazing after them in the moonlight. I threw myself upon the ground, and wept; I then sprang up, and ran out upon the terrace, and saw, under the shade of the linden-trees, her white dress disappearing near the garden-gate. I stretched out my arms, and she vanished.

Book II

We arrived here yesterday. The ambassador is indisposed, and will not go out for some days. If he were less peevish and morose, all would be well. I see but too plainly that Heaven has destined me to severe trials; but courage; a light heart may bear anything. A light heart! I smile to find such a word proceeding from my pen. A little more light-heartedness would render me the happiest being under the sun. But must I despair of my talents and faculties, whilst others of far inferior abilities parade before me with the utmost self-satisfaction? Gracious Providence, to whom I owe all my powers, why didst thou not withhold some of those blessings I possess, and substitute in their place a feeling of self-confidence and contentment?

But patience! all will yet be well; for I assure you, my dear friend, you were right: since I have been obliged to associate continually with other people, and observe what they do, and how they employ themselves, I have become far better satisfied with myself. For we are so constituted by nature, that we are ever prone to compare ourselves with others; and our happiness or misery depends very much on the objects and persons around us. On this account nothing is more dangerous than solitude; there our imagination, always disposed to rise, taking a new flight on the wings of fancy, pictures to us a chain of beings of whom we seem the most inferior. All things appear greater than they really are, and all seem superior to us. This operation of the mind is quite natural; we so continually feel our own imperfections, and fancy we perceive in others the qualities we do not possess, attributing to them also all that we enjoy our-

selves, that by this process we form the idea of a perfect,
happy man,—a man, however, who only exists in our own
imagination.

But when, in spite of weakness and disappointments, we
set to work in earnest, and persevere steadily, we often find
that, though obliged continually to tack, we make more way
than others who have the assistance of wind and tide; and
in truth, there can be no greater satisfaction than to keep
pace with others or outstrip them in the race.

Nov. 26.

I begin to find my situation here more tolerable, considering all circumstances. I find a great advantage in being much
occupied; and the number of persons I meet, and their different pursuits, create a varied entertainment for me. I have
formed the acquaintance of the Count C——, and I esteem
him more and more every day. He is a man of strong understanding and great discernment; but though he sees farther
than other people, he is not on that account cold in his manner, but capable of inspiring and returning the warmest
affection. He appeared interested in me on one occasion,
when I had to transact some business with him. He perceived, at the first word, that we understood each other, and
that he could converse with me in a different tone from
what he used with others. I cannot sufficiently esteem his
frank and open kindness to me. It is the greatest and most
genuine of pleasures to observe a great mind in sympathy
with our own.

Dec. 24.

As I anticipated, the ambassador occasions me infinite
annoyance. He is the most punctilious blockhead under
heaven. He does everything step by step, with the trifling
minuteness of an old woman; and he is a man whom it is
impossible to please, because he is never pleased with himself. I like to do business regularly and cheerfully, and,
when it is finished, to leave it. But he constantly returns my

papers to me, saying, "They will do," but recommending me to look over them again, as "one may always improve by using a better word or a more appropriate particle." I then lose all patience, and wish myself at the Devil's. Not a conjunction, not an adverb, must be omitted: he has a deadly antipathy to all those transpositions of which I am so fond; and if the music of our periods is not tuned to the established official key, he cannot comprehend our meaning. It is deplorable to be connected with such a fellow.

My acquaintance with the Count C—— is the only compensation for such an evil. He told me frankly, the other day, that he was much displeased with the difficulties and delays of the ambassador; that people like him are obstacles, both to themselves and to others. "But," added he, "one must submit, like a traveler who has to ascend a mountain; if the mountain was not there, the road would be both shorter and pleasanter; but there it is, and he must get over it."

The old man perceives the count's partiality for me; this annoys him, and he seizes every opportunity to depreciate the count in my hearing. I naturally defend him, and that only makes matters worse. Yesterday he made me indignant, for he also alluded to me. "The count," he said, "is a man of the world, and a good man of business; his style is good, and he writes with facility; but, like other geniuses, he has no solid learning." He looked at me with an expression that seemed to ask if I felt the blow. But it did not produce the desired effect; I despise a man who can think and act in such a manner. However, I made a stand, and answered with not a little warmth. The count, I said, was a man entitled to respect, alike for his character and his acquirements. I had never met a person whose mind was stored with more useful and extensive knowledge,—who had, in fact, mastered such an infinite variety of subjects, and who yet retained all his activity for the details of ordinary business. This was altogether beyond his comprehension; and

I took my leave, lest my anger should be too highly excited by some new absurdity of his.

And you are to blame for all this,—you who persuaded me to bend my neck to this yoke by preaching a life of activity to me. If the man who plants vegetables, and carries his corn to town on market-days, is not more usefully employed than I am, then let me work ten years longer at the galleys to which I am now chained.

Oh the brilliant wretchedness, the weariness, that one is doomed to witness among the silly people whom we meet in society here! The ambition of rank! How they watch, how they toil, to gain precedence! What poor and contemptible passions are displayed in their utter nakedness! We have a woman here, for example, who never ceases to entertain the company with accounts of her family and her estates. And a stranger would consider her a silly being, whose head was turned by her pretensions to rank and property; but she is in reality even more ridiculous,—the daughter of a mere magistrate's clerk from this neighborhood. I cannot understand how human beings can so debase themselves.

Every day I observe more and more the folly of judging of others by ourselves; and I have so much trouble with myself, and my own heart is in such constant agitation, that I am well content to let others pursue their own course, if they only allow me the same privilege.

What provokes me most is the unhappy extent to which distinctions of rank are carried. I know perfectly well how necessary are inequalities of condition, and I am sensible of the advantages I myself derive therefrom; but I would not have these institutions prove a barrier to the small chance of happiness which I may enjoy on this earth.

I have lately become acquainted with a Miss B——, a very agreeable girl, who has retained her natural manners in the midst of artificial life. Our first conversation pleased us both equally; and, at taking leave, I requested permission to visit her. She consented in so obliging a manner, that I waited with impatience for the arrival of the happy moment. She is not a native of this place, but resides here with her aunt. The countenance of the old lady is not prepossessing. I paid her much attention, addressing the greater part of my conversation to her; and, in less than half an hour, I discovered what her niece subsequently acknowledged to me, that her aged aunt, having but a small fortune and a still smaller share of understanding, enjoys no satisfaction except in the pedigree of her ancestors, no protection save in her noble birth, and no enjoyment but in looking from her castle over the heads of the humble citizens. She was, no doubt, handsome in her youth, and in her early years probably trifled away her time in rendering many a poor youth the sport of her caprice: in her riper years she has submitted to the yoke of a veteran officer, who, in return for her person and her small independence, has spent with her what we may designate her age of brass. He is dead; and she is now a widow, and deserted. She spends her iron age alone, and would not be approached, except for the loveliness of her niece.

Jan. 8, 1772.

What beings are men, whose whole thoughts are occupied with form and ceremony, who for years together devote their mental and physical exertions to the task of advancing themselves but one step, and endeavoring to occupy a higher place at the table! Not that such persons would otherwise want employment: on the contrary, they give themselves much trouble by neglecting important business for such petty trifles. Last week a question of precedence arose at a sledging-party, and all our amusement was spoiled.

The silly creatures cannot see that it is not place which constitutes real greatness, since the man who occupies the first place but seldom plays the principal part. How many kings are governed by their ministers, how many ministers by their secretaries? Who, in such cases, is really the chief? He, as it seems to me, who can see through the others, and possesses strength or skill enough to make their power or passions subservient to the execution of his own designs.

Jan. 20.

I must write to you from this place, my dear Charlotte, from a small room in a country inn, where I have taken shelter from a severe storm. During my whole residence in that wretched place, D——, where I lived amongst strangers,—strangers, indeed, to this heart,—I never at any time felt the smallest inclination to correspond with you; but in this cottage, in this retirement, in this solitude, with the snow and hail beating against my lattice-pane, you are my first thought. The instant I entered, your figure rose up before me, and the remembrance,—O my Charlotte, the sacred, tender remembrance! Gracious Heaven, restore to me the happy moment of our first acquaintance!

Could you but see me, my dear Charlotte, in the whirl of dissipation,—how my senses are dried up, but my heart is at no time full. I enjoy no single moment of happiness: all is vain,—nothing touches me. I stand, as it were, before the raree-show: I see the little puppets move, and I ask whether it is not an optical illusion. I am amused with these puppets, or rather, I am myself one of them; but when I sometimes grasp my neighbor's hand, I feel that it is not natural, and I withdraw mine with a shudder. In the evening I say I will enjoy the next morning's sunrise, and yet I remain in bed: in the day I promise to ramble by moonlight; and I, nevertheless, remain at home. I know not why I rise, nor why I go to sleep.

The leaven which animated my existence is gone: the charm which cheered me in the gloom of night, and aroused me from my morning slumbers, is forever fled.

I have found but one being here to interest me, a Miss B——. She resembles you, my dear Charlotte, if any one can possibly resemble you. "Ah!" you will say, "he has learned how to pay fine compliments." And this is partly true. I have been very agreeable lately, as it was not in my power to be otherwise. I have, moreover, a deal of wit : and the ladies say that no one understands flattery better, or falsehoods you will add ; since the one accomplishment invariably accompanies the other. But I must tell you of Miss B——. She has abundance of soul, which flashes from her deep blue eyes. Her rank is a torment to her, and satisfies no one desire of her heart. She would gladly retire from this whirl of fashion, and we often picture to ourselves a life of undisturbed happiness in distant scenes of rural retirement : and then we speak of you, my dear Charlotte ; for she knows you, and renders homage to your merits ; but her homage is not exacted, but voluntary,—she loves you, and delights to hear you made the subject of conversation.

Oh that I were sitting at your feet in your favorite little room, with the dear children playing around us ! If they became troublesome to you, I would tell them some appalling goblin story ; and they would crowd round me with silent attention. The sun is setting in glory ; his last rays are shining on the snow, which covers the face of the country : the storm is over, and I must return to my dungeon. Adieu ! Is Albert with you ? and what is he to you ? God forgive the question.

Feb. 8.

For a week past we have had the most wretched weather : but this to me is a blessing ; for, during my residence here, not a single fine day has beamed from the heavens but has been lost to me by the intrusion of somebody. During the severity of rain, sleet, frost, and storm, I congratulate myself that it cannot be worse in-doors than abroad, nor worse abroad than it is within doors ; and so I become reconciled. When the sun rises bright in the morning, and promises a glorious day, I never omit to exclaim, "There, now, they have another blessing from Heaven, which they will be sure to destroy : they spoil everything,—health, fame, happiness, amusement ; and they do this generally through folly, ignorance, or imbecility, and always, according to their own account, with the best intentions!" I could often beseech them, on my bended knees, to be less resolved upon their own destruction.

Feb. 17.

I fear that my ambassador and I shall not continue much longer together. He is really growing past endurance. He transacts his business in so ridiculous a manner that I am often compelled to contradict him, and do things my own way; and then, of course, he thinks them very ill done. He complained of me lately on this account at court; and the minister gave me a reprimand,—a gentle one it is true, but still a reprimand. In consequence of this I was about to tender my resignation, when I received a letter, to which I submitted with great respect, on account of the high, noble, and generous spirit which dictated it. He endeavored to soothe my excessive sensibility, paid a tribute to my extreme ideas of duty, of good example, and of perseverance in business, as the fruit of my youthful ardor,—an impulse which he did not seek to destroy, but only to moderate, that it might have proper play and be productive of good. So now I am at rest for another week, and no longer at variance with myself. Content and peace of mind are valuable things: I could wish, my dear friend, that these precious jewels were less transitory.

Feb. 20.

God bless you, my dear friends, and may he grant you that happiness which he denies to me!

I thank you, Albert, for having deceived me. I waited for the news that your wedding-day was fixed; and I intended on that day, with solemnity, to take down Charlotte's profile from the wall, and to bury it with some other papers I possess. You are now united, and her picture still remains here. Well, let it remain! Why should it not? I know that I am still one of your society, that I still occupy a place uninjured in Charlotte's heart, that I hold the second place therein; and I intend to keep it. Oh, I should become mad if she could forget! Albert, that thought is hell! Farewell, Albert,—farewell, angel of heaven,—farewell, Charlotte!

March 15.

I have just had a sad adventure, which will drive me away from here. I lose all patience! Death! It is not to be remedied; and you alone are to blame, for you urged and impelled me to fill a post for which I was by no means suited. I have now reason to be satisfied, and so have you! But, that you may not again attribute this fatality to my impetuous temper, I send you, my dear sir, a plain and simple narration of the affair, as a mere chronicler of facts would describe it.

The Count of O—— likes and distinguishes me. It is well known, and I have mentioned this to you a hundred times. Yesterday I dined with him. It is the day on which the nobility are accustomed to assemble at his house in the evening. I never once thought of the assembly, nor that we subalterns did not belong to such society. Well, I dined with the count; and after dinner we adjourned to the large hall. We walked up and down together; and I conversed with him, and with Colonel B——, who joined us; and in this manner the hour for the assembly approached. God knows, I was thinking of nothing, when who should enter but the honorable Lady S——, accompanied by her noble husband and their silly, scheming daughter, with her small waist and flat neck; and, with disdainful looks and a haughty air, they passed me by. As I heartily detest the whole race, I determined upon going away; and only waited till the count had disengaged himself from their impertinent prattle, to take leave, when the agreeable Miss B—— came in. As I never meet her without experiencing a heartfelt pleasure, I stayed and talked to her, leaning over the back of her chair, and did not perceive, till after some time, that she seemed a little confused, and ceased to answer me with her usual ease of manner. I was struck with it. "Heavens!" I said to myself, "can she, too, be like the rest?" I felt annoyed, and was about to withdraw; but I remained, notwithstanding, forming excuses for her conduct, fancying she did not mean it, and still hoping to receive some friendly recognition. The rest of the company now arrived. There was the Baron F——, in an entire suit that dated from the coronation of Francis I.; the Chancellor N——, with his deaf wife; the shabbily dressed I——, whose old-fashioned coat bore evidence of modern repairs: this crowned the whole. I conversed with some of my acquaintances, but they answered me laconically. I was engaged in observing Miss B——, and did not notice that the women were whispering at the end of the room, that the murmur extended by degrees to the men, that Madame S—— addressed the count with much warmth (this was all related to me subsequently by Miss B——); till at length the count came up to me, and took me to the window. "You know our ridiculous customs," he said. "I perceive the company is rather displeased at your being here. I would not on any account"—"I beg your excellency's pardon!" I exclaimed. "I ought to have thought of this before, but I know you will forgive this little inattention. I was going," I added, "some time ago, but my evil genius detained me." And I smiled and bowed to take my leave. He shook me by the hand, in a manner which expressed everything. I hastened at once from the illustrious assembly, sprang into a carriage, and drove to M——. I contemplated the setting sun from the top of the hill, and read that beautiful passage in Homer where Ulysses is entertained by the hospitable herdsmen. This was indeed delightful.

I returned home to supper in the evening. But few persons were assembled in the room. They had turned up a corner of the tablecloth, and were playing at dice. The good-natured A—— came in. He laid down his hat when he saw me, approached me, and said in a low tone, "You have met with a disagreeable adventure." "I!" I exclaimed. "The count obliged you to withdraw from the assembly." "Deuce take the assembly!" said I. "I was very glad to be gone." "I am delighted," he added, "that you take it so lightly. I am only sorry that it is already so much spoken of." The circumstance then began to pain me. I fancied that every one who sat down, and even looked at me, was thinking of this incident; and my heart became embittered.

And now I could plunge a dagger into my bosom when I hear myself everywhere pitied, and observe the triumph of my enemies, who say that this is always the case with vain persons, whose heads are turned with conceit, who affect to despise forms and such petty, idle nonsense.

Say what you will of fortitude, but show me the man who can patiently endure the laughter of fools, when they have obtained an advantage over him. 'T is only when their nonsense is without foundation that one can suffer it without complaint.

March 16.

Everything conspires against me. I met Miss B—— walking to-day. I could not help joining her; and when we were at a little distance from her companions, I expressed my sense of her altered manner towards me. "O Werther!" she said, in a tone of emotion, "you, who know my heart, how could you so ill interpret my distress? What did I not suffer for you from the moment you entered the room! I foresaw it all; a hundred times was I on the point of mentioning it to you. I knew that the S——s and T——s, with their husbands, would quit the room rather than remain in your company. I knew that the count would not break with them: and now so much is said about it." "How!" I exclaimed, and endeavored to conceal my emotion; for all that Adelin had mentioned to me yesterday recurred to me painfully at that moment. "Oh, how much it has already cost me!" said this amiable girl, while her eyes filled with tears. I could scarcely contain myself, and was ready to throw myself at her feet. "Explain yourself!" I cried. Tears flowed down her cheeks. I became quite frantic. She wiped them away, without attempting to conceal them. "You know my aunt," she continued; "she was present: and in what light does she consider the affair! Last night, and this morning, Werther, I was compelled to listen to a lecture upon my acquaintance with you. I have been obliged to hear you condemned and depreciated; and I could not—I dared not—say much in your defense."

Every word she uttered was a dagger to my heart. She did not feel what a mercy it would have been to conceal everything from me. She told me, in addition, all the impertinence that would be further circulated, and how the malicious would triumph; how they would rejoice over the punishment of my pride, over my humiliation for that want of esteem for others with which I had often been reproached. To hear all this, Wilhelm, uttered by her in a voice of the most sincere sympathy, awakened all my passions; and I am still in a state of extreme excitement. I wish I could find a man to jeer me about this event. I would sacrifice him to my resentment. The sight of his blood might possibly be a relief to my fury. A hundred times have I seized a dagger, to give ease to this oppressed heart. Naturalists tell of a noble race of horses that instinctively open a vein with their teeth, when heated and exhausted by a long course, in order to breathe more freely. I am often tempted to open a vein, to procure for myself everlasting liberty.

March 24.

I have tendered my resignation to the court. I hope it will be accepted, and you will forgive me for not having previously consulted you. It is necessary I should leave this place. I know you all will urge me to stay, and therefore—I beg you will soften this news to my mother. I am unable to do anything for myself: how, then, should I be competent to assist others? It will afflict her that I should have interrupted that career which would have made me first a privy councilor, and then minister, and that I should look behind me, in place of advancing. Argue as you will, combine all the reasons which should have induced me to remain,—I am going: that is sufficient. But, that you may not be ignorant of my destination, I may mention that the Prince of —— is here. He is much pleased with my company; and, having heard of my intention to resign, he has invited me to his country house, to pass the spring months with him. I shall be left completely my own master; and as we agree on all subjects but one, I shall try my fortune, and accompany him.

April 19.

Thanks for both your letters. I delayed my reply, and withheld this letter, till I should obtain an answer from the court. I feared my mother might apply to the minister to defeat my purpose. But my request is granted, my resignation is accepted. I shall not recount with what reluctance it was accorded, nor relate what the minister has written: you would only renew your lamentations. The Crown Prince has sent me a present of five and twenty ducats; and, indeed, such goodness has affected me to tears. For this reason I shall not require from my mother the money for which I lately applied.

May 5.

I leave this place to-morrow; and as my native place is only six miles from the high-road, I intend to visit it once more, and recall the happy dreams of my childhood. I shall enter at the same gate through which I came with my mother, when, after my father's death, she left that delightful retreat to immure herself in your melancholy town. Adieu, my dear friend: you shall hear of my future career.

May 9.

I have paid my visit to my native place with all the devotion of a pilgrim, and have experienced many unexpected emotions. Near the great elm-tree, which is a quarter of a league from the village, I got out of the carriage, and sent it on before, that alone and on foot I might enjoy vividly and heartily all the pleasure of my recollections. I stood there under that same elm which was formerly the term and object of my walks. How things have since changed! Then, in happy ignorance, I sighed for a world I did not know, where I hoped to find every pleasure and enjoyment which my heart could desire; and now, on my return from that wide world, O my friend, how many disappointed hopes and unsuccessful plans have I brought back!

As I contemplated the mountains which lay stretched out before me, I thought how often they had been the object of my dearest desires. Here used I to sit for hours together with my eyes bent upon them, ardently longing to wander in the shade of those woods, to lose myself in those valleys, which form so delightful an object in the distance. With what reluctance did I leave this charming spot, when my hour of recreation was over, and my leave of absence expired! I drew near to the village: all the well-known old summer-houses and gardens were recognized again: I disliked the new ones, and all other alterations which had taken place. I entered the village, and all my former feelings returned. I cannot, my dear friend, enter into details, charming as were my sensations; they would be dull in the narration. I had intended to lodge in the marketplace, near our old house. As soon as I entered, I perceived that the school-room, where our childhood had been taught by that good old woman, was converted into a shop. I called to mind the sorrow, the heaviness, the tears, and oppression of heart which I experienced in that confinement. Every step produced some particular impression. A pilgrim in the Holy Land does not meet so many spots pregnant with tender recollections, and his soul is hardly moved with greater devotion. One incident will serve for illustration. I followed the course of a stream to a farm, formerly a delightful walk of mine, and paused at the spot where, when boys, we used to amuse ourselves making ducks and drakes upon the water. I recollected so well how I used formerly to watch the course of that same stream, following it with inquiring eagerness, forming romantic ideas of the countries it was to pass through; but my imagination was soon exhausted; while the water continued flowing farther and farther on, till my fancy became bewildered by the contemplation of an invisible distance. Exactly such, my dear friend, so happy and so confined, were the thoughts of our good ancestors. Their feelings and their poetry were fresh as childhood. And when Ulysses talks of the immeasurable sea and boundless earth, his epithets are true, natural, deeply felt, and mysterious. Of what importance is it that I have learned, with every schoolboy, that the world is round? Man needs but little earth for enjoyment, and still less for his final repose.

I am at present with the prince at his hunting-lodge. He is a man with whom one can live happily. He is honest and unaffected. There are, however, some strange characters about him, whom I cannot at all understand. They do not seem vicious, and yet they do not carry the appearance of thoroughly honest men. Sometimes I am disposed to believe them honest, and yet I cannot persuade myself to confide in them. It grieves me to hear the prince occasionally talk of things which he has only read or heard of, and always with the same view in which they have been represented by others.

He values my understanding and talents more highly than my heart, but I am proud of the latter only. It is the sole source of everything—of our strength, happiness, and misery. All the knowledge I possess every one else can acquire, but my heart is exclusively my own.

May 25.

I have had a plan in my head of which I did not intend to speak to you until it was accomplished: now that it has failed, I may as well mention it. I wished to enter the army, and had long been desirous of taking the step. This, indeed, was the chief reason for my coming here with the prince, as he is a general in the —— service. I communicated my design to him during one of our walks together. He disapproved of it, and it would have been actual madness not to have listened to his reasons.

June 11.

Say what you will, I can remain here no longer. Why should I remain? Time hangs heavy upon my hands. The prince is as gracious to me as any one could be, and yet I am not at my ease. There is, indeed, nothing in common between us. He is a man of understanding, but quite of the ordinary kind. His conversation affords me no more amusement than I should derive from the perusal of a well-written book. I shall remain here a week longer, and then start again on my travels. My drawings are the best things I have done since I came here. The prince has a taste for the arts, and would improve if his mind were not fettered by cold rules and mere technical ideas. I often lose patience, when, with a glowing imagination, I am giving expression to art and nature, he interferes with learned suggestions, and uses at random the technical phraseology of artists.

June 16.

Once more I am a wanderer, a pilgrim, through the world. But what else are you!

July 18.

Whither am I going? I will tell you in confidence. I am obliged to continue a fortnight longer here, and then I think it would be better for me to visit the mines in ——. But I am only deluding myself thus. The fact is, I wish to be near Charlotte again,—that is all. I smile at the suggestions of my heart, and obey its dictates.

July 29.

No, no! it is yet well—all is well! I her husband! O God, who gave me being, if thou hadst destined this happiness for me, my whole life would have been one continued thanksgiving! But I will not murmur,—forgive these tears, forgive these fruitless wishes. She—my wife! Oh, the very thought of folding that dearest of Heaven's creatures in my arms! Dear Wilhelm, my whole frame feels convulsed when I see Albert put his arms round her slender waist!

And shall I avow it? Why should I not, Wilhelm? She would have been happier with me than with him. Albert is not the man to satisfy the wishes of such a heart. He wants a certain sensibility; he wants—in short, their hearts do not beat in unison. How often, my dear friend, in reading a passage from some interesting book, when my heart and Charlotte's seemed to meet, and in a hundred other instances when our sentiments were unfolded by the story of some fictitious character, have I felt that we were made for each other! But, dear Wilhelm, he loves her with his whole soul; and what does not such a love deserve?

I have been interrupted by an insufferable visit. I have dried my tears, and composed my thoughts. Adieu, my best friend!

Aug. 4.

I am not alone unfortunate. All men are disappointed in their hopes, and deceived in their expectations. I have paid a visit to my good old woman under the lime-trees. The eldest boy ran out to meet me: his exclamation of joy brought out his mother, but she had a very melancholy look. Her first word was: "Alas! dear sir, my little John is dead." He was the youngest of her children. I was silent. "And my husband has returned from Switzerland without any money; and if some kind people had not assisted him, he must have begged his way home. He was taken ill with fever on his journey." I could answer nothing, but made the little one a present. She invited me to take some fruit. I complied, and left the place with a sorrowful heart.

Aug. 21.

My sensations are constantly changing. Sometimes a happy prospect opens before me; but alas! it is only for a moment; and then, when I am lost in reverie, I cannot help saying to myself, "If Albert were to die?—Yes, she would become—and I should be"—and so I pursue a chimera, till it leads me to the edge of a precipice at which I shudder.

When I pass through the same gate, and walk along the same road which first conducted me to Charlotte, my heart sinks within me at the change that has since taken place. All, all is altered! No sentiment, no pulsation of my heart, is the same. My sensations are such as would occur to some departed prince whose spirit should return to visit the superb palace which he had built in happy times, adorned with costly magnificence, and left to a beloved son, but whose glory he should find departed, and its halls deserted and in ruins.

Sept. 3.

I sometimes cannot understand how she can love another, how she dares love another, when I love nothing in this world so completely, so devotedly, as I love her, when I know only her, and have no other possession than her in the world.

Sept. 4.

It is even so! As Nature puts on her autumn tints, it becomes autumn with me and around me. My leaves are sear and yellow, and the neighboring trees are divested of their foliage. Do you remember my writing to you about a peasant boy shortly after my arrival here? I have just made inquiries about him in Walheim. They say he has been dismissed from his service, and is now avoided by every one. I met him yesterday on the road, going to a neighboring village. I spoke to him, and he told me his story. It interested me exceedingly, as you will easily understand when I repeat it to you. But why should I trouble you? Why should I not reserve all my sorrow for myself? Why should I continue to give you occasion to pity and blame me? But no matter: this also is part of my destiny.

At first the peasant-lad answered my inquiries with a sort of subdued melancholy, which seemed to me the mark of a timid disposition; but as we grew to understand each other, he spoke with less reserve, and openly confessed his faults, and lamented his misfortune. I wish, my dear friend, I could give proper expression to his language. He told me, with a sort of pleasurable recollection, that after my departure his passion for his mistress increased daily, until at last he neither knew what he did nor what he said, nor what was to become of him. He could neither eat nor drink nor sleep: he felt a sense of suffocation; he disobeyed all orders, and forgot all commands involuntarily; he seemed as if pursued by an evil spirit, till one day, knowing that his mistress had gone to an upper chamber, he had followed, or rather, been drawn after her. As she proved deaf to his entreaties, he had recourse to violence. He knows not what happened; but he called God to witness that his intentions to her were honorable, and that he desired nothing more sincerely than that they should marry, and pass their lives together. When he had come to this point, he began to hesitate, as if there was something which he had not courage to utter, till at length he acknowledged with some confusion certain little confidences she had encouraged, and liberties she had allowed. He broke off two or three times in his narration, and assured me most earnestly that he had no wish to make her bad, as he termed it, for he loved her still as sincerely as ever; that the tale had never before escaped his lips, and was only now told to convince me that he was not utterly lost and abandoned. And here, my dear friend, I must commence the old song which you know I utter eternally. If I could only represent the man as he stood, and stands now before me,—could I only give his true expressions, you would feel compelled to sympathize in his fate. But enough: you, who know my misfortune and my disposition, can easily comprehend the attraction which draws me towards every unfortunate being, but particularly towards him whose story I have recounted.

On perusing this letter a second time, I find I have omitted the conclusion of my tale; but it is easily supplied. She became reserved towards him, at the instigation of her brother who had long hated him, and desired his expulsion from the house, fearing that his sister's second marriage might deprive his children of the handsome fortune they expected from her; as she is childless. He was dismissed at length; and the whole affair occasioned so much scandal that the mistress dared not take him back, even if she had wished it. She has since hired another servant, with whom, they say, her brother is equally displeased, and whom she is likely to marry; but my informant assures me that he himself is determined not to survive such a catastrophe.

This story is neither exaggerated nor embellished: indeed, I have weakened and impaired it in the narration, by the necessity of using the more refined expressions of society.

This love then, this constancy, this passion, is no poetical fiction. It is actual, and dwells in its greatest purity amongst that class of mankind whom we term rude, uneducated. We are the educated, not the perverted! But read this story with attention, I implore you. I am tranquil to-day, for I have been employed upon this narration: you see by my writing that I am not so agitated as usual. Read and re-read this tale, Wilhelm: it is the history of your friend! My fortune has been and will be similar; and I am neither half so brave nor half so determined as the poor wretch with whom I hesitate to compare myself.

Sept. 5.

Charlotte had written a letter to her husband in the country, where he was detained by business. It commenced, "My dearest love, return as soon as possible: I await you with a thousand raptures." A friend who arrived, brought word that, for certain reasons, he could not return immediately. Charlotte's letter was not forwarded, and the same evening it fell into my hands. I read it, and smiled. She asked the reason. "What a heavenly treasure is imagination!" I exclaimed; "I fancied for a moment that this was written to me." She paused, and seemed displeased. I was silent.

Sept. 6.

It cost me much to part with the blue coat which I wore the first time I danced with Charlotte. But I could not possibly wear it any longer. But I have ordered a new one, precisely similar, even to the collar and sleeves, as well as a new waistcoat and pantaloons.

But it does not produce the same effect upon me. I know not how it is, but I hope in time I shall like it better.

Sept. 12.

She has been absent for some days. She went to meet Albert. To-day I visited her: she rose to receive me, and I kissed her hand most tenderly.

A canary at the moment flew from a mirror, and settled upon her shoulder. "Here is a new friend," she observed, while she made him perch upon her hand: "he is a present for the children. What a dear he is! Look at him! When I feed him, he flutters with his wings, and pecks so nicely. He kisses me, too,—only look!"

She held the bird to her mouth; and he pressed her sweet lips with so much fervor that he seemed to feel the excess of bliss which he enjoyed.

"He shall kiss you too," she added; and then she held the bird towards me. His little beak moved from her mouth to mine, and the delightful sensation seemed like the forerunner of the sweetest bliss.

"A kiss," I observed, "does not seem to satisfy him: he wishes for food, and seems disappointed by these unsatisfactory endearments."

"But he eats out of my mouth," she continued, and extended her lips to him containing seed; and she smiled with all the charm of a being who has allowed an innocent participation of her love.

I turned my face away. She should not act thus. She ought not to excite my imagination with such displays of heavenly innocence and happiness, nor awaken my heart from its slumbers, in which it dreams of the worthlessness of life! And why not? Because she knows how much I love her.

Sept. 15.

It makes me wretched, Wilhelm, to think that there should be men incapable of appreciating the few things which possess a real value in life. You remember the walnut-trees at S——, under which I used to sit with Charlotte, during my visits to the worthy old vicar. Those glorious trees, the very sight of which has so often filled my heart with joy, how they adorned and refreshed the parsonage-yard, with their wide-extended branches! and how pleasing was our remembrance of the good old pastor, by whose hands they were planted so many years ago! The schoolmaster has frequently mentioned his name. He had it from his grandfather. He must have been a most excellent man; and, under the shade of those old trees, his memory was ever venerated by me. The schoolmaster informed us yesterday, with tears in his eyes, that those trees had been felled. Yes, cut to the ground! I could, in my wrath, have slain the monster who struck the first stroke. And I must endure this!—I, who, if I had had two such trees in my own court, and one had died from old age, should have wept with real affliction. But there is some comfort left,—such a thing is sentiment,—the whole village murmurs at the misfortune; and I hope the vicar's wife will soon find, by the cessation of the villagers' presents, how much she has wounded the feelings of the neighborhood. It was she who did it,—the wife of the present incumbent (our good old man is dead),—a tall, sickly creature, who is so far right to disregard the world as the world totally disregards her. The silly being affects to be learned, pretends to examine the canonical books, lends her aid towards the new-fashioned reformation of Christendom, moral and critical, and shrugs up her shoulders at the mention of Lavater's enthusiasm. Her health is destroyed, on account of which she is prevented from having any enjoyment here below. Only such a creature could have cut down my walnut-trees! I can never pardon it. Hear her reasons. The falling leaves made the court wet and dirty; the branches obstructed the light; boys threw stones at the nuts when they were ripe, and the noise affected her nerves, and disturbed her profound meditations, when she was weighing the difficulties of Kennicot, Semler, and Michaelis. Finding that all the parish, particularly the old people, were displeased, I asked why they allowed it. "Ah, sir!" they replied, "when the steward orders, what can we poor peasants do?" But one thing has happened well. The steward and the vicar (who for once thought to reap some advantage from the caprices of his wife) intended to divide the trees between them. The revenue-office, being informed of it, revived an old claim to the ground where the trees had stood, and sold them to the best bidder. There they still lie on the ground. If I were the sovereign, I should know how to deal with them all,—vicar, steward, and revenue-office. Sovereign, did I say? I should in that case care little about the trees that grew in the country.

Oct. 10.

Only to gaze upon her dark eyes is to me a source of happiness! And what grieves me is that Albert does not seem so happy as he—hoped to be—as I should have been— if— I am no friend to these pauses, but here I cannot express it otherwise; and probably I am explicit enough.

Oct. 12.

Ossian has superseded Homer in my heart. To what a world does the illustrious bard carry me! To wander over pathless wilds, surrounded by impetuous whirlwinds, where, by the feeble light of the moon, we see the spirits of our ancestors; to hear from the mountain-tops, mid the roar of torrents, their plaintive sounds issuing from deep caverns, and the sorrowful lamentations of a maiden who sighs and expires on the mossy tomb of the warrior by whom she was adored. I meet this bard with silver hair; he wanders in the valley; he seeks the footsteps of his fathers, and, alas! he finds only their tombs. Then, contemplating the pale moon, as she sinks beneath the waves of the rolling sea, the memory of by-gone days strikes the mind of the hero,—days when approaching danger invigorated the brave, and the moon shone upon his bark laden with spoils, and returning in triumph. When I read in his countenance deep sorrow, when I see his dying glory sink exhausted into the grave, as he inhales new and heart-thrilling delight from his approaching union with his beloved, and he casts a look on the cold earth and the tall grass which is so soon to cover him, and then exclaims, "The traveler will come,—he will come who has seen my beauty, and he will ask, 'Where is the bard, —where is the illustrious son of Fingal?' He will walk over my tomb, and will seek me in vain!" Then, O my friend, I could instantly, like a true and noble knight, draw my sword, and deliver my prince from the long and painful languor of a living death, and dismiss my own soul to follow the demigod whom my hand had set free!

Oct. 19.

Alas! the void—the fearful void, which I feel in my bosom! Sometimes I think, if I could only once—but once, press her to my heart, this dreadful void would be filled.

Oct. 26.

Yes, I feel certain, Wilhelm, and every day I become more certain, that the existence of any being whatever is of very little consequence. A friend of Charlotte's called to see her just now. I withdrew into a neighboring apartment, and took up a book; but, finding I could not read, I sat down to write. I heard them converse in an undertone: they spoke upon indifferent topics, and retailed the news of the town. One was going to be married; another was ill, very ill,—she had a dry cough, her face was growing thinner daily, and she had occasional fits. "N—— is very unwell, too," said Charlotte. "His limbs begin to swell already," answered the other; and my lively imagination carried me at once to the beds of the infirm. There I see them struggling against death, with all the agonies of pain and horror; and these women, Wilhelm, talk of all this with as much indifference as one would mention the death of a stranger. And when I look around the apartment where I now am,—when I see Charlotte's apparel lying before me, and Albert's writings, and all those articles of furniture which are so familiar to me, even to the very inkstand which I am using,—when I think what I am to this family—everything. My friends esteem me; I often contribute to their happiness, and my heart seems as if it could not beat without them; and yet—if I were to die, if I were to be summoned from the midst of this circle, would they feel—or how long would they feel—the void which my loss would make in their existence? How long! Yes, such is the frailty of man, that even there, where he has the greatest consciousness of his own being, where he makes the strongest and most forcible impression, even in the memory, in the heart of his beloved, there also he must perish,—vanish,—and that quickly.

Oct. 27.

I could tear open my bosom with vexation to think how little we are capable of influencing the feelings of each other. No one can communicate to me those sensations of love, joy, rapture, and delight which I do not naturally possess; and though my heart may glow with the most lively affection, I cannot make the happiness of one in whom the same warmth is not inherent.

Oct. 27: Evening.

I possess so much, but my love for her absorbs it all. I possess so much, but without her I have nothing.

Oct. 30.

One hundred times have I been on the point of embracing her. Heavens! what a torment it is to see so much loveliness passing and repassing before us, and yet not dare to lay hold of it! And laying hold is the most natural of human instincts. Do not children touch everything they see? And I!

Nov. 3.

Witness, Heaven, how often I lie down in my bed with a wish, and even a hope, that I may never awaken again! And in the morning, when I open my eyes, I behold the sun once more, and am wretched. If I were whimsical, I might blame the weather, or an acquaintance, or some personal disappointment, for my discontented mind; and then this insupportable load of trouble would not rest entirely upon myself. But, alas! I feel it too sadly; I am alone the cause of my own woe, am I not? Truly, my own bosom contains the source of all my sorrow, as it previously contained the source of all my pleasure. Am I not the same being who once enjoyed an excess of happiness, who at every step saw paradise open before him, and whose heart was ever expanded towards the whole world? And this heart is now dead; no sentiment can revive it. My eyes are dry; and my senses, no more refreshed by the influence of soft tears, wither and consume my brain. I suffer much, for I have lost the only charm of life: that active, sacred power which created worlds around me,—it is no more. When I look from my window at the distant hills, and behold the morning sun breaking through the mists, and illuminating the country around, which is still wrapped in silence, whilst the soft stream winds gently through the willows, which have shed their leaves; when glorious Nature displays all her beauties before me, and her wondrous prospects are ineffectual to extract one tear of joy from my withered heart,—I feel that in such a moment I stand like a reprobate before heaven, hardened, insensible, and unmoved. Oftentimes do I then bend my knee to the earth, and implore God for the blessing of tears, as the desponding laborer in some scorching climate prays for the dews of heaven to moisten his parched corn.

But I feel that God does not grant sunshine or rain to our importunate entreaties. And oh, those bygone days, whose memory now torments me! why were they so fortunate? Because I then waited with patience for the blessings of the Eternal, and received his gifts with the grateful feelings of a thankful heart.

Nov. 8.

Charlotte has reproved me for my excesses, with so much tenderness and goodness! I have lately been in the habit of drinking more wine than heretofore. "Don't do it," she said; "think of Charlotte!" "Think of you!" I answered; "need you bid me do so? Think of you—I do not think of you: you are ever before my soul! This very morning I sat on the spot where, a few days ago, you descended from the carriage, and—" She immediately changed the subject to prevent me from pursuing it farther. My dear friend, my energies are all prostrated; she can do with me what she pleases.

Nov. 15.

I thank you, Wilhelm, for your cordial sympathy, for your excellent advice; and I implore you to be quiet. Leave me to my sufferings. In spite of my wretchedness, I have still strength enough for endurance. I revere religion,—you know I do. I feel that it can impart strength to the feeble and comfort to the afflicted; but does it affect all men equally? Consider this vast universe: you will see thousands for whom it has never existed, thousands for whom it will never exist, whether it be preached to them or not; and must it, then, necessarily exist for me? Does not the Son of God himself say that they are his whom the Father has given to him? Have I been given to him? What if the Father will retain me for himself, as my heart sometimes suggests?

I pray you, do not misinterpret this. Do not extract derision from my harmless words. I pour out my whole soul before you. Silence were otherwise preferable to me, but I need not shrink from a subject of which few know more than I do myself. What is the destiny of man, but to fill up the measure of his sufferings, and to drink his allotted cup of bitterness? And if that same cup proved bitter to the God of heaven, under a human form, why should I affect a foolish pride, and call it sweet? Why should I be ashamed of shrinking at that fearful moment when my whole being will tremble between existence and annihilation; when a remembrance of the past, like a flash of lightning, will illuminate the dark gulf of futurity; when everything shall dissolve around me, and the whole world vanish away? Is not this the voice of a creature oppressed beyond all resource, self-deficient, about to plunge into inevitable destruction, and groaning deeply at its inadequate strength: "My God! my God! why hast thou forsaken me?" And should I feel ashamed to utter the same expression? Should I not shudder at a prospect which had its fears even for him who folds up the heavens like a garment?

Nov. 21.

She does not feel, she does not know that she is preparing a poison which will destroy us both; and I drink deeply of the draught which is to prove my destruction. What mean those looks of kindness with which she often—often? no, not often, but sometimes—regards me, that complacency with which she hears the involuntary sentiments which frequently escape me, and the tender pity for my sufferings which appears in her countenance?

Yesterday, when I took leave, she seized me by the hand, and said, "Adieu, dear Werther." Dear Werther! It was the first time she ever called me "dear": the sound sunk deep into my heart. I have repeated it a hundred times; and last night, on going to bed, and talking to myself of various things, I suddenly said, "Good-night, dear Werther!" and then could not but laugh at myself.

Nov. 22.

I cannot pray, "Leave her to me!" and yet she often seems to belong to me. I cannot pray, "Give her to me!" for she is another's. In this way I affect mirth over my troubles; and if I had time, I could compose a whole litany of antitheses.

Nov. 24.

She is sensible of my sufferings. This morning her look pierced my very soul. I found her alone, and she was silent; she steadfastly surveyed me. I no longer saw in her face the charms of beauty or the fire of genius; these had disappeared. But I was affected by an expression much more touching,—a look of the deepest sympathy and of the softest pity. Why was I afraid to throw myself at her feet? Why did I not dare to take her in my arms, and answer her by a thousand kisses? She had recourse to her piano for relief, and in a low and sweet voice accompanied the music with delicious sounds. Her lips never appeared so lovely: they seemed but just to open, that they might imbibe the sweet tones which issued from the instrument, and return the heavenly vibration from her lovely mouth. Oh, who can express my sensations! I was quite overcome, and bending down, pronounced this vow: "Beautiful lips, which the angels guard, never will I seek to profane your purity with a kiss." And yet, my friend, oh, I wish—but my heart is darkened by doubt and indecision—could I but taste felicity, and then die to expiate the sin! What sin?

Nov. 26.

Oftentimes I say to myself, "Thou alone art wretched: all other mortals are happy; none are distressed like thee." Then I read a passage in an ancient poet, and I seem to understand my own heart. I have so much to endure! Have men before me ever been so wretched?

Nov. 30.

I shall never be myself again! Wherever I go, some fatality occurs to distract me. Even to-day—alas, for our destiny! alas, for human nature!

About dinner-time I went to walk by the river-side, for I had no appetite. Everything around seemed gloomy; a cold and damp easterly wind blew from the mountains, and black, heavy clouds spread over the plain. I observed at a distance a man in a tattered coat; he was wandering among the rocks, and seemed to be looking for plants. When I approached, he turned round at the noise; and I saw that he had an interesting countenance, in which a settled melancholy, strongly marked by benevolence, formed the principal feature. His long black hair was divided, and flowed over his shoulders. As his garb betokened a person of the lower order, I thought he would not take it ill if I inquired about his business; and I therefore asked what he was seeking. He replied, with a deep sigh, that he was looking for flowers, and could find none. "But it is not the season," I observed, with a smile. "Oh, there are so many flowers!" he answered, as he came nearer to me. "In my garden there are roses and honeysuckles of two sorts: one sort was given to me by my father; they grow as plentifully as weeds. I have been looking for them these two days, and cannot find them. There are flowers out there, yellow, blue, and red; and that centaury has a very pretty blossom: but I can find none of them." I observed his peculiarity, and therefore asked him, with an air of indifference, what he intended to do with his flowers. A strange smile overspread his countenance. Holding his finger to his mouth, he expressed a hope that I would not betray him; and he then informed me that he had promised to gather a nosegay for his mistress. "That is right," said I. "Oh!" he replied, "she possesses many other things as well; she is very rich." "And yet," I continued, "she likes your nosegays." "Oh, she has jewels and crowns!" he exclaimed. I asked who she was. "If the states-general would but pay me," he added, "I should be quite another man. Alas! there was a time when I was so happy; but that is past, and I am now—" He raised his swimming eyes to heaven. "And you were happy once?" I observed. "Ah, would I were so still!" was his reply. "I was then as gay and contented as a man can be." An old woman, who was coming towards us, now called out: "Henry, Henry! where are you? We have been looking for you everywhere. Come to dinner." "Is he your son?" I inquired, as I went towards her. "Yes," she said; "he is my poor, unfortunate son. The Lord has sent me a heavy affliction." I asked whether he had been long in this state. She answered: "He has been as calm as he is at present for about six months. I thank Heaven that he has so far recovered. He was one whole year quite raving, and chained down in a madhouse. Now he injures no one, but talks of nothing else than kings and queens. He used to be a very good, quiet youth, and helped to maintain me; he wrote a very fine hand. But all at once he became melancholy, was seized with a violent fever, grew distracted, and is now as you see. If I were only to tell you, sir—" I interrupted her by asking what period it was in which he boasted of having been so happy. "Poor boy!" she exclaimed, with a smile of compassion, "he means the time when he was completely deranged,—a time he never ceases to regret,— when he was in the madhouse, and unconscious of everything." I was thunderstruck. I placed a piece of money in her hand, and hastened away.

"You were happy!" I exclaimed, as I returned quickly to the town, "'as gay and contented as a man can be!'" God of heaven! and is this the destiny of man? Is he only happy before he has acquired his reason or after he has lost it? Unfortunate being! And yet I envy your fate; I envy the delusion to which you are a victim. You go forth with joy to gather flowers for your princess in winter, and grieve when you can find none, and cannot understand why they do not grow. But I wander forth without joy, without hope, without design; and I return as I came. You fancy what a man you would be if the states-general paid you. Happy mortal, who can ascribe your wretchedness to an earthly cause! You do not know, you do not feel, that in your own distracted heart and disordered brain dwells the source of that unhappiness which all the potentates on earth cannot relieve.

Let that man die unconsoled who can deride the invalid for undertaking a journey to distant, healthful springs,—where he often finds only a heavier disease and a more painful death,—or who can exult over the despairing mind of a sinner who, to obtain peace of conscience and an alleviation of misery, makes a pilgrimage to the Holy Sepulchre. Each laborious step which galls his wounded feet in rough and untrodden paths pours a drop of balm into his troubled soul, and the journey of many a weary day brings a nightly relief to his anguished heart. Will you dare call this enthusiasm, ye crowd of pompous declaimers? Enthusiasm! O God! thou seest my tears. Thou hast allotted us our portion of misery: must we also have brethren to persecute us, to deprive us of our consolation, of our trust in thee and in thy love and mercy? For our trust in the virtue of the healing root or in the strength of the vine,—what is it else than a belief in thee, from whom all that surrounds us derives its healing and restoring powers? Father, whom I know not,—who wert once wont to fill my soul, but who now hidest thy face from me,—call me back to thee; be silent no longer! Thy silence shall not delay a soul which thirsts after thee. What man, what father, could be angry with a son for returning to him suddenly, for falling on his neck, and exclaiming, "I am here again, my father! Forgive me if I have anticipated my journey, and returned before the appointed time! The world is everywhere the same,—a scene of labor and pain, of pleasure and reward; but what does it all avail? I am happy only where thou art, and in thy presence am I content to suffer or enjoy." And wouldst thou, Heavenly Father, banish such a child from thy presence?

Dec. 1.

Wilhelm, the man about whom I wrote to you,—that man so enviable in his misfortunes,—was secretary to Charlotte's father; and an unhappy passion for her, which he cherished, concealed, and at length discovered, caused him to be dismissed from his situation. This made him mad. Think, whilst you peruse this plain narration, what an impression the circumstance has made upon me! But it was related to me by Albert with as much calmness as you will probably peruse it.

Dec. 4.

I implore your attention. It is all over with me. I can support this state no longer. To-day I was sitting by Charlotte. She was playing upon her piano a succession of delightful melodies, with such intense expression! Her little sister was dressing her doll upon my lap. The tears came into my eyes. I leaned down, and looked intently at her wedding-ring; my tears fell—immediately she began to play that favorite, that divine air which has so often enchanted me. I felt comfort from a recollection of the past, of those by-gone days when that air was familiar to me; and then I recalled all the sorrows and the disappointments which I had since endured. I paced with hasty strides through the room, my heart became convulsed with painful emotions. At length I went up to her, and exclaimed with eagerness, "For Heaven's sake, play that air no longer!" She stopped, and looked steadfastly at me. She then said, with a smile which sunk deep into my heart: "Werther, you are ill; your dearest food is distasteful to you. But go, I entreat you, and endeavor to compose yourself." I tore myself away. God, thou seest my torments, and wilt end them!

Dec. 6.

How her image haunts me! Waking or asleep, she fills my entire soul! Soon as I close my eyes, here, in my brain, where all the nerves of vision are concentrated, her dark eyes are imprinted. Here—I do not know how to describe it; but if I shut my eyes, hers are immediately before me: dark as an abyss they open upon me, and absorb my senses.

And what is man,—that boasted demigod? Do not his powers fail when he most requires their use? And whether he soar in joy or sink in sorrow, is not his career in both inevitably arrested? And whilst he fondly dreams that he is grasping at infinity, does he not feel compelled to return to a consciousness of his cold, monotonous existence?

THE EDITOR TO THE READER

It is a matter of extreme regret that we want original evidence of the last remarkable days of our friend; and we are, therefore, obliged to interrupt the progress of his correspondence, and to supply the deficiency by a connected narration.

I have felt it my duty to collect accurate information from the mouths of persons well acquainted with his history. The story is simple; and all the accounts agree, except in some unimportant particulars. It is true that, with respect to the characters of the persons spoken of, opinions and judgments vary.

We have only, then, to relate conscientiously the facts which our diligent labor has enabled us to collect, to give the letters of the deceased, and to pay particular attention to the slightest fragment from his pen, more especially as it is so difficult to discover the real and correct motives of men who are not of the common order.

Sorrow and discontent had taken deep root in Werther's soul, and gradually imparted their character to his whole being. The harmony of his mind became completely disturbed; a perpetual excitement and mental irritation, which weakened his natural powers, produced the saddest effects upon him, and rendered him at length the victim of an exhaustion against which he struggled with still more painful efforts than he had displayed, even in contending with his other misfortunes. His mental anxiety weakened his various good qualities; and he was soon converted into a gloomy companion—always unhappy and unjust in his ideas, the more wretched he became. This was, at least, the opinion of Albert's friends. They assert, moreover, that the character of Albert himself had undergone no change in the meantime; he was still the same being whom Werther had loved, honored, and respected from the commencement. His love for Charlotte was unbounded; he was proud of her, and desired that she should be recognized by every one as the noblest of created beings. Was he, however, to blame for wishing to avert from her every appearance of suspicion? or for his unwillingness to share his rich prize with another, even for a moment, and in the most innocent manner? It is asserted that Albert frequently retired from his wife's apartment during Werther's visits; but this did not arise from hatred or aversion to his friend, but only from a feeling that his presence was oppressive to Werther.

Charlotte's father, who was confined to the house by indisposition, was accustomed to send his carriage for her, that she might make excursions in the neighborhood. One day the weather had been unusually severe, and the whole country was covered with snow.

Werther went for Charlotte the following morning, in order that, if Albert were absent, he might conduct her home.

The beautiful weather produced but little impression on his troubled spirit. A heavy weight lay upon his soul, deep melancholy had taken possession of him, and his mind knew no change save from one painful thought to another.

As he now never enjoyed internal peace, the condition of his fellow-creatures was to him a perpetual source of trouble and distress. He believed he had disturbed the happiness of Albert and his wife; and whilst he censured himself strongly for this, he began to entertain a secret dislike to Albert.

His thoughts were occasionally directed to this point. "Yes," he would repeat to himself, with ill-concealed dissatisfaction,—"yes, this is, after all, the extent of that confiding, dear, tender, and sympathetic love, that calm and eternal fidelity! What do I behold but satiety and indifference? Does not every frivolous engagement attract him more than his charming and lovely wife? Does he know how to prize his happiness? Can he value her as she deserves? He possesses her, it is true,—I know that, as I know much more,—and I have become accustomed to the thought that he will drive me mad, or, perhaps, murder me. Is his friendship towards me unimpaired? Does he not view my attachment to Charlotte as an infringement upon his rights, and consider my attention to her as a silent rebuke to himself? I know, and indeed feel, that he dislikes me,— that he wishes for my absence,—that my presence is hateful to him."

He would often pause when on his way to visit Charlotte, stand still as though in doubt, and seem desirous of returning, but would nevertheless proceed; and, engaged in such thoughts and soliloquies as we have described, he finally reached the hunting-lodge, with a sort of involuntary consent.

Upon one occasion he entered the house; and, inquiring for Charlotte, he observed that the inmates were in a state of unusual confusion. The eldest boy informed him that a dreadful misfortune had occurred at Walheim,—that a peasant had been murdered! But this made little impression upon him. Entering the apartment, he found Charlotte engaged reasoning with her father, who, in spite of his infirmity, insisted on going to the scene of the crime, in order to institute an inquiry. The criminal was unknown; the victim had been found dead at his own door that morning. Suspicions were excited; the murdered man had been in the service of a widow, and the person who had previously filled the situation had been dismissed from her employment.

As soon as Werther heard this, he exclaimed with great

excitement, "Is it possible! I must go to the spot,—I cannot delay a moment!" He hastened to Walheim. Every incident returned vividly to his remembrance; and he entertained not the slightest doubt that that man was the murderer to whom he had so often spoken, and for whom he entertained so much regard. His way took him past the well-known lime-trees, to the house where the body had been carried; and his feelings were greatly excited at the sight of the fondly recollected spot. That threshold where the neighbors' children had so often played together was stained with blood; love and attachment, the noblest feelings of human nature, had been converted into violence and murder. The huge trees stood there leafless and covered with hoar-frost; the beautiful hedgerows which surrounded the old churchyard wall were withered; and the gravestones, half covered with snow, were visible through the openings.

As he approached the inn, in front of which the whole village was assembled, screams were suddenly heard. A troop of armed peasants was seen approaching, and every one exclaimed that the criminal had been apprehended. Werther looked, and was not long in doubt. The prisoner was no other than the servant, who had been formerly so attached to the widow, and whom he had met prowling about, with that suppressed anger and ill-concealed despair which we have before described.

"What have you done, unfortunate man?" inquired Werther, as he advanced towards the prisoner. The latter turned his eyes upon him in silence, and then replied with perfect composure, "No one will now marry her, and she will marry no one." The prisoner was taken in the inn, and Werther left the place.

The mind of Werther was fearfully excited by this shocking occurrence. He ceased, however, to be oppressed by his usual feeling of melancholy, moroseness, and indifference to everything that passed around him. He entertained a strong degree of pity for the prisoner, and was seized with an indescribable anxiety to save him from his impending fate. He considered him so unfortunate, he deemed his crime so excusable, and thought his own condition so nearly similar, that he felt convinced he could make every one else view the matter in the light in which he saw it himself. He now became anxious to undertake his defense, and commenced composing an eloquent speech for the occasion; and, on his way to the hunting-lodge, he could not refrain from speaking aloud the statement which he resolved to make to the judge.

Upon his arrival, he found Albert had been before him: and he was a little perplexed by this meeting; but he soon recovered himself, and expressed his opinion with much warmth to the judge. The latter shook his head doubtingly; and although Werther urged his case with the utmost zeal, feeling, and determination in defense of his client, yet, as we may easily suppose, the judge was not much influenced by his appeal. On the contrary, he interrupted him in his address, reasoned with him seriously, and even administered a rebuke to him for becoming the advocate of a murderer. He demonstrated that, according to this precedent, every law might be violated, and the public security utterly destroyed. He added, moreover, that in such a case he could himself do nothing, without incurring the greatest responsibility; that everything must follow in the usual course, and pursue the ordinary channel.

Werther, however, did not abandon his enterprise, and even besought the judge to connive at the flight of the prisoner. But this proposal was peremptorily rejected. Albert, who had taken some part in the discussion, coincided in opinion with the judge. At this Werther became enraged, and took his leave in great anger, after the judge had more than once assured him that the prisoner could not be saved.

The excess of his grief at this assurance may be inferred from a note we have found amongst his papers, and which was doubtless written upon this very occasion.

"You cannot be saved, unfortunate man! I see clearly that we cannot be saved!"

Werther was highly incensed at the observations which Albert had made to the judge in this matter of the prisoner. He thought he could detect therein a little bitterness towards himself personally; and although, upon reflection, it could not escape his sound judgment that their view of the matter was correct, he felt the greatest possible reluctance to make such an admission.

A memorandum of Werther's upon this point, expressive of his general feelings towards Albert, has been found amongst his papers.

"What is the use of my continually repeating that he is a good and estimable man? He is an inward torment to me, and I am incapable of being just towards him."

One fine evening in winter, when the weather seemed inclined to thaw, Charlotte and Albert were returning home together. The former looked from time to time about her, as if she missed Werther's company. Albert began to speak of him, and censured him for his prejudices. He alluded to his unfortunate attachment, and wished it were possible to discontinue his acquaintance. "I desire it on our own account," he added; "and I request you will compel him to alter his deportment towards you, and to visit you less frequently. The world is censorious, and I know that here and there we are spoken of." Charlotte made no reply, and Albert seemed to feel her silence. At least, from that time, he never again spoke of Werther; and when she introduced the subject, he allowed the conversation to die away, or else he directed the discourse into another channel.

The vain attempt Werther had made to save the unhappy murderer was the last feeble glimmering of a flame about to be extinguished. He sank almost immediately afterwards into a state of gloom and inactivity, until he was at length brought to perfect distraction by learning that he was to be summoned as a witness against the prisoner, who asserted his complete innocence.

His mind now became oppressed by the recollection of every misfortune of his past life. The mortification he had suffered at the ambassador's, and his subsequent troubles, were revived in his memory. He became utterly inactive. Destitute of energy, he was cut off from every pursuit and occupation which compose the business of common life; and he became a victim to his own susceptibility, and to his restless passion for the most amiable and beloved of women, whose peace he destroyed. In this unvarying monotony of existence his days were consumed; and his powers became exhausted without aim or design, until they brought him to a sorrowful end.

A few letters which he left behind, and which we here subjoin, afford the best proofs of his anxiety of mind and of the depth of his passion, as well as of his doubts and struggles, and of his weariness of life.

Dec. 12.

Dear Wilhelm, I am reduced to the condition of those unfortunate wretches who believe they are pursued by an evil spirit. Sometimes I am oppressed, not by apprehension or fear, but by an inexpressible internal sensation, which weighs upon my heart, and impedes my breath! Then I wander forth at night, even in this tempestuous season, and feel pleasure in surveying the dreadful scenes around me.

Yesterday evening I went forth. A rapid thaw had suddenly set in: I had been informed that the river had risen, that the brooks had all overflowed their banks, and that the whole vale of Walheim was under water! Upon the stroke of twelve I hastened forth. I beheld a fearful sight. The foaming torrents rolled from the mountains in the moonlight,—fields and meadows, trees and hedges, were confounded together; and the entire valley was converted into a deep lake, which was agitated by the roaring wind! And when the moon shone forth, and tinged the black clouds with silver, and the impetuous torrent at my feet foamed and resounded with awful and grand impetuosity, I was overcome by a mingled sensation of apprehension and delight. With extended arms I looked down into the yawning abyss, and cried, "Plunge!" For a moment my senses forsook me, in the intense delight of ending my sorrows and my sufferings by a plunge into that gulf! And then I felt as if I were rooted to the earth, and incapable of seeking an end to my woes! But my hour is not yet come: I feel it is not. Oh, Wilhelm, how willingly could I abandon my existence to ride the whirlwind, or to embrace the torrent! and then might not rapture perchance be the portion of this liberated soul?

I turned my sorrowful eyes towards a favorite spot, where I was accustomed to sit with Charlotte beneath a willow after a fatiguing walk. Alas! it was covered with water, and with difficulty I found even the meadow. And the fields around the hunting-lodge, thought I. Has our dear bower been destroyed by this unpitying storm? And a beam of past happiness streamed upon me, as the mind of a captive is illumined by dreams of flocks and herds and bygone joys of home! But I am free from blame. I have courage to die! Perhaps I have,—but I still sit here, like a wretched pauper, who collects fagots, and begs her bread from door to door, that she may prolong for a few days a miserable existence which she is unwilling to resign.

Dec. 15.

What is the matter with me, dear Wilhelm? I am afraid of myself! Is not my love for her of the purest, most holy, and most brotherly nature? Has my soul ever been sullied by a single sensual desire? But I will make no protestations. And now, ye nightly visions, how truly have those mortals understood you, who ascribe your various contradictory effects to some invincible power! This night—I tremble at the avowal—I held her in my arms, locked in a close embrace: I pressed her to my bosom, and covered with countless kisses those dear lips which murmured in reply soft protestations of love. My sight became confused by the delicious intoxication of her eyes. Heavens! is it sinful to revel again in such happiness, to recall once more those rapturous moments with intense delight? Charlotte! Charlotte! I am lost! My senses are bewildered, my recollection is confused, mine eyes are bathed in tears—I am ill; and yet I am well—I wish for nothing—I have no desires—it were better I were gone.

Under the circumstances narrated above, a determination to quit this world had now taken fixed possession of Werther's soul. Since Charlotte's return, this thought had been the final object of all his hopes and wishes; but he had resolved that such a step should not be taken with precipitation, but with calmness and tranquillity, and with the most perfect deliberation.

His troubles and internal struggles may be understood from the following fragment, which was found, without any date, amongst his papers, and appears to have formed the beginning of a letter to Wilhelm:

"Her presence, her fate, her sympathy for me, have power still to extract tears from my withered brain.

"One lifts up the curtain, and passes to the other side,— that is all! And why all these doubts and delays? Because we know not what is behind,—because there is no returning, —and because our mind infers that all is darkness and confusion, where we have nothing but uncertainty."

His appearance at length became quite altered by the effect of his melancholy thoughts; and his resolution was now finally and irrevocably taken, of which the following ambiguous letter which he addressed to his friend, may appear to afford some proof:—

Dec. 20.

I am grateful to your love, Wilhelm, for having repeated your advice so seasonably. Yes, you are right: it is undoubtedly better that I should depart. But I do not entirely approve your scheme of returning at once to your neighborhood; at least, I should like to make a little excursion on the way, particularly as we may now expect a continued frost, and consequently good roads. I am much pleased with your intention of coming to fetch me; only delay your journey for a fortnight, and wait for another letter from me. One should gather nothing before it is ripe, and a fortnight sooner or later makes a great difference. Entreat my mother to pray for her son, and tell her I beg her pardon for all the unhappiness I have occasioned her. It has ever been my fate to give pain to those whose happiness I should have promoted. Adieu, my dearest friend. May every blessing of heaven attend you! Farewell.

We find it difficult to express the emotions with which Charlotte's soul was agitated during the whole of this time, whether in relation to her husband or to her unfortunate friend; although we are enabled, by our knowledge of her character, to understand their nature.

It is certain that she had formed a determination by every means in her power to keep Werther at a distance; and if she hesitated in her decision, it was from a sincere feeling of friendly pity, knowing how much it would cost him,—indeed, that he would find it almost impossible to comply with her wishes. But various causes now urged her to be firm. Her husband preserved a strict silence about the whole matter; and she never made it a subject of conversation, feeling bound to prove to him by her conduct that her sentiments agreed with his.

The same day, which was the Sunday before Christmas, after Werther had written the last-mentioned letter to his friend, he came in the evening to Charlotte's house, and found her alone. She was busy preparing some little gifts for her brothers and sisters, which were to be distributed to them on Christmas Day. He began talking of the delight of the children, and of that age when the sudden appearance of the Christmas-tree, decorated with fruit and sweetmeats, and lighted up with wax candles, causes such transports of joy. "You shall have a gift, too, if you behave well," said

Charlotte, hiding her embarrassment under a sweet smile.
"And what do you call behaving well? What should I do,
what can I do, my dear Charlotte?" said he. "Thursday
night," she answered, "is Christmas Eve. The children are
all to be here, and my father too: there is a present for each;
do you come likewise, but do not come before that time."
Werther started. "I desire you will not: it must be so," she
continued. "I ask it of you as a favor, for my own peace and
tranquillity. We cannot go on in this manner any longer."
He turned away his face, walked hastily up and down the
room, muttering indistinctly, "We cannot go on in this manner any longer!" Charlotte, seeing the violent agitation into
which these words had thrown him, endeavored to divert
his thoughts by different questions, but in vain. "No, Charlotte!" he exclaimed; "I will never see you any more!"
"And why so?" she answered. "We may—we must see each
other again; only let it be with more discretion. Oh! why
were you born with that excessive, that ungovernable passion for everything that is dear to you?" Then, taking his
hand, she said: "I entreat of you to be more calm: your
talents, your understanding, your genius, will furnish you
with a thousand resources. Be a man, and conquer an unhappy attachment towards a creature who can do nothing
but pity you." He bit his lips, and looked at her with a
gloomy countenance. She continued to hold his hand. "Grant
me but a moment's patience, Werther," she said. "Do you
not see that you are deceiving yourself, that you are seeking
your own destruction? Why must you love me, me only,
who belong to another? I fear, I much fear, that it is only
the impossibility of possessing me which makes your desire
for me so strong." He drew back his hand, whilst he surveyed her with a wild and angry look. "'Tis well!" he exclaimed, "'tis very well! Did not Albert furnish you with
this reflection? It is profound, a very profound remark."
"A reflection that any one might easily make," she answered;
"and is there not a woman in the whole world who is at
liberty, and has the power to make you happy? Conquer

yourself : look for such a being, and believe me when I say
that you will certainly find her. I have long felt for you, and
for us all : you have confined yourself too long within the
limits of too narrow a circle. Conquer yourself ; make an
effort : a short journey will be of service to you. Seek and
find an object worthy of your love ; then return hither and
let us enjoy together all the happiness of the most perfect
friendship."

"This speech," replied Werther, with a cold smile,—"this
speech should be printed, for the benefit of all teachers. My
dear Charlotte, allow me but a short time longer, and all will
be well." "But however, Werther," she added, "do not come
again before Christmas." He was about to make some
answer, when Albert came in. They saluted each other coldly,
and with mutual embarrassment paced up and down the
room. Werther made some common remarks ; Albert did
the same, and their conversation soon dropped. Albert asked
his wife about some household matters ; and, finding that his
commissions were not executed, he used some expressions
which, to Werther's ear, savored of extreme harshness. He
wished to go, but had not power to move ; and in this situation he remained till eight o'clock, his uneasiness and discontent continually increasing. At length the cloth was laid
for supper, and he took up his hat and stick. Albert invited
him to remain ; but Werther, fancying that he was merely
paying a formal compliment, thanked him coldly and left
the house.

Werther returned home, took the candle from his servant,
and retired to his room alone. He talked for some time with
great earnestness to himself, wept aloud, walked in a state
of great excitement through his chamber ; till at length,
without undressing, he threw himself on the bed, where he
was found by his servant at eleven o'clock, when the latter
ventured to enter the room and take off his boots. Werther
did not prevent him, but forbade him to come in the morning
till he should ring.

On Monday morning, the 21st of December, he wrote to

Charlotte the following letter, which was found, sealed, on his bureau after his death, and was given to her. I shall insert it in fragments; as it appears, from several circumstances, to have been written in that manner.

"It is all over, Charlotte: I am resolved to die! I make this declaration deliberately and coolly, without any romantic passion, on this morning of the day when I am to see you for the last time. At the moment you read these lines, O best of women, the cold grave will hold the inanimate remains of that restless and unhappy being who in the last moments of his existence knew no pleasure so great as that of conversing with you! I have passed a dreadful night,— or rather, let me say, a propitious one; for it has given me resolution, it has fixed my purpose. I am resolved to die. When I tore myself from you yesterday, my senses were in tumult and disorder; my heart was oppressed, hope and pleasure had fled from me forever, and a petrifying cold had seized my wretched being. I could scarcely reach my room. I threw myself on my knees, and Heaven, for the last time, granted me the consolation of shedding tears. A thousand ideas, a thousand schemes, arose within my soul; till at length one last, fixed, final thought took possession of my heart. It was to die. I lay down to rest; and in the morning, in the quiet hour of awakening, the same determination was upon me. To die! It is not despair: it is conviction that I have filled up the measure of my sufferings, that I have reached my appointed term, and must sacrifice myself for thee. Yes, Charlotte, why should I not avow it? One of us three must die: it shall be Werther. O beloved Charlotte! this heart, excited by rage and fury, has often conceived the horrid idea of murdering your husband—you—myself! The lot is cast at length. And in the bright, quiet evenings of summer, when you sometimes wander towards the mountains, let your thoughts then turn to me: recollect how often you have watched me coming to meet you from the valley; then bend your eyes upon the churchyard which contains my grave, and, by the light of the setting sun, mark how the evening breeze waves the tall grass which grows above my tomb. I was calm when I began this letter, but the recollection of these scenes makes me weep like a child."

About ten in the morning, Werther called his servant, and, whilst he was dressing, told him that in a few days he intended to set out upon a journey, and bade him therefore lay his clothes in order, and prepare them for packing up, call in all his accounts, fetch home the books he had lent, and give two months' pay to the poor dependents who were accustomed to receive from him a weekly allowance.

He breakfasted in his room, and then mounted his horse, and went to visit the steward, who, however, was not at home. He walked pensively in the garden, and seemed anxious to renew all the ideas that were most painful to him.

The children did not suffer him to remain alone long. They followed him, skipping and dancing before him, and told him that after to-morrow—and to-morrow—and one day more, they were to receive their Christmas gift from Charlotte; and they then recounted all the wonders of which they had formed ideas in their child imaginations. "To-morrow—and to-morrow," said he, "and one day more!" And he kissed them tenderly. He was going; but the younger boy stopped him, to whisper something in his ear. He told him that his elder brothers had written splendid New Year's wishes—so large!—one for papa, and another for Albert and Charlotte, and one for Werther; and they were to be presented early in the morning, on New-Year's Day. This quite overcame him. He made each of the children a present, mounted his horse, left his compliments for papa and mamma, and, with tears in his eyes, rode away from the place.

He returned home about five o'clock, ordered his servant to keep up his fire, desired him to pack his books and linen at the bottom of the trunk, and to place his coats at the top.

He then appears to have made the following addition to the letter addressed to Charlotte :—

"You do not expect me. You think I will obey you, and not visit you again till Christmas Eve. Oh, Charlotte, to-day or never ! On Christmas Eve you will hold this paper in your hand ; you will tremble, and moisten it with your tears. I will—I must ! Oh, how happy I feel to be determined !"

In the meantime Charlotte was in a pitiable state of mind. After her last conversation with Werther, she found how painful to herself it would be to decline his visits, and knew how severely he would suffer from their separation.

She had, in conversation with Albert, mentioned casually that Werther would not return before Christmas Eve ; and soon afterwards Albert went on horseback to see a person in the neighborhood, with whom he had to transact some business which would detain him all night.

Charlotte was sitting alone. None of her family were near, and she gave herself up to the reflections that silently took possession of her mind. She was forever united to a husband whose love and fidelity she had proved, to whom she was heartily devoted, and who seemed to be a special gift from Heaven to insure her happiness. On the other hand, Werther had become dear to her. There was a cordial unanimity of sentiment between them from the very first hour of their acquaintance, and their long association and repeated interviews had made an indelible impression upon her heart. She had been accustomed to communicate to him every thought and feeling which interested her, and his absence threatened to open a void in her existence which it might be impossible to fill. How heartily she wished that she might change him into her brother,—that she could induce him to marry one of her own friends, or could re-establish his intimacy with Albert.

She passed all her intimate friends in review before her mind, but found something objectionable in each, and could decide upon none to whom she would consent to give him.

Amid all these considerations she felt deeply but indistinctly that her own real but unexpressed wish was to retain him for herself, and her pure and amiable heart felt from this thought a sense of oppression which seemed to forbid a prospect of happiness. She was wretched: a dark cloud obscured her mental vision.

It was now half-past six o'clock, and she heard Werther's step on the stairs. She at once recognized his voice, as he inquired if she were at home. Her heart beat audibly—we could almost say for the first time—at his arrival. It was too late to deny herself; and as he entered, she exclaimed, with a sort of ill-concealed confusion, "You have not kept your word!" "I promised nothing," he answered. "But you should have complied, at least for my sake," she continued. "I implore you, for both our sakes."

She scarcely knew what she said or did, and sent for some friends, who by their presence might prevent her being left alone with Werther. He put down some books he had brought with him, then made inquiries about some others, until she began to hope that her friends might arrive shortly, entertaining at the same time a desire that they might stay away.

At one moment she felt anxious that the servant should remain in the adjoining room, then she changed her mind. Werther, meanwhile, walked impatiently up and down. She went to the piano, and determined not to retire. She then collected her thoughts, and sat down quietly at Werther's side, who had taken his usual place on the sofa.

"Have you brought nothing to read?" she inquired. He had nothing. "There in my drawer," she continued, "you will find your own translation of some of the songs of Ossian. I have not yet read them, as I have still hoped to hear you recite them; but, for some time past, I have not been able to accomplish such a wish." He smiled, and went for the manuscript, which he took with a shudder. He sat down: and, with eyes full of tears, he began to read.

"Star of descending night! fair is thy light in the west! thou liftest thy unshorn head from thy cloud; thy steps are stately on thy hill. What dost thou behold in the plain? The stormy winds are laid. The murmur of the torrent comes from afar. Roaring waves climb the distant rock. The flies of evening are on their feeble wings: the hum of their course is on the field. What dost thou behold, fair light? But thou dost smile and depart. The waves come with joy around thee: they bathe thy lovely hair. Farewell, thou silent beam! Let the light of Ossian's soul arise!

"And it does arise in its strength! I behold my departed friends. Their gathering is on Lora, as in the days of other years. Fingal comes like a watery column of mist! his heroes are around; and see the bards of song,—gray-haired Ullin! stately Ryno! Alpin with the tuneful voice! the soft complaint of Minona! How are ye changed, my friends, since the days of Selma's feast, when we contended, like gales of spring as they fly along the hill, and bend by turns the feebly whistling grass!

"Minona came forth in her beauty, with downcast look and tearful eye. Her hair was flying slowly with the blast that rushed unfrequent from the hill. The souls of the heroes were sad when she raised the tuneful voice. Oft had they seen the grave of Salgar, the dark dwelling of white-bosomed Colma. Colma left alone on the hill with all her voice of song! Salgar promised to come; but the night descended around. Hear the voice of Colma, when she sat alone on the hill!

"*Colma*. It is night: I am alone, forlorn on the hill of storms. The wind is heard on the mountain. The torrent is howling down the rock. No hut receives me from the rain: forlorn on the hill of winds!

"Rise, moon, from behind thy clouds! Stars of the night, arise! Lead me, some light, to the place where my love rests from the chase alone! His bow near him unstrung, his dogs panting around him! But here I must sit alone by the rock of the mossy stream. The stream and the wind roar aloud. I hear not the voice of my love! Why delays my Salgar; why the chief of the hill his promise? Here is the rock, and here the tree; here is the roaring stream! Thou didst promise with night to be here. Ah, whither is my Salgar gone? With thee I would fly from my father, with thee from my brother of pride. Our race have long been foes: we are not foes, O Salgar!

"Cease a little while, O wind! stream, be thou silent awhile! Let my voice be heard around; let my wanderer hear me! Salgar! it is Colma who calls. Here is the tree and the rock. Salgar, my love, I am here! Why delayest thou thy coming? Lo! the calm moon comes forth. The flood is bright in the vale; the rocks are gray on the steep. I see him not on the brow. His dogs come not before him with tidings of his near approach. Here I must sit alone!

"Who lie on the heath beside me? Are they my love and my brother? Speak to me, O my friends! To Colma they give no reply. Speak to me: I am alone! My soul is tormented with fears. Ah, they are dead! Their swords are red from the fight. Oh, my brother! my brother! why hast thou slain my Salgar? Why, O Salgar! hast thou slain my brother? Dear were ye both to me! what shall I say in your praise? Thou wert fair on the hill among thousands! he was terrible in fight! Speak to me! hear my voice! hear me, sons of my love! They are silent, silent forever! Cold, cold, are their breasts of clay! Oh, from the rock on the hill, from the top of the windy steep, speak, ye ghosts of the dead! Speak, I will not be afraid! Whither are ye gone to rest? In what cave of the hill shall I find the departed? No feeble voice is on the gale: no answer half drowned in the storm!

"I sit in my grief: I wait for morning in my tears! Rear the tomb, ye friends of the dead. Close it not till Colma come. My life flies away like a dream. Why should I stay behind? Here shall I rest with my friends, by the stream of the sounding rock. When night comes on the hill,—when the loud winds arise, my ghost shall stand in the blast, and mourn the death of my friends. The hunter shall hear from his booth; he shall fear, but love my voice! For sweet shall my voice be for my friends: pleasant were her friends to Colma.

"Such was thy song, Minona, softly blushing daughter of Torman. Our tears descended for Colma, and our souls were sad! Ullin came with his harp; he gave the song of Alpin. The voice of Alpin was pleasant; the soul of Ryno was a beam of fire! But they had rested in the narrow house: their voice had ceased in Selma! Ullin had returned one day from the chase before the heroes fell. He heard their strife on the hill: their song was soft, but sad! They mourned the fall of Morar, first of mortal men! His soul was like the soul of Fingal; his sword like the sword of Oscar. But he fell, and his father mourned; his sister's eyes were full of tears. Minona's eyes were full of tears, the sister of car-borne Morar. She retired from the song of Ullin, like the moon in the west, when she foresees the shower, and hides her fair head in a cloud. I touched the harp with Ullin: the song of mourning rose!

"*Ryno*. The wind and the rain are past; calm is the noon of day. The clouds are divided in heaven. Over the green hills flies the inconstant sun. Red through the stony vale comes down the stream of the hill. Sweet are thy murmurs, O stream! but more sweet is the voice I hear. It is the voice of Alpin, the son of song, mourning for the dead! Bent is his head of age; red his tearful eye. Alpin, thou son of song, why alone on the silent hill? why complainest thou, as a blast in the wood,—as a wave on the lonely shore?

Alpin. My tears, O Ryno! are for the dead,—my voice for those that have passed away. Tall thou art on the hill; fair among the sons of the vale. But thou shalt fall like Morar; the mourner shall sit on thy tomb. The hills shall know thee no more; thy bow shall lie in thy hall unstrung!

"Thou wert swift, O Morar! as a roe on the desert; terrible as a meteor of fire. Thy wrath was as the storm; thy sword in battle as lightning in the field. Thy voice was a stream after rain, like thunder on distant hills. Many fell by thy arm: they were consumed in the flames of thy wrath. But when thou didst return from war, how peaceful was thy brow! Thy face was like the sun after rain, like the moon in the silence of night; calm as the breast of the lake when the loud wind is laid.

"Narrow is thy dwelling now! dark the place of thine abode! With three steps I compass thy grave, O thou who wast so great before! Four stones, with their heads of moss, are the only memorial of thee. A tree with scarce a leaf, long grass which whistles in the wind, mark to the hunter's eye the grave of the mighty Morar. Morar! thou art low indeed. Thou hast no mother to mourn thee, no maid with her tears of love. Dead is she that brought thee forth. Fallen is the daughter of Morglan.

"Who on his staff is this? Who is this whose head is white with age, whose eyes are red with tears, who quakes at every step? It is thy father, O Morar! the father of no son but thee. He heard of thy fame in war, he heard of foes dispersed. He heard of Morar's renown; why did he not hear of his wound? Weep, thou father of Morar! Weep, but thy son heareth thee not. Deep is the sleep of the dead,— low their pillow of dust. No more shall he hear thy voice,— no more awake at thy call. When shall it be morn in the grave, to bid the slumberer awake? Farewell, thou bravest of men! thou conqueror in the field! but the field shall see thee no more, nor the dark wood be lightened with the splendor of thy steel. Thou hast left no son. The song shall preserve thy name. Future times shall hear of thee,—they shall hear of the fallen Morar!

"The grief of all arose, but most the bursting sigh of Armin. He remembers the death of his son, who fell in the days of his youth. Carmor was near the hero, the chief of the echoing Galmal. Why burst the sigh of Armin? he said. Is there a cause to mourn? The song comes with its music to melt and please the soul. It is like soft mist that, rising from a lake, pours on the silent vale; the green flowers are filled with dew, but the sun returns in his strength, and the mist is gone. Why art thou sad, O Armin, chief of sea-surrounded Gorma?

"Sad I am! nor small is my cause of woe! Carmor, thou hast lost no son; thou hast lost no daughter of beauty. Colgar the valiant lives, and Annira, fairest maid. The boughs of thy house ascend, O Carmor! but Armin is the last of his race. Dark is thy bed, O Daura! deep thy sleep in the tomb! When shalt thou wake with thy songs,—with all thy voice of music?

"Arise, winds of autumn, arise; blow along the heath! Streams of the mountains, roar; roar, tempests in the groves of my oaks! Walk through broken clouds, O moon! show thy pale face at intervals; bring to my mind the night when all my children fell,—when Arindal the mighty fell, when Daura the lovely failed. Daura, my daughter, thou wert fair, —fair as the moon on Fura, white as the driven snow, sweet as the breathing gale. Arindal, thy bow was strong, thy spear was swift on the field, thy look was like mist on the wave, thy shield a red cloud in a storm! Armar, renowned in war, came and sought Daura's love. He was not long refused: fair was the hope of their friends.

"Erath, son of Odgal, repined: his brother had been slain by Armar. He came disguised like a son of the sea; fair was his cliff on the wave, white his locks of age, calm his serious brow. Fairest of women, he said, lovely daughter of Armin! a rock not distant in the sea bears a tree on its side: red shines the fruit afar. There Armar waits for Daura. I come to carry his love! She went,—she called on Armar. Naught answered, but the son of the rock. Armar, my love, my love! why tormentest thou me with fear? Hear, son of Arnart, hear! it is Daura who calleth thee. Erath, the traitor, fled laughing to the land. She lifted up her voice,—she called for her brother and her father. Arindal! Armin! none to relieve you, Daura.

"Her voice came over the sea. Arindal, my son, descended from the hill, rough in the spoils of the chase. His arrows rattled by his side; his bow was in his hand, five dark-gray dogs attended his steps. He saw fierce Erath on the shore; he seized and bound him to an oak. Thick wind the thongs of the hide around his limbs; he loads the winds with his groans. Arindal ascends the deep in his boat to bring Daura to land. Armar came in his wrath, and let fly the gray feathered shaft. It sung, it sunk in thy heart, O Arindal, my son! for Erath the traitor thou diest. The oar is stopped at once: he panted on the rock and expired. What is thy grief, O Daura, when round thy feet is poured thy brother's blood? The boat is broken in twain. Armar plunges into the sea to rescue his Daura, or die. Sudden a blast from a hill came over the waves; he sank, and he rose no more.

"Alone, on the sea-beat rock, my daughter was heard to complain; frequent and loud were her cries. What could her father do? All night I stood on the shore: I saw her by the faint beam of the moon. All night I heard her cries. Loud was the wind; the rain beat hard on the hill. Before morning appeared, her voice was weak; it died away like the evening breeze among the grass of the rocks. Spent with grief, she expired, and left thee, Armin, alone. Gone is my strength in war, fallen my pride among women. When the storms aloft arise, when the north lifts the wave on high, I sit by the sounding shore, and look on the fatal rock.

"Often by the setting moon I see the ghosts of my children; half viewless they walk in mournful conference together."

A torrent of tears which streamed from Charlotte's eyes, and gave relief to her bursting heart, stopped Werther's recitation. He threw down the book, seized her hand, and wept bitterly. Charlotte leaned upon her hand, and buried her face in her handkerchief: the agitation of both was excessive. They felt that their own fate was pictured in the misfortunes of Ossian's heroes,—they felt this together, and their tears redoubled. Werther supported his forehead on Charlotte's arm: she trembled, she wished to be gone; but sorrow and sympathy lay like a leaden weight upon her soul. She recovered herself shortly, and begged Werther, with broken sobs, to leave her,—implored him with the utmost earnestness to comply with her request. He trembled; his heart was ready to burst: then taking up the book again, he recommenced reading, in a voice broken by sobs.

"Why dost thou waken me, O spring? Thy voice woos me, exclaiming, I refresh thee with heavenly dews, but the time of my decay is approaching, the storm is nigh that shall wither my leaves. To-morrow the traveler shall come,—he shall come, who beheld me in beauty: his eye shall seek me in the field around, but he shall not find me."

The whole force of these words fell upon the unfortunate Werther. Full of despair, he threw himself at Charlotte's feet, seized her hands, and pressed them to his eyes and to his forehead. An apprehension of his fatal project now struck her for the first time. Her senses were bewildered: she held his hands, pressed them to her bosom; and, leaning towards him with emotions of the tenderest pity, her warm cheek touched his. They lost sight of everything. The world disappeared from their eyes. He clasped her in his arms, strained her to his bosom, and covered her trembling lips with passionate kisses. "Werther!" she cried with a faint voice, turning herself away; "Werther!" and, with a feeble hand, she pushed him from her. At length, with the firm voice of virtue, she exclaimed, "Werther!" He resisted not, but, tearing himself from her arms, fell on his knees before her. Charlotte rose, and with disordered grief, in mingled tones of love and resentment, she exclaimed, "It is the last time, Werther! You shall never see me any more!" Then, casting one last, tender look upon her unfortunate lover, she rushed into the adjoining room, and locked the door. Werther held out his arms, but did not dare to detain her. He continued on the ground, with his head resting on the sofa, for half an hour, till he heard a noise which brought him to his senses. The servant entered. He then walked up and down the room; and when he was again left alone, he went to Charlotte's door, and, in a low voice, said, "Charlotte, Charlotte! but one word more, one last adieu!" She returned no answer. He stopped, and listened and entreated; but all was silent. At length he tore himself from the place, crying, "Adieu, Charlotte, adieu forever!"

Werther ran to the gate of the town. The guards, who knew him, let him pass in silence. The night was dark and stormy,—it rained and snowed. He reached his own door about eleven. His servant, although seeing him enter the house without his hat, did not venture to say anything; and as he undressed his master, he found that his clothes were wet. His hat was afterwards found on the point of a rock overhanging the valley; and it is inconceivable how he could have climbed to the summit on such a dark, tempestuous night without losing his life.

He retired to bed, and slept to a late hour. The next morning his servant, upon being called to bring his coffee, found him writing. He was adding, to Charlotte, what we here annex.

"For the last, last time, I open these eyes. Alas! they will behold the sun no more. It is covered by a thick, impenetrable cloud. Yes, Nature! put on mourning; your child, your friend, your lover, draws near his end! This thought, Charlotte, is without parallel; and yet it seems like a mysterious dream when I repeat—This is my last day! The last! Charlotte, no word can adequately express this thought. The last! To-day I stand erect in all my strength,—to-morrow, cold, and stark, I shall lie extended upon the ground. To die! What is death? We do but dream in our discourse upon it. I have seen many human beings die; but, so straitened is our feeble nature, we have no clear conception of the beginning or the end of our existence. At this moment I am my own,—or rather I am thine, thine, my adored!—and the next we are parted, severed—perhaps forever! No, Charlotte, no! How can I, how can you, be annihilated? We exist. What is annihilation? A mere word, an unmeaning sound, that fixes no impression on the mind. Dead, Charlotte! laid in the cold earth, in the dark and narrow grave! I had a friend once who was everything to me in early youth. She died. I followed her hearse; I stood by her grave when the coffin was lowered; and when I heard the creaking of the cords as they were loosened and drawn up, when the first shovelful of earth was thrown in, and the coffin returned a hollow sound, which grew fainter and fainter till all was completely covered over, I threw myself on the ground; my heart was smitten, grieved, shattered, rent—but I neither knew what had happened nor what was to happen to me. Death! the grave! I understand not the words. Forgive, oh, forgive me! Yesterday—ah, that day should have been the last of my life! Thou angel!—for the first—first time in my existence, I felt rapture glow within my inmost soul. She loves, she loves me! Still burns upon my lips the sacred fire they received from thine. New torrents of delight overwhelm my soul. Forgive me, oh, forgive!

"I knew that I was dear to you; I saw it in your first entrancing look, knew it by the first pressure of your hand; but when I was absent from you, when I saw Albert at your side, my doubts and fears returned.

"Do you remember the flowers you sent me, when at that crowded assembly you could neither speak nor extend your hand to me? Half the night I was on my knees before those flowers, and I regarded them as the pledges of your love; but those impressions grew fainter, and were at length effaced.

"Everything passes away; but a whole eternity could not extinguish the living flame which was yesterday kindled by your lips, and which now burns within me. She loves me! These arms have encircled her waist, these lips have trembled upon hers. She is mine! Yes, Charlotte, you are mine forever!

"And what do they mean by saying Albert is your husband? He may be so for this world; and in this world it is a sin to love you, to wish to tear you from his embrace. Yes, it is a crime; and I suffer the punishment, but I have enjoyed the full delight of my sin. I have inhaled a balm that has revived my soul. From this hour you are mine; yes, Charlotte, you are mine! I go before you. I go to my Father and to your Father. I will pour out my sorrows before him, and he will give me comfort till you arrive. Then will I fly to meet you. I will claim you, and remain in your eternal embrace, in the presence of the Almighty.

"I do not dream, I do not rave. Drawing nearer to the grave, my perceptions become clearer. We shall exist; we shall see each other again; we shall behold your mother; I shall behold her, and expose to her my inmost heart. Your mother—your image!"

About eleven o'clock Werther asked his servant if Albert had returned. He answered, "Yes"; for he had seen him pass on horseback: upon which Werther sent him the following note, unsealed:—

"Be so good as to lend me your pistols for a journey. Adieu."

Charlotte had slept little during the past night. All her apprehensions were realized in a way that she could neither foresee nor avoid. Her blood was boiling in her veins, and a thousand painful sensations rent her pure heart. Was it the ardor of Werther's passionate embraces that she felt within her bosom? Was it anger at his daring? Was it the sad comparison of her present condition with former days of innocence, tranquillity, and self-confidence? How could she approach her husband, and confess a scene which she had no reason to conceal, and which she yet felt, nevertheless, unwilling to avow? They had preserved so long a silence towards each other—and should she be the first to break it by so unexpected a discovery? She feared that the mere statement of Werther's visit would trouble him, and his distress would be heightened by her perfect candor. She wished that he could see her in her true light, and judge her without prejudice; but was she anxious that he should read her inmost soul? On the other hand, could she deceive a being to whom all her thoughts had ever been

exposed as clearly as a crystal, and from whom no sentiment had ever been concealed? These reflections made her
anxious and thoughtful. Her mind still dwelt on Werther,
who was now lost to her, but whom she could not bring herself to resign, and for whom she knew nothing was left but
despair if she should be lost to him forever.

A recollection of that mysterious estrangement which had
lately subsisted between herself and Albert, and which she
could never thoroughly understand, was now beyond
measure painful to her. Even the prudent and the good
have, before now, hesitated to explain their mutual differ-
ences, and have dwelt in silence upon their imaginary griev-
ances, until circumstances have become so entangled that in
that critical juncture, when a calm explanation would have
saved all parties, an understanding was impossible. And
thus if domestic confidence had been earlier established
between them, if love and kind forbearance had mutually
animated and expanded their hearts, it might not, perhaps,
even yet have been too late to save our friend.

But we must not forget one remarkable circumstance. We
may observe, from the character of Werther's correspondence, that he had never affected to conceal his anxious desire
to quit this world. He had often discussed the subject with
Albert; and between the latter and Charlotte it had not in-
frequently formed a topic of conversation. Albert was so
opposed to the very idea of such an action, that, with a degree of irritation unusual in him, he had more than once
given Werther to understand that he doubted the seriousness
of his threats, and not only turned them into ridicule but
caused Charlotte to share his feelings of incredulity. Her
heart was thus tranquillized when she felt disposed to view
the melancholy subject in a serious point of view, though she
never communicated to her husband the apprehensions she
sometimes experienced.

Albert, upon his return, was received by Charlotte with
ill-concealed embarrassment. He was himself out of humor:
his business was unfinished; and he had just discovered

that the neighboring official, with whom he had to deal, was an obstinate and narrow-minded personage. Many things has occurred to irritate him.

He inquired whether anything had happened during his absence, and Charlotte hastily answered that Werther had been there on the evening previously. He then inquired for his letters, and was answered that several packages had been left in his study. He thereon retired, leaving Charlotte alone.

The presence of the being she loved and honored produced a new impression on her heart. The recollection of his generosity, kindness, and affection had calmed her agitation : a secret impulse prompted her to follow him ; she took her work and went to his study, as was often her custom. He was busily employed opening and reading his letters. It seemed as if the contents of some were disagreeable. She asked some questions : he gave short answers, and sat down to write.

Several hours passed in this manner, and Charlotte's feelings became more and more melancholy. She felt the extreme difficulty of explaining to her husband, under any circumstances, the weight that lay upon her heart ; and her depression became every moment greater, in proportion as she endeavored to hide her grief and to conceal her tears.

The arrival of Werther's servant occasioned her the greatest embarrassment. He gave Albert a note, which the latter coldly handed to his wife, saying, at the same time, "Give him the pistols. I wish him a pleasant journey," he added, turning to the servant. These words fell upon Charlotte like a thunder-stroke : she rose from her seat half-fainting, and unconscious of what she did. She walked mechanically towards the wall, took down the pistols with a trembling hand, slowly wiped the dust from them, and would have delayed longer, had not Albert hastened her movements by an impatient look. She then delivered the fatal weapons to the servant, without being able to utter a word. As soon as he had departed, she folded up her work, and retired at once to her room, her heart overcome with the most fearful forebodings. She anticipated some dreadful calamity. She was at one moment on the point of going to her husband, throwing herself at his feet, and acquainting him with all that had happened on the previous evening, that she might acknowledge her fault, and explain her apprehensions; then she saw that such a step would be useless, as she would certainly be unable to induce Albert to visit Werther. Dinner was served; and a kind friend whom she had persuaded to remain assisted to sustain the conversation, which was carried on by a sort of compulsion, till the events of the morning were forgotten.

When the servant brought the pistols to Werther, the latter received them with transports of delight upon hearing that Charlotte had given them to him with her own hand. He ate some bread, drank some wine, sent his servant to dinner, and then sat down to write as follows:—

"They have been in your hands—you wiped the dust from them. I kiss them a thousand times—you have touched them. Yes, Heaven favors my design—and you, Charlotte, provide me with the fatal instruments. It was my desire to receive my death from your hands, and my wish is gratified. I have made inquiries of my servant. You trembled when you gave him the pistols, but you bade me no adieu. Wretched, wretched that I am,—not one farewell! How could you shut your heart against me in that hour which makes you mine forever? Oh, Charlotte, ages cannot efface the impression, —I feel you cannot hate the man who so passionately loves you!"

After dinner he called his servant, desired him to finish the packing up, destroyed many papers, and then went out to pay some trifling debts. He soon returned home, then went out again notwithstanding the rain, walked for some time in the count's garden, and afterwards proceeded farther into the country. Towards evening he came back once more, and resumed his writing.

"Wilhelm, I have for the last time beheld the mountains, the forests, and the sky. Farewell! And you, my dearest mother, forgive me! Console her, Wilhelm. God bless you! I have settled all my affairs! Farewell! We shall meet again, and be happier than ever."

"I have requited you badly, Albert; but you will forgive me. I have disturbed the peace of your home. I have sowed distrust between you. Farewell! I will end all this wretchedness. And oh that my death may render you happy! Albert, Albert! make that angel happy, and the blessing of Heaven be upon you!"

He spent the rest of the evening in arranging his papers: he tore and burned a great many; others he sealed up, and directed to Wilhelm. They contained some detached thoughts and maxims, some of which I have perused. At ten o'clock he ordered his fire to be made up, and a bottle of wine to be brought to him. He then dismissed his servant, whose room, as well as the apartments of the rest of the family, was situated in another part of the house. The servant lay down without undressing, that he might be the sooner ready for his journey in the morning, his master having informed him that the post-horses would be at the door before six o'clock.

"Past eleven o'clock! All is silent around me, and my soul is calm. I thank thee, O God, that thou bestowest strength and courage upon me in these last moments! I approach the window, my dearest of friends; and through the clouds, which are at this moment driven rapidly along by the impetuous winds, I behold the stars which illumine the eternal heavens. No, you will not fall, celestial bodies: the hand of the Almighty supports both you and me! I have looked for the last time upon the constellation of the Greater Bear: it is my favorite star; for when I bade you farewell at night, Charlotte, and turned my steps from your door, it always shone upon me. With what rapture have I at times beheld it! How often have I implored it with uplifted hands to witness my felicity! and even still— But what object is there, Charlotte, which fails to summon up your image before me? Do you not surround me on all sides? and have I not, like a child, treasured up every trifle which you have consecrated by your touch?

"Your profile, which was so dear to me, I return to you; and I pray you to preserve it. Thousands of kisses have I imprinted upon it, and a thousand times has it gladdened my heart on departing from and returning to my home.

"I have implored your father to protect my remains. At the corner of the churchyard, looking towards the fields, there are two lime-trees,—there I wish to lie. Your father can, and doubtless will, do thus much for his friend. Implore it of him. But perhaps pious Christians will not choose that their bodies should be buried near the corpse of a poor, unhappy wretch like me. Then let me be laid in some remote valley, or near the highway, where the priest and Levite may bless themselves as they pass by my tomb, whilst the Samaritan will shed a tear for my fate.

"See, Charlotte, I do not shudder to take the cold and fatal cup, from which I shall drink the draught of death. Your hand presents it to me, and I do not tremble. All, all is now concluded; the wishes and the hopes of my existence are fulfilled. With cold, unflinching hand I knock at the brazen portals of Death.

"Oh that I had enjoyed the bliss of dying for you! how gladly would I have sacrificed myself for you, Charlotte! And could I but restore peace and joy to your bosom, with what resolution, with what joy, would I not meet my fate! But it is the lot of only a chosen few to shed their blood for their friends, and by their death to augment a thousand times the happiness of those by whom they are beloved.

"I wish, Charlotte, to be buried in the dress I wear at present: it has been rendered sacred by your touch. I have begged this favor of your father. My spirit soars above my sepulcher. I do not wish my pockets to be searched. The knot of pink ribbon which you wore on your bosom the first time I saw you, surrounded by the children— Oh, kiss them a thousand times for me, and tell them the fate of their unhappy friend! I think I see them playing around me. The dear children! How warmly have I been attached to you, Charlotte! Since the first hour I saw you, how impossible have I found it to leave you! This ribbon must be buried with me: it was a present from you on my birthday. How confused it all appears! Little did I then think that I should journey this road! But peace! I pray you, peace!

"They are loaded—the clock strikes twelve. I say amen. Charlotte, Charlotte! farewell, farewell!"

A neighbor saw the flash, and heard the report of the pistol; but as everything remained quiet, he thought no more of it.

In the morning, at six o'clock, the servant went into Werther's room with a candle. He found his master stretched upon the floor, weltering in his blood, and the pistols at his side. He called, he took him in his arms, but received no answer. Life was not yet quite extinct. The servant ran for a surgeon, and then went to fetch Albert. Charlotte heard the ringing of the bell; a cold shudder seized her. She awakened her husband, and they both rose. The servant, bathed in tears, faltered forth the dreadful news. Charlotte fell senseless at Albert's feet.

When the surgeon came to the unfortunate Werther, he was still lying on the floor; and his pulse beat, but his limbs were cold. The bullet, entering the forehead over the right eye, had penetrated the skull. A vein was opened in his right arm; the blood came, and he still continued to breathe.

From the blood which flowed from the chair, it could be inferred that he had committed the rash act sitting at his bureau, and that he afterwards fell upon the floor. He was found lying on his back near the window. He was in full-dress costume.

The house, the neighborhood, and the whole town were immediately in commotion. Albert arrived. They had laid Werther on the bed. His head was bound up, and the paleness of death was upon his face. His limbs were motionless; but he still breathed, at one time strongly, then weaker,—his death was momently expected.

He had drunk only one glass of the wine. "Emilia Galotti" lay open upon his bureau.

I shall say nothing of Albert's distress or of Charlotte's grief.

The old steward hastened to the house immediately upon hearing the news; he embraced his dying friend amid a flood of tears. His eldest boys soon followed him on foot. In speechless sorrow they threw themselves on their knees by the bedside, and kissed his hands and face. The eldest, who was his favorite, hung over him till he expired; and even then he was removed by force. At twelve o'clock Werther breathed his last. The presence of the steward, and the precautions he had adopted, prevented a disturbance; and that night, at the hour of eleven, he caused the body to be interred in the place which Werther had selected for himself.

The steward and his sons followed the corpse to the grave. Albert was unable to accompany them. Charlotte's life was despaired of. The body was carried by laborers. No priest attended.

THE SPORT OF DESTINY *

A Fragment Borrowed from Fact

By Johann von Schiller

Aloysius Von G—— was the son of a commoner of
some note in the —— Company's service. He had great
ability which was so well developed by an excellent education that, at an unusually early age, he entered the military
service of his native Prince. Both were in the full glow of
their youth and both were possessed of rash and enterpris-
ing natures, which soon endeared G—— to the Prince.
Gifted with wit, charm and good humor, as well as information, G—— soon became an agreeable addition to every
circle in which he moved, while the Prince had the good sense
to appreciate his virtues. Added to these, he showed a great
spirit of perseverance and all these qualities were heightened
by a very pleasing figure, and an appearance of blooming
health and power. He combined, in his demeanor, high spirits and natural dignity, relieved by a due share of modesty
of manner. The Prince was charmed with both the inward
and exterior qualities of his new associate, and the similarity
of age, of inclination, and of character soon led to a great
degree of intimacy between the two. G—— was advanced
very rapidly, though to the Prince, even this rate of promo-
tion seemed all too slow, so high was his opinion of his
friend. When he was not yet twenty-two, G—— had reached
heights which would have been envied by the most vener-
able statesmen at the close of their careers. But his active
spirit was incapable of contentment or repose and while the

* Translated by Marian Klopfer. Copyright, 1933, by The Modern
Library, Inc.

Prince was engaged in his pleasures, the young favorite would devote himself with unwearying assiduity to important affairs. He became, in time, so skillful and judicious that his talents were more and more constantly employed, so that, from the mere companion of his pleasures, he soon became counselor and Minister, and finally, the director of his Prince. In a short time, the only way to obtain the royal favor was through him. He had the disposal of all ranks and offices, as well as the distribution of all rewards and remunerations.

G——, however, was far too young and inexperienced, and had risen by too rapid strides, to use his power with moderation. The respectful humility and attentions shown him by the first nobles of the land, who all surpassed him in birth, fortune and reputation, awoke the slumbering embers of his pride and tyranny and he began to show a hardness of character which remained through all the vicissitudes of his fortunes. There was no service, however great, which his friends might not venture to solicit; but woe be to his enemies! He was less solicitous to enrich himself than a number of his creatures, but his choice of them was dictated by sheer whim rather than by justice. Yet, by exacting too much, by the haughtiness of his commands, and by his whole demeanor, he alienated from him even those who were most in his debt, while his rivals, and those who envied him were quickly converted into his deadliest enemies. These men, watching his every act with jealousy, were collecting materials for his future accusation and were slowly planning to undermine his greatness. Among them was a Piedmontese Count, named Joseph Martinenzo, belonging to the Prince's suite. G—— himself had promoted him, as a harmless, obedient creature, to his present post—that of attending the pleasures of his princely master, which he began to find too irksome now that he was engaged in more important occupations.

Viewing this man merely as the work of his own hands, and thinking that he could at any time again reduce him to his original unimportance, he felt assured, through motives of fear and gratitude, of the fidelity of his creature. He thus fell into the same error as was committed by Richelieu in entrusting Louis the Thirteenth to the care of the young Le Grand. Lacking Richelieu's ability of repairing so great a mistake, he had, further, to deal with a far bitterer enemy than the French Minister had to encounter. Instead of boasting of his good fortune, or allowing his patron to feel that he could dispense with his further patronage, Martinenzo was only the more cautious to maintain a show of dependence, and to bind himself constantly closer in the alliance with his benefactor. Meanwhile, he ignored no opportunity afforded him by his office to ingratiate himself with the Prince, until, from being useful, he became indispensable to him. Discovering all the avenues to his confidence and favor, he gradually made himself master of the Prince's mind. All those arts which pride and a natural elevation of character had taught the Minister to hold in contempt were brought into play by the Italian, who was utterly unscrupulous about the attainment of his object as well as about the means he employed. He was well aware that nothing is so conducive to unreserved confidence as participation in common vices and with this knowledge he proceeded to play upon the Prince, exciting passions hitherto dormant and directing them to the worst of purposes. By a train of the most seductive arts, he plunged him into excesses which admitted of no outside participation and no witnesses, and thus finally became the master of the most incriminating secrets. He then began to lay the foundation of his own fortunes upon the progressive degradation of the Prince's character ; the secrets which rendered him so formidable obtained him complete domination over the Prince's feelings before G—— even suspected that he had a rival.

It may appear strange that so important a change should escape the attention of the Minister ; but he had, unluckily, too high an opinion of his own worth to suspect that a man like Martinenzo would dare to become his opponent, while the latter was too cautious to commit the least error which might rouse his patron from his security. The same overweening confidence which had caused the downfall of so many of his predecessors from the summit of royal favor, was fast preparing the Minister's ruin. The confidential terms upon which he saw Martinenzo with his master gave him no uneasiness; he was glad to resign a species of favor which he despised, and which left his ambition unsatisfied: it was only as it smoothed his path to power that he had ever valued the Prince's friendship, and he foolishly threw down the ladder by which he had risen to his goal.

Martinenzo was not the man to play a subordinate part. At each step in the Prince's favor, his hopes rose higher, and his ambition, growing in a friendly soil, began to strike deeper and stronger roots. The greater his reputation grew, the more his rôle of humility toward his benefactor irked him. On the other hand, the Minister's deportment toward him, far from becoming more tactful as he rose in the Prince's favor, aimed at humbling his pride by admonitions reminding him of his dependence. This tyranny finally grew so intolerable to Martinenzo that he boldly plotted the destruction of his rival at a single blow. Under an impenetrable veil of dissimulation, he brought his plan to completion, still not venturing to enter into open competition with his rival. Though the first glow of the Minister's favor was at an end, the slightest circumstance could still have restored it, since the Prince showed the greatest respect for his mind and his advices and if he had once been dear to his master as a friend, he was now equally powerful as a Minister.

Fully realizing the situation, the Italian knew that the blow which he was about to strike must succeed, or else prove fatal to himself. The means by which he gained his object remained a secret with the few who aided him. It was reported that he had detected a secret correspondence of a treacherous nature, carried on by the Minister with a neighboring court; but whether his proposals had been listened to or rejected, remained a matter of doubt. The Prince felt that G—— was one of the most ungrateful and treacherous of men—that his delinquencies were fully proved and only awaited punishment. This was secretly arranged between the new favorite and his master; G—— was unconscious of the gathering storm, and continued wrapt in his fatal security until the final tragic moment, which precipitated him from the summit of princely honors into the depth of obloquy and contempt.

On the appointed day, G—— appeared as usual upon the parade. Not many years ago an ensign, he was now an officer of distinguished rank and even this was only meant as a screen for the exercise of his political power, which actually placed him above the foremost of the land. The parade was his stage—here he indulged in all the pride of patronage; here he received the obsequious attentions of his creatures, thus rewarding himself for the exertions and labors of the day. His chief dependents, all men of rank, were seen gathering around him, eager to offer their obeisance, yet evidently anxious as to the kind of reception they might meet with. The Prince himself, as he passed by, beheld his chief Minister with a relenting eye; he felt how much more dangerous it well might be to dispense with the services of such a man than with the friendship of his rival. Yet this spot, where he was flattered and adored, almost like a god, was that which had been chosen for the scene of his tragic disgrace. The Prince rejoined the Italian, and the affair was suffered to proceed. G—— mingled carelessly among his friends who, not suspecting any more than he, offered him their respects and awaited his commands. Suddenly, Martinenzo appeared, accompanied by some State officers. He was no longer the same meek, cringing, smiling courtier; the presumption and insolence of a lackey suddenly elevated into a master were visible in his haughty step and fiery eye. He marched straight up to the Prime Minister and confronted him, with his hat on, for some moments, without uttering a word; then in the Prince's name, he demanded his sword. This was handed to him with an expression of terrific emotion; then, thrusting the naked point into the ground, he split it into shivers with his foot—the fragments lay at G——'s feet. At this signal the two adjutants seized him; one strove to tear the order of the cross from his breast, the other pulled off the shoulder knots, the facings of his uniform, and even the plume of feathers from his hat. During this cruel and humiliating proceeding, which took scarcely an instant, not a single voice was raised; a breathless silence reigned throughout the immense throng. The hundreds of nobles who were present, all stood motionless, with pale cheeks and beating hearts, an expression of pained surprise on every face. Throughout this trying ordeal, G——, though anguished, bore himself with fortitude and composure.

When this procedure was ended, he was conducted through many rows of spectators, to the very end of the parade ground, where a covered carriage was waiting for him. He was motioned to ascend, an escort of mounted hussars being ready to attend him. Meanwhile, the report of what had occurred was spread on all sides; windows were opened, the streets were filled with throngs of curious people pursuing the carriage—their cries of triumph, of scorn, or of indignation, echoing far and wide.

He escaped the frightful din at last, only to meet a more fearful trial. The carriage turned out of the high road into a narrow, unfrequented by-way, towards the place of judgment and then into a more public path. Exposed to the sultry summer heat, without hearing any accusation, without attendance or consolation, he passed seven hours of misery and affliction, before he arrived at his destination. Late in the evening the carriage stopped and G——, unconscious, his gigantic strength having yielded at last to twelve hours' fast, was dragged from his seat. When he regained consciousness, he found himself consigned to a subterranean dungeon, dimly lit by the rising moon whose rays entered through a few grated openings from a great height above. Near him he found a portion of coarse bread, with a bowl of water, and a heap of straw for his bed. He endured this plight without any interruption, until noon the following day, when he heard the sash of one of the iron windows in the center of the tower drawn aside; two hands were visible, lowering down a basket like that which had contained his food the day before. For the first time since his arrest he felt some inclination to inquire into the cause, and also into the nature of his future destiny. But he received no answer from above; the hands disappeared and the sash was closed. Thus, without beholding the face, or hearing the voice of a fellow-creature; without having the least light thrown on his destiny, left in utter ignorance both as to the future and the past; never feeling the warmth of the sun nor the freshness of the air; he spent four hundred and ninety days of agony, only sustained by a small allowance of coarse bread. But this was not all, for he made a discovery one day which increased and intensified his wretchedness. He recognized the place; he had ordered it constructed only a short while ago, in a rage of vengeance against a worthy officer who had had the misfortune to displease him, and he had even suggested the manner in which it might be made more horrible and revolting. What added the last bitter sting to his punishment was that the same officer who had been destined to occupy it, had just succeeded the late commander of the fortress, and by a sort of retributive justice, was made the master of his enemy's destiny. He was deprived of the last poor comfort, the right of commiserating with himself. He knew he did not deserve it; he felt himself an object of disgust and of the bitterest self-contempt; and, worst of all, dependent upon the magnanimity of a man to whom he had shown none.

His jailer was, fortunately for him, a man of noble feelings, who scorned to take a mean revenge. He felt sorry at the idea of fulfilling the part assigned to him; yet, as a faithful subject and an old soldier, he did not think himself justified in departing from the usual rules, and he feared to swerve from his instructions. Still, he pitied him, and pointed him out to a benevolent assistant, the preacher of the prison, who, having been able to ascertain nothing against the prisoner beyond mere report, resolved, as far as possible, to mitigate his sufferings. This excellent man, whose name I willingly suppress, believed that he could best fulfill his pious charge by bestowing his spiritual support and consolations upon a being deprived of all other hopes of mercy.

As he could not obtain permission from the commandant himself to visit the prisoner, he proceeded to the capital to solicit the consent of the Prince. He fell at his feet, appealing for some mitigation of the prisoner's sufferings. He insisted, in the name of his pious calling, on free admittance to the prisoner, whom he claimed as a penitent, and for whose soul he was responsible. His subject made him eloquent and he soon made some impression upon the Prince, who had at first refused his request. The result of his efforts won him, at last, full permission to visit the wretched prisoner and administer to his spiritual needs.

The first human face G—— saw, after a lapse of sixteen months, was that of his new benefactor and he was eloquent in his gratitude, for this was the only friend he had in the world; all his prosperity had never brought him one. The pastor was filled with horror and astonishment on entering the vault. His eyes sought a human form, but beheld, creeping towards him, a white and wild-looking living skeleton, whose couch resembled the den of a beast of prey rather than a human resting-place. All signs of life seemed absent from his countenance; on which despair and grief had traced deep furrows; his beard and nails had grown to a frightful length; his clothing was falling about him in tatters and, due to the lack of water and all means of cleanliness, the air was foul and contaminated. Almost terrified at the terrible state in which he found the prisoner, the pastor quickly hastened back to the Governor to solicit a second alleviation of his sufferings, since he feared that without it, the first concession would be of little use. Since this, however, was in opposition to the strict letter of the Governor's instructions, the pastor resolved on a second journey to the capital, in the hope of obtaining some further concessions from the Prince. He declared that he could not, without violating the sacred character of the sacrament, administer it to a wretch who had not even the semblance of a human being. He gained his object and from that day on, the prisoner's lot was much ameliorated.

For many subsequent years, however, G—— continued to languish in captivity, though its trials were much less agonizing than those he had suffered previously; especially after the short reign of the new favorite was over and he was succeeded by others, who either were more humane or had no motive for revenge. Yet ten years passed, without any judicial investigation or any formal acquittal, before he was finally released. He was presented with his freedom as a sort of princely gift, but was requested at the same time, to banish himself from his native country. Here, the oral traditions which I have been able to collect begin to fail and I find myself compelled to omit an intervening period of about twenty years. During this period, he took up his military career once more, this time in foreign service, and by combined skill and industry he achieved the same heights which he had formerly attained in his native land. Time, likewise, helped; the Prince's days of pleasure and of passion were over; humanity gradually resumed its sway over him, and when his hair turned white, and he trembled at the brink of the grave, the friend of his youth appeared to him and constantly haunted his rest. He invited the banished man to revisit his native land, in order to repair, so far as possible, the injuries which had been done him. G——, of course, had long been anxious to return, but the meeting, though apparently warm and cordial, was extremely trying. The Prince gazed earnestly, as if trying to recall features so well known and yet so strange; he seemed to be numbering the deep furrows which he himself had traced there. But nowhere in that aged, grief-worn countenance could he recognize the features of his former companion and friend.

The welcome and the looks of confidence were quite evidently forced on both sides; mutual shame and dread had separated them irrevocably. A single look, which brought back to his soul the full sense of his guilt, hurt the Prince, while G—— felt that he could no longer have any regard for the author of his misfortune.

The Prince attempted to salve his conscience by reinstating him in all his old honors and authority, but he never succeeded in winning back the sincere good-will and fondness which had characterized their friendship. His failure so distressed him that he found his heart closed to all the enjoyments of life and ended his days in the shadow of unhappiness.

G——, on his part, continued his troubled existence for nineteen years: neither time nor fate had quenched the fire of passion, nor wholly obscured the lively spirit of his character. In his seventieth year, he was still in pursuit of the shadow of a happiness which he had really possessed when he was only twenty. He died, finally, as the Governor of a fortress for the confinement of State prisoners. It was to be expected that he would behave with true humanity towards these unfortunates but, on the contrary, he treated them with the greatest harshness and ill-temper. If he remembered his own miseries as a prisoner, he gave not the slightest sign of it either by word or action. It was in one of his increasingly frequent fits of temper, in his eightieth year, that G—— collapsed and died without regaining consciousness, a victim, finally, to the passions that had wrecked his character and his career.

THE HISTORY OF KRAKATUK *

By Ernst T. W. Hoffmann

PERLIPAT'S mother was the wife of a king—that is, a queen; and, in consequence, Perlipat, the moment she was born, was a princess by birth. The king was beside himself for joy as he saw his beautiful little daughter lying in her cradle; he danced about, and hopped on one leg, and sang out, "Was anything ever so beautiful as my Perlipatkin?" And all the ministers, presidents, generals, and staff-officers, hopped likewise on one leg, and cried out, "No, never!" However, the real fact is, that it is quite impossible, as long as the world lasts, that a princess should be born more beautiful than Perlipat. Her little face looked like a web of the most beautiful lilies and roses, her eyes were the brightest blue, and her hair was like curling threads of shining gold. Besides all this, Perlipat came into the world with two rows of pearly teeth, with which, two hours after her birth, she bit the lord chancellor's thumb so hard that he cried out, "O gemini!" Some say he cried out, "O dear!" but on this subject people's opinions are very much divided, even to the present day. In short, Perlipat bit the lord chancellor on the thumb, and all the kingdom immediately declared that she was the wittiest, sharpest, cleverest little girl, as well as the most beautiful. Now, everybody was delighted except the queen—she was anxious and dispirited, and nobody knew the reason; everybody was puzzled to know why she caused Perlipat's cradle to be so strictly guarded. Besides having guards at the door, two nurses always sat close to the cradle, and six other nurses sat every night round the

---

* Translated by William Makepeace Thackeray.

131

room; and what was most extraordinary, each of these six nurses was obliged to sit with a great tom-cat in her lap, and keep stroking him all night, to amuse him, and keep him awake.

Now, my dear little children, it is quite impossible that *you* should know why Perlipat's mother took all these precautions; but *I* know, and will tell you all about it. It happened that, once on a time, a great many excellent kings and agreeable princesses were assembled at the court of Perlipat's father, and their arrival was celebrated by all sorts of tournaments, and plays, and balls. The king, in order to show how rich he was, determined to treat them with a feast which should astonish them. So he privately sent for the upper court cook-master, and ordered him to order the upper court astronomer to fix the time for a general pig-killing, and a universal sausage-making; then he jumped into his carriage, and called, himself, on all the kings and queens; but he only asked them to eat a bit of mutton with him, in order to enjoy their surprise at the delightful entertainment he had prepared for them. Then he went to the queen, and said, "You already know, my love, the partiality I entertain for sausages." Now the queen knew perfectly well what he was going to say, which was that she herself (as indeed she had often done before) should undertake to superintend the sausage-making. So the first lord of the treasury was obliged to hand out the golden sausage-pot and the silver saucepans; and a large fire was made of sandal-wood; the queen put on her damask kitchen-pinafore; and soon after the sausage soup was steaming and boiling in the kettle. The delicious smell penetrated as far as the privy-council-chamber; the king was seized with such extreme delight, that he could not stand it any longer. "With your leave," said he, "my lords and gentlemen"—jumped over the table, ran down into the kitchen, gave the queen a kiss, stirred about the sausage-brew with his golden scepter, and then returned back to the privy-council-chamber in an easy and contented state of mind. The queen had now come to the point in the sausage-making, when the bacon was cut into little bits and roasted on little silver spits. The ladies of honor retired from the kitchen, for the queen, with a proper confidence in herself, and consideration for her royal husband, performed *alone* this important operation. But just when the bacon began to roast, a little whispering voice was heard, "Sister, I am a queen as well as you, give me some roasted bacon, too"; then the queen knew it was Mrs. Mouserinks who was talking. Mrs. Mouserinks had lived a long time in the palace; she declared she was a relation of the king's, and a queen into the bargain, and she had a great number of attendants and courtiers underground. The queen was a mild, good-natured woman; and although she neither acknowledged Mrs. Mouserinks for a queen nor for a relation, yet she could not, on such a holiday as this, grudge her a little bit of bacon. So she said, "Come out, Mrs. Mouserinks, and eat as much as you please of my bacon." Out hops Mrs. Mouserinks, as merry as you please, jumped on the table, stretched out her pretty little paw, and ate one piece of bacon after the other, until, at last, the queen got quite tired of her. But then out came all Mrs. Mouserinks' relations, and her seven sons, ugly little fellows, and nibbled all over the bacon; while the poor queen was so frightened that she could not drive them away. Luckily, however, when there still remained a little bacon, the first lady of the bedchamber happened to come in; she drove all the mice away, and sent for the court mathematician, who divided the little that was left as equally as possible among all the sausages. Now sounded the drums and the trumpets; the princes and potentates who were invited rode forth in glittering garments, some under white canopies, others in magnificent coaches, to the sausage feast. The king received them with hearty friendship and elegant politeness; then, as master of the land, with scepter and crown, sat down at the head of the table. The first course was polonies. Even then it was remarked that the king grew paler and paler; his eyes were raised to heaven, his breast heaved with sighs; in fact, he seemed to be agitated by some deep and inward sorrow. But when the blood-puddings came on, he fell back in his chair, groaning and moaning, sighing and crying. Everybody rose from table; the physicians in ordinary in vain endeavored to feel the king's pulse: a deep and unknown grief had taken possession of him.

At last—at last, after several attempts had been made, several violent remedies applied, such as burning feathers under his nose, and the like, the king came to himself, and almost inaudibly gasped out the words, "Too little bacon!" Then the queen threw herself in despair at his feet: "Oh, my poor unlucky royal husband," said she, "what sorrows have you had to endure! but see here the guilty one at your feet; strike—strike—and spare not. Mrs. Mouserinks and her seven sons, and all her relations, ate up the bacon, and—and——" Here the queen tumbled backwards in a fainting-fit! But the king arose in a violent passion, and said he, "My lady of the bedchamber, explain this matter." The lady of the bedchamber explained as far as she knew, and the king swore vengeance on Mrs. Mouserinks and her family for having eaten up the bacon which was destined for the sausages.

The lord chancellor was called upon to institute a suit against Mrs. Mouserinks and to confiscate the whole of her property; but as the king thought that this would not prevent her from eating his bacon, the whole affair was entrusted to the court machine and watch maker. This man promised, by a peculiar and extraordinary operation, to expel Mrs. Mouserinks and her family from the palace forever. He invented curious machines, in which pieces of roasted bacon were hung on little threads, and which he set round about the dwelling of Mrs. Mouserinks. But Mrs. Mouserinks was far too cunning not to see the artifices of the court watch and machine maker; still all her warnings, all her cautions, were vain; her seven sons, and a great number of her relations, deluded by the sweet smell of the bacon, entered the watchmaker's machines, where, as soon as they bit at the bacon, a trap fell on them, and then they were quickly sent to judgment and execution in the kitchen. Mrs. Mouserinks, with the small remnants of her court, left the place of sorrow, doubt, and astonishment. The court was rejoiced; but the queen alone was sorrowful; for she knew well Mrs. Mouserinks' disposition, and that she would never allow the murder of her sons and relations to go unrevenged. It happened as she expected. One day, whilst she was cooking some tripe for the king, a dish to which he was particularly partial, appeared Mrs. Mouserinks and said, "You have murdered my sons, you have killed my cousins and relations, take good care that the mouse, queen, does not bite your little princess in two. Take care." After saying this, she disappeared; but the queen was so frightened, that she dropped the tripe into the fire, and thus for the second time Mrs. Mouserinks spoiled the dish the king liked best; and of course he was very angry. And now you know why the queen took such extraordinary care of princess Perlipatkin: was not she right to fear that Mrs. Mouserinks would fulfill her threat, come back, and bite the princess to death?

The machines of the machine-maker were not of the slightest use against the clever and cunning Mrs. Mouserinks; but the court astronomer, who was also upperastrologer and star-gazer, discovered that only the Tom-cat family could keep Mrs. Mouserinks from the princess's cradle; for this reason each of the nurses carried one of the sons of this family on her lap, and, by continually stroking him down the back, managed to render the otherwise unpleasant court service less intolerable.

It was once at midnight, as one of the two chief nurses, who sat close by the cradle, awoke as it were from a deep sleep; everything around lay in profound repose; no purring, but the stillness of death; but how astonished was the chief nurse when she saw close before her a great ugly mouse, who stood upon his hind legs, and already had laid his hideous head on the face of the princess. With a shriek of anguish, she sprung up; everybody awoke; but Mrs.

Mouserinks (for she it was who had been in Perlipat's cradle), jumped down, and ran into the corner of the room. The tom-cats went after, but too late; she had escaped through a hole in the floor. Perlipat awoke with the noise, and wept aloud. "Thank heaven," said the nurses, "she lives!" But what was their horror, when, on looking at the before beautiful child, they saw the change which had taken place in her! Instead of the lovely white and red cheeks which she had had before, and the shining golden hair, there was now a great deformed head on a little withered body; the blue eyes had changed into a pair of great green gogglers, and the mouth had stretched from ear to ear. The queen was almost mad with grief and vexation, and the walls of the king's study were obliged to be wadded, because he was always dashing his head against them for sorrow, and crying out, "O luckless monarch!" He might have seen how that it would have been better to have eaten the sausage without bacon, and to have allowed Mrs. Mouserinks quietly to stay underground. Upon this subject, however, Perlipat's royal father did not think at all, but he laid all the blame on the court watchmaker, Christian Elias Drosselmeier, of Nuremberg. He therefore issued this wise order, that Drosselmeier, should before four weeks restore the princess to her former state, or at least find out a certain and infallible means for so doing; or, in failure thereof, should suffer a shameful death under the ax of the executioner.

Drosselmeier was terribly frightened; but, trusting to his learning and good fortune, he immediately performed the first operation which seemed necessary to him. He carefully took Princess Perlipat to pieces, took off her hands and feet, and thus was able to see the inward structure; but there, alas! he found that the princess would grow uglier as she grew older, and he had no remedy for it. He put the princess neatly together again, and sunk down in despair at her cradle; which he never was permitted to leave.

The fourth week had begun,—yes, it was Wednesday! when the king, with eyes flashing with indignation, entered the room of the princess; and, waving his scepter, he cried out, "Christian Elias Drosselmeier, cure the princess, or die!" Drosselmeier began to cry bitterly, but little Princess Perlipat went on cracking her nuts. Then first was the court watchmaker struck with the princess's extraordinary partiality for nuts, and the circumstance of her having come into the world with teeth. In fact, she had cried incessantly since her metamorphosis, until some one by chance gave her a nut; she immediately cracked it, ate the kernel, and was quiet.

From that time the nurses found nothing so effectual as to bring her nuts. "O holy instinct of natural, eternal and unchangeable sympathy of all beings; thou showest me the door to the secret. I will knock, and thou wilt open it." He then asked permission to speak to the court astronomer, and was led out to him under a strong guard. These two gentlemen embraced with many tears, for they were great friends; they then entered into a secret cabinet, where they looked over a great number of books which treated of instincts, sympathies, and antipathies, and other deep subjects. The night came; the court astronomer looked to the stars, and made the horoscope of the princess, with the assistance of Drosselmeier, who was also very clever in this science. It was a troublesome business, for the lines were always wandering this way and that; at last, however, what was their joy to find that the princess Perlipat, in order to be freed from the enchantment which made her so ugly, and to become beautiful again, had only to eat the sweet kernel of the nut Krakatuk.

Now the nut Krakatuk had such a hard shell that an eight-and-forty-pound cannon could drive over without breaking it. But this nut was only to be cracked by a man who had never shaved, and never worn boots; he was to break it in the princess's presence, and then to present the kernel to her with his eyes shut; nor was he to open his eyes until he had walked seven steps backwards without stumbling. Drosselmeier and the astronomer worked without stopping three days and three nights; and, as the king was at dinner on Saturday, Drosselmeier (who was to have had his head off Sunday morning early), rushed into the room, and declared he had found the means of restoring the princess Perlipat to her former beauty. The king embraced him with fervent affection, promised him a diamond sword, four orders, and two new coats for Sundays. "We will go to work immediately after dinner," said the king in the most friendly manner, "and thou, dear watchmaker, must see that the young unshaven gentleman in shoes be ready with the nut Krakatuk. Take care, too, that he drink no wine before, that he may not stumble as he walks his seven steps backwards like a crab; afterwards he may get as tipsy as he pleases." Drosselmeier was very much frightened at this speech of the king's; and it was not without fear and trembling that he stammered out that it was true that the means were known, but that both the nut Krakatuk, and the young man to crack it, were yet to be sought for; so that it was not impossible that nut and cracker would never be found at all. In tremendous fury the king swung his scepter over his crowned head, and cried, with a lion's voice, "Then you must be beheaded, as I said before."

It was a lucky thing for the anxious and unfortunate Drosselmeier that the king had found his dinner very good that day, and so was in a disposition to listen to any reasonable suggestions, which the magnanimous queen, who deplored Drosselmeier's fate, did not fail to bring forward. Drosselmeier took courage to plead that, as he had found out the remedy and the means whereby the princess might be cured, he was entitled to his life. The king said this was all stupid nonsense; but, after he had drunk a glass of cherry-brandy, concluded that both the watchmaker and the astronomer should immediately set off on their journey, and never return, except with the nut Krakatuk in their pocket. The man who was to crack the same was, at the queen's suggestion, to be advertised for in all the newspapers, in the country and out of it.

Drosselmeier and the court astronomer had been fifteen years on their journey without finding any traces of the nut Krakatuk. The countries in which they were, and the wonderful sights they saw, would take me a month at least to tell of. This, however, I shall not do: all I shall say is, that at last the miserable Drosselmeier felt an irresistible longing to see his native town Nuremberg. This longing came upon him most particularly as he and his friend were sitting together smoking a pipe in the middle of a wood; in Asia. "O Nuremberg, delightful city! Who's not seen thee, him I pity! All that beautiful is, in London, Petersburg, or Paris, are nothing when compared to thee! Nuremberg, my own city!" As Drosselmeier deplored his fate in this melancholy manner, the astronomer, struck with pity for his friend, began to howl so loudly that it was heard all over Asia. But at last he stopped crying, wiped his eyes, and said, "Why do we sit here and howl, my worthy colleague? Why don't we set off at once for Nuremberg? Is it not perfectly the same where and how we seek this horrid nut Krakatuk?" "You are right," said Drosselmeier; so they both got up, emptied their pipes, and walked from the wood in the middle of Asia to Nuremberg at a stretch.

As soon as they had arrived in Nuremberg, Drosselmeier hastened to the house of a cousin of his, called Christopher Zachariah Drosselmeier, who was a carver and gilder, and whom he had not seen for a long, long time. To him the watchmaker related the whole history of Princess Perlipat, of Mrs. Mouserinks, and the nut Krakatuk; so that Christopher Zachariah clapped his hands for wonder, and said, "O, cousin, cousin, what extraordinary stories are these!" Drosselmeier then told his cousin of the adventures which befell him on his travels: how he had visited the grand duke of Almonds, and the king of Walnuts; how he had inquired of the Horticultural Society of Acornshausen; in short, how he had sought everywhere, but in vain, to find some traces of the nut Krakatuk. During this recital Christopher Zachariah had been snapping his fingers, and

opening his eyes, calling out, hum! and ha! and oh! and
ah! At last, he threw his cap and wig up to the ceiling, embraced his cousin, and said, "Cousin, I'm very much mistaken, *very* much mistaken, I say, if I don't myself possess
this nut Krakatuk!" He then fetched a little box, out of
which he took a gilded nut, of a middling size. "Now,"
said he, as he showed his cousin the nut, "the history of
this nut is this: Several years ago, a man came here on
Christmas Eve with a sackful of nuts, which he offered
to sell cheap. He put the sack just before my booth, to
guard it against the nut-sellers of the town, who could not
bear that a foreigner should sell nuts in their native city.
At that moment a heavy wagon passed over his sack, and
cracked every nut in it except one, which the man, laughing in an extraordinary way, offered to sell me for a silver
half-crown of the year 1720. This seemed odd to me. I
found just such a half-crown in my pocket, bought the nut,
and gilded it, not knowing myself why I bought it so dear
and valued it so much." Every doubt with respect to its
being the nut which they sought was removed by the
astronomer, who, after removing the gilding, found written
on the shell, in Chinese characters, the word Krakatuk.

The joy of the travelers was excessive, and Drosselmeier's cousin, the gilder, the happiest man under the sun,
on being promised a handsome pension and the gilding of
all the gold in the treasury into the bargain. The two
gentlemen, the watchmaker and the astronomer, had put
on their night caps and were going to bed, when the latter
(that is, the astronomer) said, "My worthy friend and
colleague, you know one piece of luck follows another, and
I believe that we have not only found the nut Krakatuk, but
also the young man who shall crack it, and present the kernel of beauty to the princess; this person I conceive to be
the son of your cousin!" "Yes," continued he, "I am determined not to sleep until I have cast the youth's horoscope."
With these words he took his night cap from his head, and
instantly commenced his observations. In fact, the gilder's

son was a handsome well-grown lad, who had never shaved, and never worn boots.

At Christmas he used to wear an elegant red coat embroidered with gold; a sword, and a hat under his arm, besides having his hair beautifully powdered and curled. In this way he used to stand before his father's booth, and with a gallantry which was born with him, crack the nuts for the young ladies, who, from this peculiar quality of his, had already called him "Nutcrackerkin."

Next morning the astronomer fell delighted on the neck of the watchmaker, and cried, "We have him,—he is found! but there are two things, of which, my dear friend and colleague, we must take particular care: first, we must strengthen the under-jaw of your excellent nephew with a tough piece of wood, and then, on returning home, we must carefully conceal having brought with us the young man who is to bite the nut; for I read by the horoscope that the king, after several people have broken their teeth in vainly attempting to crack the nut, will promise to him who shall crack it, and restore the princess to her former beauty,— will promise, I say, to this man the princess for a wife, and his kingdom after his death." Of course the gilder was delighted with the idea of his son marrying the Princess Perlipat and becoming a prince and king; and delivered him over to the two deputies. The wooden jaw which Drosselmeier had fixed in his young and hopeful nephew answered to admiration, so that in cracking the hardest peach-stones he came off with distinguished success.

As soon as Drosselmeier and his comrade had made known the discovery of the nut, the requisite advertisements were immediately issued; and as the travelers had returned with the means of restoring the princess's beauty, many hundred young men, among whom several princes might be found, trusting to the soundness of their teeth, attempted to remove the enchantment of the princess. The ambassadors were not a little frightened when they saw the princess again. The little body with the wee hands and

feet could scarcely support the immense deformed head!
The hideousness of the countenance was increased by a
woolly beard, which spread over mouth and chin. Everything happened as the astronomer had foretold. One dandy
in shoes after another broke teeth and jaws upon the nut
Krakatuk, without in the slightest degree helping the princess, and as they were carried away half-dead to the den-
tist (who was always ready), groaned out—that was a hard
nut!

When now the king in the anguish of his heart had promised his daughter and kingdom to the man who would
break the enchantment, the gentle Drosselmeier made himself known, and begged to be allowed the trial. No one had
pleased the princess so much as this young man; she laid her
little hand on her heart, and sighed inwardly, Ah! if *he*
were the person destined to crack Krakatuk, and be my
husband! Young Drosselmeier, approaching the queen, the
king, and the princess Perlipat in the most elegant manner, received from the hands of the chief master of cere-
monies the nut Krakatuk, which he immediately put into
his mouth,—and crack! crack!—broke the shell in a dozen
pieces; he neatly removed the bits of shell which yet remained on the kernel, and then with a most profound bow
presented it to the princess, shut his eyes, and proceeded to
step backwards. The princess swallowed the kernel; and
oh! wonderful wonder! her ugliness disappeared, and, instead, was seen a form of angel beauty, with a countenance
like lilies and roses mixed, the eyes of glancing azure, and
the full locks curling like threads of gold. Drums and
trumpets mingled with the rejoicings of the people. The
king and the whole court danced upon one leg, as before,
at Perlipat's birth, and the queen was obliged to be sprinkled all over with eau de Cologne, since she had fainted
with excessive joy. This great tumult did not a little disturb young Drosselmeier, who had yet his seven steps to
accomplish: however, he recollected himself, and had just
put his right foot back for the seventh step, when Mrs.

Mouserinks, squeaking in a most hideous manner, raised herself from the floor, so that Drosselmeier, as he put his foot backwards, trod on her, and stumbled,—nay, almost fell down. What a misfortune! The young man became at that moment just as ugly as ever was the princess Perlipat. The body was squeezed together, and could scarcely support the thick deformed head, with the great goggling eyes and wide gaping mouth. Instead of the wooden roof for his mouth, a little wooden mantel hung out from behind his back. The watchmaker and astronomer were beside themselves with horror and astonishment; but they saw how Mrs. Mouserinks was creeping along the floor all bloody. Her wickedness, however, was not unavenged, for Drosselmeier had struck her so hard on the neck with the sharp heel of his shoe, that she was at the point of death; but just as she was in her last agonies, she squeaked out in the most piteous manner, "O Krakatuk, from thee I die! but Nutcracker dies as well as I; and thou, my son, with the seven crowns, revenge thy mother's horrid wounds! Kill the man who did attack her, that naughty, ugly wicked Nutcracker!" Quick with this cry died Mrs. Mouserinks, and was carried off by the royal housemaid. Nobody had taken the least notice of young Drosselmeier. The princess, however, reminded the king of his promise, and he immediately ordered the young hero to be brought before him. But when that unhappy young man appeared in his deformed state, the princess put her hands before her and cried out, "Away with that nasty Nutcracker!" So the court marshal took him by his little shoulder and pushed him out of the door.

The king was in a terrible fury that anybody should ever think of making a nutcracker his son-in-law: he laid all the blame on the watchmaker and astronomer, and banished them both from his court and kingdom. This had not been seen by the astronomer in casting his horoscope; however, he found, on reading the stars a second time, that young Drosselmeier would so well behave himself in his new station, that, in spite of his ugliness, he would become prince and king. In the meantime, but with the fervent hope of soon seeing the end of these things, Drosselmeier remains as ugly as ever; so much so, that the nutcrackers in Nuremberg have always been made after the exact model of his countenance and figure.

HANSEL AND GRETEL *

By Jacob Ludwig Grimm and Wilhelm Karl Grimm

Once upon a time there dwelt near a large wood a poor wood cutter with his wife and two children by his former marriage, a little boy called Hansel, and a girl named Gretel. He had little enough to break or bite, and once, when there was a great famine in the land, he could not procure even his daily bread; and as he lay thinking in his bed one evening, rolling about for trouble, he sighed, and said to his wife, "What will become of us? How can we feed our children when we have no more than we can eat ourselves?"

"Know, then, my husband," answered she, "we will lead them away quite early in the morning into the thickest part of the wood, and there make them a fire, and give them each a little piece of bread; then we will go to our work and leave them alone, so they will not find the way home again, and we shall be freed from them." "No, wife," replied he, "that I can never do; how can you bring your heart to leave my children all alone in the wood, for the wild beasts will soon come and tear them to pieces?"

"Oh, you simpleton!" said she, "then we must all four die of hunger; you had better plane the coffins for us." But she left him no peace till he consented, saying, "Ah, but I shall regret the poor children."

The two children, however, had not gone to sleep for

---

* "Hansel and Gretel" and "Cinderella" demand inclusion in any volume of representative German stories. They are among the oldest bits of German folk-lore that have come down to us, and the Brothers Grimm, by setting them down on paper, have made them famous in every household in the civilized world.—Editor's Note.

very hunger, and so they overheard what the stepmother said to their father. Gretel wept bitterly, and said to Hansel, "What will become of us?" "Be quiet, Gretel," said he; "do not cry, I will soon help you." And as soon as their parents had fallen asleep, he got up, put on his coat, and, unbarring the backdoor, slipped out. The moon shone brightly, and the white pebbles which lay before the door seemed like silver pieces, they glittered so brightly. Hansel stooped down, and put as many into his pocket as it would hold, and then going back he said to Gretel, "Be comforted, dear sister, and sleep in peace; God will not forsake us"; and so saying he went to bed again.

The next morning, before the sun arose, the wife went and awoke the two children. "Get up, you lazy things; we are going into the forest to chop wood." Then she gave them each a piece of bread, saying, "There is something for your dinner; do not eat it before the time, for you will get nothing else." Gretel took the bread in her apron, for Hansel's pocket was full of pebbles; and so they all set out upon their way. When they had gone a little distance Hansel stood still and peeped back at the house; and this he repeated several times, till his father said, "Hansel, what are you peeping at, and why do you lag behind? Take care, and remember your legs."

"Ah! father," said Hansel, "I am looking at my white cat sitting upon the roof of the house, and trying to say good-by." "You simpleton!" said the wife, "that is not a cat; it is only the sun shining on the white chimney." But in reality Hansel was not looking at a cat; but every time he stopped he dropped a pebble out of his pocket upon the path.

When they came to the middle of the wood the father told the children to collect wood, and he would make them a fire, so that they should not be cold; so Hansel and Gretel gathered together quite a little mountain of twigs. Then they set fire to them, and as the flame burnt up high the wife said, "Now, you children, lie down near the fire and

rest yourselves, whilst we go into the forest and chop
wood; when we are ready, I will come and call you."

Hansel and Gretel sat down by the fire, and when it was
noon each ate the piece of bread, and, because they could
hear the blows of an ax, they thought their father was
near; but it was not an ax, but a branch which he had
bound to a withered tree, so as to be blown to and fro by
the wind. They waited so long that at last their eyes closed
from weariness, and they fell fast asleep. When they awoke
it was quite dark, and Gretel began to cry: "How shall we
get out of the wood?" But Hansel tried to comfort her by
saying, "Wait a little while till the moon rises, and then we
will quickly find the way." The moon soon shone forth,
and Hansel, taking his sister's hand, followed the pebbles,
which glittered like new-coined silver pieces, and showed
them the path. All night long they walked on, and as day
broke they came to their father's house. They knocked at
the door, and when the wife opened it, and saw Hansel
and Gretel, she exclaimed, "You wicked children! why
did you sleep so long in the wood? We thought you were
never coming home again." But their father was very glad,
for it had grieved his heart to leave them all alone.

Not long afterwards there was again great scarcity in
every corner of the land; and one night the children overheard their mother saying to their father, "Everything is
again consumed; we have only half a loaf left, and then
the song is ended: the children must be sent away. We
will take them deeper into the wood, so that they may not
find the way out again; it is the only means of escape for
us."

But her husband felt heavy at heart, and thought, "It
were better to share the last crust with the children." His
wife, however, would listen to nothing that he said, and
scolded and reproached him without end.

He who says A must say B too; and he who consents
the first time must also the second.

The children, however, had heard the conversation as

they lay awake, and as soon as the old people went to sleep Hansel got up, intending to pick up some pebbles as before; but the wife had locked the door, so that he could not get out. Nevertheless he comforted Gretel, saying, "Do not cry; sleep in quiet; the good God will not forsake us."

Early in the morning the stepmother came and pulled them out of bed, and gave them each a slice of bread, which was still smaller than the former piece. On the way Hansel broke his in his pocket, and stopping every now and then, dropped a crumb upon the path. "Hansel, why do you stop and look about?" said the father. "Keep in the path." "I am looking at my little dove," answered Hansel, "nodding a good-by to me." "Simpleton!" said the wife, "that is no dove, but only the sun shining on the chimney." So Hansel still kept dropping crumbs as he went along.

The mother led the children deep into the wood, where they had never been before, and there making an immense fire she said to them, "Sit down here and rest, and when you feel tired you can sleep for a little while. We are going into the forest to hew wood, and in the evening, when we are ready, we will come and fetch you."

When noon came Gretel shared her bread with Hansel, who had strewn his on the path. Then they went to sleep; but the evening arrived, and no one came to visit the poor children, and in the dark night they awoke, and Hansel comforted his sister by saying, "Only wait, Gretel, till the moon comes out, then we shall see the crumbs of bread which I have dropped, and they will show us the way home." The moon shone and they got up, but they could not see any crumbs, for the thousands of birds which had been flying about in the woods and fields had picked them all up. Hansel kept saying to Gretel, "We will soon find the way"; but they did not, and they walked the whole night long and the next day, but still they did not come out of the wood; and they got so hungry, for they had nothing to eat but the berries which they found upon the bushes. Soon they got so tired that they could not drag themselves along, so they laid down under a tree and went to sleep.

It was now the third morning since they had left their father's house and they still walked on; but they only got deeper and deeper into the wood, and Hansel saw that if help did not come very soon they would die of hunger. As soon as it was noon they saw a beautiful snow-white bird sitting upon a bough, which sang so sweetly that they stood still and listened to it. It soon left off, and spreading its wings flew off; and they followed it until it arrived at a cottage, upon the roof of which it perched; and when they went close up to it they saw that the cottage was made of bread and cakes, and the window panes were of clear sugar.

"We will go in there," said Hansel, "and have a glorious feast. I will eat a piece of the roof, and you can eat the window. Will they not be sweet?" So Hansel reached up and broke a piece off the roof, in order to see how it tasted; while Gretel stepped up to the window and began to bite it. Then a sweet voice called out in the room, "Tip-tap, tip-tap, who raps at my door?" and the children answered, "The wind, the wind, the child of heaven"; and they went on eating without interruption. Hansel thought the roof tasted very nice, and so he tore off a great piece; while Gretel broke a large round pane out of the window, and sat down quite contentedly. Just then the door opened, and a very old woman, walking upon crutches, came out. Hansel and Gretel were so frightened that they let fall what they had in their hands; but the old woman, nodding her head, said, "Ah, you dear children, what has brought you here? Come in and stop with me, and no harm shall befall you"; and so saying she took them both by the hand, and led them into her cottage. A good meal of milk and pancakes, with sugar, apples, and nuts, was spread on the table, and in the back room were two nice little beds, covered with white, where Hansel and Gretel laid themselves down, and thought themselves in heaven. The old woman had be- haved very kindly to them, but in reality she was a wicked witch who waylaid children, and built the bread-house in order to entice them in; but as soon as they were in her power she killed them, cooked and ate them, and made a great festival of the day. Witches have red eyes, and cannot see very far; but they have a fine sense of smelling, like wild beasts, so that they know when children approach them. When Hansel and Gretel came near the witch's house she laughed wickedly, saying, "Here come two who shall not escape me." And early in the morning, before they awoke, she went up to them, and saw how lovingly they lay sleeping, with their chubby red cheeks; and she mumbled to herself, "That will be a good bite." Then she took up Hansel with her rough hand, and shut him up in a little cage with a lattice-door; and although he screamed loudly it was of no use. Gretel came next, and, shaking her till she awoke, she said, "Get up, you lazy thing, and fetch some water to cook something good for your brother, who must remain in that stall and get fat; when he is fat enough I shall eat him." Gretel began to cry, but it was all useless, for the old witch made her do as she wished. So a nice meal was cooked for Hansel, but Gretel got nothing else but a crab's claw.

Every morning the old witch came to the cage and said, "Hansel, stretch your finger that I may feel whether you are getting fat." But Hansel used to stretch out a bone, and the old woman, having very bad sight, thought it was his finger, and wondered very much that it did not get fat. When four weeks had passed, and Hansel still kept quite lean, she lost all her patience and would not wait any longer. "Gretel," she called out in a passion, "get some water quickly; be Hansel fat or lean, this morning I will kill and cook him." Oh, how the poor little sister grieved, as she was forced to fetch the water, and how fast the tears ran down her cheeks! "Dear good God, help us now!" she exclaimed. "Had we only been eaten by the wild beasts in the wood then we should have died together." But the old witch called out, "Leave off that noise; it will not help you a bit."

So early in the morning Gretel was forced to go out and fill the kettle, and make a fire. "First we will bake, however," said the old woman; "I have already heated the oven and kneaded the dough"; and so saying she pushed poor Gretel up to the oven, out of which the flames were burning fiercely. "Creep in," said the witch, "and see if it is hot enough, and then we will put in the bread"; but she intended when Gretel got in to shut up the oven and let her bake, so that she might eat her as well as Hansel. Gretel perceived what her thoughts were, and said, "I do not know how to do it; how shall I get in?" "You stupid goose," said she, "the opening is big enough. See, I could even get in myself!" and she got up and put her head into the oven. Then Gretel gave her a push, so that she fell right in, and then shutting the iron door she bolted it. Oh! how horribly she howled; but Gretel ran away, and left the ungodly witch to burn to ashes.

Now she ran to Hansel, and, opening his door, called out, "Hansel, we are saved; the old witch is dead!" So he sprang out, like a bird out of his cage when the door is opened; and they were so glad that they fell upon each other's neck, and kissed each other over and over again. And now, as there was nothing to fear, they went into the witch's house, where in every corner were caskets full of pearls and precious stones. "These are better than pebbles," said Hansel, putting as many into his pocket as it would hold; while Gretel thought, "I will take some home too," and filled her apron full. "We must be off now," said Hansel, "and get out of this bewitched forest"; but when they had walked for two hours they came to a large piece of water. "We cannot get over," said Hansel. "I can see no bridge at all." "And there is no boat either," said Gretel; "but there swims a white duck, I shall ask her to help us over"; and she sang,

"Little duck, good little duck,
    Gretel and Hansel, here we stand,
    There is neither stile nor bridge,
    Take us on your back to land."

So the duck came to them, and Hansel sat himself on, and
bade his sister sit behind him. "No," answered Gretel,
"that will be too much for the duck, she will take us over
one at a time." This the good little bird did, and when both
were happily arrived on the other side, and had gone a little
way, they came to a well-known wood, which they knew
the better every step they went, and at last they perceived
their father's house. Then they began to run, and, bursting
into the house, they fell on their father's neck. He had not
had one happy hour since he had left the children in the
forest; and his wife was dead. Gretel shook her apron, and
the pearls and precious stones rolled out upon the floor,
and Hansel threw down one handful after the other out of
his pocket. Then all their sorrows were ended, and they
lived together in great happiness.

My tale is done. There runs a mouse: whoever catches
her may make a great, great cap out of her fur.

CINDERELLA

By the Brothers Grimm

THERE was once a rich man, whose wife died, leaving him with one little girl. After some years, hoping to give his child a mother's love and care, he married again, this time a widow, with two grown-up daughters. But his second wife was haughty and proud, and her two daughters were even worse than their mother; and the poor little girl had a very unhappy time with her new relations. Her step-sisters were jealous of her, for she was very beautiful, and they themselves were plain and ugly. They did all they could to make her miserable; and, at length, through their wicked spite and envy, her life became a burden to her. The poor child was sent to live in the kitchen, where she had to do all the rough and dirty work; and because she was always dressed in rags, and sat beside the cinders in the grate, they called her Cinderella.

It happened that the King of the country had an only son. He was very anxious that the Prince should be married; so he gave a great ball, and invited all the grand ladies in the country to come to it. It was to be a very splendid affair, lasting for three nights, and people were very eager to be invited to it, for it was known that the Prince would choose his bride from among the ladies present.

Cinderella's sisters received invitations; and from the day they arrived they talked of nothing but of what they should wear, for each of them secretly hoped that she would be chosen as the Prince's bride.

When the great day came at last, they began to dress for the ball directly after breakfast. Cinderella had to help them; and they kept her busy all day doing their hair, and running messages, and helping them to lace up their fine dresses.

When Cinderella saw their beautiful clothes she wished that she could go to the ball as well; but when she timidly asked if she might, they laughed in mocking scorn.

"You go to the ball!" they cried. "What would you do at the ball, with your rags and tatters and your dirty face? No, no, Cinderella, go back to your seat amongst the ashes —that is the place for a little kitchen girl like you!"

So the two sisters and their mother drove away in a carriage and pair to the King's palace, and Cinderella was left behind. She sat down on the hearth before the kitchen fire and began to cry softly to herself, because she felt so very lonely and miserable.

As she sat there in the dusk, with the firelight dancing over her, and her face buried in her hands, she heard a voice calling:

"Cinderella, Cinderella!" and with a start she looked up to see who it could be.

There on the hearth in front of her stood an old woman, leaning upon a stick. She was dressed in a long red cloak, and she wore high-heeled shoes and a tall black hat.

Where she had come from Cinderella could not imagine. She certainly had not come in through the door, nor yet through the window, for both were shut.

Cinderella was so surprised to see her that she stopped crying and stared at her in astonishment.

"What are you crying for?" asked the old woman.

"Because my mother and sisters have gone to the ball, and I am left here all alone," said Cinderella.

"Do you want to go to the ball, too?" said the old lady.

"Yes, but it is no good; I have nothing but rags to wear," sobbed poor Cinderella.

"Well, well, be a good child and don't cry any more," said the old woman, briskly. "I am your Fairy Godmother, and if you do what I tell you, perhaps you shall go after all. Run out into the garden and bring me in a pumpkin!"

Cinderella ran out into the garden and brought in the biggest pumpkin that she could find.

"Now go and fetch the mouse-trap out of the cellar," said her Godmother, and Cinderella hurried to get it. There were six mice in the trap, and the old woman harnessed them to the pumpkin, put a rat on the top to drive them, and two lizards behind, and then waved her wand over them. Immediately the pumpkin turned into a gorgeous coach, the mice into six beautiful horses, the rat into a stately coachman, and the lizards into tall footmen, with powdered hair and silk stockings. "There," said the old woman; "there's a carriage to take you to the ball."

"Alas," said Cinderella, "how can I go to the ball? I have nothing to wear but this!" and she touched her ragged frock.

"Is that all?" said the Fairy Godmother. Once more she waved her wand, and Cinderella's rags turned into the most beautiful dress in the world, all shining with gold and silver threads and covered with costly gems. In her hair was a circlet of pearls, and her feet were shod with the prettiest and daintiest pair of glass slippers that ever were seen.

"Now," said the Fairy Godmother, "now you can go to the ball. But mind you come away before the clock strikes twelve, for should you linger beyond that hour, all your splendor will vanish and your dress will turn into rags again."

Cinderella promised to obey her Godmother's instructions. Then she got into the beautiful coach. The footman shut the door, the coachman whipped up the horses, and away she went to the ball.

When she arrived there was a great stir in the Palace. So lovely a face and so costly and rich a dress had never before been seen, and everybody thought it must be some great Princess arrived from foreign lands.

All the courtiers and other guests stood back to let her pass, and when the Prince caught sight of her he fell in love with her on the spot. He danced with her the whole of the evening, and people thought there was no doubt as to whom he would choose for his bride.

At a quarter to twelve, Cinderella, remembering her Godmother's instructions, said good-by to the Prince and came away.

She arrived home just as the clock struck twelve. At once the coachman and footmen turned back into rats and mice, and the coach into a pumpkin; and when the sisters came home a little later, there was Cinderella, dressed in her old shabby frock, sitting in her usual place amongst the cinders.

The two ugly sisters were full of the strange Princess who had come to the ball. They talked about her all the next day, little dreaming that all the while the beautiful lady was their despised sister Cinderella.

In the evening after they had gone again to the ball, the Fairy Godmother made her appearance. Once more Cinderella drove to the Palace in her coach and six; this time arrayed in a still more gorgeous and beautiful dress; and once more the Prince danced with her all the evening.

But when the third night came Cinderella was enjoying herself so much that she quite forgot what her Fairy Godmother had said, until suddenly she heard the clock begin to strike twelve. She remembered that as soon as it finished striking, all her fine clothes would turn to rags again; and, jumping up in alarm, she ran out of the room. The Prince ran after her, trying to overtake her; and Cinderella in her fright ran so fast that she left one of her little glass slippers on the floor behind her.

The Prince stopped to pick it up, and this gave Cinderella time to escape; but she was only just in time. Just as she was crossing the Palace yard, the clock finished striking, and immediately all her finery vanished; and there she was, dressed in her old ragged frock again.

When the Prince came out upon the Palace steps, he could see no sign of the lovely Princess. The guards at the gate told him that nobody at all had passed that way, except a little ragged kitchen-maid; and the Prince had to go back to the ball with only a little glass slipper to remind him of the beautiful lady with whom he was so desperately in love.

The next day the King sent out all his heralds and trumpeters with a Proclamation, saying that the Prince would marry the lady whose foot the slipper fitted. But though all the ladies in the land tried on the slipper it would fit none of them—their feet were all too big!

At last the heralds came to the house where Cinderella lived. The eldest stepsister tried the slipper on first, but it was quite impossible for her to get her foot into it, for her great toe was too big. Then her mother, who was watching eagerly, fetched a carving-knife.

"Be quick, cut the toe off," she said; "what does it matter if you are lame—if you are the Prince's bride you will always ride in a carriage!"

So the eldest sister cut off her big toe, but it was no use, the slipper would not fit, and at last she was obliged to hand it to her sister.

But the other sister had no better luck. She did, indeed, get her toes inside, but her foot was much too long, and her heel stuck out behind. The mother urged her to cut it off.

"What does it matter?" she said. "If you are the Prince's bride you will never need to walk any more."

But although she cut her heel off, the slipper was still too small; and at length she, too, had to give up the attempt to force her foot into it.

Then Cinderella came shyly out from behind the door where she had been standing out of sight, and asked if she might try on the slipper. Her stepmother and sisters were very angry, and were about to drive her away with blows, but the herald stopped them.

"The Prince wishes every woman in the land to try on this slipper," he said; and asking Cinderella to sit on a chair, he knelt down and tried the slipper on her foot.

And it fitted her exactly!

While every one stood and stared in astonishment, Cinderella drew from her pocket the other slipper and put it on. No sooner had she done so than her ragged frock changed into the beautiful ball dress again, and she stood up before them all—the beautiful lady with whom the Prince had fallen in love at the ball.

The Prince was overjoyed to find her again; and they were married at once with much pomp amid great rejoicings.

As for the wicked sisters, they were so jealous that they both turned green with envy. They grew uglier and uglier every day, until at last they grew so dreadfully ugly that nobody could bear to look at them any longer. But Cinderella became more and more beautiful, and lived happily with the Prince forever afterwards.

GODS IN EXILE *

By Heinrich Heine

I MEAN to tell of that metamorphosis into demons which the Greek and Roman gods underwent when Christianity achieved supreme control of the world. The superstition of the people ascribed to those gods a real but cursed existence, coinciding entirely in this respect with the teaching of the Church. The latter by no means declared the ancient gods to be myths, inventions of falsehood and error, as did the philosophers, but held them to be evil spirits, who, through the victory of Christ, had been hurled from the summit of their power, and now dragged along their miserable existences in the obscurity of dismantled temples or in enchanted groves, and by their diabolic arts, through lust and beauty, particularly through dancing and singing, lured to apostasy unsteadfast Christians who had lost their way in the forest . . . I will remind the reader that the perplexities into which the poor old gods fell at the time of the final triumph of Christendom—that is, in the third century —offer striking analogies to former sorrowful events in their god-lives; for they found themselves plunged into the same sad predicament in which they had once before been placed in that most ancient time, in that revolutionary epoch when the Titans broke loose from their confinement in Orcus and, piling Pelion on Ossa, scaled high Olympus. At that time the poor gods were compelled to flee ignominiously and conceal themselves under various disguises on earth. Most of them repaired to Egypt, where, as is well known, for greater safety, they assumed the forms of animals. And in a like manner, when the true Lord of the uni-

* Translated by M. Fleishman.

verse planted the banner of the cross on the heavenly heights, and those iconoclastic zealots, the black band of monks, hunted down the gods with fire and malediction and razed their temples, then these unfortunate heathen divinities were again compelled to take to flight, seeking safety under the most varied disguises and in the most retired hiding-places. Many of these poor refugees, deprived of shelter and ambrosia, were now forced to work at some plebeian trade in order to earn a livelihood. Under these circumstances several, whose shrines had been confiscated, became wood-choppers and day-laborers in Germany, and were compelled to drink beer instead of nectar. It appears that Apollo was reduced to this dire plight, and stooped so low as to accept service with cattle-breeders, and as once before he had tended the cows of Admetus, so now he lived as a shepherd in Lower Austria. Here, however, he aroused suspicion through the marvelous sweetness of his singing, and, being recognized by a learned monk as one of the ancient magic-working heathen gods, he was delivered over to the ecclesiastical courts. On the rack he confessed that he was the god Apollo. Before his execution he begged that he might be permitted for the last time to play the zither and sing to its accompaniment. But he played so touchingly and sang so enchantingly, and was so handsome in face and form, that all the women wept; and many of them indeed afterwards sickened. After some lapse of time, it was decided to remove his body from the grave under the impression that he was a vampire, and impale it upon a stake, this being an approved domestic remedy certain to effect the cure of the sick women; but the grave was found empty.

I have but little to communicate concerning the fate of Mars, the ancient god of war. I am not disinclined to believe that during the feudal ages he availed himself of the then prevailing doctrine that might makes right. Lank Schimmelpennig, nephew of the executioner of Münster, once met Mars at Bologna, and conversed with him. Shortly before he had served as a peasant under Froudsberg, and was present at the storming of Rome. Bitter thoughts must have filled his breast when he saw his ancient, favorite city, and the temples wherein he and his brother gods had been so revered, now ignominiously laid waste.

Better than either Mars or Apollo fared the god Bacchus at the great stampede, and the legends relate the following: —In Tyrol there are very large lakes, surrounded by magnificent trees that are mirrored in the blue waters. Trees and water murmur so that one experiences strange feelings of awe when one wanders there alone. On the bank of such a lake stood the hut of a young fisherman, who lived by fishing, and who also acted as ferryman to any travelers who wished to cross the lake. He had a large boat, that was fastened to the trunk of an old tree not far from his dwelling. Here he lived quite alone. Once, about the time of the autumnal equinox, towards midnight, he heard a knocking at his window, and on opening the door he saw three monks, with their heads deeply muffled in their cowls, who seemed to be in great haste. One of them hurriedly asked him for the boat, promising to return it within a few hours. The monks were three, and the fisherman could not hesitate; so he unfastened the boat, and when they had embarked and departed, he went back to his hut and lay down. He was young, and soon fell asleep; but in a few hours he was awakened by the returning monks. When he went out to them, one of them pressed a silver coin into his hand, and then all three hastened away. The fisherman went to look at his boat, which he found made fast. Then he shivered, but not from the night-air. A peculiarly chilling sensation had passed through his limbs, and his heart seemed almost frozen, when the monk who paid the fare touched his hand; the monk's fingers were cold as ice. For some days the fisherman could not forget this circumstance; but youth will soon shake off mysterious influences, and the fisherman thought no more of the occurrence until the following year, when, again just at the time of the autumnal equinoxes, towards midnight, there was a knocking at the window of the hut, and again the three cowled monks appeared, and again demanded the boat. The fisherman delivered up the boat with less anxiety this time, but when after a few hours they returned, and one of the monks again hastily pressed a coin into his hand, he again shuddered at the touch of the icy cold fingers. This happened every year at the same time and in the same manner. At last, as the seventh year drew near, an irresistible desire seized on the fisherman to learn, at all costs, the secret that was hidden under these three cowls. He piled a mass of nets into the boat, so as to form a hiding-place into which he could slip while the monks were preparing to embark. The somber expected travelers came at the accustomed time, and the fisherman succeeded in hiding himself under the nets unobserved. To his astonishment, the voyage lasted but a short time, whereas it usually took him over an hour to reach the opposite shore; and greater yet was his surprise when here, in a locality with which he had been quite familiar, he beheld a wide forest-glade which he had never before seen, and which was covered with flowers that, to him, were of quite strange kind. Innumerable lamps hung from the trees, and vases filled with blazing rosin stood on high pedestals; the moon, too, was so bright that the fisherman could see all that took place, as distinctly as if it had been mid-day. There were many hundreds of young men and young women, most of them beautiful as pictures, although their faces were all as white as marble, and this circumstance, together with their garments, which consisted of white, very white tunics with purple borders, girt up, gave them the appearance of moving statues. The women wore on their heads wreaths of vine leaves, either natural or wrought of gold and silver, and their hair was partly plaited over the brow into the shape of a crown, and partly fell in wild locks on their necks. The young men also wore wreaths of vine-leaves. Both men and women swinging in their hands golden staffs covered with vine leaves, hastened joyously to greet the newcomers. One of the latter threw aside his cowl, revealing an impertinent fellow of middle age, with a repulsive, libidinous face, and pointed goat-ears, and scandalously extravagant sexuality. The second monk also threw aside his cowl, and there came to view a big-bellied fellow, not less naked, whose bald pate the mischievous women crowned with a wreath of roses. The faces of the two monks, like those of the rest of the assemblage, were white as snow. White as snow also was the face of the third monk, who laughingly brushed the cowl from his head. As he unbound the girdle of his robe, and with a gesture of disgust flung off from him the pious and dirty garment, together with crucifix and rosary, lo! there stood, robed in a tunic brilliant as a diamond, a marvelously beautiful youth with a form of noble symmetry, save that there was something feminine in the rounded hips and the slender waist. His delicately curved lips, also, and soft, mobile features gave him a somewhat feminine appearance; but his face expressed also a certain daring, almost reckless heroism. The women caressed him with wild enthusiasm, placed an ivy-wreath upon his head, and threw a magnificent leopard-skin over his shoulders. At this moment came swiftly dashing along, drawn by two lions, a golden two-wheeled triumphal chariot. Majestically, yet with a merry glance, the youth leaped on the chariot, guiding the wild steeds with purple reins. At the right of the chariot strode one of his uncassocked companions, whose lewd gestures and unseemly form delighted the beholders, while his comrade, with the bald pate and fat paunch, whom the merry women had placed on an ass, rode at the left of the chariot, carrying in his hand a golden drinking-cup, which was constantly refilled with wine. On moved the chariot, and behind it whirled the romping, dancing, vine-crowned men and women. At the head of the triumphal procession marched the orchestra; the pretty, chubby-cheeked youth, playing the double flute; then the nymph with the high-girt tunic, striking the jingling tambourine with her knuckles; then the equally gracious beauty, with the triangle; then the goat-footed trumpeters, with handsome but lascivious faces, who blew their fanfares on curious sea-shells and fantastically shaped horns; then the lute players.

But, dear reader, I forgot that you are a most cultured and well-informed reader, and have long since observed that I have been describing a Bacchanalia and a feast of Dionysus. You have often seen on ancient bas-reliefs, or in the engravings of archæological works, pictures of the triumphal processions held in honor of the god Bacchus; and surely, with your cultivated and classic tastes, you would not be frightened even if at dead of night, in the depths of a lonely forest, the lonely specters of such a Bacchanalian procession, together with the customary tipsy *personnel,* should appear bodily before your eyes. At the most you would only give way to a slight voluptuous shudder, an æsthetic awe, at sight of this pale assemblage of graceful phantoms, who have risen from their monumental sarcophagi, or from their hiding-places amid the ruins of ancient temples, to perform once more their ancient, joyous, divine service; once more, with sport and merry-making, to celebrate the triumphal march of the divine liberator, the Savior of the senses; to dance once more the merry dance of paganism, the *can-can* of the antique world—to dance it without any hypocritical disguise, without fear of the interference of the police of a spiritualistic morality, with the wild abandonment of the old days, shouting, exulting, rapturous. Evoe Bacche!

But alas, dear reader, the poor fisherman was not, like yourself, versed in mythology; he had never made archæological studies; and terror and fear seized upon him when he beheld the Triumphator and his two wonderful acolytes emerge from their monks' garb. He shuddered at the immodest gestures and leaps of the Bacchantes, Fauns, and Satyrs, who, with their goats' feet and horns, seemed to him peculiarly diabolical, and he regarded the whole assemblage as a congress of specters and demons, who were seeking by their mysterious rites to bring ruin on all Christians. His hair stood on end at sight of the reckless impossible posture of a Mænad, who, with flowing hair and head thrown back, only balanced herself by the weight of her thyrsus. His own brain seemed to reel as he saw the Corybantes in mad frenzy wounding their own bodies with short swords, seeking voluptuousness in pain itself. The soft and tender, yet so terrible, tones of the music seemed to penetrate to his very soul, like a burning, consuming, excruciating flame. But when he saw that defamed Egyptian symbol of exaggerated size and crowned with flowers, borne upon a tall pole by an unashamed woman, then sight and hearing forsook the poor fisherman—and he darted back to the boat, and crept under the nets, with chattering teeth and trembling limbs, as though Satan already held him fast by the foot. Soon after, the three monks also returned to the boat and shoved off. When they had disembarked at the original starting-place, the fisherman managed to escape unobserved from his hiding-place, so that they supposed he had merely been behind the willows awaiting their return. One of the monks, as usual, with icy-cold fingers pressed the fare into the fisherman's hand, then all three hurried away.

For the salvation of his own soul, which he believed to be endangered, and also to guard other good Christians from ruin, the fisherman held it his duty to communicate a full account of the mysterious occurrence to the Church authorities; and as the superior of a neighboring Franciscan monastery was in great repute as a learned exorcist, the fisherman determined to go to him without delay. The rising sun found him on his way to the monastery, where, with modest demeanor, he soon stood before his excellency the superior, who received him seated in an easy-chair in the library, and with hood drawn closely over his face, listened meditatively while the fisherman told his tale of horror. When the recital was finished, the superior raised his head, and as the hood fell back, the fisherman saw, to his dismay, that his excellency was one of the three monks who annually sailed over the lake—the very one, indeed, whom he had the previous night seen as a heathen demon riding in the golden chariot drawn by lions. It was the same marble-white face, the same regular, beautiful features, the same mouth with its delicately curved lips. And these lips now wore a kindly smile, and from that mouth now issued the gracious and melodious words, "Beloved son in Christ, we willingly believe that you have spent the night in company of the god Bacchus. Your fantastic ghost story gives ample proof of that. Not that we would say aught unpleasant of this god: at times he is undoubtedly a care-dispeller, and gladdens the heart of man. But he is very dangerous for those who cannot bear much; and to this class you seem to belong. We advise you to partake in future very sparingly of the golden juice of the grape, and not again to trouble the spiritual authorities with the fantasies of a drunken brain. Concerning this last vision of yours, you had better keep a very quiet tongue in your head; otherwise the secular arm of our beadle shall measure out to you twenty-five lashes. And now, beloved son in Christ, go to the kitchen, where brother butler and brother cook will set before you a slight repast."

With this, the reverend father bestowed the customary benediction on the fisherman, and when the latter, bewildered, took himself off to the kitchen and suddenly came face to face with brother cook and brother butler, he almost fell to the earth in affright, for they were the same monks who had accompanied the superior on his midnight excursions across the lake. He recognized one by his fat paunch and bald head, and the other by his lascivious grin and goat-ears. But he held his tongue, and only in later years did he relate his strange story.

Several old chronicles which contain similar legends locate the scene near the city of Speyer, on the Rhine.

Along the coast of East Friesland an analogous tradition is found, in which the ancient conception of the transportation of the dead to the realm of Hades, which underlies all those legends, is most distinctly seen. It is true that none of them contain any mention of Charon, the steersman of the boat: this old fellow seems to have entirely disappeared from folk-lore, and is to be met with only in puppet-shows. But a far more notable mythological personage is to be recognized in the so-called forwarding agent, or dispatcher, who makes arrangements for the transportation of the dead, and pays the customary passage-money into the hands of the boatman; the latter is generally a common fisherman, who officiates as Charon. Notwithstanding his quaint disguise, the true name of this dispatcher may readily be guessed, and I shall therefore relate the legend as faithfully as possible.

The shores of East Friesland that border on the North Sea abound with bays, which are used as harbors, and are called fiords. On the farthest projecting promontory of land generally stands the solitary hut of some fisherman, who here lives, peaceful and contented, with his family. Here nature wears a sad and melancholy aspect. Not even the chirping of a bird is to be heard, only now and then the shrill screech of a sea-gull flying up from its nest among the sand-hills, that announces the coming storm. The monotonous plashings of the restless sea harmonize with the somber, shifting shadows of the passing clouds. Even the human inhabitants do not sing here, and on these melancholy coasts the strain of a *volkslied* is never heard. The people who live here are an earnest, honest, matter-of-fact race, proud of their bold spirit and of the liberties which they have inherited from their ancestors. Such a people are not imaginative, and are little given to metaphysical speculations. Fishing is their principal support, added to which is an occasional pittance of passage-money for transporting some traveler to one of the adjacent islands.

It is said that at a certain period of the year, just at midday, when the fisherman and his family are seated at table eating their noonday meal, a traveler enters and asks the master of the house to vouchsafe him an audience for a few minutes to speak with him on a matter of business. The fisherman, after vainly inviting the stranger to partake of the meal, grants his request, and they both step aside to a little table. I shall not describe the personal appearance of the stranger in detail, after the tedious manner of novel-writers: a brief enumeration of the salient points will suffice. He is a little man, advanced in years but well preserved. He is, so to say, a youthful graybeard: plump, but not corpulent; cheeks ruddy as an apple; small eyes, which blink merrily and continually, and on his powdered little head is set a three-cornered little hat. Under his flaming yellow cloak, with its many collars, he wears the old-fashioned dress of a well-to-do Dutch merchant, such as we see depicted in old portraits—namely, a short silk coat of a parrot-green color, a vest embroidered with flowers, short black trousers, striped stockings, and shoes ornamented with buckles. The latter are so brightly polished that it is hard to understand how the wearer could trudge a-foot through the slimy mud of the coast and yet keep them so clean. His voice is a thin, asthmatic treble, sometimes inclining to be rather lachrymose; but the address and bearing of the little man are as grave and measured as beseem a Dutch merchant. This gravity, however, appears to be more assumed than natural, and is in marked contrast with the searching, roving, swift-darting glances of the eye, and with the ill-repressed fidgetiness of the legs and arms. That the stranger is a Dutch merchant is evidenced not only by his apparel, but also by the mercantile exactitude and caution with which he endeavors to effect as favorable a bargain as possible for his employers. He is, as he says, a forwarding agent, and has received from some of his mercantile friends a commission to transport a certain number of souls, as many as can find room in an ordinary boat, from the coast of East Friesland to the White Island. In fulfillment of this commission, he adds, he wishes to know if the fisherman will this night convey in his boat the aforesaid cargo to the aforesaid island; in which case he is authorized to pay the passage money in advance, confidently hoping that, in Christian fairness, the fisherman will make his price very moderate. The Dutch merchant (which term is, in fact, a pleonasm, since every Dutchman is a merchant) makes this proposition with the utmost nonchalance, as if it referred to a cargo of cheeses, and not to the souls of the dead. The fisherman is startled at the word "souls," and a cold chill creeps down his back, for he immediately comprehends that the souls of the dead are here meant, and that the stranger is none other than the phantom Dutchman, who has already entrusted several of his fellow-fishermen with the transportation of the souls of the dead, and paid them well for it, too.

These East Frieslanders are, as I have already remarked, a brave, healthy, practical people; in them is lacking that morbid imagination which makes us so impressible to the ghostly and supernatural. Our fisherman's weird dismay lasts but a moment; suppressing the uncanny sensation that is stealing over him, he soon regains his composure, and, intent on securing as high a sum as possible, he assumes an air of supreme indifference. But after a little chaffering the two come to an understanding, and shake hands to seal the bargain. The Dutchman draws forth a dirty leather pouch, filled entirely with little silver pennies of the smallest denomination ever coined in Holland, and in these tiny coins counts out the whole amount of the fare. With instructions to the fisherman to be ready with his boat at the appointed place about the midnight hour when the moon becomes visible, the Dutchman takes leave of the whole family, and, declining their repeated invitations to dine, the grave little figure, dignified as ever, trips lightly away.

At the time agreed upon the fisherman appears at the appointed place. At first the boat is rocked lightly to and fro by the waves; but by the time the full moon has risen above the horizon the fisherman notices that his bark is less easily swayed, and so it gradually sinks deeper and deeper in the stream, until finally the water comes within a hand's-breadth

of the boat's bow. This circumstance apprises him that his
passengers, the souls, are now aboard, and he pushes off
from shore with his cargo. Although he strains his eyes to
the utmost, he can distinguish nothing but a few vapory
streaks that seem to be swayed hither and thither, and to
intermingle with one another, but assume no definite forms.
Listen intently as he may, he hears nothing but an indescribably faint chirping and rustling. Only now and then a
sea-gull with a shrill scream flies swiftly over his head; or
near him a fish leaps up from out the stream, and for a
moment stares at him with a vacuous look. The night-
winds sigh, and the sea-breezes grow more chilly. Everywhere only water, moonlight, and silence! and silent as all
around him is the fisherman, who finally reaches the White
Island and moors his boat. He sees no one on the strand,
but he hears a shrill, asthmatic, wheezy, lachrymose voice,
which he recognizes as that of the Dutchman. The latter
seems to be reading off a list of proper names, with a peculiar, monotonous intonation, as if rehearsing a roll-call.
Among the names are some which are known to the fisherman as belonging to persons who have died that year. During
the reading of the list, the boat is evidently being gradually
lightened of its load, and as soon as the last name is called
·it rises suddenly and floats free, although but a moment before it was deeply imbedded in the sand of the sea-shore.
To the fisherman this is a token that his cargo has been
properly delivered, and he calmly rows back to his wife and
child, to his beloved home on the fiord.

. . . Notwithstanding this clever disguise, I have ventured
to guess who the important mythological personage is that
figures in this tradition. It is none other than the god Mercury, Hermes Psychopompos, the whilom conductor of the
dead to Hades. Verily, under that shabby yellow cloak and
prosaic tradesman's figure is concealed the youthful and
most accomplished god of heathendom, the cunning son of
Maia. On his little three-cornered hat not the slightest tuft
of a feather is to be seen which might remind the beholder

of the winged cap, and the clumsy shoes with steel buckles fail to give the least hint of the winged sandals. This grave and heavy Dutch lead is quite different from the mobile quicksilver, from which the god derived his very name. But the contrast is so exceedingly striking as to betray the god's design, which is the more effectually to disguise himself. Perhaps this mask was not chosen out of mere caprice. Mercury was, as you know, the patron god of thieves and merchants, and, in all probability, in choosing a disguise that should conceal him, and a trade by which to earn his livelihood, he took into consideration his talents and his antecedents.

... And thus it came to pass that the shrewdest and most cunning of the gods became a merchant, and, to adapt himself most thoroughly to his rôle, became the *ne plus ultra* of merchants—a Dutch merchant. His long practice in the olden time as Psychopompos, as conveyor of the dead to Hades, marks him out as particularly fitted to conduct the transportation of the souls of the dead to the White Island, in the manner just described.

The White Island is occasionally also called Brea, or Britannia. Does this perhaps refer to White Albion, to the chalky cliffs of the English coast? It would be a very humorous idea if England was designated as the land of the dead, as the Plutonian realm, as hell. In such a form, in truth, England has appeared to many a stranger.

In my essay on the Faust legend I discussed at full length the popular superstition concerning Pluto and his dominion. I showed how the old realm of shadows became hell, and how its old gloomy ruler became more and more diabolical. Neither Pluto, god of the nether regions, nor his brother, Neptune, god of the sea, emigrated like the other gods. Even after the final triumph of Christendom they remained in their domains, their respective elements. No matter what silly fables concerning him were invented here above on earth, old Pluto sat by his Proserpine, warm and cozy down below.

Neptune suffered less from calumny than his brother Pluto, and neither church-bell chimes nor organ-strains could offend his ears in the depths of old ocean, where he sat peacefully by the side of his white-bosomed wife, Dame Amphitrite, surrounded by his court of dripping nereids and tritons. Only now and then, when a young sailor crossed the equator, he would dart up from the briny deep, in his hand brandishing the trident, his head crowned with seaweed, and his flowing, silvery beard reaching down to the navel. Then he would confer on the neophyte the terrible sea-water baptism, accompanying it with a long unctuous harangue, interspersed with coarse sailor jests, to the great delight of the jolly tars. The harangue was frequently interrupted by the spitting of amber quids of chewed tobacco, which Neptune so freely scattered around him. A friend, who gave me a detailed description of the manner in which such a sea-miracle is performed, assured me that the very sailors that laughed most heartily at the droll antics of Neptune never for a moment doubted the existence of such a god, and sometimes when in great danger they even prayed to him.

Neptune, as we have seen, remained monarch of the watery realm; and Pluto, notwithstanding his metamorphosis into Satan, still continued to be prince of the lower regions. They fared better than did their brother Jupiter, who, after the overthrow of their father, Saturn, became ruler of heaven, and as sovereign of the universe resided at Olympus, where, surrounded by his merry troop of gods, goddesses, and nymphs-of-honor, he carried on his ambrosial rule of joy. But when the great catastrophe occurred,—when the rule of the cross, that symbol of suffering, was proclaimed, —then the great Kronides fled, and disappeared amid the tumults and confusion of the transmigration of races. All traces of him were lost, and I have in vain consulted old chronicles and old women: none could give me the least information concerning his fate. With the same purpose in view, I have ransacked many libraries, where I was shown the magnificent codices ornamented with gold and precious stones, true odalisques in the harem of science. To the learned eunuchs who, with such affability, unlocked for me those brilliant treasures, I here return the customary thanks. It appears as if no popular tradition of a medieval Jupiter exists; and all that I could gather concerning him consists of a story told me by my friend, Niels Andersen.

. . . The events that I am about to relate, said Niels Andersen, occurred on an island, the exact situation of which I cannot tell. Since its discovery no one has been able again to reach it, being prevented by the immense icebergs that tower like a high wall around the island, and seldom, probably, permit a near approach. Only the crew of a Russian whaling-vessel, which a storm had driven so far to the north, ever trod its soil; and since then over a hundred years have elapsed. When the sailors had, by means of a small boat, effected a landing, they found the island to be wild and desolate. Sadly waved the blades of tall sedgy grass over the quicksands; here and there grew a few stunted fir-trees, or barren shrubs. They saw a multitude of rabbits springing around, on which account they named it the Island of Rabbits. Only one miserable hut gave evidence that a human being dwelt there. As the sailors entered the hut they saw an old, very old man, wretchedly clad in a garment of rabbit skins rudely stitched together. He was seated in a stone chair in front of the hearth, trying to warm his emaciated hands and trembling knees by the flaring brushwood fire. At his right side stood an immense bird, evidently an eagle, but which had been roughly treated by time, and shorn of all its plumage save the long bristly quills of its wings, that gave it a highly grotesque, and, at the same time, hideous appearance. At the old man's left, squatted on the earth, was an extraordinarily large hairless goat, which seemed to be very old; although full milky udders, with fresh, rosy nipples, hung at its belly.

Among the sailors were several Greeks, one of whom, not thinking that his words would be understood by the

aged inhabitant of the hut, remarked in the Greek language
to a comrade, "This old fellow is either a specter or an evil
demon." But at these words the old man suddenly rose from
his seat, and to their great surprise the sailors beheld a
stately figure, which, in spite of its advanced age, raised
itself erect with commanding, yes, with king-like dignity,
his head almost touching the rafters. The features, too,
although rugged and weather-beaten, showed traces of
original beauty, they were so noble and well-proportioned.
A few silvery locks fell over his brow, which was furrowed
by pride and age. His eyes had a dim and fixed look, but
occasionally they would still gleam piercingly; and from
his mouth were heard in the melodious and sonorous words
of the ancient Greek language, "You are mistaken, young
man; I am neither a specter nor an evil demon; I am an
unhappy old man, who once knew better days. But who
are ye?"

The sailors explained the accident which had befallen
them, and then inquired concerning the island. The information, however, was very meager. The old man told them that
since time immemorial he had inhabited this island, whose
bulwark of ice served him as a secure asylum against his
inexorable foes. He subsisted principally by catching rabbits, and every year, when the floating icebergs had settled,
a few bands of savages crossed over on sleds, and to them
he sold rabbit-skins, receiving in exchange various articles
of indispensable necessity. The whales, which sometimes
came swimming close to the island, were his favorite company. But it gave him pleasure to hear again his native
tongue, for he too was a Greek. He entreated his country-
men to give him an account of the present condition of
Greece. That the cross had been torn down from the battle-
ments of Grecian cities apparently caused the old man a
malicious satisfaction; but it did not altogether please him
when he heard that the crescent had been planted there
instead. It was strange that none of the sailors knew the
names of the cities concerning which the old man inquired,

and which, as he assured them, had flourished in his time. In like manner the names of the present cities and villages in Greece, which were mentioned by the sailors, were unknown to him; at this the old man would shake his head sadly, and the sailors looked at one another perplexed. They noticed that he knew exactly all the localities and geographical peculiarities of Greece; and he described so accurately and vividly the bays, the peninsulas, the mountain-ridges, even the knolls and most trifling rocky elevations, that his ignorance of these localities was all the more surprising. With especial interest, with a certain anxiety even, he questioned them concerning an ancient temple, which in his time, he assured them, had been the most beautiful in all Greece; but none of his hearers knew the name, which he pronounced with a loving tenderness. But finally, when the old man had again described the site of the temple, with the utmost particularity, a young sailor recognized the place by the description.

The village wherein he was born, said the young man, was situated hard by, and when a boy he had often tended his father's swine at the very place where there had been found ruins of an ancient structure, indicating a magnificent grandeur in the past. Now, only a few large marble pillars remained standing; some were plain, unadorned columns, others were surmounted by the square stones of a gable. From the cracks of the masonry the blooming honeysuckle vines and red bell-flowers trailed downwards. Other pillars —among the number some of rose-colored marble—lay shattered on the ground, and the costly marble head-pieces, ornamented with beautiful sculpture, representing foliage and flowers, were overgrown by rank creepers and grasses. Half buried in the earth lay huge marble blocks, some of which were squares, such as were used for the walls; others were three-cornered slabs for roof-pieces. Over them waved a large, wild fig-tree, which had grown up out of the ruins. Under the shadow of that tree, continued the young man, he had passed whole hours in examining the strange figures

carved on the large marble blocks; they seemed to be pic-
torial representations of all sorts of sports and combats, and
were very pleasing to look at, but, alas! much injured by
exposure, and overgrown with moss and ivy. His father,
whom he had questioned in regard to the mysterious signifi-
cation of these pillars and sculptures, told him that these
were the ruins of an ancient pagan temple, and had once
been the abode of a wicked heathen god, who had here
wantoned in lewd debauchery, incest, and unnatural vices.
Notwithstanding this, the unenlightened heathen were accustomed to slaughter in his honor a hundred oxen at a
time, and the hollowed marble block into which was gathered the blood of the sacrifices was yet in existence. It was,
in fact, the very trough which they were in the habit of using
as a receptacle for refuse wherewith to feed the swine.

So spoke the young sailor. But the old man heaved a sigh
that betrayed the most terrible anguish. Tottering, he sank
into his stone chair, covered his face with his hands, and
wept like a child. The great, gaunt bird, with a shrill screech,
flapped its immense wings, and menaced the strangers with
claws and beak. The old goat licked its master's hands, and
bleated mournfully as in consolation.

At this strange sight, an uncanny terror seized upon the
sailors: they hurriedly left the hut, and were glad when
they could no longer hear the sobbing of the old man, the
screaming of the bird, and the bleating of the goat. When
they were safely on board the boat, they narrated their adventure. Among the crew was a learned Russian, professor
of philosophy at the university of Kazan; and he declared
the matter to be highly important. With his forefinger held
knowingly to the side of his nose, he assured the sailors that
the old man of the island was undoubtedly the ancient god
Jupiter, son of Saturn and Rhea. The bird at his side was
clearly the eagle that once carried in its claws the terrible
thunderbolts. And the old goat was, in all probability, none
other than Althea, Jupiter's old nurse, who had suckled him

in Crete, and now in exile again nourished him with her milk.

This is the story as told to me by Niels Andersen; and I must confess that it filled my soul with a profound melancholy. Decay is secretly undermining all that is great in the universe, and the gods themselves must finally succumb to the same miserable destiny. The iron law of fate so wills it, and even the greatest of the immortals must submissively bow his head. He of whom Homer sang, and whom Phidias sculptured in gold and ivory, he at whose glance earth trembled, he, the lover of Leda, Alcmena, Semele, Danaë, Callisto, Io, Leto, Europa, etc.—even he is compelled to hide himself behind the icebergs of the North Pole, and in order to prolong his wretched existence must deal in rabbit-skins, like a shabby Savoyard!

I do not doubt that there are people who will derive a malicious pleasure from such a spectacle. They are, perhaps, the descendants of these unfortunate oxen who, in hecatombs, were slaughtered on the altars of Jupiter. Rejoice! avenged is the blood of your ancestors, those poor martyrs of superstition. But we, who have no hereditary grudge rankling in us, we are touched at the sight of fallen greatness, and withhold not our holiest compassion.

IMMENSEE *

By Theodor W. Storm

The Old Man

One afternoon in the late autumn a well-dressed old man was walking slowly down the street. He appeared to be returning home from a walk, for his buckle-shoes, which followed a fashion long since out of date, were covered with dust.

Under his arm he carried a long, gold-headed cane; his dark eyes, in which the whole of his long-lost youth seemed to have centered, and which contrasted strangely with his snow-white hair, gazed calmly on the sights around him or peered into the town below as it lay before him, bathed in the haze of sunset.

He appeared to be almost a stranger, for of the passers-by only a few greeted him, although many a one involuntarily was compelled to gaze into those grave eyes.

At last he halted before a high, gabled house, cast one more glance out toward the town, and then passed into the hall. At the sound of the door-bell some one in the room within drew aside the green curtain from a small window that looked out on to the hall, and the face of an old woman was seen behind it. The man made a sign to her with his cane.

"No light yet!" he said in a slightly southern accent, and the housekeeper let the curtain fall again.

The old man now passed through the broad hall, through an inner hall, wherein against the walls stood huge oaken chests bearing porcelain vases; then through the door opposite he entered a small lobby, from which a narrow staircase

* Translated by C. W. Bell.

178

led to the upper rooms at the back of the house. He climbed the stairs slowly, unlocked a door at the top, and landed in a room of medium size.

It was a comfortable, quiet retreat. One of the walls was lined with cupboards and bookcases; on the other hung pictures of men and places; on a table with a green cover lay a number of open books, and before the table stood a massive armchair with a red velvet cushion.

After the old man had placed his hat and stick in a corner, he sat down in the armchair and, folding his hands, seemed to be taking his rest after his walk. While he sat thus, it was growing gradually darker; and before long a moonbeam came streaming through the window-panes and upon the pictures on the wall; and as the bright band of light passed slowly onward the old man followed it involuntarily with his eyes.

Now it reached a little picture in a simple black frame. "Elisabeth!" said the old man softly; and as he uttered the word, time had changed: *he was young again.*

THE CHILDREN

Before very long the dainty form of a little maiden advanced toward him. Her name was Elisabeth, and she might have been five years old. He himself was twice that age. Round her neck she wore a red silk kerchief which was very becoming to her brown eyes.

"Reinhard!" she cried, "we have a holiday, a holiday! No school the whole day and none to-morrow either!"

Reinhard was carrying his slate under his arm, but he flung it behind the front door, and then both the children ran through the house into the garden and through the garden gate out into the meadow. The unexpected holiday came to them at a most happily opportune moment.

It was in the meadow that Reinhard, with Elisabeth's help, had built a house out of sods of grass. They meant to live in it during the summer evenings; but it still wanted a bench. He set to work at once; nails, hammer, and the necessary boards were already to hand.

While he was thus engaged, Elisabeth went along the dyke, gathering the ring-shaped seeds of the wild mallow in her apron, with the object of making herself chains and necklaces out of them; so that when Reinhard had at last finished his bench in spite of many a crookedly hammered nail, and came out into the sunlight again, she was already wandering far away at the other end of the meadow.

"Elisabeth!" he called, "Elisabeth!" and then she came, her hair streaming behind her.

"Come here," he said; "our house is finished now. Why, you have got quite hot! Come in, and let us sit on the new bench. I will tell you a story."

So they both went in and sat down on the new bench. Elisabeth took the little seed-rings out of her apron and strung them on long threads. Reinhard began his tale: "There were once upon a time three spinning-women . . ." *

"Oh!" said Elisabeth, "I know that off by heart; you really must not always tell me the same story."

Accordingly Reinhard had to give up the story of the three spinning-women and tell instead the story of the poor man who was cast into the den of lions.

"It was now night," he said, "black night, you know, and the lions were asleep. But every now and then they would yawn in their sleep and shoot out their red tongues. And then the man would shudder and think it was morning. All at once a bright light fell all about him, and when he looked up an angel was standing before him. The angel beckoned to him with his hand and then went straight into the rocks.

Elisabeth had been listening attentively. "An angel?" she said. "Had he wings, then?"

"It is only a story," answered Reinhard; "there are no angels, you know."

"Oh, fie! Reinhard!" she said, staring him straight in the face.

* The beginning of one of the best known of Grimm's fairy tales.

He looked at her with a frown, and she asked him hesitatingly: "Well, why do they always say there are? Mother, and Aunt, and at school as well?"

"I don't know," he answered.

"But tell me," said Elisabeth, "are there no lions either?"

"Lions? Are there lions? In India, yes. The heathen priests harness them to their carriages, and drive about the desert with them. When I'm big, I mean to go out there myself. It is thousands of times more beautiful in that country than it is here at home; there's no winter at all there. And you must come with me. Will you?"

"Yes," said Elisabeth; "but Mother must come with us, and your mother as well."

"No," said Reinhard, "they will be too old then, and cannot come with us."

"But I mayn't go by myself."

"Oh but you may right enough; you will then really be my wife, and the others will have no say in the matter."

"But Mother will cry!"

"We shall come back again, of course," said Reinhard impetuously. "Now just tell me straight out, will you go with me? If not, I will go all alone, and then I shall never come back again."

The little girl came very near to crying. "Please don't look so angry," said she; "I will go to India with you."

Reinhard seized both her hands with frantic glee, and rushed out with her into the meadow.

"To India, to India!" he sang, and swung her round and round, so that her little red kerchief was whirled from off her neck. Then he suddenly let her go and said solemnly:

"Nothing will come of it, I'm sure; you haven't the pluck."

"Elisabeth! Reinhard!" some one was now calling from the garden gate. "Here we are!" the children answered, and raced home hand in hand.

IN THE WOODS

So the children lived together. She was often too quiet for him, and he was often too headstrong for her, but for all that they stuck to one another. They spent nearly all their leisure hours together: in winter in their mothers' tiny rooms, during the summer in wood and field.

Once when Elisabeth was scolded by the teacher in Reinhard's hearing, he angrily banged his slate upon the table in order to turn upon himself the master's wrath. This failed to attract attention.

But Reinhard paid no further attention to the geography lessons, and instead he composed a long poem, in which he compared himself to a young eagle, the schoolmaster to a gray crow, and Elisabeth to a white dove; the eagle vowed vengeance on the gray crow, as soon as his wings had grown.

Tears stood in the young poet's eyes: he felt very proud of himself. When he reached home he contrived to get hold of a little parchment-bound volume with a lot of blank pages in it; and on the first pages he elaborately wrote out his first poem.

Soon after this he went to another school. Here he made many new friendships among boys of his own age, but this did not interrupt his comings and goings with Elisabeth. Of the stories which he had formerly told her over and over again he now began to write down the ones which she had liked best, and in doing so the fancy often took him to weave in something of his own thoughts; yet, for some reason he could not understand, he could never manage it.

So he wrote them down exactly as he had heard them himself. Then he handed them over to Elisabeth, who kept them carefully in a drawer of her writing-desk, and now and again of an evening when he was present it afforded him agreeable satisfaction to hear her reading aloud to her mother these little tales out of the notebooks in which he had written them.

Seven years had gone by. Reinhard was to leave the town

in order to proceed to his higher education. Elisabeth could not bring herself to think that there would now be a time to be passed entirely without Reinhard. She was delighted when he told her one day that he would continue to write out stories for her as before; he would send them to her in the letters to his mother, and then she would have to write back to him and tell him how she liked them.

The day of departure was approaching, but ere it came a good deal more poetry found its way into the parchment-bound volume. This was the one secret he kept from Elisabeth, although she herself had inspired the whole book and most of the songs which gradually had filled up almost half of the blank pages.

It was the month of June, and Reinhard was to start on the following day. It was proposed to spend one more festive day together, and therefore a picnic was arranged for a rather large party of friends in an adjacent forest.

It was an hour's drive along the road to the edge of the wood, and there the company took down the provision baskets from the carriages and walked the rest of the way. The road lay first of all through a pine grove, where it was cool and darksome, and the ground was all strewed with pine needles.

After half an hour's walk they passed out of the gloom of the pine trees into a bright fresh beech wood. Here everything was light and green; every here and there a sunbeam burst through the leafy branches, and high above their heads a squirrel was leaping from branch to branch.

The party came to a halt at a certain spot, over which the topmost branches of ancient beech trees interwove a transparent canopy of leaves. Elisabeth's mother opened one of the baskets, and an old gentleman constituted himself quartermaster.

"Round me, all of you young people," he cried, "and attend carefully to what I have to say to you. For lunch each one of you will now get two dry rolls; the butter has been left behind at home. The extras every one must find

for himself. There are plenty of strawberries in the wood—
that is, for any one who knows where to find them. Unless
you are sharp, you'll have to eat dry bread; that's the way
of the world all over. Do you understand what I say?"

"Yes, yes," cried the young folks.

"Yes, but look here," said the old gentleman, "I have not
done yet. We old folks have done enough roaming about
in our time, and therefore we will stay at home now, here,
I mean, under these wide-spreading trees, and we'll peel the
potatoes and make a fire and lay the table, and by twelve
o'clock the eggs shall be boiled.

"In return for all this you will be owing us half of your
strawberries, so that we may also be able to serve some
dessert. So off you go now, east and west, and mind be
honest."

The young folks cast many a roguish glance at one another.

"Wait," cried the old gentleman once again. "I suppose
I need not tell you this, that whoever finds none need not
produce any; but take particular note of this, that he will
get nothing out of us old folks either. Now you have had
enough good advice for to-day; and if you gather strawberries to match you will get on very well for the present
at any rate."

The young people were of the same opinion, and pairing
off in couples set out on their quest.

"Come along, Elisabeth," said Reinhard. "I know where
there is a clump of strawberry bushes; you shan't eat dry
bread."

Elisabeth tied the green ribbons of her straw hat together
and hung it on her arm. "Come on, then," she said, "the
basket is ready."

Off into the wood they went, on and on; on through
moist shady glens, where everything was so peaceful, except
for the cry of the falcon flying unseen in the heavens far
above their heads; on again through the thick brushwood,
so thick that Reinhard must needs go on ahead to make a

track, here snapping off a branch, there bending aside a trailing vine. But ere long he heard Elisabeth behind him calling out his name. He turned round.

"Reinhard!" she called, "do wait for me! Reinhard!"

He could not see her, but at length he caught sight of her some way off struggling with the undergrowth, her dainty head just peeping out over the tops of the ferns. So back he went once more and brought her out from the tangled mass of briar and brake into an open space where blue butterflies fluttered among the solitary wood blossoms.

Reinhard brushed the damp hair away from her heated face, and would have tied the straw hat upon her head, but she refused; yet at his earnest request she consented after all.

"But where are your strawberries?" she asked at length, standing still and drawing a deep breath.

"They were here," he said, "but the toads have got here before us, or the martens, or perhaps the fairies."

"Yes," said Elisabeth, "the leaves are still here; but not a word about fairies in this place. Come along, I'm not a bit tired yet; let us look farther on."

In front of them ran a little brook, and on the far side the wood began again. Reinhard raised Elisabeth in his arms and carried her over. After a while they emerged from the shady foliage and stood in a wide clearing.

"There must be strawberries here," said the girl, "it all smells so sweet."

They searched about the sunny spot, but they found none. "No," said Reinhard, "it is only the smell of the heather."

Everywhere was a confusion of raspberry-bushes and holly, and the air was filled with a strong smell of heather, patches of which alternated with the short grass over these open spaces.

"How lonely it is here!" said Elisabeth: "I wonder where the others are?"

Reinhard had never thought of getting back.

"Wait a bit," he said, holding his hand aloft; "where is the wind coming from?" But wind there was none.

"Listen!" said Elisabeth; "I think I heard them talking. Just give a call in that direction."

Reinhard hollowed his hand and shouted: "Come here!"

"Here!" was echoed back.

"They answered," cried Elisabeth, clapping her hands.

"No, that was nothing; it was only the echo."

Elisabeth seized Reinhard's hand. "I'm frightened!" she said.

"Oh! no, you must not be frightened. It is lovely here. Sit down there in the shade among the long grass. Let us rest awhile: we'll find the others soon enough."

Elisabeth sat down under the overhanging branch of a beech and listened intently in every direction. Reinhard sat a few paces off on a tree stump, and gazed over at her in silence.

The sun was just above their heads, shining with the full glare of midday heat. Tiny, gold-flecked, steel-blue flies poised in the air with vibrating wings. Their ears caught a gentle humming and buzzing all round them, and far away in the wood were heard now and again the tap-tap of the wood-pecker and the screech of other birds.

"Listen," said Elisabeth, "I hear a bell."

"Where?" asked Reinhard.

"Behind us. Do you hear it? It is striking twelve o'clock."

"Then the town lies behind us, and if we go straight through in this direction we are bound to fall in with the others."

So they started on their homeward way; they had given up looking for strawberries, for Elisabeth had become tired. And at last there rang out from among the trees the laughing voices of the picnic party; then they saw too a white cloth spread gleaming on the ground; it was the luncheon-table and on it were strawberries enough and to spare.

The old gentleman had a table-napkin tucked in his button-hole and was continuing his moral sermon to the young folks and vigorously carving a joint of roast meat.

"Here come the stragglers," cried the young people when they saw Reinhard and Elisabeth advancing among the trees.

"This way," shouted the old gentleman. "Empty your handkerchiefs, upside down with your hats! Now show us what you have found."

"Only hunger and thirst," said Reinhard.

"If that's all," replied the old man, lifting up and showing them the bowl full of fruit, "you must keep what you've got. You remember the agreement: nothing here for lazybones to eat."

But in the end he was prevailed on to relent; the banquet proceeded, and a thrush in a juniper bush provided the music.

So the day passed. But Reinhard had, after all, found something, and though it was not strawberries yet it was something that had grown in the wood. When he got home this is what he wrote in his old parchment-bound volume:

> Out on the hillside yonder
>   The wind to rest is laid;
> Under the drooping branches
>   There sits the little maid.
>
> She sits among the wild thyme,
>   She sits in the fragrant air;
> The blue flies hum around her,
>   Bright wings flash everywhere.
>
> And through the silent woodland
>   She peers with watchful eyen,
> While on her hazel ringlets
>   Sparkles the glad sunshine.
>
> And afar, far off the cuckoo
>   Laughs out his song. I ween
> Hers are the bright, the golden
>   Eyes of the woodland queen.

So she was not only his little sweetheart, but was also the expression of all that was lovely and wonderful in his opening life.

By the Roadside the Child Stood

The time is Christmas Eve. Before the close of the afternoon Reinhard and some other students were sitting together at an old oak table in the Ratskeller. The lamps on the wall were lighted, for down here in the basement it was already growing dark; but there was only a thin sprinkling of customers present, and the waiters were leaning idly up against the pillars let into the walls.

In a corner of the vaulted room sat a fiddler and a fine-featured gypsy-girl with a zither; their instruments lay in their laps, and they seemed to be looking about them with an air of indifference.

A champagne cork popped off at the table occupied by the students. "Drink, my gypsy darling!" cried a young man of aristocratic appearance, holding out to the girl a glass full of wine.

"I don't care about it," she said, without altering her position.

"Well, then, give us a song," cried the young nobleman, and threw a silver coin into her lap. The girl slowly ran her fingers through her black hair while the fiddler whispered in her ear. But she threw back her head, and rested her chin on her zither.

"For him," she said, "I'm not going to play."

Reinhard leapt up with his glass in his hand and stood in front of her.

"What do you want?" she asked defiantly.

"To have a look at your eyes."

"What have my eyes to do with you?"

Reinhard's glance flashed down on her.

"I *know* they are false."

She laid her cheek in the palm of her hand and gave him a searching look. Reinhard raised his glass to his mouth.

"Here's to your beautiful, wicked eyes!" he said, and drank.

She laughed and tossed her head.

"Give it here," she said, and fastening her black eyes on his, she slowly drank what was left in the glass. Then she struck a chord and sang in a deep, passionate voice:

To-day, to-day thou think'st me
  Fairest maid of all;
To-morrow, ah! then beauty
  Fadeth past recall.
While the hour remaineth,
  Thou art yet mine own;
Then when death shall claim me,
  I must die alone.

While the fiddler struck up an allegro finale, a new arrival joined the group.

"I went to call for you, Reinhard," he said. "You had already gone out, but Santa Claus had paid you a visit."

"Santa Claus?" said Reinhard. "Santa Claus never comes to me now."

"Oh, yes, he does! The whole of your room smelt of Christmas tree and ginger cakes."

Reinhard dropped the glass out of his hand and seized his cap.

"Well, what are you going to do now?" asked the girl.

"I'll be back in a minute."

She frowned. "Stay," she said gently, casting an amorous glance at him.

Reinhard hesitated. "I can't," he said.

She laughingly gave him a tap with the toe of her shoe and said: "Go away, then, you good-for-nothing; you are one as bad as the other, all good-for-nothings." And as she turned away from him, Reinhard went slowly up the steps of the Ratskeller.

Outside in the street deep twilight had set in; he felt the cool winter air blowing on his heated brow. From some window every here and there fell the bright gleam of a Christmas tree all lighted up, now and then was heard from within some room the sound of little pipes and tin trumpets mingled with the merry din of children's voices.

Crowds of beggar children were going from house to house or climbing up on to the railings of the front steps, trying to catch a glimpse through the window of a splendor that was denied to them. Sometimes too a door would suddenly be flung open, and scolding voices would drive a whole swarm of these little visitors away out into the dark street. In the vestibule of yet another house they were singing an old Christmas carol, and little girls' clear voices were heard among the rest.

But Reinhard heard not; he passed quickly by them all, out of one street into another. When he reached his lodging it had grown almost quite dark; he stumbled up the stairs and so gained his apartment.

A sweet fragrance greeted him; it reminded him of home; it was the smell of the parlor in his mother's house at Christmas time. With trembling hand he lit his lamp; and there lay a mighty parcel on the table. When he opened it, out fell the familiar ginger cakes. On some of them were the initial letters of his name written in sprinkles of sugar; no one but Elisabeth could have done that.

Next came to view a little parcel containing neatly embroidered linen, handkerchiefs and cuffs; and finally letters from his mother and Elisabeth. Reinhard opened Elisabeth's letter first, and this is what she wrote:

"The pretty sugared letters will no doubt tell you who helped with the cakes. The same person also embroidered the cuffs for you. We shall have a very quiet time at home this Christmas Eve. Mother always puts her spinning-wheel away in the corner as early as half-past nine. It is so very lonesome this winter now that you are not here.

"And now, too, the linnet you made me a present of died last Sunday. It made me cry a good deal, though I am sure I looked after it well.

"It always used to sing of an afternoon when the sun shone on its cage. You remember how often mother would hang a piece of cloth over the cage in order to keep it quiet when it sang so lustily.

"Thus our room is now quieter than ever, except that your old friend Eric now drops in to see us occasionally. You told us once that he was just like his brown top-coat. I can't help thinking of it every time he comes in at the door, and it is really too funny; but don't tell mother, it might easily make her angry.

"Guess what I am giving your mother for a Christmas present! You can't guess! Well, it is myself! Eric is making a drawing of me in black chalk; I have had to give him three sittings, each time for a whole hour.

"I simply loathed the idea of a stranger getting to know my face so well. Nor did I wish it, but mother pressed me, and said it would very much please dear Frau Werner.

"But you are not keeping your word, Reinhard. You haven't sent me any stories. I have often complained to your mother about it, but she always says you now have more to do than to attend to such childish things. But I don't believe it; there's something else perhaps."

After this Reinhard read his mother's letter, and when he had read them both and slowly folded them up again and put them away, he was overcome with an irresistible feeling of homesickness. For a long while he walked up and down his room, talking softly to himself, and then, under his breath, he murmured:

> I have err'd from the straight path,
>   Bewildered I roam;
> By the roadside the child stands
>   And beckons me home.

Then he went to his desk, took out some money, and stepped down into the street again. During all this while it had become quieter out there; the lights on the Christmas trees had burnt out, the processions of children had come to an end. The wind was sweeping through the deserted streets; old and young alike were sitting together at home in family parties; the second period of Christmas Eve celebrations had begun.

As Reinhard drew near the Ratskeller he heard from below the scraping of the fiddle and the singing of the zither girl. The restaurant door bell tinkled and a dark form staggered up the broad dimly-lighted stair.

Reinhard drew aside into the shadow of the houses and then passed swiftly by. After a while he reached the well-lighted shop of a jeweler, and after buying a little cross studded with red corals, he returned by the same way he had come.

Not far from his lodgings he caught sight of a little girl, dressed in miserable rags, standing before a tall door, in a vain attempt to open it.

"Shall I help you?" he said.

The child gave no answer, but let go the massive door-handle. Reinhard had soon opened the door.

"No," he said; "they might drive you out again. Come along with me, and I'll give you some Christmas cake."

He then closed the door again and gave his hand to the little girl, who walked along with him in silence to his lodgings.

On going out he had left the light burning.

"Here are some cakes for you," he said, pouring half of his whole stock into her apron, though he gave none that bore the sugar letters.

"Now, off you go home, and give your mother some of them too."

The child cast a shy look up at him; she seemed unaccustomed to such kindness and unable to say anything in reply. Reinhard opened the door, and lighted her way, and then the little thing like a bird flew downstairs with her cakes and out of the house.

Reinhard poked the fire in the stove, set the dusty inkstand on the table, and then sat down and wrote and wrote letters the whole night long to his mother and Elisabeth.

The remainder of the Christmas cakes lay untouched by his side, but he had buttoned on Elisabeth's cuffs, and odd they looked on his shaggy coat of undyed wool. And there he was still sitting when the winter sun cast its light on the frosted window-panes, and showed him a pale, grave face reflected in the looking-glass.

HOME

When the Easter vacation came Reinhard journeyed home. On the morning after his arrival he went to see Elisabeth.

"How tall you've grown!" he said, as the pretty, slender girl advanced with a smile to meet him. She blushed, but made no reply; he had taken her hand in his own in greeting, and she tried to draw it gently away. He looked at her doubtingly, for never had she done that before; but now it was as if some strange thing was coming between them.

The same feeling remained, too, after he had been at home for some time and came to see her constantly day after day. When they sat alone together there ensued pauses in the conversation which distressed him, and which he anxiously did his best to avoid. In order to have a definite occupation during the holidays, he began to give Elisabeth some instruction in botany, in which he himself had been keenly interested during the early months of his university career.

Elisabeth, who was wont to follow him in all things and was, moreover, very quick to learn, willingly entered into the proposal. So now several times in the week they made excursions into the fields or the moors, and if by midday they brought home their green field-box full of plants and flowers, Reinhard would come again later in the day and share with Elisabeth what they had collected in common.

With this same object in view, he entered the room one afternoon while Elisabeth was standing by the window and sticking some fresh chickweed in a gilded birdcage which he had not seen in the place before. In the cage was a canary, which was flapping its wings and shrilly chirruping as it pecked at Elisabeth's fingers. Previously to this Reinhard's bird had hung in that spot.

"Has my poor linnet changed into a goldfinch after its death?" he asked jovially.

"Linnets are not accustomed to do any such thing," said Elisabeth's mother, who sat spinning in her armchair. "Your friend Eric sent it this noon from his estate as a present for Elisabeth."

"What estate?"

"Why, don't you know?"

"Know what?"

"That a month ago Eric took over his father's second estate by the Immensee." *

"But you have never said a word to me about it."

"Well," said the mother, "you haven't yet made a single word of inquiry after your friend. He is a very nice, sensible young man."

The mother went out of the room to make the coffee. Elisabeth had her back turned to Reinhard, and was still busy with the making of her little chickweed bower.

"Please, just a little longer," she said. "I'll be done in a minute."

As Reinhard did not answer, contrary to his wont, she turned round and faced him. In his eyes there was a sudden expression of trouble which she had never observed before in them.

"What is the matter with you, Reinhard?" she said, drawing nearer to him.

"With me?" he said, his thoughts far away and his eyes resting dreamily on hers.

"You look so sad."

"Elisabeth," he said, "I cannot bear that yellow bird."

She looked at him in astonishment, without understanding his meaning. "You are so strange," she said.

He took both her hands in his, and she let him keep

* *i.e.* the "Lake of the Bees."

them there. Her mother came back into the room shortly after; and after they had drunk their coffee she sat down at her spinning-wheel, while Reinhard and Elisabeth went off into the next room to arrange their plants.

Stamens were counted, leaves and blossoms carefully opened out, and two specimens of each sort were laid to dry between the pages of a large folio volume.

All was calm and still this sunny afternoon; the only sounds to be heard were the hum of the mother's spinning-wheel in the next room, and now and then the subdued voice of Reinhard, as he named the orders of the families of the plants, and corrected Elisabeth's awkward pronunciation of the Latin names.

"I am still short of that lily of the valley which I didn't get last time," said she, after the whole collection had been classified and arranged.

Reinhard pulled a little white vellum volume from his pocket. "Here is a spray of the lily of the valley for you," he said, taking out a half-pressed bloom.

When Elisabeth saw the pages all covered with writing, she asked: "Have you been writing stories again?"

"These aren't stories," he answered, handing her the book.

The contents were all poems, and the majority of them at most filled one page. Elisabeth turned over the leaves one after another; she appeared to be reading the titles only. "When she was scolded by the teacher." "When they lost their way in the woods." "An Easter story." "On her writing to me for the first time." Thus ran most of the titles.

Reinhard fixed his eyes on her with a searching look, and as she kept turning over the leaves he saw that a gentle blush arose and gradually mantled over the whole of her sweet face. He would fain have looked into her eyes, but Elisabeth did not look up, and finally laid the book down before him without a word.

"Don't give it back like that," he said.

She took a brown spray out of the tin case. "I will put your favorite flower inside," she said, giving back the book into his hands.

At length came the last day of the vacation and the morning of his departure. At her own request Elisabeth received permission from her mother to accompany her friend to the stage-coach, which had its station a few streets from their house.

When they passed out of the front door Reinhard gave her his arm, and thus he walked in silence side by side with the slender maiden. The nearer they came to their destination the more he felt as if he had something he must say to her before he bade her a long farewell, something on which all that was worthy and all that was sweet in his future life depended, and yet he could not formulate the saving word. In his anguish, he walked slower and slower.

"You'll be too late," she said; "it has already struck ten by St. Mary's clock."

But he did not quicken his pace for all that. At last he stammered out:

"Elisabeth, you will not see me again for two whole years. Shall I be as dear to you as ever when I come back?"

She nodded, and looked affectionately into his face.

"I stood up for you," she said, after a pause.

"Me? And against whom had you to stand up for me?"

"Against my mother. We were talking about you a long time yesterday evening after you left. She thought you were not so nice now as you once were."

Reinhard held his peace for a moment: then he took her hand in his, and looking gravely into her childish eyes, he said:

"I am still just as nice as I ever was; I would have you firmly believe that. Do you believe it, Elisabeth?"

"Yes," she said.

He freed her hand and quickly walked with her through the last street. The nearer he felt the time of parting approach, the happier became the look on his face; he went almost too quickly for her.

"What is the matter with you, Reinhard?" she asked.

"I have a secret, a beautiful secret," said Reinhard, looking at her with a light in his eyes. "When I come back again in two years' time, then you shall know it."

Meanwhile they had reached the stage-coach; they were only just in time. Once more Reinhard took her hand. "Farewell!" he said, "farewell, Elisabeth! Do not forget!"

She shook her head. "Farewell," she said. Reinhard climbed up into the coach and the horses started. As the coach rumbled round the corner of the street he saw her dear form once more as she slowly wended her way home.

A LETTER

Nearly two years later Reinhard was sitting by lamp-light with his books and papers around him, expecting a friend with whom he used to study in common. Some one came upstairs. "Come in." It was the landlady. "A letter for you, Herr Werner," and she went away.

Reinhard had never written to Elisabeth since his visit home, and he had received no letter from her. Nor was this one from her; it was in his mother's handwriting.

Reinhard broke the seal and read, and ere long he came to this paragraph:

"At your time of life, my dear boy, nearly every year still brings its own peculiar experience; for youth is apt to turn everything to the best account. At home, too, things have changed very much, and all this will, I fear, cause you much pain at first, if my understanding of you is at all correct.

"Yesterday Eric was at last accepted by Elisabeth, after having twice proposed in vain during the last three months. She had never been able to make up her mind to it, but now in the end she has done so. To my mind she is still

far too young. The wedding is to take place soon, and her
mother means to go away with them."

IMMENSEE

Again years have passed. One warm afternoon in spring
a young man, whose sunburnt face was the picture of health,
was walking along a shady road through the wood leading
down to the valley below.

His grave dark eyes looked intently into the distance, as
though he was expecting to find every moment some change
in the monotony of the road, a change, however, which
seemed reluctant to come about. At length he saw a cart
slowly coming up from below.

"Hullo! my friend," shouted the traveler to the farmer,
who was walking by the side of the cart, "is this the right
road to Immensee?"

"Yes, straight on," answered the man, touching his
slouch hat.

"Is it still far off?"

"You are close to the place, sir. In less time than it takes
to smoke half a pipe of tobacco you'll be at the lake side,
and the manor is hard by."

The farmer passed on, while the other quickened his
pace as he went along under the trees. After a quarter of an
hour's walk the shade to the left of him suddenly came to
an end; the road led along a steep slope from which the
ancient oaks growing below hardly reared their topmost
branches.

Away over their crests opened out a broad, sunny landscape. Far below lay the peaceful, dark-blue lake, almost
entirely surrounded by green sun-lit woods, save where on
one spot they divided and afforded an extensive view until
it closed in the distant blue mountains.

Straight opposite, in the middle of all this forest verdure,
there lay a patch of white, like driven snow. This was an
expanse of blossoming fruit-trees, and out of them, up on

the high lake shore, rose the manor-house, shining white, with tiles of red. A stork flew up from the chimney, and circled slowly above the waters.

"Immensee!" exclaimed the traveler.

It almost seemed as if he had now reached the end of his journey, for he stood motionless, looking out over the tops of the trees at his feet, and gazing at the farther shore, where the reflection of the manor-house floated, rocking gently, on the bosom of the water. Then he suddenly started on his way again.

His road now led almost steeply down the mountain-side, so that the trees that had once stood below him again gave him their shade, but at the same time cut off from him the view of the lake, which only now and then peeped out between the gaps in the branches.

Soon the way went gently upwards again, and to left and right the woods disappeared, yielding place to vine-clad hills stretching along the pathway; while on either side stood fruit-trees in blossom, filled with the hum of the bees as they busily pried into the blossoms. A tall man wearing a brown overcoat advanced to meet the traveler. When he had almost come up to him, he waved his cap and cried out in a loud voice:

"Welcome, welcome, brother Reinhard! Welcome to my Immensee estate!"

"God's greeting to you, Eric, and thank you for your welcome," replied the other.

By this time they had come up close to one another, and clasped hands.

"And is it really you?" said Eric, when he at last got a near sight of the grave face of his old school-fellow.

"It is I right enough, Eric, and I recognize you too; only you almost look cheerier than you ever did before."

At these words a glad smile made Eric's plain features all the more cheerful.

"Yes, brother Reinhard," he said, as he once more held

out his hand to him, "but since those days, you see, I have won the great prize; but you know that well enough."

Then he rubbed his hands and cried cheerily, "This *will* be a surprise! You are the last person she expects to see."

"A surprise?" asked Reinhard. "For whom, pray?"

"Why, for Elisabeth."

"Elisabeth! You haven't told her a word about my visit?"

"Not a word, brother Reinhard; she has no thought of you, nor her mother either. I invited you entirely on the quiet, in order that the pleasure might be all the greater. You know I always had little quiet schemes of my own."

Reinhard turned thoughtful; he seemed to breathe more heavily the nearer they approached the house.

On the left side of the road the vineyards came to an end, and gave place to an extensive kitchen-garden, which reached almost as far as the lake-shore. The stork had meanwhile come to earth and was striding solemnly between the vegetable beds.

"Hullo!" cried Eric, clapping his hands together, "if that long-legged Egyptian isn't stealing my short pea-sticks again!"

The bird slowly rose and flew on to the roof of a new building, which ran along the end of the kitchen-garden, and whose walls were covered with the branches of the peach and apricot trees that were trained over them.

"That's the distillery," said Eric. "I built it only two years ago. My late father had the farm buildings rebuilt; the dwelling-house was built as far back as my grand-father's time. So we go ever forward a little bit at a time."

Talking thus they came to a wide, open space, enclosed at the sides by farm-buildings, and in the rear by the manor-house, the two wings of which were connected by a high garden wall. Behind this wall ran dark hedges of yew trees, while here and there syringa trees trailed their blossoming branches over into the courtyard.

Men with faces scorched by the sun and heated with

toil were walking over the open space and gave a greeting to the two friends, while Eric called out to one or another of them some order or question about their day's work.

By this time they had reached the house. They entered a high, cool vestibule, at the far end of which they turned to the left into a somewhat darker passage.

Here Eric opened a door and they passed into a spacious room that opened into a garden. The heavy mass of leafage that covered the opposite windows filled this room at either end with a green twilight, while between the windows two lofty wide-open folding-doors let in the full glow of spring sunshine, and afforded a view into a garden, laid out with circular flower-beds and steep hedgerows and divided by a straight, broad path, along which the eye roamed out on to the lake and away over the woods growing on the opposite shore.

As the two friends entered, a breath of wind bore in upon them a perfect stream of fragrance.

On a terrace in front of the door leading to the garden sat a girlish figure dressed in white. She rose and came to meet the two friends as they entered, but half-way she stood stock-still as if rooted to the spot and stared at the stranger. With a smile he held out his hand to her.

"Reinhard!" she cried. "Reinhard! Oh! is it you? It is such a long time since we have seen each other."

"Yes, a long time," he said, and not a word more could he utter; for on hearing her voice he felt a keen, physical pain at his heart, and as he looked up to her, there she stood before him, the same slight, graceful figure to whom he had said farewell years ago in the town where he was born.

Eric had stood back by the door, with joy beaming from his eyes.

"Now, then, Elisabeth," he said, "isn't he really the very last person in the world you would have expected to see?"

Elisabeth looked at him with the eyes of a sister. "You are so kind, Eric," she said.

He took her slender hand caressingly in his. "And now that we have him," he said, "we shall not be in a hurry to let him go. He has been so long away abroad, we will try to make him feel at home again. Just see how foreign-looking he has become, and what a distinguished appearance he has!"

Elisabeth shyly scanned Reinhard's face. "The time that we have been separated is enough to account for that," she said.

At this moment in at the door came her mother, key basket on arm.

"Herr Werner!" she cried, when she caught sight of Reinhard; "ah! you are as dearly welcome as you are unexpected."

And so the conversation went smoothly on with questions and answers. The ladies sat over their work, and while Reinhard enjoyed the refreshment that had been prepared for him, Eric had lighted his huge meerschaum pipe and sat smoking and conversing by his side.

Next day Reinhard had to go out with him to see the fields, the vineyards, the hop-garden, the distillery. It was all well appointed; the people who were working on the land or at the vats all had a healthy and contented look.

For dinner the family assembled in the room that opened into the garden, and the day was spent more or less in company just according to the leisure of the host and hostess. Only during the hours preceding the evening meal, as also during the early hours of the forenoon, did Reinhard stay working in his own room.

For some years past, whenever he could come across them, he had been collecting the rhymes and songs that form part of the life of the people, and now set about arranging his treasure, and wherever possible increasing it by means of fresh records from the immediate neighborhood.

Elisabeth was at all times gentle and kind. Eric's con-

stant attentions she received with an almost humble gratitude, and Reinhard thought at whiles that the gay, cheerful
child of bygone days had given promise of a somewhat
less sedate womanhood.

Ever since the second day of his visit he had been wont
of an evening to take a walk along the shore of the lake.
The road led along close under the garden. At the end of
the latter, on a projecting mound, there was a bench under
some tall birch trees. Elisabeth's mother had christened it
the Evening Bench, because the spot faced westward, and
was mostly used at that time of the day in order to enjoy
a view of the sunset.

One evening Reinhard was returning from his walk along
this road when he was overtaken by the rain. He sought
shelter under one of the linden trees that grew by the water-
side, but the heavy drops were soon pelting through the
leaves. Wet through as he was he resigned himself to his
fate and slowly continued his homeward way.

It was almost dark; the rain fell faster and faster. As he
drew near to the Evening Bench he fancied he could make
out the figure of a woman dressed in white standing among
the gleaming birch tree trunks. She stood motionless, and,
as far as he could make out on approaching nearer, with
her face turned in his direction, as if she was expecting
some one.

He thought it was Elisabeth. But when he quickened his
pace in order that he might catch up to her and then return
together with her through the garden into the house, she
turned slowly away and disappeared among the dark side-
paths.

He could not understand it; he was almost angry with
Elisabeth, and yet he doubted whether it had really been
she. He was, however, shy of questioning her about it—
nay, he even avoided going into the garden-room on his
return to the house for fear he should happen to see Elisabeth enter through the garden-door.

By my Mother's Hard Decree

Some days later, as evening was already closing in, the family was, as usual at this time of the day, sitting all together in their garden-room. The doors stood wide open, and the sun had already sunk behind the woods on the far side of the lake.

Reinhard was invited to read some folk-songs which had been sent to him that afternoon by a friend who lived away in the country. He went up to his room and soon returned with a roll of papers which seemed to consist of detached neatly written pages.

So they all sat down to the table, Elisabeth beside Reinhard. "We shall read them at random," said the latter, "I have not yet looked through them myself."

Elisabeth unrolled the manuscript. "Here's some music," she said, "you must sing it, Reinhard."

To begin with he read some Tyrolese ditties, and as he read on he would now and then hum one or other of the lively melodies. A general feeling of cheeriness pervaded the little party. "And who, pray, made all these pretty songs?" asked Elisabeth.

"Oh," said Eric, "you can tell that by listening to the rubbishy things—tailors' apprentices and barbers and such-like merry folk."

Reinhard said: "They are not made; they grow, they drop from the clouds, they float over the land like gossamer, hither and thither, and are sung in a thousand places at the same time. We discover in these songs our very inmost activities and sufferings: it is as if we all had helped to write them."

He took up another sheet: "I stood on the mountain height . . ."

"I know that one," cried Elisabeth; "begin it, do, Reinhard, and I will help you out."

So they sang that famous melody, which is so mysterious that one can hardly believe that it was ever conceived by the heart of man, Elisabeth with her slightly clouded contralto taking the second part to the young man's tenor.

The mother meanwhile sat busy with her needlework, while Eric listened attentively, with one hand clasped in the other. The song finished, Reinhard laid the sheet on one side in silence. Up from the lake-shore came through the evening calm the tinkle of the cattle bells; they were all listening without knowing why, and presently they heard a boy's clear voice singing:

> I stood on the mountain height
> And viewed the deep valley beneath...

Reinhard smiled. "Do you hear that now? So it passes from mouth to mouth."

"It is often sung in these parts," said Elisabeth.

"Yes," said Eric, "it is Casper the herdsman; he is driving the heifers home."

They listened a while longer until the tinkle of the bells died away behind the farm buildings. "These melodies are as old as the world," said Reinhard; "they slumber in the depths of the forest; God knows who discovered them."

He drew forth a fresh sheet.

It had now grown darker; a crimson evening glow lay like foam over the woods in the farther side of the lake. Reinhard unrolled the sheet, Elisabeth caught one side of it in her hand, and they both examined it together. Then Reinhard read:

> By my Mother's hard decree
> Another's wife I needs must be;
> Him on whom my heart was set,
> Him, alas! I must forget;
> My heart protesting, but not free.
>
> Bitterly did I complain
> That my mother brought me pain.
> What mine honor might have been,
> That is turned to deadly sin.
> Can I ever hope again?

> For my pride what can I show,
> And my joy, save grief and woe?
> Ah! could I undo what's done,
> O'er the moor scorched by the sun
> Beggarwise I'd gladly go.

During the reading of this Reinhard had felt an imperceptible quivering of the paper; and when he came to an end Elisabeth gently pushed her chair back and passed silently out into the garden. Her mother followed her with a look. Eric made as if to go after, but the mother said: "Elisabeth has one or two little things to do outside," so he remained where he was.

But out of doors the evening brooded darker and darker over garden and lake. Moths whirred past the open doors through which the fragrance of flower and bush floated in increasingly; up from the water came the croak of the frogs, under the windows a nightingale commenced his song answered by another from within the depths of the garden; the moon appeared over the tree-tops.

Reinhard looked for a little while longer at the spot where Elisabeth's sweet form had been lost to sight in the thick-foliaged garden paths, and then he rolled up his manuscript, bade his friends good-night and passed through the house down to the water.

The woods stood silent and cast their dark shadow far out over the lake, while the center was bathed in the haze of a pale moonlight. Now and then a gentle rustle trembled through the trees, though wind there was none: it was but the breath of summer night.

Reinhard continued along the shore. A stone's throw from the land he perceived a white water-lily. All at once he was seized with the desire to see it quite close, so he threw off his clothes and entered the water. It was quite shallow; sharp stones and water plants cut his feet, and yet he could not reach water deep enough for him to swim in.

Then suddenly he stepped out of his depth: the waters

swirled above him, and it was some time before he rose to
the surface again. He struck out with hands and feet and
swam about in a circle until he had made quite sure from
what point he had entered the water. And soon too he
saw the lily again floating lonely among the large, gleaming
leaves.

He swam slowly out, lifting every now and then his
arms out of the water so that the drops trickled down and
sparkled in the moonlight. Yet the distance between him
and the flower showed no signs of diminishing, while the
shore, as he glanced back at it, showed behind him in a
hazy mist that ever deepened. But he refused to give up the
venture and vigorously continued swimming in the same
direction.

At length he had come so near the flower that he was
able clearly to distinguish the silvery leaves in the moonlight; but at the same time he felt himself entangled in a
net formed by the smooth stems of the water plants which
swayed up from the bottom and wound themselves round
his naked limbs.

The unfamiliar water was black all round about him, and
behind him he heard the sound of a fish leaping. Suddenly
such an uncanny feeling overpowered him in the midst of
this strange element that with might and main he tore
asunder the network of plants and swam back to land in
breathless haste. And when from the shore he looked back
upon the lake, there floated the lily on the bosom of the
darkling water as far away and as lonely as before.

He dressed and slowly wended his way home. As he
passed out of the garden into the room he discovered Eric
and the mother busied with preparations for a short journey
which had to be undertaken for business purposes on the
morrow.

"Wherever have you been so late in the dark?" the
mother called out to him.

"I?" he answered; "oh, I wanted to pay a call on the
water-lily, but I failed."

"That's beyond the comprehension of any man," said Eric. "What on earth had you to do with the water-lily?"

"Oh, I used to be friends with the lily once," said Reinhard; "but that was long ago."

ELISABETH

The following afternoon Reinhard and Elisabeth went for a walk on the farther side of the lake, strolling at times through the woodland, at other times along the shore where it jutted out into the water. Elisabeth had received injunctions from Eric, during the absence of himself and her mother, to show Reinhard the prettiest views in the immediate neighborhood, particularly the view toward the farm itself from the other side of the lake. So now they proceeded from one point to another.

At last Elisabeth got tired and sat down in the shade of some overhanging branches. Reinhard stood opposite to her, leaning against a tree trunk; and as he heard the cuckoo calling farther back in the woods, it suddenly struck him that all this had happened once before. He looked at her and with an odd smile asked:

"Shall we look for strawberries?"

"It isn't strawberry time," she said.

"No, but it will soon be here."

Elisabeth shook her head in silence; then she rose and the two strolled on together. And as they wandered side by side, his eyes ever and again were bent toward her; for she walked gracefully and her step was light. He often unconsciously fell back a pace in order that he might feast his eyes on a full view of her.

So they came to an open space overgrown with heather where the view extended far over the country-side. Reinhard bent down and plucked a bloom from one of the little plants that grew at his feet. When he looked up again there was an expression of deep pain on his face.

"Do you know this flower?" he asked.

She gave him a questioning look. "It is an erica. I have often gathered them in the woods."

"I have an old book at home," he said; "I once used to write in it all sorts of songs and rhymes, but that is all over and done with long since. Between its leaves also there is an erica, but it is only a faded one. Do you know who gave it me?"

She nodded without saying a word; but she cast down her eyes and fixed them on the bloom which he held in his hand. For a long time they stood thus. When she raised her eyes on him again he saw that they were brimming over with tears.

"Elisabeth," he said, "beyond yonder blue hills lies our youth. What has become of it?"

Nothing more was spoken. They walked dumbly by each other's side down to the lake. The air was sultry; to westward dark clouds were rising. "There's going to be a storm," said Elisabeth, hastening her steps. Reinhard nodded in silence, and together they rapidly sped along the shore till they reached their boat.

On the way across Elisabeth rested her hand on the gunwale of the boat. As he rowed Reinhard glanced along at her, but she gazed past him into the distance. And so his glance fell downward and rested on her hand, and the white hand betrayed to him what her lips had failed to reveal.

It revealed those fine traces of secret pain that so readily mark a woman's fair hands, when they lie at nights folded across an aching heart. And as Elisabeth felt his glance resting on her hand she let it slip gently over the gunwale into the water.

On arriving at the farm they fell in with a scissors grinder's cart standing in front of the manor-house. A man with black, loosely-flowing hair was busily plying his wheel and humming a gypsy melody between his teeth, while a dog that was harnessed to the cart lay panting hard by. On the threshold stood a girl dressed in rags, with features of faded beauty, and with outstretched hand she asked alms of Elisabeth.

Reinhard thrust his hand into his pocket, but Elisabeth was before him, and hastily emptied the entire contents of her purse into the beggar's open palm. Then she turned quickly away, and Reinhard heard her go sobbing up the stairs.

He would fain have detained her, but he changed his mind and remained at the foot of the stairs. The beggar girl was still standing at the doorway, motionless, and holding in her hand the money she had received.

"What more do you want?" asked Reinhard.

She gave a sudden start: "I want nothing more," she said; then, turning her head toward him and staring at him with wild eyes, she passed slowly out of the door. He uttered a name, but she heard him not; with drooping head, with arms folded over her breast, she walked down across the farmyard:

> Then when death shall claim me,
> I must die alone.

An old song surged in Reinhard's ears, he gasped for breath; a little while only, and then he turned away and went up to his chamber.

He sat down to work, but his thoughts were far afield. After an hour's vain attempt he descended to the parlor. Nobody was in it, only cool, green twilight; on Elisabeth's work-table lay a red ribbon which she had worn round her neck during the afternoon. He took it up in his hand, but it hurt him, and he laid it down again.

He could find no rest. He walked down to the lake and untied the boat. He rowed over the water and trod once again all the paths which he and Elisabeth had paced together but a short hour ago. When he got back home it was dark. At the farm he met the coachman, who was about to turn the carriage horses out into the pasture; the travelers had just returned.

As he came into the entrance hall he heard Eric pacing

up and down the garden-room. He did not go in to him; he stood still for a moment, and then softly climbed the stairs and so to his own room. Here he sat in the armchair by the window. He made himself believe that he was listening to the nightingale's throbbing music in the garden hedges below, but what he heard was the throbbing of his own heart. Downstairs in the house every one went to bed, the night-hours passed, but he paid no heed.

For hours he sat thus, till at last he rose and leaned out of the open window. The dew was dripping among the leaves, the nightingale had ceased to trill. By degrees the deep blue of the darksome sky was chased away by a faint yellow gleam that came from the east; a fresh wind rose and brushed Reinhard's heated brow; the early lark soared triumphant up into the sky.

Reinhard suddenly turned and stepped up to the table. He groped about for a pencil and when he had found one he sat down and wrote a few lines on a sheet of white paper. Having finished his writing he took up hat and stick, and leaving the paper behind him, carefully opened the door and descended to the vestibule.

The morning twilight yet brooded in every corner; the big house-cat stretched its limbs on the straw mat and arched its back against Reinhard's hand, which he unthinkingly held out to it. Outside in the garden the sparrows were already chirping their patter from among the branches, and giving notice to all that the night was now past.

Then within the house he heard a door open on the upper floor; some one came downstairs, and on looking up he saw Elisabeth standing before him. She laid her hand upon his arm, her lips moved, but not a word did he hear.

Presently she said: "You will never come back. I know it; do not deny it; you will never come back."

"No, never," he said.

She let her hand fall from his arm and said no more.

He crossed the hall to the door, then turned once more. She was standing motionless on the same spot and looking at him with lifeless eyes. He advanced one step and opened his arms toward her; then, with a violent effort, he turned away and so passed out of the door.

Outside the world lay bathed in morning light, the drops of pearly dew caught on the spiders' webs glistened in the first rays of the rising sun. He never looked back; he walked rapidly onward; behind him the peaceful farmstead gradually disappeared from view as out in front of him rose the great wide world.

THE OLD MAN

The moon had ceased to shine in through the windowpanes, and it had grown quite dark; but the old man still sat in his armchair with folded hands and gazed before him into the emptiness of the room.

Gradually the murky darkness around him dissolved away before his eyes and changed into a broad dark lake; one black wave after another went rolling on farther and farther, and on the last one, so far away as to be almost beyond the reach of the old man's vision, floated lonely among its broad leaves a white water-lily.

The door opened, and a bright glare of light filled the room.

"I am glad that you have come, Bridget," said the old man. "Set the lamp upon the table."

Then he drew his chair up to the table, took one of the open books and buried himself in studies to which he had once applied all the strength of his youth.

THE NAUGHTY SAINT VITALIS *

By Gottfried Keller

AT the beginning of the eighth century there lived in Alexandria of Egypt an extraordinary monk, by name Vitalis, who had made it his particular task to reclaim the souls of lost women from the ways of sin and lead them back to virtue. But the method which he pursued was so peculiar, and the fondness, nay enthusiasm with which he unceasingly prosecuted his ends, was alloyed with such remarkable self-abasement and simulation, that the like was scarcely ever known in the world.

He kept an exact roll of all those wantons on a neat slip of parchment, and, whenever he discovered a new quarry in the city or its environs, he immediately noted her name and dwelling on it; so that the frivolous young patricians of Alexandria could have found no better guide than the industrious Vitalis, had he been disposed to harbor less saintly aims. As it was, the monk wormed out much news and information for his business from his sly conversations with them; but he never suffered the scamps to pick up any information of the sort from him.

He carried this directory in his cowl, rolled up in a silver case, and drew it out repeatedly to add a newly-discovered light name, or to run over those already inscribed, count them, and reckon which of the occupants should have her turn next.

Then he would seek her hurriedly and half ashamed, and say hastily, "Keep the night after to-morrow for me, and promise no one else!" When he entered the house at the

* Translated by Martin Wyness.

appointed time, he would leave the fair one standing, and betake him to the farthest corner of the room, fall on his knees, and pray fervently and at the pitch of his voice all night long for the occupant of the house. In the early morning he would leave her, and charge her strictly not to tell any one what had passed between them.

So he went on for a good while, and got himself into very ill odor indeed. For while in secret, behind the closed doors of the wantons, he alarmed and touched many a lost woman by his fiery words of thunder and the fervent sweetness of his murmured prayers, so that she came to herself and began to lead a holy life; in the public eye, on the contrary, he appeared to have laid himself out of set purpose to merit the reputation of a vicious and sinful monk, who wallowed gleefully in all the debaucheries of the world, and flaunted his religious habit as a banner of shame.

If he found himself of an evening at dusk in respectable company, he would exclaim abruptly, "Oh, what am I about? I had almost forgotten that the brunette Doris is waiting for me, the little dear! The deuce! I must be off, or she will be vexed!"

If any one reproached him, he would cry out as if incensed, "Do you think that I am a stone? Do you imagine that God did not create a little woman for a monk?" If any one said, "Father, you would be better to lay aside your frock and marry, so as not to offend others," he would answer, "Let them be offended if they choose, and run their heads against a wall! Who is my judge?"

All this he used to say with great vehemence and all the address of an actor, like one who defends a bad cause with a multitude of bold words.

And he would go off and quarrel with the other suitors before the girls' doors. He would even come to blows with them, and administered many a rude buffet when they said, "Away with the monk! Does the cleric mean to dispute the ground with us? Get out, bald-pate!"

But he was so obstinate and persistent that in most cases

he got the better of them, and slipped into the house before they knew where they were.

When he returned to his cell in the gray of the morning, he would cast himself down before the Mother of God, to whose sole honor and praise he undertook those adventures and drew down on himself the world's blame; and, did he succeed in bringing back some lost lamb and placing her in some holy convent, he felt more blissful in the presence of Heaven's Queen than if he had converted a thousand heathen. For this was his very remarkable taste, to endure the martyrdom of appearing in the eye of the world as an unclean profligate, while all the time Our Undefiled Lady in Heaven was well aware that he had never touched a woman, and that he wore an invisible crown of white roses on his much-maligned head.

Once he heard of a peculiarly dangerous person, who by her beauty and unusual charms had occasioned much trouble, and even bloodshed, inasmuch as a ferocious military dandy laid siege to her door, and struck down all who attempted to dispute her possession with him. Vitalis immediately proposed the attack and conquest of this hell. He did not wait to write the fair sinner's name in his list, but went straight off to the notorious house, and at the door, sure enough, encountered the soldier, who was stalking along, clad in scarlet, and with a javelin in his hand.

"Dodge aside, monkling!" he shouted contemptuously to the pious Vitalis. "How dare you come sneaking about my lion's den? Heaven is your place; the world is ours!"

"Heaven and earth and all that therein is," said Vitalis, "belong to the Lord, and to his merry servants! Pack, you gaudy lout, and let me go where I choose."

The warrior wrathfully raised the shaft of his javelin to bring it down on the monk's pate; but he suddenly pulled out a peaceful olive-branch from beneath his frock, parried the blow, and smote the bully so roughly on the crown that he well-nigh lost his senses, after which the fighting cleric gave him several raps on the muzzle, until the soldier, completely dumbfounded, made off cursing.

Thereupon Vitalis forced his way triumphantly into the house, where, at the head of a narrow staircase, the woman stood with a light in her hand, listening to the noise and shouting. She was an uncommonly fine figure of a woman, with beautiful, strong but rather defiant, features, about which her reddish hair floated in abundant loose waves, like a lion's mane.

She looked down contemptuously on Vitalis as he ascended, and said, "Where are you going?" "To you, my dove!" he answered. "Have you never heard of the tender monk Vitalis, the jolly Vitalis?" But she answered harshly, as she blocked the staircase with her powerful figure, "Have you money, monk?" Disconcerted, he said, "Monks do not carry money about with them." "Then trot off," she said, "or I'll have you beaten out of the house with firebrands!"

Vitalis scratched his head, completely nonplussed, for he had never reckoned on this happening. The creatures whom he had hitherto converted had naturally thought no more of the price of iniquity, and those whom he failed to convert contented themselves with hard words in compensation for the precious time which he had made them lose. But here he could get no footing inside to begin his pious work; and yet there was something hugely attractive in the prospect of breaking in this red-haired daughter of Satan; for large and beautiful figures of men and women always mislead the judgment, so that we attribute greater qualities to them than they really possess. In desperation he searched through his frock, and came upon the silver case, which was adorned with an amethyst of some value. "I have nothing but this," he said; "let me in for it!" She took the case, examined it carefully, then bade him come with her. Arrived at her bedchamber, he did not favor her with another glance; but knelt down in a corner after his custom, and began to pray aloud.

The harlot, who believed that from force of habit the holy

man meant to begin his worldly performance with prayer,
broke into uncontrollable laughter, and sat down on her
couch to look at him, for his behavior amused her mon-
strously. But as the business never came to an end, and was
beginning to weary her, she bared her shoulders immodestly,
went up to him, clasped him in her strong, white arms, and
pressed the good Vitalis with his shorn and tonsured head
so roughly against her breast that he was like to choke, and
began to gasp as if the flames of purgatory had taken hold
of him. But it did not last long; he began to kick out in all
directions like a young horse in a smithy, until he freed
himself from the hellish embrace. Then he took the long
cord which he wore about his waist, and caught hold of the
woman, to bind her hands behind her back, and have peace
from her. He had to wrestle hard with her before he succeeded in tying her up. He bound her feet together as well,
and threw the whole bundle with a mighty heave upon the
bed; after which he betook himself to his corner again, and
continued his prayers as if nothing had happened.

The captive lioness at first turned about angrily and restlessly, endeavoring to release herself, and uttered a hundred
curses. Then she became quieter as the monk never ceased
to pray, to preach, to adjure her, and towards morning she
uttered manifest sighs, which, as it seemed, were soon followed by contrite sobbing. In short, when the sun rose, she
was lying like a Magdalene at his feet, released from her
bonds, and bedewing the hem of his garment with tears.
With dignity, yet with gladness, Vitalis stroked her head,
and promised to pay her another visit as soon as it was
dark, to inform her in what convent he had found a penitent's cell for her. Then he left, not forgetting first to
impress upon her that she was to say nothing in the meantime about her conversion, but only tell any one who might
inquire, that he had been very merry with her.

But judge of his surprise, when he reappeared at the appointed time, and found the door shut fast, and the female
freshly bedizened in all her glory looking out of the window.

"What do you want, priest?" she cried down. And in astonishment he answered in an undertone, "What does this mean, my lamb? Put away those sinful baubles, and let me in to prepare you for your penance." "You want me, you naughty monk?" she said with a smile, as if she had misunderstood him. "Have you money, or money's worth, about you?" Vitalis stared up open-mouthed, then shook the door desperately; but it remained shut as fast as ever, and the woman too disappeared from the window.

At last the laughter and imprecations of the passers-by drove the apparently depraved and shameless monk away from the door of the house of ill fame. But his thought and endeavor ran entirely upon making his way into the house again, and finding some means or other to overcome the devil by which the woman was possessed.

Absorbed in such thoughts, he turned his steps to a church, where, instead of praying, he thought over ways and means by which he might contrive to gain access to the lost woman. While thus engaged, his eye fell upon the box in which the charitable offerings were kept, and scarcely was the church deserted (it had become dark), when he burst the box violently open with his fist, poured the contents, which consisted of a lot of small silver coins, into his tucked-up frock, and hastened faster than any lover to the sinful woman's abode.

A foppish admirer was about to slip in at the opening door. Vitalis seized him from behind by his perfumed locks, flung him into the street, slammed the door in his face as he sprang in himself, and in another instant found himself once again in the presence of the disreputable person, who glared at him with flaming eyes when he appeared instead of her expected admirer. But Vitalis promptly poured the stolen money out on the table, saying, "Is that enough for to-night?" Without a word, but carefully, she counted the sum, said, "It is enough!" and put it away.

Now they confronted each other in the strangest fashion. Biting her lips to restrain a laugh, she looked at him with a simulated air of utter ignorance; while the monk scrutinized her with undecided and anxious glances, not knowing how he should begin to bring her to book. But when she suddenly proceeded to alluring gestures, and made to stroke his dark, glossy beard, the storm of his saintly character broke out in all its fury, he struck her hand indignantly away, and flung her upon the couch so that it shook. Then kneeling upon her, and grasping her hands, unaffected by her charms, he began to speak home to her in such fashion that at last her obduracy seemed to soften.

She desisted from her violent struggles to free herself. Copious tears flowed over her strong and lovely features, and, when at length the zealous man of God released her, and stood erect beside her sinful couch, the great form lay upon it with weary, relaxed limbs, as if broken by repentance and remorse, sobbing and turning her tear-dimmed eyes upon him, as if in astonishment at her unwilling transformation.

Then the tempest of his eloquent wrath changed likewise to tender emotion and deep sympathy. In his heart he gave praise to his Heavenly protectress, in whose honor this hardest of all his victories had been gained; and now his words of forgiveness and consolation flowed like the mild breath of spring over the broken ice of her heart.

More delighted than if he had enjoyed the sweetest favors of love, he hastened thence, not to snatch a brief slumber on his hard bed, but to throw himself down before the Virgin's altar, and pray for the poor repentant soul until the day had fully dawned. Then he vowed not to close an eye until the strayed lamb was finally safe within the shelter of the convent-walls.

The morning was scarcely astir when he was again on the way to her house. But he saw approaching at the same moment from the other end of the street the fierce warrior, who, after a riotous night, had taken it into his half-drunken head to wind up with a fresh conquest of the harlot.

Vitalis was the nearer to the unhallowed door, and he

sprang nimbly forward to reach it. Thereupon the other
hurled his spear at him, which buried itself just beside the
monk's head in the door so that its shaft quivered. But, before it had ceased quivering, the monk wrenched it out of
the wood with all his force, faced the infuriated soldier as
he sprang towards him brandishing a naked sword, and
quick as lightning drove the spear through his breast. The
man sank in a heap, dead, and Vitalis was almost instantly
seized and bound by a troop of soldiers, who were returning
from the night-watch and had seen his deed, and he was
led away to jail.

In genuine anguish he looked back to the house, where
he could no longer accomplish his good work. The watch
thought that he was simply deploring his evil star which had
balked him of his wicked purpose, and treated the apparently incorrigible monk to blows and hard words until he
was safely in ward.

He had to lie there for many days, and was several times
brought before the judge. True, he was at length discharged
without punishment, seeing that he had killed the man in
self-defense. But nevertheless he came out of the affair with
the reputation of a homicide, and every one cried out that
now, surely, they must unfrock him. But Bishop Joannes,
who was then chief at Alexandria, must have had some
inkling of the real state of affairs, or else have cherished
some deeper design; for he declined to expel the disreputable
monk from the clergy, and ordered that for the present he
was to be allowed to continue his extraordinary career.

He lost no time in returning to the converted sinner, who
in the interval had gone back to her old ways, and would
not admit the horrified and distressed Vitalis until he had
appropriated another object of value and brought it to her.
She repented and converted a third, and likewise a fourth
and fifth time, for she found these conversions more lucra-
tive than anything else, and moreover the evil spirit in her
found an infernal satisfaction in mocking the poor monk
with an endless variety of devices and inventions.

As for him, he now became a veritable martyr inwardly and outwardly; for, the more cruelly he was deceived, the more he felt compelled to exert himself, and it seemed to him as if his own eternal welfare depended on the reformation of this one person. He was already a homicide, a violator of churches, a thief; but he would rather have cut off his hand than part with the least portion of his reputation as a profligate; and, though all this became harder and harder for his heart to bear, he strove all the more eagerly to maintain his wicked exterior in the world's eye by means of frivolous speech. For this was the special form of martyrdom which he had elected. All the same, he became pale and thin, and began to flit about like a shadow on the wall, though always with a laughing face.

Now over against that house of torment dwelt a rich Greek merchant who had an only daughter called Iole, who could do what she liked, and consequently never knew what to do with herself all the livelong day. For her father, who was retired from business, studied Plato, and when tired of him he would compose neat epigrams on the ancient engraved gems of which he had a large collection; but Iole, when she had laid aside her music, could think of no outlet for her lively fancies, and would peep out restlessly at the sky and at the distance, from every peep-hole she found.

So it came about that she discovered the monk's coming and going in the street, and ascertained how matters stood with the notorious cleric. Startled and shy, she peeped at him from her safe concealment, and could not help commiserating his handsome form and manly appearance. When she learned from one of her maids, who was intimate with a maid of the wicked strumpet, how Vitalis was being deceived by her, and what was the real truth about him, she was amazed beyond measure, and, far from respecting his martyrdom, was overcome by a strange indignation, and considered this sort of holiness little conducive to the honor of her sex. She dreamed and puzzled over it a while, and became always the more displeased, while, at the same time, her partiality for the monk increased and conflicted with her wrath.

All of a sudden she resolved that if the Virgin Mary had not sense enough to lead the erring monk back to more respectable ways, she would undertake the task herself, and lend the Virgin a hand in the business, little dreaming that she was the unwitting instrument of the Queen of Heaven, who had now begun to intervene. Forthwith she went to her father, and complained bitterly to him of the unseemly proximity of the lady of pleasure, and adjured him to employ his wealth in getting her out of the way immediately, at any price.

In obedience to her directions, the old gentleman addressed himself to the person, and offered her a certain sum for her house, on condition that she handed it over at once, and left the neighborhood entirely. She desired nothing better; and that same forenoon she had disappeared from the quarter, while the old merchant was sitting once more over his Plato and had dismissed the whole affair from his mind.

Not so Iole, who was in the utmost eagerness to rid the house from top to bottom of every trace of its former occupant. When it was all swept and garnished, she had it fumigated with rare spices so that the fragrant clouds poured out from all the windows.

Then she furnished the empty room with nothing but a carpet, a rose-bush, and a lamp, and, as soon as her father, who went to bed with the sun, was asleep, she went across, with a wreath of roses adorning her hair, and took her seat alone on the outspread carpet, while two trusty old servants kept watch at the door.

They turned away several night-revelers, but, whenever they saw Vitalis approach, they hid themselves and allowed him to pass in unhindered by the open door. With many sighs, he climbed the stair, full of fear lest he should see himself made a fool of once again, full of hope that he might be freed at last from this burden by the genuine repentance of a creature who was hindering him from rescuing so many other souls. But judge of his astonishment, when he entered the room, and found it stripped of all the wild red lioness's trumpery, and instead of her a sweet and tender form sitting on the carpet with the rose-bush opposite her on the floor.

"Where is the wretched creature who used to live here?" he exclaimed, looking about him in wonder, and finally letting his eyes rest on the lovely apparition which he saw before him.

"She has gone out into the Desert," answered Iole, without looking up. "There she means to live as an anchorite and do penance. It came upon her suddenly this morning, and broke her like a straw, and her conscience is awakened at last. She cried out for a certain priest Vitalis, who could have helped her. But the spirit which had entered into her would not suffer her to wait. The fool gathered all her possessions together, sold them, and gave the money to the poor, then went off hot-foot with a hair-cloth shift, and shorn hair, and a staff in her hand, the way of the Desert."

"Glory to thee, O Lord, and praise to thy Gracious Mother!" cried Vitalis, his hands folded in glad devotion, while a burden as of stone fell from his heart. But at the same time he looked more narrowly at the maiden with her rose-wreath, and said, "Why do you call her a fool? and who are you? and where do you come from? and what are you about?"

At that the lovely Iole cast her dark eyes to the ground lower than ever. She hung her head, and a bright flush of modesty spread over her face, for she thought shame of herself for the sad things she was going to say before a man.

"I am an outcast orphan, who have neither father nor mother. This lamp and carpet and rose-bush are the last remnants of my inheritance, and I have settled in this house with them to take up the life which my predecessor here has abandoned."

"Ah, so you would——!" the monk exclaimed, and clapped his hands. "Just see how busy the Devil is! And this innocent creature says the thing as indifferently as if I were not Vitalis! Now, my kitten, how do you mean to do? Just tell me!"

"I mean to devote myself to love and serve the men as long as this rose lives!" she said, pointing hastily at the flower-pot. Still, she could hardly get the words out, and almost sank on the floor for shame, so deeply did she droop her head. This natural modesty served the little rogue well; for it convinced the monk that he had to do this time with a childish innocent, who was possessed by the Devil and was on the point of jumping plump into the abyss. He caressed his beard in satisfaction at having arrived on the scene so opportunely for once, and, to enjoy his satisfaction still longer, he said slowly and jestingly, "Then afterwards, my dove?"

"Afterwards I will go, a poor lost soul, to Hell where beauteous Dame Venus is; or perhaps, if I meet a good preacher, I may even enter a convent later on, and do penance!"

"Better and better!" he cried. "That is an orderly plan of campaign, indeed, and not badly thought out. For, so far as the preacher is concerned, he is here now, he is standing before you, you black-eyed Devil's tit-bit! And the convent is all ready rigged up for you, like a mousetrap, only you'll go into it without having sinned, do you see? Without having sinned in anything but the pretty intention, which after all may make a very toothsome bone of repentance for you to gnaw all your days, and may serve your turn. For without it, you little witch, you would be too comical and light-hearted for a real penitent! But now!" he continued seriously, "first off with the roses, and then listen attentively!"

"No!" answered Iole, somewhat more pertly. "I will listen first, and then see whether I'll take off the roses. Now that I have once overcome my womanly feelings, mere words will not suffice to restrain me until I know the sin. And, without sin, I can know nothing about repentance. I give you this to think over before you begin your efforts. But still I am willing to hear you."

Then Vitalis began the finest exhortation he had ever delivered. The maiden listened good-naturedly and attentively, and the sight of her had, unknown to him, a considerable influence on his choice of language; for the beauty and daintiness of the prospective convert were themselves enough to evoke a lofty eloquence. But, as she was not the least bit in earnest about the project which she had so outrageously advertised, the monk's oration could not have any very serious effect upon her. On the contrary, a charming laugh flitted about her mouth, and, when he had concluded, and expectantly wiped the sweat from his brow, Iole said, "I am only half moved by your words, and cannot decide to give up my project; for I am only too curious to know what it is like to live in sin and pleasure!"

Vitalis stood as if petrified, and could not get so much as one word out. It was the first time that his powers of conversion had failed so roundly. Sighing and thoughtful, he paced up and down the room, and took another look at the little candidate for Hell. The power of the Devil seemed to have combined in some bewildering fashion with the power of innocence to thwart him. But he was all the more passionately anxious to overcome them.

"I do not leave this place until you repent," he cried at length, "not though I should spend three days and three nights here!"

"That would only make me more obstinate," responded Iole. "But I will take time to think, and will hear you again to-morrow night. The day will soon be dawning now. Go your way. Meantime I promise to do nothing in the matter, and to remain in my present condition; in return for which you must promise on no account to mention me to anybody, and to come here only under cover of darkness."

"So be it!" exclaimed Vitalis, and took his departure, while Iole slipped quickly back into her father's house.

She did not sleep long, and awaited the coming evening

with impatience. For the monk, now that he had been so close to her throughout the night, pleased her better than he had done at a distance. She saw now what a fire of enthusiasm glowed in his eyes, and how resolute all his movements were, despite his monkish garments. And when she represented to herself his self-abnegation, his perseverance in the course he had once chosen, she could not help wishing that those good qualities were utilized to her own pleasure and profit, in the shape of a cherished and faithful husband. Her project, accordingly, was to make a brave martyr into a still better husband.

The next night she found Vitalis at her carpet in good time, and he continued his exertions on behalf of her virtue with undiminished zeal. He had to stand all the time, except when he knelt to pray. Iole, on the contrary, made herself comfortable. She laid herself back on the carpet, clasped her hands behind her head, and kept her half-closed eyes steadily fixed upon the monk as he stood and preached. Sometimes she closed them as if overcome by drowsiness, and, as soon as Vitalis saw this, he pushed her with his foot to waken her. But this harsh measure always turned out milder than he intended; for, as soon as his foot neared the maiden's slender side, it spontaneously moderated its force, and touched her tender ribs quite gently; not to mention that a most unusual sensation ran along the whole length of the monk, a sensation which he had never before experienced in the slightest degree from any of the numerous fair sinners with whom he had had to deal.

As morning approached, Iole nodded more and more frequently, till at last Vitalis exclaimed indignantly, "Child, you are not listening! I can't keep you awake. You are utterly sunk in sloth!"

"Not so!" she said, as she suddenly opened her eyes, and a sweet smile flitted across her face, as if the approaching day were already reflected in it. "I have been paying attention; I am beginning to hate that wretched sin, which is all the more repulsive to me that it causes you vexation, dear monk; for nothing could be pleasing to me that is displeasing to you."

"Really?" he queried, full of joy. "So I have really succeeded? Come away to the convent at once, that we may make sure of you. This time we'll strike while the iron's hot."

"You do not understand me aright," Iole answered, and, blushing, cast her eyes again to the ground. "I am enamored of you, and have conceived a tender inclination towards you!"

For a moment, Vitalis felt as if a hand had smitten his heart; yet he did not feel that it caused him pain. Paralyzed, he opened wide his mouth and eyes, and stood stock-still.

But Iole, blushing redder than ever, went on to say gently and softly, "You must now lecture me and charm away this new mischief from me, in order to deliver me entirely from the malady, and I hope you may succeed!"

Vitalis, without saying a word, turned tail and ran out of the house. Instead of seeking his bed, he rushed out into the silvery gray morning, and debated whether he should leave this dangerous young woman to her fate and have done with her, or should endeavor to cast out this latest whim also, which appeared to be the most reprehensible of all her notions, and not altogether without danger to himself. But a wrathful flush of shame flew to his head at the thought that anything of the sort could be perilous for him. Then again it occurred to him that the Devil might have set a snare for him, in which case it were best to avoid it betimes. But to become a deserter in the face of such a wisp of a temptress! And supposing the poor creature were in earnest, and could be cured of her latest unseemly delusion by a few rough words? In short, Vitalis could not settle within himself, all the more that at the bottom of his heart a dim wave was beginning to cause the skiff of his reason to be unsteady.

In his perplexity he slipped into a little chapel where a beautiful ancient marble statue of the goddess Juno had recently been set up with a golden nimbus as an image of the Virgin Mary, so as not to waste such a gift of divine art. He cast himself down before this Mary, and laid his doubts fervently before her, and prayed his patroness for a token. If she nodded, he would complete Iole's conversion; if she shook her head, he would desist.

But the image left him in the most cruel uncertainty, and did neither one thing nor the other; it neither nodded nor shook its head. Only when the red gleam of some flying morning clouds passed over the marble, its face seemed to smile most propitiously; whether it was that the ancient goddess, as guardian deity of connubial love and chastity, was giving a sign, so that the new one could not refrain from smiling at her adorer's troubles; for both were women at heart, and such are always tickled when a love-affair is in train. But Vitalis knew nothing of all this. On the contrary, the beauty of the expression raised his courage amazingly, and, still more remarkable to relate, the statue appeared to assume the features of the blushing Iole, who was challenging him to expel her love of him from her mind.

Meantime, at the same hour, Iole's father was strolling beneath the cypresses of his garden. He had acquired some very fine new gems, the engraving on which had brought him out of bed at that early hour. He was handling them rapturously, and making them play in the beams of the rising sun. There was a dark amethyst, on which Luna drove her car through the heavens, unwitting that Love was squatted behind her, while flying Cupids called to her the Greek for "Whip behind!" A handsome onyx showed Minerva lost in meditation, holding Love on her knee, who was busy polishing her breast-plate with his hand to see his own reflection.

And lastly, on a cornelian, Love, in the form of a salamander, was tumbling about in a vestal fire and throwing its guardian virgins into perplexity and alarm.

These scenes tempted the old man to compose some distichs, and he was considering which he should attack first when his daughter Iole came through the garden, pale and unslept. Anxious and surprised, he called her to him and inquired what had robbed her of her slumbers. But, before she could answer, he began to show her his gems and explain them to her.

At that she heaved a deep sigh and said, "Ah, if all those great powers, Chastity herself, Wisdom, and Religion, could not defend themselves against Love, how is a poor insignificant creature like me to fortify herself against him?"

The old gentleman was not a little astonished at these words. "What do I hear?" he said. "Is it that the dart of mighty Eros has smitten thee?"

"It has pierced me to the heart," she responded, "and, if I am not in possession of the man whom I love within a day and a night, I shall be the bride of Death!"

Although her father was accustomed to let her have her own way in everything she desired, this haste was rather too violent for him, and he recommended repose and reflection to his daughter. But she had no lack of the latter, and she employed it so well that the old man exclaimed, "So I must discharge the most unpleasant of all a father's duties, I must go to your choice, to your man, and lead him by the nose up to the best that I can call mine, and beg him to be so kind as to take possession? Here is a tidy little woman, my dear sir! I pray you, don't despise her! I had much rather give you a box or two on the ear, but my little daughter will die, so I must be civil! So be graciously pleased, for Heaven's sake, to taste the pasty which is offered you. It has been well baked, and will fairly melt in your mouth!"

"All that is spared us," said Iole, "for, if you will only allow me, I hope to bring him to it that he will come himself and ask for my hand."

"And what if this man, whom I know nothing of, turns out to be a wastrel and a good-for-nothing?"

"Then let him be driven away with scorn! But he is a saint!"

"Then run away, and leave me to the Muses," said the good old man.

When evening came, the night did not follow the dusk so promptly as Vitalis appeared at Iole's heels in the familiar house. But he had never entered the house in the same fashion as now. His heart beat, and he was forced to feel what it meant to see again a person who had played such a trump. It was another Vitalis than the one who had descended in the early morning, who now came up the steps, although he himself was the most unconscious of the fact; for the poor converter of frail women and monk of evil renown had never learned the difference between the smile of a harlot and that of an honorable woman.

Yet he came with the best of intentions, and with the old purpose of driving all the idle notions out of the little monster's head for good and all. Only he had a vague idea that once his task was accomplished he might be permitted a pause in his martyr activity; all at once he began to be very tired of it.

But it was determined that some new surprise should always await him in that enchanted dwelling. When he entered the room, he found it beautifully decorated, and furnished with all usual furniture. A delicate, insidious odor of flowers pervaded the room, and was in keeping with a certain modest worldliness. On a snow-white couch, not a fold out of place in its silk coverings, sat Iole, splendidly arrayed, in sweet troubled melancholy, like an angel in meditation. Under the trim pleats of her robe her bosom heaved like the foam on a milking pail, and, though the white arms, which she folded beneath her breast, shone so fair, yet all those charms looked so lawful and permissible in the order of things that Vitalis's accustomed eloquence stuck in his throat.

"You are amazed, my pretty monk," began Iole, "to find all this show and finery here! Know that this is the farewell which I mean to take of the world, and, at the same time, I will lay aside the inclination which, unfortunately, I cannot help feeling for you. But you must help me to this end to the best of your ability, and after the fashion that I have devised and request of you. I mean that when you address me in these garments and as a cleric it is always the same. The bearing of a churchman fails to convince me, for I belong to the world. I cannot be cured of love by a monk, who is unacquainted with love, and does not know what he is talking about. If you really mean to afford me rest and put me on the way to Heaven, go into that closet, where you will find secular clothes laid out ready for you. Exchange your monk's clothes there for them, array yourself like a man of the world, then seat yourself beside me to partake of a little repast with me, and in such worldly externals exert all your acuteness and understanding to wean me from you and incline me to piety."

Vitalis made no reply, but bethought himself a while. Then he decided to end all his difficulties at one stroke, and to put the devil of this world to flight with his own weapons by acceding to Iole's eccentric proposal.

So he actually betook himself into an adjoining closet, where a couple of servants awaited him with splendid garments of purple and fine linen. Scarcely had he put them on, when he looked a good head taller, and it was with a noble mien that he strode back to Iole, who could not take her eyes off him, and clapped her hands for joy.

Now, however, a real miracle and a strange transformation was wrought on the monk. For scarcely had he sat down in his worldly array beside the charming woman, when the immediate past was blown away like a dream from his mind, and he forgot all about his purpose. Instead of speaking so much as a word, he listened eagerly to what was said by Iole, who had taken possession of his hand and begun to tell him her true story, who she was, where she lived, and how it was her most heart-felt desire that he should give over his strange manner of life, and ask her father for her

hand, so that he might become a good husband, well-pleasing
to God. She also said many wonderful things in the most
beautiful words about the history of a happy and chaste
love, but concluded with a sigh that she saw well how hopeless her desire was, and that he was now at liberty to argue
her out of all those ideas, but not before he had fortified
himself duly for his task with meat and drink.

Then at her signal the servants set drinking-vessels on
the table together with a basket of cakes and fruits. Iole
mixed a goblet of wine for the silent Vitalis, and affectionately handed him something to eat, so that he felt quite
at home, and was reminded of his childhood, when as a little
boy he was tenderly fed by his mother. He ate and drank,
and, when he had done so, it seemed to him as if he might
now venture to rest from his long, weary toil, and lo! our
Vitalis leant his head to one side, towards Iole, and without
more ado fell asleep, and lay till sunrise.

When he awoke, he was alone, and no one was to be seen
or heard. He sprang up hastily, and was horrified at the
splendid garment in which he was dressed. He rushed madly
through the house from top to bottom, seeking for his
monk's frock. But not the smallest trace of it could he find,
until he chanced to see a little heap of cinders and ashes,
on which a sleeve of his priest's dress was lying half consumed, whereupon he rightly concluded that there it had
been solemnly burned.

Next he put his head out cautiously, first at one, then at
another of the windows which looked on to the street, drawing it in every time that any one approached. At last he
flung himself down upon the silken couch as comfortable
and at ease as if he had never lain on a monk's hard bed.
Then he roused himself, put his dress straight, and stole in
high excitement to the street-door. There he still hesitated
a moment; but suddenly he flung it wide open, and went
out into the world a magnificent and imposing figure. No
one recognized him; every one took him for some fine gen-

tleman from abroad, who was enjoying a few gay days at Alexandria.

He looked neither to right nor left, else he would have seen Iole on her house-top. So he went straight back to his convent, where, however, all the monks and their superior had just resolved to expel him from their fellowship; for the measure of his iniquities was now full, and he contributed only to the scandal and disgrace of the Church. The sight of him, actually coming among them in his worldly gallant's attire, knocked the bottom out of the tub of their patience; they drenched him and doused him with water from all sides, and drove him with crosses, besoms, pitchforks and kitchen-ladles out of the convent.

Once on a time this rough handling would have been the height of felicity to him, and a triumph of his martyrdom True, he laughed inwardly even now, but for a somewhat different reason. He took one more stroll round about the city-walls, and let his red cloak wave in the wind. A fine breeze from the Holy Land blew across the sparkling sea; but Vitalis was becoming more and more worldly-minded. Suddenly he retraced his steps into the bustling streets of the city, sought the house where Iole dwelt, and did what she wished.

He now made as excellent and complete a layman and husband as he had been a martyr. The Church, however, when she understood the real facts of the case, was inconsolable over the loss of such a saint, and made every endeavor to recall the fugitive to her bosom. But Iole held him fast and gave it to be understood that he was in very good hands with her.

THE NEW YEAR'S EVE CONFESSION

By Hermann Sudermann

Ah, dear lady, it's good to be here, with you again, sitting so peacefully in this comfortable chair, ready for a cozy chat. Thank goodness, the holiday hubbub is over and done with, and you have a little leisure for me again.

Oh, the Christmas season! I do believe it was invented by the devil especially for the annoyance of us bachelors, to impress upon us the dreariness of our homeless lives. The thing that is a source of delight to others is a torture to us. Of course, of course, we're not all of us lonely. The joy of bestowing joy blooms for most of us, too. But the pure pleasure of sharing pleasure with others is embittered partly by a dose of ironical self-criticism, partly by that acid yearning which I might call, instead of homesickness, marriage-sickness.

Why did I not come and pour my heart out to you? you ask, you sympathetic soul, who bestow consolation as generously as most of your sex bestow petty spite. Ah, but you see, the matter is not so simple. Don't you know what Speidel says in his charmingly chatty *Lonely Sparrows,* which you, correctly divining the state of my soul, sent me on the third day of the holiday? He says, "The genuine bachelor does not *want* to be consoled. Once having become unhappy, he wants to indulge his unhappiness."

Besides Speidel's lonely sparrow, there is also a species of confirmed old bachelors, family friends. I do not mean those professional destroyers of the family who insinuate themselves hypocritically with evil intent while making themselves comfortable at the hospitable hearth. I mean the good old uncle, papa's whilom schoolmate, who dandles baby on his knees while respectably reading aloud to mamma the story in the evening paper—with omission of the indecent passages.

I know of men whose whole life goes in the service of a family with which they have become friendly, men who pass their days without desire beside a lovely woman whom they secretly adore.

You are skeptical? Oh, it is the "without desire" that you object to? You may be right. In the depths of even the tamest heart there probably lurks a wild desire, but a desire —it is understood—that is held in check.

I should like to give you an example and tell you of a conversation that two ancient gentlemen had with each other this very New Year's Eve. You must not ask me how I found out about the conversation, and you must not tell it to any one else. May I begin?

Picture, as the scene, a high-ceilinged room furnished in an old-fashioned style and dimly lighted by a green-shaded, brightly polished, hanging lamp, such as our parents used before the era of kerosene; the light falling upon a round table covered with a white cloth and set with the ingredients for mixing a New Year's punch, and in the center a few drippings of oil spreading slowly.

My two ancient gentlemen sat half in the dimness cast by the green shade. Moldy ruins they were of a time long past, each tremulously sunk in himself, and each staring into space with the dim eyes and the dull look of old age. The one, the host, was a military man, as was clear at first glance from his close-fitting stock, his pointed mustache, shaved off under the points, and his eyebrows knitted in a martial frown. He sat huddled in a rolling chair and clutched the handle of the steering rod with both hands like a crooked walking-stick. Nothing about him stirred except his lower jaw, which went up and down incessantly with a chewing movement. The other, who was sitting beside him on the sofa, was tall and thin, with narrow shoulders and the head of a thinker, angular and broad of brow. He drew skimpy clouds of smoke from a long pipe that was about to go out. Snowy white curls framed his face, and in the thousand fine lines of his smooth, dried-up skin nestled a soft, quiet smile, such as nothing but the peace of renunciation can impress upon an aged countenance.

They sat without talking. In the silence you could hear the slight bubbling of the burning oil mingled with the slight bubbling of the tobacco juice. Then the clock on the wall in the dark background wheezed and struck eleven.

"This is about the time you usually brew the punch," said the man with the thinker's head. His voice sounded soft and quavered a little.

"Yes, this is the time," the other rejoined. His tone was harsh, as if again resounding with the strident shouts of command.

"I should never have thought," the guest continued, "that it would be so sad without her."

The host nodded and chewed on.

"She made the New Year's punch for us forty-four times."

"Yes," the old soldier put in, "ever since I have been living here in Berlin and you have been coming to see us."

"Last year at this time," the guest continued, "we three were still together, so happily. She sat there in the easy chair, knitting socks for Paul's oldest child, and hurrying as fast as she could. They had to be finished by twelve o'clock, she said. And they were. Then we drank the punch and very comfortably discussed death. And two months later she actually was carried out to the cemetery. You know, I wrote a thick volume on the immortality of the idea. You never could bear it. And I cannot bear it any more either, since your wife died. As a matter of fact, I don't give a fig for any ideas any more."

"Yes, she was a good woman," said the husband of the deceased. "She took good care of me. When I had to be out for service by five o'clock in the morning, she was always up ahead of me and saw to it that I had a good cup of coffee before I left. To be sure, she had her faults, too. When once she got to philosophizing with you—whew!"

"You simply never understood her," murmured the guest, something like restrained resentment quivering about the corners of his mouth, though the look he allowed to rest on his friend a long time was mild and sad, as though his soul carried the secret consciousness of guilt.

After a period of silence, he began:

"Listen, Franz, I must tell you something—something that has been gnawing at me a long while. I cannot possibly go down into the grave carrying it along with me."

"Fire away, then," said Franz, picking up the long pipe leaning against his rolling chair and stuffing its bowl with tobacco.

"Once—something happened—between me and—your wife."

"Please don't joke, Doc," said Franz.

"I'm in grim earnest, Franz. I have been carrying it round with me for more than forty years, and now the time has come at last to make a clean breast of it."

"Do you mean to say my wife deceived me?" the old soldier shouted in a rage.

"Shame on you, Franz," said the philosopher, with his sad, mild smile.

Franz mumbled and muttered a little, and then lighted his pipe.

"No, she was pure as an angel," the philosopher went on. "You and I are the criminals. Listen to me. It was forty-three years ago. You had just been ordered to Berlin as a captain, and I was teaching at the University. You know what a wild fellow you were then."

"Hm," said Franz, and raised his shaking hand to twist the points of his mustache.

"There was a beautiful actress with big black eyes and small white teeth. Do you remember?"

"Do I remember! Bianca was her name." A feeble smile flitted across the old man's weather-beaten countenance with the marks on it of hard and fast living. "She could bite, I tell you, she could bite!"

"You deceived your wife, and she suspected it. But she never said anything, and suffered in silence. You did not notice it, but I did. She was the first woman I got to know after my mother's death. She came into my life like a shining star, and I looked up to her as to a shining star. Finally I summoned up the courage to ask her what was troubling her. She smiled and said she was not feeling quite well yet. You remember, it was only a short while before that that Paul had been born. Then came New Year's Eve—exactly forty-three years ago this very night. I came to your house at about eight o'clock, as usual. She sat embroidering, and I read to her while we waited for you. The hours passed, one by one. You did not come. I saw how uneasy she became and how she began to tremble, and I trembled with her. I knew what was keeping you, and I was afraid that you would forget twelve o'clock in that woman's arms. It was getting very near the hour. She stopped embroidering, and I stopped reading, and an awful silence descended on us. I saw a tear creep out slowly between her lashes and fall down on her embroidery. I jumped up and wanted to go out, and bring you home. I felt capable of tearing you by force from that woman's side. But at the same instant your wife jumped up, too, from this very seat I am sitting on.

"Where are you going?" she cried. There was unspeakable dread in her face.

" 'I am going to get Franz,' I said.

"At that she fairly screamed.

" 'For goodness' sake, stay with me. At least *you* stay with me. Don't *you* leave me.'

"And she threw herself on me and laid her hands on my shoulders and hid her wet face on my chest. My whole body quivered. Never before had a woman been so close to me. But I held on to myself and spoke to her comfortingly. She so needed comforting. Soon after, you came back. You did not notice my confusion. Your cheeks were flushed and there was a love-drunken weariness in your eyes.

"That New Year's Eve produced a change in me which filled me with alarm. Since I had felt her soft arms around my neck and had drawn in the perfume of her hair, the star had fallen from heaven, and instead of the star it was the *woman,* the woman, beautiful, and breathing love. I knew there was ardor in my glances; and I denounced myself as a blackguard, a deceiver; and to make at least partial atonement to my conscience, I went to work to separate you from your mistress. Fortunately, I had some money, which I had inherited, and she was satisfied with the sum I offered her, and——"

"By Jingo," the old soldier interjected, "so you're the one to blame for Bianca's writing me that touching good-by letter in which she told me it was with a breaking heart that she had to forego my love?"

"Yes, I am the one to blame for it. But listen. I had expected to purchase peace with the money I gave her. I was mistaken. The wild thoughts kept going round and round in my brain worse and worse. I buried myself in my work. It was just then that I conceived the central thought for my *Immortality of the Idea.* No use. Peace did not come that way.

"And so a whole year went by, and another New Year's Eve arrived. I was sitting beside her on this seat once again. This time you were at home, but you were lying asleep on the sofa in the next room, tired out by a jollification at the club. Sitting there, close beside her, looking at her pale face, the recollection of the New Year's Eve before came back and overwhelmed me irresistibly. Just to feel her head at my neck once again, just to kiss her once again, and then let come what may! Our glances met for an instant. It seemed to me that a secret understanding flashed into her eyes. I could not control myself any longer. I dropped at her feet and hid my burning face in her lap.

"I lay there like that, motionless, for possibly two sec-

onds, when I felt her hand cool on my head and heard her
say softly and gently:

" 'You must be good.'

"Yes, I must be good. I must not deceive the man sleeping in the next room so trustfully. I jumped up and looked
about, disconcerted. She picked up a book from the table and
handed it to me. I knew what she meant, and opened the
book at random and started to read aloud. I do not know
what I read. The letters danced before my eyes. But gradually the storm in my soul subsided, and when it struck
twelve, and you, with a sleepy look in your eyes, came in
to wish us a Happy New Year, I felt as though that instant
of sin lay far, far behind me, in an era long past.

"From that time on I became calmer. I knew she did not
return my love, and I had nothing to hope for from her
but compassion. The years went by. Your children grew up
and married. We three grew old. You gave up sowing wild
oats and lived for only the one woman, like myself. I did
not stop loving her. No, that was impossible. But my love
took on other forms. It discarded earthly desires and turned
into a spiritual communion. You often used to laugh when
you heard us philosophizing. But had you divined how my
soul became one with hers, it would have made you very
jealous. And now she's dead. Perhaps by next New Year's
Eve we shall have followed her. That is why it is high time
for me to unburden myself of my secret and say to you,
'Franz, I once did you a wrong. Forgive me!' "

He held out his hand to his friend pleadingly, but Franz
answered testily:

"Bah, stuff and nonsense! A lot to forgive! This news of
yours, this confession, is stale. I've known it for ages. She
herself told me all about it forty years ago. And now I'll
tell you the reason I ran after women the way I did until I
was an old man—because, when she told me, she also said
that you were the only man she had ever loved."

His guest stared at him in silence. The clock on the wall
wheezed and struck twelve o'clock.

THE FATE OF THE BARON *

By Arthur Schnitzler

It was on a mild evening in May that Kläre Hell made her first reappearance as Queen of the Night. The circumstances that had kept the singer away from the stage for nearly two months were well known. On March 15th the Prince Richard Bedenbruck had been thrown from his horse, and after lingering for a few hours, during which Kläre had not stirred from his side, had died in her arms. Kläre's despair had been so terrible that her friends feared first for her life, then for her reason, and, until lately, for her voice. The last anxiety proved as unfounded as the first two. When she appeared on the stage she was greeted with friendly curiosity, but after the first great aria it was clear that her intimate friends could safely accept the congratulations of her more distant acquaintances. In the gallery the childish face of little Fräulein Fanny Ringeiser could be seen glowing with delight, and the regular opera-goers in the upper tiers smiled knowingly at their little friend. They all knew that Fanny, although she was only the daughter of a shop assistant on the Mariahilferstrasse, belonged to the beloved singer's inner circle, had often been invited to parties at her house and had been secretly in love with the dead Prince. In the interval, Fanny explained to her many male and female friends that Baron von Leisenbohg had suggested to Kläre the idea of choosing the Queen of the Night for her first part—thinking that the dark costume would be most in harmony with her state of mind.

The Baron himself took his usual stall, the corner seat

* Translated by Eric Sutton. Copyright, 1929, by Simon and Schuster, Inc.

on the gangway in the first row, and acknowledged the greetings of his acquaintances with a cordial, but almost melancholy smile. His mind was full of many memories that evening. He had first met Kläre ten years ago. At that time he was making himself responsible for the artistic training of a slim young lady with red hair, and had looked in one evening for a performance at the Eisenstein School of Singing, in which his protégée was making her first public performance as Mignon. On that same evening he saw and heard Kläre who was singing Philine in the same scene. He was then twenty-five years old, independent, and impulsive. He took no further interest in Mignon, made Frau Natalie Eisenstein introduce him to Philine after the performance and told her that his heart, his fortune, and his influence with the management of the Opera were all at her disposal. At that time Kläre was living with her mother, the widow of a higher official in the Post Office, and was in love with a young medical student, with whom she often went to tea in his room out in the Alser district. She rejected the Baron's impetuous proposals, but Leisenbohg's homage inclined her to a more complaisant attitude of mind, and she became the medical student's mistress. She made no secret of this to the Baron, who returned to his red-haired protégée, but pursued his acquaintance with Kläre. On all festivals that gave him any sort of excuse, he sent her presents of flowers and sweets, and from time to time he paid a formal call at the house of the postal official's widow.

In the autumn of that year, Kläre got her first engagement at Detmold. Baron von Leisenbohg, who at that time still had a post under the Government, took advantage of his first Christmas leave to pay Kläre a visit in her new abode. He knew that the medical student had become a doctor and had married in September, and he was tempted to hope once more. But Kläre, with her usual straightforwardness, told the Baron immediately he arrived that she had established tender relations with the tenor at the Court Theatre : thus it befell, therefore, that the only memories Leisenbohg could carry away from Detmold were of a platonic stroll in the little public park, and a supper at the theater restaurant with a few fellow artists of both sexes. In spite of this, he made several more journeys to Detmold, took great pleasure in Kläre's devotion to her art and the unmistakable progress that she made, and, moreover, hoped for better luck next season, for which the tenor was under contract to sing in Hamburg. But that year, too, he was disappointed, as Kläre felt obliged to yield to the solicitations of a Dutch merchant in a large way of business, by the name of Louis Verhajen.

When Kläre, in her third season, was offered an engagement at the Dresden Court Theatre, in spite of his youth the Baron gave up a very promising official career and migrated to Dresden. He spent every evening with Kläre and her mother, who had always known how to maintain the most admirable detachment in all her relations with her daughter, and began to hope again. Unfortunately the Dutchman had the unpleasant habit whenever he wrote of announcing his arrival for the following day, and informing his beloved that she was surrounded by an army of spies, and threatening her with every variety of painful death, if she was not faithful to him. As he never came, and Kläre was gradually getting into an extremely nervous state, Leisenbohg decided to end the business at any cost, and went to Detmold to try to see the man personally. To his amazement, the Dutchman explained that he had sent these passionate and threatening missives purely from a sense of chivalry, and that he would really be exceedingly relieved to be freed from any further responsibility. In high satisfaction Leisenbohg took the train back to Dresden, and informed Kläre of the agreeable outcome of the interview. She thanked him warmly, but avoided the Baron's attempts at tender advances in so decided a manner that he was quite taken aback. After a few brief and searching questions she finally admitted that during his absence no less a person than Prince Kajetan had conceived a violent passion for her and had sworn to do himself an injury if she did not take pity on him. So, of course, she had had at last to give way, to avoid plunging the ruling family and the nation into the most unspeakable grief.

With a heart that showed signs of breaking, Leisenbohg left the city and went back to Vienna. Here he began to pull wires, and it was not a little due to his persistent efforts that Kläre received an offer from the Vienna Opera for the very next year. After a successful tour, she took up her engagement in October, and the Baron's magnificent basket of flowers, that she found on the evening when she first entered her dressing-room, seemed like the expression of an entreaty and a hope. But her generous admirer had once again to endure the experience of having come too late. The fair-haired gentleman who played for her while she had been practicing during the last few weeks—he was pretty well known as a song composer—had acquired rights over her which she was bound in honor to respect. Since then seven years had passed. The accompanist had been succeeded by Herr Klemens von Rhodoewyl, the dashing gentleman-jockey; Herr von Rhodoewyl was followed by Vincenz Klaudi, the conductor, who often sang the music of the operas he was conducting, so loudly that the singers could not be heard; after him came the Count von Alban-Rattony, who had gambled away his Hungarian estates at cards, but had made up for it by winning a castle in Lower Austria; the next was Herr Edgar Wilhelm, who wrote ballet librettos (for which highly paid composers wrote the music), tragedies produced at his own expense at the Jansch theater, and poems printed in elegant type in the stupidest kind of Court journal. Herr Wilhelm was succeeded by a gentleman named Amandus Meier, who had nothing to recommend him but his age, which was nineteen, and his appearance, which was charming, and whose sole possession was a fox-terrier that could stand on its head; after Herr Meier came the best dressed man in the kingdom—Prince Richard Bedenbruck.

Kläre had never made any secret of these affairs. Hers was, and continued to be, a simple bourgeois household in which the master changed from time to time. Her public popularity was extraordinary. In higher circles she was looked on with not a little favor for going to Mass every Sunday, confessing twice a month, wearing on her bosom as an amulet a picture of the Madonna blessed by the Pope, and never going to bed without saying her prayers. There were few bazaars at which she was not in charge of a stall, and ladies of the aristocracy, as well as those of Jewish financial circles, were delighted to be able to offer their wares under the same marquee as Kläre. She bestowed fascinating smiles on youthful enthusiasts of both sexes who waited for her by the stage door. She distributed her bouquets among the patient crowd, and once, when she had left the flowers behind her in her dressing-room, she said in that refreshing Viennese of hers that seemed to suit her looks so well: "Oh, God, I've left the stuff up in my room; come to-morrow afternoon, my dears, if you still want any." Then she jumped into her carriage, put her head out of the window, and cried as she drove off: "You'll get some coffee, too!"

Fanny Ringeiser had been one of the few who had had the nerve to accept this invitation. Kläre fell into a chaffing conversation with her, inquired about her family with all the affability of an archduchess, and found the ingenuous and adoring girl's chatter so much to her liking that she asked her to come again soon. Fanny did so, and it came about that she soon achieved a position of importance in the singer's household; and she managed to keep it, mainly because, though Kläre was very ready with her confidences, Fanny never fully confided in her in return. In the course of years, Fanny had received a succession of proposals, mostly from the young sons of the Mariahilferstrasse shopkeepers with whom she used to go to dances. But she rejected them all, owing to the fact that she fell, with irrevocable regularity, in love with Kläre's admirer for the time being.

Kläre had in fact loved Prince Bedenbruck just as faith-

fully but much more passionately than his predecessors, and
Leisenbohg, who in spite of his innumerable disappointments had never given up hope, had begun to be seriously
afraid that the happiness he had yearned for these ten long
years would never blossom now. Whenever he saw any one
falling out of her favor, he had always discharged his mistress so as to be ready for all contingencies, and at any
moment. And he did so after Prince Richard's sudden
death; but, for the first time, more from habit than conviction. For Kläre's grief seemed so boundless that every one
could not help believing that she had finished for ever with
the delights of love. She drove out to the cemetery every day
and laid flowers on the grave of the departed. She flung
away all her gay clothes and locked up her jewelry in the
innermost drawers of her writing-table. Much serious ex-
postulation was needed to dissuade her from leaving the
stage for ever.

After her first reappearance, which had gone off so brilliantly, her life, outwardly at any rate, resumed its wonted
course. Her original circle of less intimate acquaintances
gathered round once more. The music critic, Bernhard
Feuerstein, appeared, his coat stained with spinach or to-
mato, in accordance with what he might have had for lunch,
and, to Kläre's unconcealed delight, abused her fellow
artists of both sexes, including the Director himself. She
allowed Prince Richard's two cousins, Lucius and Christian,
Bedenbrucks of the other line, to make love to her in their
usual light-hearted but respectful way; a gentleman from
the French Embassy and a young Czech pianist were
brought to see her, and on June 11th she drove to the races
again for the first time. But, as Prince Lucius, who had a
touch of poetry about him, expressed it, only her soul was
awake, her heart was still sunk in slumber. It was true that
if one of her younger or older friends ventured the slightest
suggestion that there were such things as love and passion
in the world, every trace of a smile vanished from her face,
she stared darkly in front of her, and from time to time

raised her hand in a strange gesture of repulsion which
seemed intended to apply to all men, and for ever.

In the latter half of the month of June it so happened
that a singer from the north, named Sigurd Ölse, sang Tristan at the Opera. His voice was clear and powerful, though
it was not really first-rate; he was almost a giant in stature,
though inclining towards stoutness, and, in repose, his face
was lacking in individual expression; but as soon as he began to sing, his steel-gray eyes flashed with a sort of secret
inner light, and his voice and look seemed to reduce everybody, more especially women, to a state of ecstatic admiration.

Kläre sat in the theater-box with some of her fellow
artists who were not singing that night. She alone seemed
to remain unmoved. Next morning Sigurd Ölse was introduced to her in the manager's office. She spoke kindly, but
quite coldly about his performance on the previous evening.
The same afternoon he called upon her, though she had not
invited him to do so. Leisenbohg and Fanny Ringeiser were
present and Sigurd drank tea with them. He spoke of his
parents who were fisher-folk living in a little Norwegian
village, of the marvelous discovery of his talent as a singer
by a passing Englishman who had landed from a white
yacht in that far-distant fjord; of his wife, an Italian, who
had died on the Atlantic Ocean during their honeymoon and
who had been buried at sea. After he had taken his departure
the others stayed for some time in silence. Fanny stared
gravely into her empty tea cup, Kläre sat down at the piano
with her elbows on the closed keyboard, while the Baron
sank into a silent and anxious meditation as to why, during
the account of Sigurd's honeymoon, Kläre had omitted that
strange gesture by which, since the Prince's death, she indicated that any suggestion of passion or affection could
have no place whatever in her future life.

The next parts that Sigurd Ölse sang were Siegfried and
Lohengrin. On each occasion Kläre sat in her box and made
no sign. But the singer, whose only other acquaintance was

the Norwegian Ambassador, appeared at Kläre's house every afternoon; Fräulein Fanny Ringeiser was usually there, and the Baron von Leisenbohg always.

On June 27th he sang Tristan for the last time. Kläre sat in the theater-box and made no sign. The next day she drove with Fanny to the cemetery and laid a gigantic cross on the Prince's grave; and in the evening she gave a party in honor of the singer who was to leave Vienna on the morrow.

Her circle of friends was present in full strength. The passion that Sigurd had conceived for Kläre was obvious to every one; as his custom was, he was voluble and excited. He mentioned incidentally that while on the ship crossing to the Continent an Arabian lady, married to a Russian Grand Duke, had read his hand and prophesied that the immediate future would be the most fateful period in his life. He believed firmly in this prophecy, and, indeed, superstition seemed to him something more than a means of exciting interest. He also said it was generally known that last year, on landing in New York, where he had gone to fulfill an engagement, that very day—that very hour in fact—notwithstanding the enormous fine involved, he boarded a ship for Europe simply because a black cat had walked between his legs on the gangway. He had certainly every reason to believe in the secret connections between such inexplicable omens and the fates of men. One evening at the Covent Garden Theater in London, before going on the stage he had omitted to repeat a certain magic formula he had received from his grandmother, and his voice had suddenly failed him. One night a winged genius in pink tights had appeared to him in a dream and predicted the death of his favorite barber, and sure enough the unfortunate man was found hanged the next morning. Moreover, he always carried about with him a short but highly significant missive which had been handed to him at a spiritualist séance in Brussels by the spirit of the dead singer, Cornelia Lujan, and contained a prophecy, in fluent Portuguese, that he was destined to become the greatest singer in the Old and New Worlds.

All these experiences he related that evening; and when the spirit letter (written on rose-colored paper manufactured by Glienwood & Co.) was passed from hand to hand, the effect on the company was profound and universal. Kläre did not move a muscle, but merely nodded indifferently once or twice. In spite of this Leisenbohg's anxiety grew more and more acute. To his penetrating eyes the signs of threatening danger grew ever more ominous. Worst of all, Sigurd, like all Kläre's previous lovers, conceived an extraordinary liking for him during supper, invited him to his house on the Molde-Fjord, and ended by addressing him as "du." Moreover, Fanny trembled all over when Sigurd spoke a word to her, her color came and went when he looked at her with his great steel-gray eyes, and when he spoke of his approaching departure she burst openly into tears. But Kläre remained perfectly quiet and serious. She barely returned Sigurd's burning glances, she spoke to him no more eagerly than to the rest, and when he at last kissed her hand and then looked up at her with eyes that seemed full of prayers and promises and desperation, her own remained veiled and her expression unmoved. Leisenbohg observed all this with suspicion and anxiety. But when the party came to an end and all the guests departed, something unexpected happened that took the Baron completely by surprise. He was the last of all to take Kläre's hand in farewell, and hurried to depart; but she held his hand fast and whispered: "Come back again." He thought he could not have heard her rightly. But she pressed his hand again, and, with her lips quite close to his ear, repeated, "Come back again; I shall expect you in an hour."

In a state bordering on ecstasy he went out with the rest. He and Fanny accompanied Sigurd to his hotel, and as though from a far distance he heard the tenor raving about Kläre. Then he took Fanny Ringeiser back through the silent streets, in soft cool night air, to Mariahilferstrasse, and he saw, as though through a mist, her girlish cheeks wet with foolish tears. Then he got into a cab and drove up to

Kläre's door. He saw the light glimmering through the curtains of her bedroom, he saw her shadow glide past, her head appeared in the gap between the curtain and the window, and she nodded to him. He had not been dreaming: she was waiting for him.

Next morning Baron von Leisenbohg went for a ride in the Prater. He felt young and happy. In the late fulfillment of his passion there seemed to be some deeper meaning. His experience of the past night had been the most marvelous surprise—and yet, again, it was nothing but the climax and the inevitable conclusion of his relations with Kläre hitherto. He now felt that it could not have happened otherwise, and fell to making plans for the immediate and more distant future. "How long will she stay on the stage?" he wondered. . . . "Perhaps for a few years. Then, but not until then, we will get married. We will live together somewhere in the country not far from Vienna, perhaps in St. Veit or in Lainz. I will buy a small house there, or build one to her liking. We shall live a rather retired life, but often take long trips abroad . . . to Spain, Egypt or India. . . ." Thus he dreamed, as he let his horse canter across the meadows towards the hay-stall. Then he trotted back into the main avenue and got into his carriage at the crossroads. He told his coachman to stop at Fossatti's and sent Kläre a bouquet of beautiful dark roses. He breakfasted at home alone, as his custom was, in his house on the Schwarzenbergplatz, and when he had finished he lay down on the divan. He was filled with the most fervent longing for Kläre. What meaning had all the other women had for him? . . . They had served to pass the time, nothing more. And he felt a day would come when Kläre too would say to him: "What were all the others to me? You are the first and only one I ever loved. . . ." And while he lay on the divan with closed eyes, he let the whole succession of them glide past his inner vision. He was sure she had loved none of them before him

—perhaps she had loved him always, and in each and all of them! . . .

The Baron then dressed himself and walked slowly through the familiar streets towards her house, as though to savor their first reunion for a few more seconds. There were a good many people about on the Ring, but still it was observable that the season was coming to an end. And Leisenbohg was glad that summer was there, that he could travel with Kläre and they could see the sea and the mountains together—indeed he had very nearly shouted aloud in his delight.

He stood before her house and looked up at her windows. The light of the afternoon sun was reflected from them and almost blinded him. He walked up the two flights of stairs to her door and rang. No one opened. He rang again. No one opened. Then Leisenbohg noticed that the door was padlocked. What did it mean? Had he made a mistake? . . . As a matter of fact there was no plate on her door, but opposite was the one he knew so well: "Lt.-Colonel von Jeleskowitz." . . . There could be no doubt: this was her flat and it was shut up. He hurried down the stairs and flung open the door of the porter's lodge. The porter's wife was sitting in the half-darkness on a bed, one child was peering up at the street through the small underground window, the other was blowing an unrecognizable tune on a comb.

"Is Fräulein Hell not at home?" asked the Baron.

The woman stood up. "No, Herr Baron, Fräulein Hell has gone away."

"What!" cried the Baron. . . . "Oh, yes, of course," he added quickly. "She went about three o'clock, didn't she?"

"No, Herr Baron, about eight o'clock this morning."

"Where did she go? . . . I mean did she go straight . . ." he was talking at random . . . "did she go straight to Dresden?"

"No, Herr Baron; she left no address. She said she would write and say where she was."

"Ah . . . yes—yes . . . of course. Thank you very much."

He hurried away and went out into the street: unconsciously he looked back at the house. The evening sunlight shining in those windows looked very different now! And the sultry summer evening lay like a pall of oppression over the city. Kläre had gone?... Why?... Had she fled from him? What did it mean?... His first thought was to go to the Opera House. But it occurred to him that the vacation began the day after to-morrow, and that Kläre was not singing the last two days. Then he went to 76 Mariahilfer-strasse where the Ringeisers lived. An elderly cook opened the door to him and looked at the well-dressed visitor with a certain mistrust. He asked her to call Frau Ringeiser.

"Is Fräulein Fanny at home?" he asked in a tone of excitement that he could no longer control.

"I beg your pardon?" said Frau Ringeiser sharply.

He introduced himself.

"Ah, of course," said Frau Ringeiser. "Please come in, Herr Baron."

He remained standing in the hall and asked once more:

"Is Fräulein Fanny not at home?"

"But the Herr Baron must come in." Leisenbohg had to follow her, and found himself in a dark, low-ceilinged room with furniture covered in blue velvet and rep window curtains of the same color. "No," said Frau Ringeiser, "Fanny is not at home. Fräulein Hell has taken her away for a holiday trip."

"Where?" asked the Baron, and stared at a photograph of Kläre that stood on the piano in a gold frame.

"I don't know where," said Frau Ringeiser. "Fräulein Hell was here at eight o'clock this morning and begged me to let Fanny go with her.... And she begged so nicely that I could not say 'No.'"

"But where have they gone—where have they gone?" persisted Leisenbohg.

"That I can't tell you. Fanny is going to telegraph as soon as Fräulein Hell has made up her mind where she is going to stay. Perhaps to-morrow or the day after."

"Ah," said Leisenbohg, and dropped on to a kind of cane

stool in front of the piano. He was silent for a few moments, then he suddenly stood up, shook hands with Frau Ringeiser, asked her to excuse him for having disturbed her, and went slowly down the dark staircase of the old house.

He shook his head. She had indeed been careful . . . more careful than was necessary. . . . She might have known that he would not come where he was not wanted.

"Where to now, Herr Baron?" asked the coachman, and Leisenbohg realized that he had been sitting in the open carriage, staring in front of him, for some minutes. And, following a sudden instinct, he answered: "Hotel Bristol."

Sigurd Ölse had not yet gone. He invited the Baron up to his rooms, greeted him eagerly and asked him to spend the last evening in Vienna in his company. Leisenbohg was much struck by the fact that Sigurd Ölse was still actually in Vienna, and the singer's friendliness positively stirred him to tears. Sigurd began at once to talk about Kläre. He asked Leisenbohg to tell him all he knew about her—he knew that the Baron was her oldest and most faithful friend. So Leisenbohg sat down on one of his host's trunks and began to speak of Kläre. It did him good to be able to talk about her. He told the singer almost everything, except such matters as he felt bound in honor not to mention. Sigurd listened and appeared enraptured.

At supper the singer invited his friend to leave Vienna with him that very evening, and go with him to his estate near Molde. The Baron felt wonderfully comforted. He excused himself for the time being, but promised Ölse to visit him in the course of the summer.

They drove to the station together. "You will take me for a simpleton," said Sigurd, "but I want to pass her window once again."

Leisenbohg threw a sidelong glance at him. Was this perhaps an attempt to make a fool of him, or was it a final proof of the singer's honesty? . . . As they went by Kläre's house, Sigurd flung a kiss at the closed windows. Then he said: "Say good-by for me once more."

Leisenbohg nodded. "I will give her your message when she comes back."

Sigurd looked at him in amazement.

"As a matter of fact she has gone away," Leisenbohg continued. "She went off early this morning—without a word to any one. It is a habit of hers," he added, untruthfully.

"Gone away?" repeated Sigurd, and sank into thought. Then they were both silent.

Before the departure of the train they embraced like old friends.

That night the Baron wept as he lay in bed, more bitterly than he had done since his childhood. The hour of delight that he had spent with Kläre seemed to him beset by gloom and terror. There had been, he thought, a gleam of madness in her eyes last night. Now he understood. He had obeyed her summons too soon. The shadow of Prince Bedenbruck still had power over her, and Leisenbohg felt that he had possessed Kläre only to lose her for ever.

He wandered about Vienna for a few days without knowing what to do with his days and nights: everything that used to occupy his time—the newspapers, bridge and riding, had become completely indifferent to him. He realized that the meaning of his whole existence depended on Kläre, and even that his relations with other women had their being only as reflections of his passion for her. An eternal gray mist seemed to hang over the city; the people to whom he spoke had hushed voices and stared at him in a strange, almost treacherous way. One evening he drove to the station and almost mechanically took a ticket to Ischl. There he met acquaintances who asked him unsuspectingly for news of Kläre; he answered in an irritable and offensive tone, and had to fight a duel with one man who did not interest him in the least. He went nonchalantly into the field, heard the bullet whistle past his ear, fired in the air and left Ischl half an hour afterwards. He traveled to Tyrol, the Engadine and the Bernese Oberland, and to Lake Geneva, swam, crossed mountain passes, climbed mountains, and remembered nothing from one day to the next.

One day he received a telegram that had been sent on from Vienna. He opened it with feverish fingers. In it were these words: "If you are my friend, keep your word and come to me quickly, for I need a friend. Sigurd Ölse." Leisenbohg did not doubt for a moment that the contents of this telegram must have some sort of connection with Kläre. He packed as quickly as possible and left Aix, where he then happened to be, at the earliest opportunity. He traveled straight through to Hamburg via Munich, and took the boat via Stavanger to Molde, where he arrived on a fine summer evening. The journey had seemed interminable, and the beauties of the scenery had left him quite unmoved. Moreover, latterly he had not been able to remember Kläre's voice when she sang, or even her features. It seemed like a year, ten years, since he had left Vienna. But when he saw Sigurd standing on the shore in a white flannel suit and white cap, he felt as though he had seen him only the evening before. And, disheveled as he was, he smilingly returned Sigurd's greeting from where he was standing on the deck, and walked cheerfully down the gangway.

"I thank you a thousand times for coming so promptly," said Sigurd; and then he added simply: "I'm done for."

The Baron eyed him. Sigurd looked very pale and the hair on his temples had grown astonishingly gray. Over his arm he was carrying a green rug of dimly iridescent material.

"What is it? What has happened?" asked Leisenbohg with a fixed smile.

"I will tell you the whole story," said Sigurd Ölse. It struck the Baron that Sigurd's voice was less resonant than it had been. They drove in a small carriage along the lovely avenue along the shore of the blue sea. Both were silent. Leisenbohg did not dare to ask a question. He stared vacantly at the water which was almost motionless. The strange and (as it proved) impossible idea of counting the ripples came into his mind; then he looked up into the sky and it seemed as though the stars were dropping slowly down to earth. At last it also occurred to him that a singer, by name Kläre Hell, was wandering somewhere about in the wide world—a fact which did not matter much. Then the carriage stopped with a jerk before a simple white house entirely surrounded by trees and foliage. In the evening they dined upon a veranda that looked out upon the sea. A servant with a stern, and, as he poured out the wine, almost a menacing expression, waited on them. The distant horizon slept under the clear northern light.

"Well?" asked Leisenbohg, in a sudden burst of impatience.

"I am a lost man," said Sigurd Ölse, and stared in front of him.

"What do you mean by that?" asked Leisenbohg in a toneless voice, "and what can I do for you?" he added mechanically.

"Not much. I don't know yet," and he looked beyond the tablecloth, the balustrade, the garden and the garden fence, the road, and the sea into the far distance.

Leisenbohg felt numb within him . . . all manner of notions flashed across his mind . . . what was going to happen? . . . was Kläre dead? . . . had Sigurd murdered her? . . . thrown her into the sea? . . . Or was Sigurd dead? . . . No, that was impossible—there he was sitting opposite. . . . But why didn't he speak? . . . and suddenly, in an access of terror, Leisenbohg burst out, "Where is Kläre?"

The singer turned slowly towards him. His rather fleshy face began to light up with a sort of inner glow and seemed to smile, unless it was the moonlight playing over it. In any case, at that moment, it seemed to Leisenbohg that the man sitting near him leaning back in his chair with his hands in his pockets and his legs outstretched under the table, and gazing at him with veiled eyes, looked exactly like a Pierrot. The green shawl hung down over the balustrade of the veranda and at that moment seemed to the Baron so like an old acquaintance. . . . But what on earth had this ridiculous

old shawl to do with him? Was he dreaming perhaps?...he
was in Molde; it was all very strange; if he had been sensible he ought really to have telegraphed to the singer from
Aix: "What is the matter? What do you want me to do for
you, Pierrot?" And he suddenly repeated his earlier question only in a much politer and calmer tone: "Where is
Kläre?"

The singer nodded several times. "Yes," he said, "it is
something to do with her, of course. Are you a friend of
mine?"

Leisenbohg nodded, he felt slightly chilly; a light wind
was blowing in from the sea. "I am your friend. What do
you want of me?"

"Do you remember the evening I left Vienna, Baron,
when we had supper together at the Bristol, and you went
with me to the station?"

Leisenbohg nodded once more.

"You had no idea, of course, that Kläre Hell was leaving
Vienna in that same train?"

Leisenbohg let his head sink heavily on his chest....

"Nor had I," went on Sigurd. "I saw Kläre for the first
time next morning at the station where we stopped for
breakfast. She was sitting with Fanny Ringeiser in the
dining-room drinking coffee. Her demeanor led me to suppose that this meeting was a fortunate accident. It was not
an accident at all."

"Go on," said the Baron, looking at the green shawl which
was moving slightly.

"Later on, of course, she confessed that it was not an accident. From that morning we all stayed together, Kläre,
Fanny and I. We settled down by one of your enchanting
little Austrian lakes, in a charming house between the shore
and the forest, quite by ourselves. We were very happy."

He spoke so slowly that Leisenbohg thought he was going mad.

"Why did he send for me?" he thought. "What does he
want of me? Had she confessed? What's the matter with

him? Why is he staring at me like that?... Why am I sitting here at Molde on a veranda with a Pierrot? Can it be all a dream after all? Perhaps I am still asleep in Kläre's arms. Perhaps that night of ours has not yet ended after all." ... And he unconsciously opened his eyes wide.

"Will you avenge me?" said Sigurd, suddenly.

"Avenge you? Whatever for? What has happened?" asked the Baron, and his words sounded as if they came from a distance.

"Because she has destroyed me, and I am a lost man."

"Tell me all about it," said Leisenbohg in a hard, dry voice.

"Fanny Ringeiser was with us," Sigurd went on. "She is a good girl, isn't she?"

"Yes, she is a good girl," answered Leisenbohg, and all at once he saw a dim room with furniture covered in blue velvet and rep curtains where, several hundred years before, he had spoken to Fanny's mother.

"She is rather a stupid girl, is she not?"

"I believe she is," answered the Baron.

"I am sure of it," answered Sigurd. "She did not realize how happy we were." And he was silent for some while.

"Go on," said Leisenbohg, and waited.

"One morning Kläre was still asleep," began Sigurd afresh. "She always slept late into the morning. But I had gone for a walk into the forest. Suddenly Fanny came running up behind me: "Fly, Herr Ölse, before it is too late; leave this place, for you are in dreadful danger!" Strangely enough, to begin with she absolutely refused to say any more. But I persisted and at last found out what kind of danger it was that she believed to be threatening me. You see, she believed that I could still be saved or she would certainly have told me nothing!"

The green shawl on the balustrade bellied out like a sail, and the lamp flickered a little on the table.

"What did Fanny tell you?" asked Leisenbohg in a rasping tone.

"Do you remember the evening," asked Sigurd, "when we were all at Kläre's house? On the next day Kläre drove out with Fanny to the cemetery, and on the Prince's grave she confided the dreadful secret to her friend."

"The dreadful secret . . . ?" stammered the Baron.

"Yes. You know how the Prince died? He was thrown from his horse and lingered for an hour."

"I know."

"Nobody was with him but Kläre."

"That also I know."

"He would see no one but her, and on his deathbed he uttered a curse."

"A curse?"

"A curse. 'Kläre,' said the Prince, 'do not forget me. I shall have no peace in the grave if you forget me.'—'I will never forget you,' replied Kläre.—'Do you swear you will never forget me?'—'I swear it.'—'Kläre, I love you and I must die!'"

"Who is it speaking?" cried the Baron.

"I am," said Sigurd; "I am telling you what Fanny said; Fanny told me what Kläre said, and Kläre told her what the Prince said. Don't you understand?"

Leisenbohg listened with strained attention: it seemed as though he could hear the voice of the dead Prince ringing out from the triply-sealed coffin into the night.

" 'Kläre, I love you, and I must die! You are so young, and I must die. . . . And after me another man will come. . . . I know it will be so, another man will hold you in his arms and be happy with you . . . he must not be—shall not be—I lay my curse on him, do you hear, Kläre? I curse him!—The first man that kisses those lips and holds that body in his arms when I am gone shall go down to hell! Kläre, Heaven hears the curses of dying men. Beware—and let him be- ware; he shall go down to hell in madness, misery and death! Woe be to that man—woe!' "

Sigurd, from whose mouth the dead man's voice thundered out, had got up from his chair and stood, a tall heavy figure in his white flannel suit, staring into the clear night. The green shawl slipped down from the balustrade into the garden. An icy chill came over the Baron; he felt as though his whole body was growing stiff; he would gladly have cried out, but though he opened his mouth wide no sound came . . . in a flash he was back again in Frau Eisenstein, the singing teacher's, little room where he had seen Kläre for the first time. On the stage stood a Pierrot, and shouted out: "With this curse on his lips Prince Bedenbruck died, and the unhappy man in whose arms she lay, the wretch upon whom the curse must be fulfilled, is I—I !"

Then the stage collapsed with a loud crash and sank before Leisenbohg's eyes into the sea. But he, without a word, fell backwards with his chair, like a marionette.

Sigurd leapt up and shouted for help. Two servants came, picked up the unconscious man and laid him out in an arm-chair that stood beside the table; one of them went for a doctor, and the other brought some water and vinegar. Sigurd rubbed the Baron's forehead and temples, but he did not stir. Then the doctor came and began his examination. It did not last long. When he had finished he said: "This gentleman is dead."

Sigurd Ölse was much upset, asked the doctor to make the necessary arrangements and left the veranda. He walked through the drawing-room, went upstairs, entered his bed-room, lit a lamp and hurriedly wrote the following words: "Kläre! I found your telegram waiting for me in Molde where I had fled without stopping on the way. I will confess that I did not believe you; I thought that you were trying to set my mind at rest by a lie. Forgive me; I no longer doubt you. Baron von Leisenbohg has been here. I asked him to come, but I did not question him because as an honorable man he would have had to lie. I had an ingenious idea. I told him about the dead Prince's curse. The effect was amazing. The Baron fell backwards as he sat, and died on the spot."

Sigurd paused for a moment, looked very serious and seemed to be reflecting. Then he took up his stand in the middle of the room and began to sing. At first his voice sounded timid and subdued, but gradually it grew clearer and rang out strong and splendid into the night—so powerfully at last that it seemed full of the thunder of the sea. A satisfied smile spread over Sigurd's features and he breathed a deep sigh of relief. Once more he sat down at the writing table, and added the following words to his letter:

"Darling Kläre! Forgive me—all is well again. I shall be with you in three days...."

FLAGMAN THIEL *

By Gerhart Hauptmann

I

Every Sunday Thiel, the flagman, was to be seen sitting
in a pew in the church at Neu Zittau. If he was absent, you
might be sure he was on Sunday duty or else—as happened
twice in the course of ten years—at home ill in bed. Once a
great lump of coal from the tender of a passing locomotive
had struck his leg and sent him rolling into the ditch at the
bottom of the embankment. The second time the trouble
was a wine bottle that had come flying from an express and
had hit him in the middle of his chest. Nothing but these two
mishaps had ever succeeded in keeping Thiel from church
the instant he was off duty.

The first five years he had had to come alone to Neu
Zittau from Schön-Schornstein, a small collection of homes
on the Spree. Then, one fine day, he appeared in the company
of a delicate, sickly looking woman. The people thought she
ill suited his herculean build. And on a later Sunday afternoon, at the altar of the church, he solemnly gave her his
hand and pledged his troth.

So, for two years, the delicate young creature sat beside
him in the pew. For two years her fine, hollow-cheeked face
bent over the ancient hymnal beside his weather-tanned
face.

And suddenly the flagman was to be seen sitting alone, as
of old.

On one of the preceding weekdays the bell had tolled for
the dead. That was all.

* Translated by Adele S. Seltzer. Copyright, 1933, by The Modern
Library, Inc.

Scarcely any change, so the people declared, was to be observed in the flagman. The brass buttons of his clean Sunday uniform were as brightly polished as before, his red hair as sleekly pomaded and as neatly parted, military fashion. Only he held his broad, hairy neck a little bent, and sang more eagerly, and listened to the sermon more devoutly. The general opinion was that his wife's death had not hit him very hard. A view that was strengthened when in the course of the year he married again. The second wife was a strong, stout milkmaid from Altegrund.

Even the pastor felt free to express his doubts when Thiel came to announce his engagement.

"So soon again? You really want to marry so soon again?"

"I can't keep my house running, sir, with the wife who's gone."

"To be sure. But I mean—aren't you in a bit of a hurry?"

"It's on account of the boy."

Thiel's wife had died in childbirth. The boy had lived and been named Tobias.

"Yes, yes, to be sure, the boy," said the pastor, with a gesture clearly revealing that he had not thought of the infant until that moment. "That throws a different light on the matter. What have you been doing with him until now while you are at work?"

Thiel explained that he left Tobias in the care of an old woman. Once she had nearly let him get burned, and another time had let him roll from her lap to the floor. Fortunately the child had not been badly hurt—only a big surface bruise. Such a state of things could not continue, the flagman said, especially as the child, being delicate, required particular attention. For that reason and also because he had sworn to his wife on her deathbed that he would always take exceedingly good care of the child, he had decided to marry again.

The people found absolutely nothing to cavil with in the new couple that now visited the church regularly on Sundays. The milkmaid seemed to have been made for the flagman. She was but a few inches shorter than he and exceeded him in girth, while her features were just as coarsely molded as his, though, in contrast, they lacked soul.

If Thiel had cherished the desire for an inveterate worker and paragon of a housewife in his second wife, then his hopes were surprisingly fulfilled. However, without knowing it, he had purchased three other qualities, too, a hard, domineering disposition, quarrelsomeness, and brutal passion.

Within half a year the whole place knew who was lord and master in the flagman's little house. Thiel became the object of general pity. It was a piece of good luck for the "creature," the exercised husbands said, that she had got such a gentle lamb as Thiel for a husband. With other men she wouldn't come off so easy, she'd receive some hard knocks. An animal like that had to be managed—with blows, if need be—a good sound thrashing to make her behave herself.

But Thiel, despite his sinewy arms, was not the man to thrash his wife. What got the people so annoyed seemed to cause him no perturbation. As a rule, he let his wife's endless sermonizings pass without a word, and when he did occasionally make a response, the slow drag of his speech and the quiet coolness of his tone contrasted oddly with her high-pitched bawling.

The outside world seemed scarcely to touch him. It was as though he carried something within him that heavily overbalanced all of the evil it brought by good.

Nevertheless, for all his phlegm, there were occasions on which he would not allow things to pass—when little Toby was concerned. Then his childlike goodness, his yieldingness took on a dash of determination that even so untamed a temperament as Lena's did not dare to oppose.

The moments, however, in which he revealed this side of his character became rarer and rarer, and finally ceased completely. During the first year of his marriage he had shown a certain suffering resistance to Lena's tyranny. In the second year this also ceased completely. After a quarrel he no longer left for his work with his earlier indifference in case he had not previously placated her. Often he even stooped to beg her to be kind again. His solitary post in the heart of the Brandenburg pine forest was no longer, as it had been, the place where he would rather be than anywhere else on earth. The quiet devout thoughts of his dead wife were crossed by thoughts of the living wife. It was not with repugnance, as in the first months of his marriage, that he trod the homeward way, but often with passionate haste, after having counted the hours and minutes till the time of his release.

He who had been united to his first wife by a more spiritual love fell into his second wife's grip through the power of crude impulses. He became almost wholly dependent upon her.

At times he experienced pangs of conscience at this turn, and resorted to a number of unusual devices to bring about a change. For one thing, he declared his hut and his beat to be holy ground, dedicated exclusively to the shades of the dead. And he actually succeeded by all sorts of pretexts in preventing Lena from accompanying him there. He hoped he should always be able to keep her off. The very number of his hut and the direction in which it lay were still unknown to her.

Thus, by conscientiously dividing the time at his disposal between the living and the dead, Thiel actually succeeded in soothing his conscience.

Often, to be sure, especially in moments of solitary devotion, when he felt the tie between him and his dead wife deeply and warmly, he beheld his present condition in the light of truth, and he experienced disgust.

If he was doing day duty, his spiritual intercourse with her was limited to dear recollections of their life together. But in the dark, when a snowstorm raged among the pines and along the embankment, his hut at midnight, by the light of his lantern, became a chapel.

With a faded photograph of the departed before him on the table, and the hymnal and the Bible turned open, he alternately read and sang the whole night long, interrupted only at intervals by the trains rushing past. He would attain a state of ecstasy in which he had visions of his wife standing there in person.

In its remoteness this post, which Thiel had held for ten years, contributed to the intensification of his mystic inclinations. To the north, east, south and west, it was separated by a walk of at least three quarters of an hour from the nearest habitation. It lay in the very heart of the forest. But there was a grade crossing there, and Thiel's duty was to lower and raise the gates.

In the summer days passed, in the winter weeks without a single person except other railroad workers setting foot on Thiel's beat. Almost the only changes in the solitude came from the weather and the periodic mutations of the seasons. It was not difficult to recall the events—besides the two mishaps to his body—that had broken into the regular course of the hours of service.

Four years previous the imperial special bearing the Kaiser to Breslau had gone dashing by. Once on a winter's night an express had run over a stag. And once on a hot summer's day, as Thiel was making an inspection of his beat, he had found a corked bottle of wine. It was scorching hot to the touch, and Thiel had esteemed its contents because when he uncorked it a geyser spouted out, showing that the stuff was well fermented. Thiel had laid the bottle on the edge of a pond in the woods to cool off. Somehow it had disappeared from the spot, and even after the passage of years Thiel never thought of that bottle without a pang of regret.

A bit of diversion was provided by a spring behind the hut. From time to time men at work on the road bed or on the telegraph lines came for a drink, and stayed, of course, to talk a while. Sometimes the forest ranger would also come when he was thirsty.

Tobias developed slowly. It was not until he was two years old that he learned to walk and talk. For his father he displayed unusual affection, and as he grew more understanding Thiel's old love for his child was re-awakened. Accordingly Lena's love for the child decreased, turning into unmistakable dislike when the next year a baby boy was born to her, too.

After that bad times began for Tobias. In his father's absence he was particularly made to suffer. He had to dedicate his feeble powers unrewarded to the service of the little cry-baby. He became more and more exhausted. His head grew too large round, and his fiery red hair, with the chalky face beneath, on top of his wretched little body, made an unlovely and pitiful impression. When the backward mite was seen dragging himself down to the Spree with his baby brother bursting with health in his arms, curses were muttered behind the windows of the cottages. But no one ever ventured to utter the curses in the open.

Thiel, who was most of all concerned, seemed to have no eyes for what was going on, and refused to understand the hints of well-meaning neighbors.

II

Once Thiel returned from night duty at seven o'clock of a June morning. Directly Lena had greeted him, she burst into her usual complaining.

A few weeks before notice had been given that they could no longer cultivate the piece of land which they rented for planting potatoes for their own use, and no other land had been found to replace it. Though everything pertaining to the land was part of Lena's duty, Thiel none the less had to listen to a hundred iterations that he would be to blame if they had to buy ten sacks of potatoes for dear money. Thiel merely muttered a word or two. Paying slight attention to Lena's tirade, he went straight over to Tobias's bed, which he shared with the boy on nights when he was off duty.

He sat down and watched the sleeping child with an anxious expression on his good face. For a while he contented himself with chasing away the persistent flies, then he woke him up. A touching joy lighted up the boy's blue, deep-set eyes. He snatched for his father's hand, and a pitiful smile drew the corners of his mouth. Thiel helped him put on his few bits of clothing. Suddenly a shadow chased across his face. He noticed that his son's right cheek was slightly swollen and bore finger marks designed white on red.

At breakfast Lena brought up the same subject again, pursuing it with even more vigor. Thiel cut her off by telling her that the railroad inspector had given him for nothing the use of a stretch of land alongside the tracks not far from his hut, probably because it was too distant for the inspector to use for himself.

Lena was incredulous, then gradually her doubts melted away and she became noticeably good-humored. How big was the lot? How good was the soil? She plied him with questions. And when she learned that there were actually two dwarf fruit trees on the land, she fairly lost her head. At length the questions were all asked, and as the shopkeeper's bell, which could be heard in every house in the place, kept ringing incessantly, Lena ran forth to ferret out the latest news.

While she remained in the dark shop crowded with wares, Thiel occupied himself at home with Tobias, who sat on his knee playing with pine cones that his father had brought from the woods.

"What do you want to be when you grow up?" asked Thiel. The stereotyped question was invariably answered by the equally stereotyped reply, "Railroad inspector." It was not asked in fun. The flagman's dreams actually soared so high. It was in all seriousness that he cherished the hope that with God's help Tobias would become something extraordinary. The instant "railroad inspector" left the child's bloodless lips, Thiel's face brightened, fairly radiated bliss.

"Go play now, Tobias," he said soon afterward, lighting

his pipe with a shaving kindled at the hearth fire. The boy showing shy pleasure went out.

Thiel undressed and got into bed. For a long while he lay staring up at the low, cracked ceiling. Finally he fell asleep and woke up shortly before twelve o'clock. While Lena in her noisy fashion prepared the midday meal, he dressed and went out on the street to fetch Tobias, whom he found scratching plaster out of a hole in the wall and stuffing it into his mouth. Thiel led him by the hand past the eight houses that constituted the hamlet down to the Spree. The stream lay dark and glassy between sparsely foliaged poplars. Thiel sat down on a block of granite close to the water's edge.

Every fair day the villagers were accustomed to see him on this spot. The children were devoted to him. They called him Father Thiel. He taught them games that he remembered from his own childhood, reserving, however, the best of his memories for Tobias. He whittled him arrows that flew farther than those of the other boys, he carved him willow pipes, and even deigned to sing ditties in his rusty bass, and tap the beat with the horn handle of his knife against the bark of a tree.

The people thought him silly. They blamed him. They could not understand how he could go to so much trouble for the little brats. Though they should have been richly content, seeing that the children were well taken care of when in his charge. Besides, Thiel did more than play with them. He took up serious things, too. He heard the older ones recite their lessons, helped them study their Bible and hymn verses, and spelled out c-a-t and d-o-g with the younger ones.

After the midday meal Thiel rested again a while, drank a cup of coffee, and began to prepare for work. It took him a lot of time, as for everything he did. Each move had been regulated for years. The objects carefully spread out on the walnut dresser went into his various pockets always in the same order—knife, notebook, comb, a horse's tooth, an old watch in a case, and a small book wrapped in red paper. The last was handled with especial care. During the night it lay under Thiel's pillow, and by day was carried in his breast pocket. On a label pasted on the cover was written in Thiel's awkward yet flourished hand, "Savings Account of Tobias Thiel."

The clock on the wall with the long pendulum and sickly yellow face indicated a quarter to five when Thiel left. A small boat, his own property, ferried him across the Spree. Arrived at the further side, he stood still a moment and listened back in the direction he had come from. Then he turned into a broad path through the woods and within a few moments reached the depths of the deep-booming pine forest, its mass of needles like a dark green undulating sea.

The moist layers of needles and moss made a carpet as inaudible to the tread as felt. Thiel made his way without looking up, now past the rusty brown columns of the older trees, now between the thickly enmeshed younger growth, and farther on across broad stretches of nursery, over-shadowed by a few tall slim pines for the protection of the young saplings. A transparent bluish haze rising from the earth laden with mingled fragrances blurred the forms of the trees. A heavy, drab sky hung low over the tops. Flocks of cawing crows seemed to bathe in the gray of the atmosphere. Black puddles filled the depressions in the path and cast a still drearier reflection of a dreary nature.

"Fearful weather," thought Thiel when he roused out of deep reflection and looked up.

Suddenly his thoughts were deflected. A dim feeling came to him that he must have forgotten something. And surely enough, when he searched his pockets, he discovered that he had not brought along the sandwich that he required on account of the long hours on duty. For a while he stood undecided. Then turned and hurried back.

In a short while he reached the Spree, rowed himself across in a few powerful strokes, and without delay, per-spiring from every pore, ascended the gradual slope of the village street. The shopkeeper's old, mangy poodle lay in the middle of the road. On the tarred board fence around a cottager's yard perched a hooded crow. It spread its feathers, shook itself, nodded, uttered an ear-splitting caw, caw, and with a slapping sound of its wings rose in the air and let the wind drive it in the direction of the forest.

Nothing was to be seen of the villagers—about twenty fishermen and lumbermen with their families.

The stillness was broken—by a high-pitched voice. The flagman involuntarily stopped. A volley of violent, jangling tones assailed his ears. It seemed to come from the open dormer window of a low house that he knew only too well.

Treading as silently as possible, he glided nearer. Now he quite clearly recognized his wife's voice. Only a few steps more, and he could understand almost everything she said.

"You horrid little beast, you! Is the poor baby to scream its belly inside out from hunger? What? Just you wait—just you wait. I'll teach you to mind. You'll never forget."

For a few moments there was silence. Then a sound could be heard like the beating out of clothes. And the next instant another hailstorm of abuse was let loose.

"You miserable little puppy, you! Do you think I'll let my own child die of hunger because of a mean little thing like you?—Shut your mouth!" A slight whimper had been audible. "If you don't shut your mouth, I'll give you something that'll keep you going a whole week."

The whimpering did not subside.

The flagman felt his heart pounding in irregular beats. He began to tremble slightly. His glance fastened on the ground as though his mind were wandering, and again and again his coarse, hard hand went up to his freckled forehead to brush back a dank strand of hair. For a second he was about to give way. He stood shaken by a convulsion that swelled his muscles and drew his fingers into a clenched ball. The convulsion subsided. He was left in a state of dull exhaustion.

With unsteady steps he entered the narrow, brick-paved

vestibule and slowly, wearily mounted the creaking wooden
stairs.

"Pugh, pugh, pugh!" You could hear how with every
sign of scorn and fury some one spat out three times in
succession. "You horrid, mean, sneaking, cowardly, low-
down good-for-nothing!" The epithets followed one another in crescendo, the voice that uttered them breaking
several times from strain. "You want to hit my boy, do
you? You ugly little brat you, don't you dare to hit the
poor helpless child on its mouth. What's that? Huh? If I
wanted to soil my hands on you, I'd——"

At that moment the door to the living room was opened,
and the rest of the sentence remained unspoken on the
frightened woman's tongue. She was livid with passion, her
lips twitched evilly. Her right hand raised in the air sank
and grasped the saucepan with milk in it. She tried to pour
some into the baby's bottle, but desisted as the larger part of
the milk flowed down the outside of the bottle on to the
table. She clutched at various objects without being able to
hold them any length of time. Finally she recovered herself
sufficiently to address her husband with violence. What did
he mean by coming home at this unusual hour? Was he
thinking of spying on her? That would be too much. This
last was directly followed by the asseveration that she had
a clear conscience and need not lower her eyes before any
one.

Thiel scarcely heard what she said. He gave a hasty look
at Toby, who was crying aloud, and for a few moments he
had to restrain forcibly a something dreadful rising within
him. Then the old phlegm spread over his taut features, and
at the same time a furtive, lustful light came into his eyes.
His glance played over his wife's heavy limbs while she,
with averted face, bustled about still making an effort to
be composed. Her full, half-bared breasts swelled with excitement and threatened to burst her corset. Her drawn-up
skirts accentuated the width of her broad hips. A force
seemed to emanate from the woman, indomitable, inesca-

pable. Thiel felt himself powerless to cope with it. Tightly, like a cobweb, yet firmly as a mesh of steel, it laid itself around him, chaining him down, robbing him of his strength. In this condition he was incapable of saying a word to her, much less a harsh word.

Thus it was that Tobias, bathed in tears, cowering in a corner, saw his father go over to the oven bench without looking round at him, pick up the forgotten sandwich, hold it out to Lena by way of the only explanation, give a short, distraught nod of his head in good-by, and disappear.

III

Thiel made all possible haste back to his solitary post in the woods. Even so he was a quarter of an hour late. The assistant who relieved him, a consumptive, the victim of the unavoidably rapid changes in temperature to which the work subjected one, was waiting prepared to leave on the sanded little platform of the hut, on which the number, black on white, gleamed from a distance between the tree trunks.

The two men shook hands, exchanged a few brief reports, and parted, the one disappearing within the hut, the other taking the continuation of the road by which Thiel had come. His convulsive cough sounded further and further away among the trees, until finally the one human sound in the solitude fell silent.

Thiel as always, after his fashion, set about preparing the small square room for the night. He worked mechanically, his mind occupied with the impression of the past hour.

First he laid his supper on the narrow, brown-painted table beside one of the windows like slits through which the stretch of track could be conveniently viewed. Next he kindled a fire in the small, rusty stove and placed a pot of cold water on top. After that he straightened out his utensils, a shovel, a spade, a wrench and a few other things, and then cleaned his lantern and filled it with fresh oil.

Scarcely were his arrangements completed when the signal rang shrilly, three times, and three times again, to announce that a train from the direction of Breslau was pulling out of the near station. Thiel showed no hurry, allowing a few minutes to pass before emerging from the hut with flag and cartridge case in his hand. And it was with a lazy, dragging shuffle that he walked along the narrow strip of sand to the crossing, about sixty feet away. Though there was scarcely any traffic along the road at that point, still he conscientiously let down and raised the gates before and after the passage of each train.

This operation now concluded, he leaned idly on one of the black-and-white barred anchor-posts.

The tracks cut in a straight line right and left into the green forest stretching beyond the reach of the eye. On each side the mass of needles stood apart to leave, as it were, an avenue free for the reddish-brown graveled embankment. The black tracks running parallel looked like the strands of a huge iron net drawn together to a point on the horizon in the extreme south and north.

The wind had risen, it drove light waves of mist along the edge of the forest into the distance. A humming came from the telegraph poles alongside the tracks. On the wires that stretched from pole to pole like the sustaining cords spun by a huge spider perched swarms of chirping birds. A woodpecker flew with a laugh over Thiel's head. The man did not so much as look up.

The sun hanging from under the edge of vast masses of clouds and about to sink into the dark-green sea of treetops poured streams of purple over the forest. The pillared arcades of the pine trunks on the yon side of the embankment took fire as from within and glowed like metal. The tracks, too, began to glow, turning into the semblance of fiery snakes. They were the first to pale. The glow, leaving the ground, slowly ascended upward, resigning first the bodies of the trees, then the lower tops to the cold light of dissolution. For a while a reddish sheen lingered on the extreme crowns.

Silently and solemnly was the exalted drama enacted.

The flagman still stood at the gates motionless. At length he made a step forward. A dark point on the horizon where the tracks joined, became more than a point. Increasing from second to second it yet seemed to stand still. Then of a sudden it acquired movement, and drew nearer. A vibrating and humming went through the tracks, a rhythmic clang, a muted thunder. It grew louder and louder until at length it sounded not unlike the hoof beats of a storming cavalry regiment. From a distance the air pulsated intermittently with a panting and a blustering. Then suddenly the serenity of the forest snapped. A mad uproar filled the welkin, the tracks curved, the earth shook—a blast of air, a cloud of dust and steam and smoke—and the snorting monster had gone by.

The noises waned as they had waxed. The exhalations thinned away. Shrunken to a point again the train vanished in the distance, and the old solemn hush again settled upon this corner of the forest.

"Minna," whispered the flagman, as if coming out of a dream.

He returned to the hut, where he brewed himself some weak coffee, then sat down, sipping from time to time and all the while staring at a dirty piece of newspaper that he had picked up on his round.

Gradually a curious unrest came upon him. Attributing it to the heat from the stove, he tore off his coat and waistcoat. That proving to be of no help, he got up, took a spade from a corner, and went out to the lot that the inspector had presented to him.

It was a narrow strip of soil, overgrown with weeds. The blossoms on the two fruit trees were like snowy white foam. Thiel calmed down, a quiet content possessed him.

To work now.

The spade cut into the earth with a crunch. The wet clods flew and crumbled as they fell.

For a long while he dug uninterruptedly. Then he paused and said to himself audibly, shaking his head gravely:

"No, no, it won't do. No, it won't do."

The thought had suddenly struck him that Lena would be coming there often to look after the lot, and his accustomed life would be seriously disturbed. At one blow pleasure in the possession of the bit of ground turned into distaste. Hastily, as if he had been about to do wrong, he ripped the spade out of the earth and carried it back to the hut.

Again he sank into gloomy reflections. Almost without knowing why, he could not endure the prospect of Lena's presence for whole days at a stretch while he was on duty. Much as he might try he could not reconcile himself to the idea. It seemed to him he had something valuable to defend, against some one who was attempting to violate his holiest sanctuary. Involuntarily his muscles tautened in a slight cramp, and a short, defiant laugh escaped him.

The sound of his own laughter was alarming. He looked about and lost the thread of his thoughts. Finding it again he went back to the same dismal broodings.

Then suddenly a heavy black curtain was torn apart, his eyes so long befogged had now a clear view. He had the sensation of awakening from a deathlike sleep that had lasted two years. With an incredulous shake of the head he contemplated all the awful things he must have been guilty of in that condition. The long-suffering of his child, which the impressions of the earlier afternoon should only have confirmed, now were clearly revealed to his soul. Pity and penitence overcame him, and also great shame, that all this long while he had lived in disgraceful resignation, never taking the dear, helpless child's part, not even finding the strength to admit how much the child suffered.

From the self-tormenting contemplation of his sins of omission a great tiredness came over him. He fell asleep, bent over the table with his forehead resting on his hand.

For a long while he lay like that, and several times uttered the name Minna in a choked voice.

A rushing and roaring filled his ears, as of great masses of water. He tore his eyes open and looked about. Darkness enveloped him. His limbs gave way, the sweat of terror oozed from every pore, his pulse beat irregularly, his face was wet with tears.

He wanted to look toward the door, but in the inky darkness did not know which way to turn. He rose reeling. And still terror possessed him. The woods outside boomed like the ocean, the wind drove rain and sleet against the panes. Thiel groped about helplessly. For a moment he felt himself to be drowning. Then suddenly there was a dazzling bluish flare, as of drops of supernatural light falling down into the earth's atmosphere to be instantly extinguished by it.

The moment sufficed to restore the flagman to reason. He fumbled for his lantern and found it. At the same instant the thunder awoke on the farthest edge of the heavens over Brandenburg. At first a dull, restrained rumble, it rolled nearer in surging metallic waves, until overhead it discharged itself in great peals, menacing roars that shook the earth to its foundations.

The window panes clattered. Thiel lighted the lantern, and his first glance after he regained self-control was at the clock. In a bare five minutes the express was due. Thinking he had failed to hear the signal, he made for the crossing as quickly as the dark and the storm permitted. Just as he was letting down the gates the signal rang—the sound was scattered by the wind in all directions.

The pine-trees bent over, their branches scraped against each other with uncanny creakings and squeakings. For a few moments the moon was visible, a pale yellow chalice amid the torn clouds. By its light could be seen the wind's mauling of the black treetops. The foliage of the birches along the embankment waved and fluttered like ghostly horses' tails. Beneath them lay the rails gleaming wet, absorbing the pale moonlight in spots here and there.

Thiel tore the cap from his head. The rain soothed him. It ran down his face mingled with tears.

His brain was in a ferment with confused recollections of his dream. Tobias seemed to be undergoing maltreatment, and such horrible maltreatment that the mere thought of it stopped his heart. Another vision was clearer, of his dead wife. She had come from somewhere along the railroad tracks. She had looked very ill and was wearing rags for clothes. Without looking round she passed the hut, and then —here his memory became vague—she had great difficulty somehow in proceeding, she even collapsed several times.

Thiel pondered. And then he knew that she was in flight. No doubt of it. Else why those anxious backward glances as she dragged herself forward with her legs giving way under her? Oh, those awful looks of hers!

But there was something that she was carrying, wrapped in cloths, something limp, bloody, pale. And the way she looked down on it reminded him of a past scene.

A dying woman who kept her gaze fixed on her new-born babe with an expression of the deepest pain, intolerable torture. It was an expression he could no more forget than that he had a father and a mother.

Where had she gone? He did not know. But one thing was clear in his soul: she had withdrawn from him, disregarded him, dragged herself further and further away into the dark, stormy night. "Minna, Minna," he had cried, and the sound of his own cry awakened him.

Two round red lights like the staring eyes of a huge monster penetrated the dark. A bloody sheen glided in advance, transforming the drops of rain in its course into drops of blood. A veritable rain of blood seemed to descend from heaven.

Horror fell upon Thiel, mounting and mounting as the train drew nearer. Dream and reality fused into one. He still saw the woman wandering down the tracks. His hand wavered toward the cartridge case, as if to stop the speeding train. Fortunately it was too late. Lights flared before his eyes, the train had rushed past.

The remainder of the night there was little peace for Thiel. He felt a great urgency to be at home, a great longing to see little Toby, from whom, it seemed to him, he had been separated for years. Several times, in his growing anxiety over the child's condition he was tempted to quit duty.

To shorten the hours until his release he determined as soon as day dawned to walk his beat. So, with a cane in one hand and a large iron wrench in the other, he went out into the dirty-gray twilight and stepped along on the spine of a rail, halting every now and then to tighten a bolt with the wrench or to hammer at one of the fish-plates that held the rails together.

The wind and rain had stopped, fragments of a pale blue sky became visible between rifts in the banked clouds. The monotonous tap-tap of his soles on the hard metal and the sleepy drip-drop from the wet trees gradually calmed Thiel.

At six o'clock he was relieved. Without delay he started home.

It was a glorious Sunday morning. The clouds had broken and drifted beyond the horizon. The sun, gleaming like a great blood-red gem, poured veritable masses of light upon the forest. Through the network of the branches the beams shot in sharp straight lines casting a glow upon islets of lacy ferns and here and there turning silvery gray patches on the ground into bits of coral. The tops of the trees, the trunks, the grass shed fire like dew. The world seemed to lie under a deluge of light. And the freshness of the air penetrated to the very core of one's being.

Even in Thiel's brain the fantasies of the night could not but grow pale. And when he entered the room where little Toby was lying in bed with the sun shining on him and more color in his cheeks than usual, they disappeared completely.

To be sure, in the course of the day Lena thought she

noticed something odd about him. At church instead of looking in the book he observed her sidewise, and in the middle of the day, when Toby was supposed as usual to carry the baby out on the street, he took it from the boy's arms and laid it in her lap. Otherwise there was nothing conspicuously different about him.

Having no chance to take a nap and as he was to do day duty that week, he went to bed early, at nine o'clock. Exactly as he was about to fall asleep, his wife told him that she intended to accompany him the next morning to dig the lot and plant potatoes.

Thiel winced. He awoke completely, but kept his eyes shut.

Lena went on. If the potatoes were to amount to anything, she said, it was high time to do the planting. And she would have to take the children along because it would probably occupy her the entire day.

Thiel muttered a few unintelligible words, to which she paid no attention. She had turned her back and by the light of a tallow candle was occupied with unfastening her corset and letting down her skirts. Suddenly, without herself knowing why, she turned round and beheld her husband's ashen face distorted by a play of passions. He had raised himself partly, supporting himself by his hands on the edge of the bed, his burning eyes fastened upon her.

"Thiel!" cried the woman, half in anger, half in fear.

Like a somnambulist who hears his name called, Thiel came out of his daze. He stammered something, threw his head back on the pillow, and pulled the quilt over his ears.

Lena was the first to get up the next morning. She went about noiselessly, making the necessary preparations for the excursion. The baby was put into the perambulator, then Tobias was awakened and dressed. He smiled when he was told where he was going.

When everything was ready and even the coffee was made and set on the table, Thiel awoke. His first sensation on seeing the arrangements was of displeasure. He wanted to

protest, but the proper opening refused to frame itself.
Besides, what arguments could he advance that would weigh
with Lena? And there was his child's little face beaming
with joy, growing happier and happier each instant, until
Thiel, from the sight of his delight in the approaching excursion, could not think of opposing it.

Nevertheless, on the way through the woods, as he pushed
the baby-carriage with difficulty through the deep soil, Thiel
was not free from anxiety.

Tobias gathered flowers and laid them in the carriage. He
was happier than almost any time his father had seen him.
In his little brown plush cap he hopped about among the
ferns and tried, helplessly to be sure, to catch the glassy-
winged dragon flies that darted above them.

As soon as they reached the spot, Lena made a survey.
She threw the sack of seed potatoes on the grassy edge of a
small grove of birches, kneeled down, and let the darkish
soil run between her fingers.

Thiel watched her eagerly.

"Well," he said, "how is it?"

"Every bit as good as the corner on the Spree."

A burden fell from the flagman. He contentedly scratched
the stubble on his face. He had feared she would be dissatisfied.

After hastily devouring a thick slice of bread the woman
tossed aside head cloth and jacket, and began to spade up the
earth with the speed and endurance of a machine. At regular
intervals she straightened up and took several deep breaths.
But the pauses were never for long, except when she had to
suckle the baby, which she did quickly, with panting, per-
spiring breasts.

After a while the flagman called to her from the platform
in front of the hut:

"I must inspect the beat. I'm taking Tobias with me."

"What!" she screamed back. "Nonsense! Who'll stay
with the baby? You'll come here," she shouted still louder.

But the flagman as if not hearing walked off with Toby.

For a moment she considered whether she should not run after the two, then desisted because of the loss of time.

Thiel walked down the tracks with his son. The boy was quite excited, everything was so new and strange. Those narrow black rails warmed by the sun—he could not comprehend what they could be meant for. And he kept up an incessant stream of funny questions. What struck him as strangest of all was the resonance of the telegraph poles.

Thiel knew the sound of each pole on his beat so well that with closed eyes he could tell at exactly what spot he stood. And now he stopped several times, holding Tobias by the hand, to listen to the wonderful tones that came from the wood like sonorous chorals from inside a church. The pole at the extreme south end made a particularly full, beautiful sound. It was a mingling of tones that seemed to come without pausing for breath.

Tobias ran round the weathered post to see if he could not through some hole discover the originators of the lovely music. His father listening sank into a devout mood, as in church. He distinguished a voice that reminded him of his dead wife, and fancied it was a choir of blessed spirits, her voice mingling with the others. A deep emotion, a great yearning brought the tears to his eyes.

Tobias asked to be allowed to gather the flowers in the field alongside the tracks. Thiel as always let the child have his way.

Fragments of the blue sky seemed to have dropped on to the meadow, so thickly was it strewn with small, blue blossoms. Like colored pennants the butterflies fluttered and floated among the shining white trunks of the birches. The delicate green foliage gave forth a soft rustle.

Tobias plucked flowers. His father watched him meditatively. Occasionally the flagman raised his eyes and searched between the leaves for a glimpse of the sky, which held the golden sunlight like a huge, spotless bowl.

"Father," said the child, pointing to a brown squirrel

which with small scratching sounds was darting up a solitary pine-tree, "father, is that the good Lord?"

"Silly boy," was all that Thiel could find to reply as bits of loosened bark fell from the trunk of the tree to his feet.

Lena was still digging when Thiel and Tobias returned. She had already spaded up half the plot!

The trains passed at intervals. Each time they rushed by Tobias watched with mouth agape. Even his stepmother was amused by the funny faces he made.

The midday meal, consisting of potatoes and a remnant of roast pork, was consumed inside the hut. Lena was in good spirits. Even Thiel seemed ready to resign himself to the inevitable with good grace. While they ate, he entertained his wife by telling her various things connected with his work. Could she, for instance, imagine that there were forty-six screws in one rail, and more like that.

By mealtime the spading had been done, and in the afternoon Lena was going to sow the potatoes. This time, insisting that Tobias must look after the baby, she took him along.

"Watch out!" Thiel called after her, suddenly gripped by concern. "Watch out that he doesn't go too close to the tracks."

A shrug of Lena's shoulders was her only answer.

The signal rang for the Silesian express. Scarcely had Thiel taken his place in readiness at the gates when the approaching rumble became audible. Within a fraction of a minute he could see the train. On it came, the black funnel spitting steam in countless puffs, one chasing upward after the other. There! One—two—three milk-white geysers gushing up straight as candles—the engine whistling. Three times in succession, short, shrill, alarming.

"They're putting on the brakes," Thiel said to himself. "I wonder why."

He stepped out beyond the gates to look down the tracks.

mechanically pulling the red flag from its case and holding it straight in front of him.

Good heavens! Had he been blind? God, O God, what was that? There—between the rails.

"Stop!" he screamed with every atom of breath in his lungs.

Too late. A dark mass had gone down under the train and was being tossed between the wheels like a rubber ball.

Only a few seconds more and with a grating and squeaking of the brakes, the train came to a standstill.

Instantly the lonely stretch became a scene of animation. The conductor and brakeman ran along the gravel path beside the tracks back to the rear end. From every window curious faces peered. And then the crowd that had gathered in the rear formed into a cluster, and moved forward.

Thiel panted. He had to hold on to something not to sink to the ground like a slaughtered steer.

How's that? Were they actually waving to him?

"No!"

A scream came from the spot where the accident had occurred, followed by a howling as from an animal. Who was that? Lena? It was not her voice, yet—

A man came hurrying down the tracks.

"Flagman!"

"What's the matter?"

"An accident."

The messenger shrank before the strange expression in the flagman's eyes. His cap hung on the side of his head, his red hair stood straight up.

"He's still alive. Maybe something can be done."

A rattle in the flagman's throat was the only answer.

"Come quickly—quickly."

With a tremendous effort Thiel pulled himself together. His slack muscles tautened, he drew himself to his full height, his face was empty and dead.

He followed the man at a run, oblivious of the pale, frightened faces at the windows. A young woman looked out, a traveling salesman with a fez on his head, a young couple apparently on their honeymoon. What were they to him? The contents of those rattling, thumping boxes on wheels had never concerned him. His ears were filled with Lena's lamentations.

Yellow dots swam before his eyes, countless yellow dots like fireflies. He shrank back, he stood still. From out of the dance of fireflies it came toward him, pale, limp, bloody —a forehead beaten black and blue, blue lips with dark blood trickling from them. Tobias!

Thiel said nothing. His face went a dirty white. He grinned as if out of his senses. At length he bent over, he felt the limp, dead limbs heavy in his arms. The red flag went round them.

He started to leave.

Where?

"To the railroad doctor, to the railroad doctor, came from all sides.

"We'll take him," called the baggage-master, and turned to prepare a couch of coats and books in his car. "Well?"

Thiel made no move to let go of the boy. They urged him In vain. The baggage-master had a stretcher handed out from the car and ordered a man to remain with the father. Time was precious. The conductor's whistle shrilled. Coins rained from the windows.

Lena raved like a madwoman. "The poor woman," they said in the coaches, "the poor, poor mother."

The conductor whistled several times, the engine blew a signal, sent white clouds hissing up from its cylinders, and stretched its sinews of iron. In a few seconds, the mail express, with floating flags of smoke, was dashing with redoubled speed through the forest.

The flagman, whose mood had altered, laid the half-dead child on the stretcher.

There he lay with his racked tiny body. Every now and then a long wheeze raised the bony chest, which was visible under the tattered shirt. The little arms and legs, broken not only at the joints, assumed the most unnatural positions. The heel of one small foot was twisted to the front, the arms hung over the sides of the stretcher.

Lena kept up a continuous whimper. Every trace of her former insolence had disappeared. Over and over again she repeated a story to exonerate herself.

Thiel seemed not to notice her. With an expression of awful anxiety he kept his eyes riveted on the child.

A hush had fallen, a deadly hush. The tracks rested hot and black on the glaring gravel. The noon had stifled the wind, and the forest stood motionless, as if carved in stone.

In muffled voices the two men took counsel. The quickest way to reach Friedrichshagen would be to go back to the neighboring station in the direction of Breslau, because the next train, a fast commutation, did not stop at the station that was nearer to Friedrichshagen.

Thiel seemed to consider if he should go along. At the time there was no one there who understood the duties of the position, so with a mute motion of his head he indicated to his wife that she should take hold of the stretcher. She did not dare to refuse though she was concerned about having to leave the baby behind.

Thiel accompanied the cortège of two to the end of his beat, then stood still and looked after them long. Suddenly he clapped his hand to his forehead with a blow that resounded afar. It might wake him up, he thought. Because this was a dream like the one he had had yesterday. No use. Reeling rather than walking he reached his hut. There he fell face downward on the floor. His cap flew into a corner, his carefully kept watch fell from his pocket, the case sprang open, the glass broke. An iron fist seemed to be clamped on his neck, so tight that he could not move no matter how he moaned and groaned and tried to free himself. His forehead was cold, his throat parched.

The ringing of the signal roused him. Under the influence of those three repeated sounds the attack abated. Thiel could rise and do his duty. To be sure, his feet were heavy as lead, and the stretch of rails circled about him like the spokes of an enormous wheel with his head for its axis. But at least he could stand up a while.

The commutation train approached. Tobias must be in it. The nearer it drew the more the pictures before Thiel's eyes blurred. Finally all he saw was the mutilated boy with the bloody mouth. Then darkness fell.

After a while he awoke from the swoon. He found himself lying in the hot sun close to the gates. He rose, shook the sand from his clothes and spat it from his mouth. His head cleared a bit, he could think more quietly.

In the hut he immediately picked his watch up from the floor and laid it on the table. It was still going. For two hours he counted the seconds, then the minutes, while representing to himself what was happening to Tobias. Now Lena was arriving with him, now she stood in front of the doctor. The doctor observed the boy and felt him all over, and shook his head.

"Bad, very bad—but perhaps—who can tell?"

He made a more thorough examination.

"No," he then said, "no, it's all over."

"All over, all over," groaned the flagman. But then he drew himself up, raised his unconsciously clenched fist, rolled his eyes to the ceiling, and shouted as if the narrow little room must burst with the sound of his voice. "He must live, he must. I tell you, he must live."

He flung open the door of the hut—the red glow of evening fell through—and ran rather than walked to the gates. Here he stood still seemingly bewildered. Then suddenly spreading his arms he went to the middle of the road-bed, as if to stop something that was coming from the same direction as the commutation. His wide-open eyes made the impression of blindness. While stepping backward to make way for something, a stream of half-intelligible words came from between his gritted teeth.

"Listen. Don't go. Listen, listen. Don't go. Stay here. Give him back to me. He's beaten black and blue. Yes, yes.

All right. I'll beat her black and blue, too. Do you hear? Stay. Give him back to me."

Something seemed to move past him, because he turned and made as if to follow.

"Minna, Minna,"—his voice was weepy like a small child's—"Minna, listen. Give him back to me. I will—" He groped in the air as if to catch and hold some one fast. "My little wife—yes, yes—and I'll—and I'll beat her—so she's black and blue, too—I'll beat her, too—with the hatchet— you see?—with the kitchen hatchet—I'll beat her with the kitchen hatchet. And that'll be the end of her. And then— yes, yes—with the hatchet—yes, with the kitchen hatchet— black blood."

Foam gathered on his lips, his glassy eyeballs rolled incessantly.

A gentle breath of the evening blew steadily over the forest, a rosy cloud mass hung in the western sky.

He had followed the invisible something about a hundred paces when he stood still, apparently having lost courage. With fearful dread in his eyes, he stretched out his arms, pleading, adjuring. He strained his eyes, shaded them with his hand, as if to discern the inessential being in the far distance. Finally his head sank, and the tense expression of his face changed into apathy. He turned and dragged himself the way he had come.

The sunlight laid its final glow over the forest, then was extinguished. The trunks of the pines rose among the tops like pale, decayed bones, and the tops weighed upon them like grayish black layers of mold. The hammering of a woodpecker penetrated the silence. Up above one last dilatory pink cloud traversed the steely blue of the sky. The breath of the wind turned dankly cold as if blowing from a cellar.

The flagman shivered. Everything was new and strange. He did not know what he was walking on, or what was about him. A squirrel hopped along the road-bed. Thiel pondered. He had to think of the Lord. But why? "The Lord is hop-

ping along the tracks, the Lord is hopping along the tracks."
He said it several times as if to get at something associated
with it. He interrupted himself. A ray of illumination fell
upon his brain. "Good heavens! That's madness." He forgot everything else and turned upon this new enemy. He
tried to order his thoughts. In vain. They'd come and go and
ramble away and shoot off at a tangent. He caught himself
in the absurdest fancies, and shuddered at the consciousness
of his impotence.

The sound of a child crying came from the birch grove
near by. It was the signal for madness. Almost against his
will he had to hurry to the spot where the baby, whom everybody had neglected, was crying and kicking on the un-
blanketed floor of its carriage.

What did he mean to do? What had driven him there?
The questions were submerged in a whirling eddy of
thoughts and emotions.

"The Lord is hopping along the tracks." Now he knew.
Tobias—she had murdered him—Lena—the child had been
entrusted to her care. "Stepmother! Beast of a mother!" he
hissed between clenched teeth. "And her brat lives."

A red mist enveloped his senses. Two baby eyes penetrated through it. He felt something soft, fleshy between his
fingers. He heard gurgling, whistling sounds, mingled with
hoarse cries that came from he did not know whom.

Then something fell upon his brain like hot drops of seal-
ing wax, and his spirit was cleared as from a cataleptic
trance. Aroused to consciousness, he caught the quiver in
the air that was the final reverberation of the signal, and in
a trice he realized what he had been about to do. His hand
relaxed its grip on the throat, under which the infant had
writhed and squirmed. It gasped for breath, then began to
cough and bawl.

"It's alive. Thank the Lord, it's alive."

He let it lie and hastened to the crossing. Dark clouds of
smoke rolled in the distance, the wind drove them to the
ground. He distinguished the panting of an engine that

sounded like the intermittent, tortured breathing of a giant.

The stretch was shrouded in a cold twilight. But after a while the clouds of smoke parted, and Thiel recognized the train as being the freight that was returning with open empty cars and bringing home the men who had been working on the road-bed during the day. It had ample running time to stop at each station to drop or pick up the men.

Quite a distance from Thiel's hut the brakes began to be put on, and a loud clanking and clanging and rattling and screeching tore the silence before the train came to a standstill with a single shrill, long-drawn whistle.

About fifty men and women were in the different cars. Nearly all of them stood, some of the men with bared heads. There was a mystifying air of solemnity about them. When they caught sight of the flagman, a whispering began among them, and the old men drew their pipes from between their yellow teeth and held them respectfully in their hands. Here and there a woman would turn to blow her nose.

The conductor descended and advanced toward Thiel. The workmen saw him solemnly shake the flagman's hand, and then saw Thiel with slow steps almost military in their stiffness go back to the rear. None of them dared to address him, though they all knew him.

From the rear wagon they were lifting little Toby.

He was dead.

Lena followed. Her face was a bluish white, brown rings underlined her eyes.

Thiel did not so much as cast a glance at her. She, however, was shocked at sight of her husband. His cheeks were hollow, his eyelashes and beard were plastered, his hair, it seemed to her, was gone grayer. Traces of dried tears all over his face. And an unsteady light in his eyes that made her shudder.

The stretcher had been brought back for transporting the body home.

For a while there was gruesome silence. Thiel lost himself in black depths of awful thoughts. Darkness deepened.

A herd of deer started to cross the embankment. The stag stood still between the rails and turned his agile neck curiously. The engine whistled. He and the rest of the herd disappeared in a flash.

At the moment that the train was about to start Thiel collapsed. The train stood still, and counsel was held as to what had now best be done. Since every effort they made to bring the flagman back to his senses, proved futile, they decided to let the child's body lie in the hut temporarily, and use the stretcher for conveying the flagman instead. Two men carried the stretcher, Lena followed, pushing the baby carriage, sobbing the whole way, the tears running down her cheeks.

The great purplish ball of the moon shone low between the trunks of the pine-trees. As it rose it paled and diminished in size until finally it hung high in the heavens like a swinging lamp, and cast a pale sheen over the forest, through every chink and cranny of the foliage, painting the faces of the processionists a livid white.

Cautiously but sturdily they made their way through the close second growth, then past broad nurseries with the larger trees scattered among the younger ones. Here the pale light seemed to have collected itself in great dark bowls.

Occasionally a rattle came from the unconscious man's throat, and occasionally he raved. Several times he clenched his fists and tried to raise himself, his eyes all the time remaining closed. Getting him across the Spree was difficult, and a return trip had to be made to fetch Lena and the baby.

As they ascended the slight eminence on which the hamlet was situated, they met a few of the inhabitants, who forthwith spread the news of the misfortune. The whole colony came running.

Among her gossips Lena broke into fresh lamentations.

Thiel was with difficulty carried up the narrow stairway of his home and put to bed. And the men returned immediately to bring little Toby's body back.

Some of the old, experienced people advised cold

compresses. Lena carried out their prescription eagerly, properly, dropping cloths into icy cold spring water and renewing them as soon as the unconscious man's burning forehead had heated them. Anxiously she observed his breathing. It seemed to come more regularly and to continue to improve each minute.

However, the day's excitement had told upon her, and she decided to try to get a little sleep. No use! Whether she held her eyes open or shut, she kept seeing the events of the past hours. The baby slept. Contrary to her wont, she had not paid much attention to it. Altogether she had turned into a different person. Not a trace of her former arrogance. The sick man with the colorless face shining with sweat dominated her even in sleep.

A cloud passed, obscuring the moon and throwing the room into complete darkness. Lena heard nothing but her husband's heavy though regular breathing. She felt creepy in the dark and considered whether she should not rise and kindle a light. But as she attempted to get up, a leaden weight on her limbs pulled her back, her lids drooped, she fell asleep.

Some time later the men returning with the boy's body found the front door wide open. Surprised at this, they mounted and found the upstairs door also open. They called the woman by her name. No answer. They struck a match. The flare of it revealed awful havoc.

"Murder, murder!"

Lena lay in her blood, her face unrecognizable, her skull broken open.

"He murdered his wife, he murdered his wife!"

They ran about witless. Neighbors came. One bumped against the cradle.

"Good heavens!" He shrank back, ashen pale, his eyes fixed in a horrified stare. The baby lay with its throat cut.

The flagman had disappeared. The search made for him that night proved fruitless. The next morning, however, the man who replaced him found him on the tracks at the spot where little Toby had been run over, holding the shaggy brown cap in his arm and caressing it as if it were a living thing.

The block signaler, apprised of his discovery, telegraphed for help. Several men tried with kindly inducements to lure Thiel from the tracks. He was not to be budged. The express then due had to be stopped, and it was only by the united efforts of the entire crew and the use of force that the man, who had begun to rave fearfully, could be removed from the railroad. They had to bind him hands and feet, and the policeman summoned to the spot guarded his transportation the whole way to Berlin, where he was examined in the jail and the next day was sent to a free psychopathic ward. He never let go of the shaggy brown cap. He watched over it with jealous tenderness.

LUKARDIS *

By Jacob Wassermann

In the course of the long drawn out revolution which afflicted the Russian Empire in the last decade but one, a brawl took place in the streets of Moscow. The immediate cause of this brawl was the exile to Siberia of thirty-five students of both sexes, who had been celebrating with excessive exuberance the jubilee of a professor whom they revered and who was the object of police suspicion. A contributing cause was the fact that the preparation for this celebration had been made in a series of secret meetings. Certain of the most highly respected families of Moscow were affected by this harsh measure, and the sorrow and indignation of so many hitherto peaceful citizens created an atmosphere more fraught with danger than if it had resulted merely from the instigation of political agitators.

Among the students deported with such cruel haste was a girl named Anna Pavlovna Nadinsky. She had a brother living in Moscow, Eugene—or, as the Russians say, Evgen Pavlovitch—who was an officer in a regiment of dragoons. Eugene was a proud, handsome young man, twenty-three years old, and apparently assured of a brilliant future. He was exceedingly fond of his sister, who had been his close friend and confidante throughout his life. Seeing her now lost to herself and to the world, a prey to the want and humiliation which the years in Siberia would bring, his sorrow was so great, his sense of justice was so deeply outraged, that the very foundation of his existence crumbled, and he determined to protest against the institution in whose

* Translated by Lewis Galantière. Copyright, 1927, by Boni and Liveright, Inc.

services he had, until now, been so eager. What followed
seemed to happen of its own accord, and astonished him as
much as anybody else. A few days after the arbitrary action
of the police, his regiment was ordered out to quell a revolt
in the streets. Of a sudden he left the column at the head of
which he was riding, jumped down from his horse, and ran
towards a barricade which had been hastily erected out of
paving-blocks, wheelbarrows, baskets, and articles of furniture. As he ran, he gestured frantically to its defenders in a
way they could not misunderstand, particularly since deser-
tions from the army to their ranks, even in the midst of
battle, were not uncommon. But scarcely had Nadinsky
reached the top of the barricade from whose shelter he
hoped to fight against the real enemies of his country, when
he was struck by two bullets from the guns trained on him
by his dragoons. Hands stretched towards him, eyes filled
with enthusiasm welcomed him; he seemed to hear a chant
of thanksgiving which stilled his last doubts. Even his name
was called aloud, as if some of these revolutionists knew
him. Despite his weakness, the joy in their voices seemed to
him sufficient reward. He turned, drew his revolver, fired
upon the assailants, his former comrades, then plunged forward on his face, the fingers of one hand caught in a cane
chair wedged into the barricade.

He was seized immediately by two young men who bore
his unconscious form away and laid him on the stone stoop
of a house near by. Hastily, they ripped open his coat and
shirt, bound up his wound, which was bleeding freely, and
looked about in search of help. A peddler's cart stood at the
curb. Its owner had vanished, and its lean little horse seemed
frozen in the shafts. Quickly they laid the officer on a bed of
vegetables and greens, and covered him with leaves. One of
them returned to the barricade while the other led the cart
down the street, through numerous alleys, and finally into an
open square where stood the University hospital. He went
on into the courtyard and called an interne, who gave orders
at once to place Nadinsky in one of the wards. His wound

was severe. One of the bullets had merely grazed his throat, but the other was lodged in his lung and had to be removed by an operation. On the third day, Nadinsky awoke out of a feverish unconsciousness. It was some time before he knew where he was and what had befallen him.

Meanwhile, all Moscow had been talking of the young officer's desertion, and the police, through one of its numerous spies, had discovered his hiding-place. An Ispravnik turned up at the hospital to arrest the fatally wounded man. Although the critical condition of the patient was clear even to the policeman's eye, he flourished his written order and insisted upon taking Nadinsky away. An interne was still arguing with him when the surgeon stepped forward, glanced at Nadinsky's apathetic countenance, was touched by his youth, and said: "If he is removed now he will die within fifteen minutes. The police will do better to wait." The Ispravnik stood irresolute. He was still a novice and not yet hardened. Moreover, in the maze of his multiple orders and commissions, he had lost his head. He thought a while, and then declared himself willing to leave the officer in the hospital until his strength had returned in sufficient measure to permit of removal.

Thus, a few days were gained by Nadinsky. During these days the surgeon's sympathy for him grew greater, and he made efforts to interest others in the fate of his patient. Friends appeared who were willing to help him escape. One morning he was taken into a private room. In the evening, a young man arrived with an orderly's uniform in which Nadinsky was to be conveyed to Sokolnikin, a park in the environs of Moscow. In his weakened condition, there was still a life and death chance of saving him. Nadinsky agreed to accompany the young man, for to remain meant the certainty either of death or of life imprisonment in remotest Siberia. In the dead of night, amid snow and ice (for it was the middle of March), he was taken to Sokolnikin, where he lived in the villa of a scientist who was presumed to be above suspicion by the police. But twenty-four hours had

scarcely passed when messengers appeared from the city
who, after strolling casually and unconcernedly about, entered the villa and announced that the police were again on
Nadinsky's track and were planning to swoop down and
arrest him the following night. No choice remained, therefore, but to seek another refuge. This scientist, who was of
German birth, had living with him his sister, Anastasia
Karlovna, a woman whose courage was as great as her
kindly spirit. She had been living in Moscow for more than
forty years, enjoyed a great many influential and benevolent
friends in high position, and was, besides, greatly loved by
many of the common folk. It was she who kept house for
her brother, nursed the young officer, tended him, and arranged cleverly to conceal his presence in the villa. Her first
concern was to procure for Nadinsky a new disguise. Having attired him as a laborer, she conveyed him, with the aid
of a total stranger who had offered his services, to the house
of a wood-turner in the suburbs. He was able to remain
there only the night, for by morning the wood-turner had
become fearful for himself and his family, and refused to
harbor the fugitive any longer. Nadinsky was dragged in
this way for five days from one house to another, to a coachman's, a widow's, a gardener's, and finally to a laboratory
worker's. Each time, at the end of a few hours these people
realized to whom they were giving asylum. Fear of the
police outweighed considerations of pity and hardened them
against the eloquence of Anastasia, whose zeal never flagged.
She spent her nights with Nadinsky, for he was not in a
condition to be left by himself. He had to be washed,
dressed, and have his bandages changed twice a day; the
irregularity and excitation of his mode of living prevented
his wound from healing rapidly. And now that the laboratory worker, who had been plied with gold and eloquence,
refused any longer to shelter Nadinsky, Anastasia Karlovna
feared that there was nothing more to be done. Those
friends who had stood by her until now could do no more;
the police were on their track and every fresh step led in the

direction of their ruin. Anastasia herself felt that she was
being spied upon and was menaced. She tried for the last
time, by prayer and entreaty, to soften the laboratory
worker: would he not practice Christian indulgence for
only one night more? The life of her brother—for so she
represented Nadinsky—was at stake. But her words served
only to increase the man's distrust of the business, and she
secured merely a respite of three hours. If, at the end of that
period, Nadinsky had not been removed from the house,
the man would go to the police.

It was now three o'clock in the afternoon. By six, therefore, Anastasia would have to find another hiding-place for
her ward. She drifted for a time through the streets, stopping first before one house and then another, but turning
back each time at the door in fear of an unfavorable response, or even of betrayal. At last, in her distress, she fell
back upon the idea of taking Nadinsky to one of those
assignation houses in which rooms are let out to lovers.
In such a place only could she introduce a man who carried
no passport. Given two days of rest and care, he would pull
through, the doctor had told her that morning. Thereafter,
he could get to the frontier by himself.

But to carry out this plan she would need an accomplice,
a creature who could make the love-affair seem plausible,
who was strong, discreet, and intelligent. She thought of all
the young women she knew, but none of them seemed suited
to such an undertaking. Anastasia had no friends among the
revolutionists; moreover, it would be folly to confide in a
person who might be under police surveillance. Nor was it
possible to consider a woman of the lower class, or any
woman to whom one might offer money; it had to be a lady
or a girl of good family.

The exertion of the past few days had wearied her.
Rather more to be seated somewhere than for refreshment,
she went into a little pastry shop and stepped into a twilit
back room. Two women sat at a small table, drinking choco-
late. Anastasia took a seat absent-mindedly, but she saw

presently that the elder of the two women was looking in
her direction and greeting her with a friendly nod. She
recognized the woman as Anna Ivanovna Schmoll, the deaf-
mute wife of a retired general. With her was her daughter
Lukardis, a nineteen-year-old girl of unusual beauty.
Scarcely had Anastasia glanced at Lukardis when she said
to herself : there is the only girl who can do it. Years before
she had been a frequent guest at the Schmolls', when
Lukardis Nikolaievna was a little girl. She had often played
and chatted with the child and remembered her well. She
remembered that, already at the age of thirteen, this child
had impressed her as do only those people who possess a
peculiar quality, a peculiar strength. What sort of quality
or strength that was, she had never been able to fathom,
much as she had reflected upon it. The mother, Anna Ivanovna, was a rather simple-minded person, pious, apathetic,
harmless, conscious in a vague way of her infirmity.

Anastasia took a seat at their table and, having inquired
by look and gesture about the health of the general's wife,
began to speak to Lukardis Nikolaievna in a low tone. The
general's wife looked inquiringly at Anastasia's lips, but,
unable to follow the conversation, she lowered her eyes
modestly and refrained from interrupting their speech by
any sign of curiosity. Anastasia was conscious of the boldness of her design, and anxious about it. She had no time to
lose. It was essential that she speak briefly. In a few sentences she had to tell her story, make an extraordinary
demand, arouse Lukardis's innermost sympathies, and at
the same time move with care and cunning, for one word,
one awkward gesture, could frustrate the whole plan.
Lukardis knew nothing of revolutionary intrigues. She suspected much, but she had no information about these matters. She lived in a sphere of gentle dreaming, with the dolls
of her past and the jewel-cases of her present, with echoes
of the comical gallantries of married men and the careful
protestations of scented, unmarried men. Yet, there was
something in her of the young animal in the forest that

listens to the sound of the distant hunt, the tremendous commotion of pain and blood and death. She was ready for action, but unaware of her expectancy. There were moments when she was seized by a vehement unrest, an unreasoning desire, an impulse to escape from the realm of hypocritical calm in which her life was taking shape. But she was afraid of the world, of people; she trembled at each strange hand that was stretched forth to her. It seemed to her that everything that lay outside her home, even outside her room, was troubled, soiled. She never overheard people in conversation in the street without a shudder; never opened a newspaper without the sense that, side by side with all that was savage and mysterious to her in the outer world, there was something unclean, something that would soil her. Even the books she read, a snatch of verse, a street song, a jest, awakened in her this terrible, unconquerable impression.

Motionless, she listened while Anastasia spoke. There was no lure for her in the story; she felt no girlish impurity or lust for excitement. All that she could read in the stern features of Anastasia Karlovna was a call to duty. She had no decision to make. What there was for her to do was immediately and unalterably clear to her.

Lukardis had been engaged these six weeks past to a Petersburg nobleman, a privy councilor named Alexander Mikhailovitch Kussin. Her parents and their friends felt that as the wife of this rich nobleman an enviable future lay before her; and indeed she herself was happy about it. If anything could make her hesitate, it was the thought of him to whom she felt herself bound by a sisterly affection. But when Anastasia, who divined her preoccupation, suggested that she might be tranquil on this point, she wrinkled her forehead and replied that she did not need this assurance. Her fiancé, she said, would never dream for a moment that she might do anything evil or ugly.

"I take it, then, that you have made up your mind to do it," said Anastasia in a low voice, her gray eyes fixed on the girl.

"I have made up my mind to do it," Lukardis answered in an equally low tone without raising her eyes. "But there is one difficulty—"

"Can there still be a difficulty when one has made up one's mind?" Anastasia interrupted sharply, with a note of fanaticism in her voice.

"But how am I to explain my remaining away from home for two days and nights?" asked Lukardis, crossing the fingers of her white hands.

Anastasia stared, gloomily pondering, at a plate of cakes Lukardis went on in a whisper. "The only thing possible is to disappear quietly, to leave a letter for mother— "

"Yes, yes. A few lines. Anything. And beg them to keep it secret. Say you will explain everything on your return. But you too must be silent, Lukardis Nikolaievna," she added almost menacingly. "You must be as silent as though it had never happened."

Lukardis merely nodded. Her eyes were now wide open and gazing straight in front of her. Anastasia explained down to the last detail how she was to dress and act. After telling her where to come and at what time, she added to their serious conversation—which despite its gravity had lasted but a quarter of an hour—a few jesting remarks, in order that Lukardis might smile and divert any suspicion which might have arisen in the mind of her mother. Then she arose with a lighter heart and went her way.

She returned to Nadinsky and told him what she had planned. He lay on a sofa in the wretched room of the laboratory worker, and pressed her hand. "My life," he said, "is no longer worth such great effort, Anastasia Karlovna. It is a lost life." She retorted that she had hoped for livelier thanks than were contained in these spiritless phrases, and set about changing his dressing. Nadinsky sighed. "What is the use?" he said in a tired voice. "Everything about me is changed, eye, hand, and emotions. I seem to be surrounded by ghosts. I do not seem to mind being cut off from the world. I can see my mother on our estate. As yet, she

suspects nothing. I see her opening a locket and looking at a
picture in it. It is a picture of me. She does not know that
she will never see me again, she has no idea of that, and yet
she sheds tears on the locket. But I have no feelings whatever. The world is to me unreal, because I can no longer
love anything."

To Anastasia, these words were the ravings of a feverish
mind. She shook her head indignantly. After a while, when
it had grown dark, a carriage drove up before the door.
Anastasia had bought some handsome clothes for Nadinsky, had helped him with his toilette, and now she looked at
him critically before once more escorting him downstairs.
In the carriage sat Lukardis Nikolaievna Schmoll, heavily
veiled. Anastasia handed her a package of gauze bandages,
and said to Nadinsky that she would be waiting for him on
the second morning thereafter at a certain hour and at a
particular place in the railway station. Meanwhile, she
added, she would set about procuring him a passport to
foreign countries. She gave an address to the coachman,
waved her hand in farewell, and the carriage drove off.

Lukardis and Nadinsky sat in silence. Their situation
was too unreal, too threatening, too fateful for embarrassment. When the occasional street lamps lit up the interior
of the carriage, Lukardis saw that Nadinsky's eyes were
closed and his face was pallid. He had given her his hand on
first sitting down beside her; that was all. She discovered
that his proximity was not frightening her and that silence
was easy.

The house to which they drove stood in a remote street.
Nadinsky had to summon all his strength to get out of the
carriage. He offered Lukardis his arm, but it was rather she
who supported him than he her. He asked for two rooms,
and was received with great assiduity. Dragging himself
with an effort up the stairs, he strove to preserve the air of
a man of the world engaged in a passing adventure. In accordance with the custom of the house, a servant was placed
at their especial disposal. This person, suffocating in silver-

embroidered livery, had malicious pop eyes, wore an un-
varyingly insipid smile on his thick lips, and was obsequious
in his humility. Lukardis felt her heart contract at his
glance. He set the table and stood listening in a doglike
manner while Nadinsky, exhausted and indifferent, ordered
the dinner, the wines, the champagne. His appraising glance
seemed to insist that they be really what they pretended to
be. Lukardis was rouged and wore a low cut gown. It was
difficult for her to be anything else than herself. She was
forced to put off the childlike innocence which shone ordi-
narily in her face and put on an air of frivolity. She had to
chatter, coquette, laugh, throw her arms about Nadinsky, and
sit from time to time on his knees. She had to sketch passionate, wanton, seductive gestures. All those things that she had
never noticed, never wished to see, never thought about save
with horror, known only through careless words and pictures, the things from which she had hitherto averted her
mind and her eye, she had now to do in order to deceive this
man who came in with plates, bowls, glasses, and bottles,
who chilled the champagne, served the food, and then,
silently, smilingly, spying from under lowered eyelids,
awaited further orders. She had to fit herself into the volup
tuous lights, the multicolored cushions, the mirrored walls,
for this house with its sham and glitter put her mind in a
tumult. Nor was that all. She had to act so as to arouse no
doubt about the reality and naturalness of her behavior.
Everything had to be done casually, cunningly, and trans-
parently, with no overt shudder or haste. She had to eat
what was set before her, to drink the wines placed before
her, and not only the wine in her glass but, when the waiter
was out, in Nadinsky's, too, for he might neither drink nor
leave his glass filled. She was entirely unaccustomed to
drinking, and it filled her with fright and depression to have
to continue in this rôle which she played instinctively and
out of a spirit of self-sacrifice. Whenever the waiter left the
room she got up. The terrific tension that strained the muscles of her face gave way to an expression of bewilderment

and even of frightened recollection, for it seemed to her that many years had elapsed since she had driven away from the home of her parents. Nadinsky gazed at her in pain and astonishment, sought her as behind a mask, pitied her dumbly, accused himself in a gesture,—and then, with an effort, brought back the studied smile to his lips and continued his acting when the fellow returned.

After the table had been cleared away, a maid came in, wearing a little white cap. She was young, but she appeared old. Her face had grown gray from this life in lamplight and in badly aired rooms. She brought water, tended the fire, asked if there was anything else she could do. Her voice was sweet, but her features were stony with hatred of the upper world, hatred of those who came to this house to indulge themselves in contemptible, quickly snatched pleasures. Lukardis's knees trembled whenever her glance fell on the maid. She was ashamed of her feet, her hands, her neck, and her shoulders. At last this trial too ended, and she was able to lock the door. They were alone. A clock in a tower somewhere struck ten, its tones vibrating through the apartment. Nadinsky went into the adjoining room where stood a double bed over which was stretched a blue satin counterpane. Bereft of strength, he fell upon the bed, and it was only after he had rested thus a quarter of an hour that Lukardis could help him undress. The cover drawn half way up, he lay there with his chest bare. This is a human thing, said Lukardis to herself. Suddenly the tears started in her eyes and she thought with a kind of fright of the red-cheeked face of Alexander Mikhailovitch, her fiancé. She bathed Nadinsky's wound and bound it. As in a dream one sees perfumes, so Nadinsky saw her delicate hand. He was incapable of thanking her. He was afraid to catch her eye, afraid that a glance of gratitude might offend her. He wished that she might be able to look upon him as nothing but a body, a thing devoid of feature and of feeling. And while Lukardis, half shocked and half in pity, was thinking

—a human being! he, half blissful and half in fear for her, thought—an unearthly being!

He fell asleep. Lukardis sat motionless in an armchair. She had brought a book in her little bag, but she knew she would be unable to read. She tried to think of her mother, her father, her friends, the last ball, of the opera she had last heard, but she could think of nothing. Everything faded out, everything eluded her. She heard Nadinsky's deep breathing, saw his pale, fine face, wearied by pain,—but he too, he whom she was to tend and guard, seemed out of reach of her thoughts. It was as if miles separated her chair from his bed. She heard tittering on the stairs and shuffling steps in the hall. Voices, women's voices and men's voices, pierced in muffled tones through the walls, from above and from below. Glasses clinked. Then came the sound of a waltz played on a piano with, doubtless, one string missing, for at a certain point there was a hole in the melody, like a gap between two teeth in a smiling mouth. Shrieks arose. The piano was silent. Beyond the wall to the left arose a creaking, and then a sighing note at the sound of which Lukardis's blood curdled in her veins. The smell of perfumes came in from the locked rooms; garments rustled; doors banged open and shut. Every sound called up a picture from which she could not turn away. She trembled, yet, trembling, she had to look. She had never imagined that the world was like this, that this was life. Encounters in the darkness, strange hands clasping one another, forms reeling against suddenly illuminated mirrors, consent given in shameless words, the unknown unveiled, the crypt of mystery emptied, the consecrated soiled, the secret treasures of the imagination cheapened. She covered her face with her hands; the blood rushed to her rouged cheeks and her heart filled with horror.

Nadinsky opened his eyes and moaned. She walked the many miles to his bedside and held forth a glass of water. His forehead was hot. She put a damp cloth over it. At that moment he awoke and began to speak. He spoke in broken sentences of the hospital, the surgeon, Anastasia Karlovna. Whenever he paused, Lukardis interjected a timid word. He said: "To-morrow I shall be strong enough to leave here!" to which she replied: "That is impossible. You are still feverish. Besides, Anastasia Karlovna is not expecting you until the morning after, early, at seven o'clock." These softly spoken words seemed suddenly to show him her soul, her hitherto unclouded youth, her strong clean instincts; but he could not see that she had not stopped trembling. Once more the piano was being played, but this time by a different hand, a rough, riotous, drunken hand. Throughout the performance Nadinsky and Lukardis gazed in torment into each other's eyes. It was past midnight. Out of the silence that fell came a hollow knocking at the street door. Nadinsky half raised himself. His fingers stiffened and his face was full of dark expectancy. Lukardis stood up and listened breathlessly. It was long before the door was opened. Steps sounded on the stair. They gazed in fear at the latched door, waited for the knock that was to decide their terrible fate. Voices reached them from the hall in a hurried exchange of words. Then all grew calm again and their pulses commenced once more to beat regularly. In these three or four minutes they felt themselves strangely united, their strength and their fear were directed against a common enemy. It was as if they had been lifted into the air by a hurricane, propelled against one another breast to breast, and had thrown their arms about each other in order to help avert the crash that threatened. Lukardis forgot herself; Nadinsky forgot himself. He felt only the intensity of her fear, the forfeiture of her happiness, the shame and the misery of her. She, for her part, was thinking courageously of his fate, realizing now for the first time why his life hung in the balance.

Meanwhile sleep had once more overcome the feverish man. But he could not sleep soundly while the glaring electric lights shone upon him. He said nothing about his desire for darkness, out of consideration for Lukardis, but she saw the nervous flicker of his eyelids and guessed what the matter was. She lighted a candle in the adjoining room and switched off the lights. She too was weary. The late hour was like a paralyzing poison, and she sought a place to lie down. There was no bed in this room, merely a sofa, whose plush covering filled her with repugnance. She was repelled also by the chairs and the carpet. She rolled back the carpet from the threshold of Nadinsky's room, spread her fur coat on the floor, and lay down. The candle still glowed, but it seemed to bring nearer to her each sound in the house that had until now been vague—a call, a laugh, a single word. And she heard also the beating of the snow on the windowpane; its mildly crackling noise quieted her. She heard the breathing of Nadinsky, and was reminded of her responsibility. Each breath chained her more closely to his destiny. The things that had once been significant became meaningless to her; what she had done, wanted, and been in the course of her life now seemed childish and frivolous. She gazed back longingly, as from the deck of a ship, to the home that faded into the distance. She was asleep, and yet not asleep. Nadinsky had spoken words of comfort and encouragement to her—that was a dream; his throat had rattled feverishly—that was a fact. In dream she bent over him, nursed him; in fact she was chained to the floor, listening to the Bacchic cry of a woman. In the gray light of dawn she saw a rat running across the carpet. It seemed to her fantastically large, and moved, she thought, like a ghost. She rose to her knees and sought the sky in the parting of the curtains, but all that she could see was a vague blot of gray and below it a window out of which peered an angular face. There was a second of crushing helplessness, and then she crept, nay fled, to Nadinsky's bed. His right arm was hanging limp. Beads of perspiration stood on his forehead. He looked frighteningly strange. A painful sense of hatred flared up in her. Yet there was no longer anybody in the world at whom she could look in this fashion. She had much to demand of him, everything, in fact; except for him, her world was but this house.

They had said nothing on their arrival about how long they wished to remain in these rooms. It was customary to let them only for the night. Anastasia's plan had been that they should lock themselves in until noon, and then declare their wish to spend a second night in the house. A gold-piece to the waiter and another to the chambermaid would suffice for this. But fresh water was needed for Nadinsky's wound; his condition demanded nourishment. If they arose early, how were they to justify staying all day? Nadinsky, who had been lying open-eyed and silent, was the first to broach this subject. He asked her to hand him his coat, drew out his wallet, and gave it to her. Two gold-pieces, he thought, would not be enough; fifty roubles would be better. Lukardis remarked that such extravagance would create suspicion and induce the proprietor to spy upon them. She held the note between trembling fingers. Never had money seemed to her at once so real and so incomprehensible. They were behaving with outward coolness, but their voices seemed smothered. Lukardis said something about the nastiness in the waiter's face, which induced Nadinsky to retort, more spitefully than he intended, that she had certainly led a life excessively sheltered in cotton-wool, since none of these people who lived in dirt and squalor could please her. He was revolting against the yoke of gratitude which she had laid upon him, and at the same time, trying to draw her out of herself and let light and darkness play about her features. But she gazed sadly at the floor. She granted his point, and thus disarmed him. Her gentleness touched him, but also it goaded him into further cruelty. He protested against the idea that chance alone was responsible for making her his companion during these twenty-eight hours; she seemed to him herself guilty of the humiliation she was suffering, and he was angry with her because of that. He thought of her as having worn, before she met him, only robes of purest white, as having spoken, with those beautiful lips, only

meaningless words, the dregs of her pampered class. It was
only now, beside her, that he became a true revolutionist.
His flight and concealment seemed to him now ignominious,
and he imagined that very likely they lowered him in Lukardis's eyes. And therefore he declared suddenly his determination to get up and leave the house. He was trying
to show her that it meant nothing to him, indeed, it was his
duty, to share the lot of so many of the condemned, who had
accomplished more and dared more than he. Once across the
frontier, to whom could he be of use? Not to the Russian
people, not to his friends, not to his unfortunate sister!

Lukardis begged him to control himself and tried vainly
to reason with him, though she had only a child's reasons to
present. Then, seeing that he remained obdurate, she assumed a tone of command, the air of a young queen. Of a
sudden she was silent. She had heard steps. She raised her
finger and pressed it to her lips. Some one stood listening
at the door. Her proud glance became a plea for protection,
and Nadinsky hung his head. Then Lukardis accepted the
inevitable. She tiptoed to the door, unbolted it, hurried back
to the bed, and slipped quickly in beside Nadinsky. Pulling
the covers up under her chin, she reached for the electric
bell-cord and rang. They lay breathless until a knock came.
It was the maid. She stood in the doorway with an air of
Nornlike gloom and took Nadinsky's order to bring fresh
water and call the waiter so that breakfast might be ordered.
Back she came with two jugs of water, followed by the
waiter. His watchful eye took in the first room and as much
of the next as it could see, and to Lukardis it appeared as
if he were seeking the clothes she wore as she lay in bed, a
circumstance she thought proper to arouse his suspicion.
She shut her eyes, for the sight of this man was horrible to
her. Nadinsky held out the fifty-rouble note. "Twenty for
the maid and thirty for you," he said in a tone of studied
indifference. "We shall stay until to-morrow morning, if it
can be arranged." The waiter bowed nearly to the ground.
He had not looked for so generous a tip. The maid, who was

feeding the fire, came over and tried to kiss his hand, but Nadinsky warded it off. "If it please the lady and gentleman, and there is nothing against it," said the waiter with a catlike gesture and a wink. Nadinsky ordered breakfast, and at the end of a quarter of an hour the tea and things were brought in. Meanwhile, Lukardis lay on coals of fire. Her whole body was penetrated with something for which she found no name, a feeling composed of grief and fear, that clouded her face with a deathly pallor. Nadinsky lay motionless, sharing her sensation. He understood her agony and averted his eyes from her. The waiter had set the table, bowed again to the ground, and left. When the maid had gone, Lukardis threw back the cover and rose as if fleeing from flames. She bolted the door and opened a window. Her hair had come unbound, and she let it hang freely, for it covered her bare shoulders. An hour earlier she would have resented appearing thus before Nadinsky, but since she had lain beside him, uncovered despite all covering, immeasurably his, her blood now revolted at the notion of his mercy. It was no longer improper that her hair hang loose about her shoulders.

When the room was filled with fresh air, she shut the window and said to Nadinsky that it was time to change the dressing. Silently, he uncovered the sheet. Even to Lukardis's untrained eyes it was clear that the wound was healing rapidly and that Nadinsky's fever had passed. She was already more adroit than yesterday in the dressing and the binding of the wound. When she had finished, she offered him bread and milk. He asked to have a little tea in his milk, and she gave it to him. She herself swallowed something in great haste, as if she begrudged her body its hunger. The house was strangely silent. In the street, wagons rolled and children shouted. Nadinsky fell asleep, and Lukardis went into the other room. She pulled off her slippers in order to make no noise, and walked back and forth for hours, holding the strands of her hair in both hands. From time to time she would stand still and muse. Then she would stare at the pictures on the wall without really seeing them. One represented a Leda, holding the swan between her knees. By the door hung another: a German student with a rucksack on his back, flourishing his cap in the direction of a girl with two long braids, looking out of a window. The two rooms were reflected on both sides in the mirrors with the effect of an endless succession of rooms, all of them peopled by the fat, ugly nakedness of Leda, the sentimental student, the bed in which Nadinsky lay asleep, and the portrait of Czar Nicholas that hung above it. Endless, multiple reflections, far into the dim, dim distance. Often, too, she would stand at the window and look at the vehicles and the children, at the snow on the ledges and the faces seen faintly behind window-panes, and it would seem to her that all this, too, was endlessly repeated in the faint distance. Where had the world vanished to? Where was everything she had loved, embraced with harmless affection? Where was she herself, Lukardis, who had spent her life in the elegant boudoir of a general's daughter? Where was Alexander Mikhailovitch, ever ruddy and ever smiling? And where was brilliant Moscow with the tempting displays of its shops, the friendly acquaintances who turned up on every hand, the distinguished young officers and the gay women? Where had the world vanished to? She could see only the man who lay before her in the many mirrors of the many rooms; she could see only his wound on his white skin, his wound that was like a flitting flame which she, with an enchantment put upon her, was forced to follow.

The chimes struck twelve, and it was a long time thereafter, how long she could not judge, before Nadinsky awoke. He sat up, and she came forward with some hesitation. More determinedly than she had expected, he said that she must leave this same evening. He felt strong enough now to stay alone and would intimate to the waiter that she would be back later in the night. And in the night, nobody would bother to think about it again. Lukardis shook her head and said that it was as much for her own sake as for

his that she preferred to stay. The scar had only just begun
to form, and the wound would need to be dressed at least
twice again before he could stir. If she left and he met with
an accident, she would never forgive herself. Nadinsky
gazed searchingly into her face; then he stretched forth his
arm in such fashion that she held out her hand to him. At
that moment they both grew frightened. It was like some
blissful but disastrous transformation which each underwent in the eyes of the other. Then Lukardis stepped with
beating heart before one of the mirrors and pinned up her
hair. Her fingers shook. If at this moment he had ordered
her to leave, she would probably have gone without protest.
But instead he began to lament that he had not died an honorable death in battle; what was he to do in foreign lands,
eternally wandering, gnawed by grief and by the ever-pres-
ent thought of his tortured comrades, worried by the business of earning a bare living? For he was not rich. He had
many debts. His mother's estate belonged to his creditors,
really. Discouraged by so much discouragement, Lukardis
stood still before the mirror and examined her tired face.
He went on. He reviled his deed: he had not known what
he was taking upon himself; it had been the result of impulse, not of decision; heroes did not act this way, did not
deliver themselves up to chance, in order to be crushed.
And here was she who had fled with him to this sewer: had
she acted with a clear sense of what she was doing, or had
she not, in reality, allowed herself to be swept away by sentiment, by pity, by the temptation of the unusual, the seduc-
tion of an enthusiastic friend? Had she not been uprooted
and shaken, robbed of all her strength by Medusa-like
visions? "So are we all," he cried, throwing himself back
upon his pillows; "all of us, delivered up, cast down, beggars
of fantasy, sacrifices to the moment, deceived by our actions!"

Lukardis moved over and sat on the edge of his bed.
Quietly and firmly, she looked into his face. Her eyes gave
the lie to his words: there was a soulful harmony in the ex-

pression of her features. It was as though, in the simple silence of bewilderment, a godlike nature had come to the aid of his heart. A beam of happiness sped across Nadinsky's brow. His skeptical spirit bowed in shame before the confidence and serenity of this girl, who was able to take him out of himself, out of this house. Night fell. They sat in silence amid the darkness. When it came time to continue the comedy demanded by their situation, Lukardis switched on the light, drew the curtains together, and went out of the room in order that Nadinsky might dress. He called to her after a moment to help him on with his coat. Dinner was served as on the previous evening by the liveried waiter, with even more humility, with a smile even more insipid and an eye even more alert behind his evil grimaces, than before. They sat at table mirthlessly and avoided one another's glance. Only their hands moved,—mute obedient spirits, passing to and fro, pretending a casual innocuousness under the eyes of the spy. This evening Lukardis was playing her part badly. Her laughter was artificial, her frivolity was even less convincing. Nadinsky came to her rescue by whispering, when they were alone, that they should pretend to quarrel. He invented the name of a Countess Shuilov and insisted that the collar of pearls she had worn at Princess Karamsin's last reception was false. Lukardis contradicted him. He persisted peevishly in his opinion, and with such success that a crimson glow overspread Lukardis's cheeks. She was astounded at this hypocrisy within hypocrisy and suddenly was afraid of Nadinsky. The waiter came and went, poured champagne, with a look in his face that seemed to implore them to be friends, as if he were afraid of anything else than dovelike cooing. Finally Nadinsky got up ill-humoredly and ordered the waiter to clear out. He was amazed by Lukardis's pleading glance. Acting as though he regretted his impetuosity, he stepped towards her with outstretched hands. The waiter grinned with joy. Lukardis too stood up. She let her head fall on his shoulder, but only in order to whisper to him not to forget that the carriage must be ordered for the next morning.

All at once a piercing shriek resounded through the house, followed by a second and then a third cry. Lukardis clasped her hands in fright while Nadinsky looked uneasily in the direction of the door. The waiter stood with a metal tray in the open doorway. A half naked woman ran by. "Shut the door," breathed Lukardis faintly. A shot sounded and the ghostly howl of a man filled the air. Nadinsky pushed the servant out and slammed the door. In a few minutes all was quiet; then steps ran to and fro, voices murmured, a tone of command arose from below and was answered by a wail of lament from above. This was followed by sobs so heartrending that Lukardis ran, wringing her hands, to the sofa, and flung herself face downward upon it. A lively tumult arose in the street, in the midst of which the voice of a policeman was clearly audible. Heavy feet through the hall indicated that some one was being carried out. The waiter came in with a look of contrition in his face and said: "I beg your Excellency to be without anxiety: I beg the lady to calm herself. It is nothing. An insignificant accident has occurred. Your Excellency will not be disturbed again." With this he vanished.

Nadinsky went over to Lukardis and sat down beside her, stroking her hair with a trembling hand. She shrank from his touch and moved her head away. He withdrew his hand, weary of life. A storm rattled at the windows. As if in defiance, the piano sounded again; some one was playing the same waltz, the same gap-toothed melody. Was it only one day, one day and one night, since they had last heard that air? Had not years elapsed? years filled with images and moods, joy and pain, splendor and wretchedness, expectancy and disappointment, greed and deprivation, dream and death? And was this already the end? Was not another night imminent? An endless, mysterious night? To Nadinsky it seemed that in the moment when he had climbed the barricade and been shot, he had stepped into another existence,

conditioned by hitherto unknown laws and demands; and
that his earlier existence with all that it comported had been
shed like a cloak; that on coming into this house he had
taken upon himself his destined life, divorced from past and
future, devoid of bridges leading either backward or forward.

Oppressed and nerve-racked, he fell upon his bed. Lukardis came in. A lamp burned in the sitting-room, but in this
room there was no light. The rooms repeated themselves in
the mirrors, gray and vague. Lukardis found that one jug
of water was still full, and again she dressed Nadinsky's
wound. In drawing the fresh bandage from her bag, she
pulled out a book, and when Nadinsky had been bandaged
he asked if she would read to him. The book was a volume
of Lermontov's poems. Lukardis, in her chair, had read
only for a few minutes when her arms fell to her sides, her
head sank, and sleep overcame her. Thus, without resistance or transition do children fall asleep. Nadinsky was
careful not to stir. His eyes clung to her face, and it seemed
to him that his own face must follow the change of expression to which her features were being subjected. A sense of
ineffable peace entered his soul. He stretched his legs and
breathed deeply, as in a garden. Her lips were moving. She
was whispering, smiling gently. Her hands opened and the
book fell from her lap. She started, opened her eyes, glanced
in horror at the dim room, and slept on. Sleep mastered her
completely and her body lost its equilibrium so that she
would have fallen to the floor had not Nadinsky caught her
in his arms. He laid her across his bed, her feet on the chair.
Her head rested on his knees, her arms were crossed above
it, and her breast rose and fell in a powerful rhythm. Gradually Nadinsky commenced to feel her weight; the blood
ceased to circulate in his thighs, and it was hard for him to
remain motionless. He let himself fall back on his pillows,
slipped his hands under the covers and under the girl's back,
and tried thus to hold up the unconscious body. In this way
the burden fell in rotation on the arms, the thighs, and the

knees. A glow of happiness went through him. He felt that
he was repaying her care and trouble, and also he was happy
because she was so close to him, so utterly under his protection. His eyes dwelt long on the sleeping girl while his
mind was filled with a rapturous gratitude. Her life, her
slumber, the lines of her relaxed and unconscious form, each
of which seemed a sort of spiritual barrier against the
chaos of the world, filled him with a sense of limitless bliss
and poured new strength into his heart.

She had been asleep for hours when she was awakened
by the drums of a military patrol marching through the
street. Nadinsky was pulling himself up to a sitting posture
when he saw that her eyes were full of dull astonishment.
They seemed to be trying to glow serenely, and then to be
covered by a veil of shame. Lukardis uttered a little cry, and
sprang up. Her face was suffused with blood. She pressed
her hands to her breast and looked mutely ahead; and
although Nadinsky spoke to her, she continued to appear
embarrassed. He made an effort to speak casually, inquiring
about the weather and the hour. She answered absent-mindedly, her face revealing alternately shyness and fright, and
gratitude and secret questioning. For the last time she
washed and bound Nadinsky's wound, maintaining, meanwhile, her composure with difficulty. The world outside
seemed to her like the open jaws of a savage beast. It was a
quarter to six. They had to make themselves ready. Nadinsky
was growing more and more calm; he was very pale, when,
having dressed, he went into the other room where Lukardis
stood. They sat opposite each other at the table. Lukardis
was wearing her hat and fur coat; her hand-bag lay at her
feet. Thus they waited in silence and with averted eyes for
the time of their deliverance.

The clatter of wheels sounded finally in the street, and in
a moment there was a knock on their door. The waiter came
in wearing not his livery but a greasy bathrobe. His hair
hung in oily strands over his forehead and his face was
sullen and evil. He presented the bill, which Nadinsky paid,

including at the same time the coachman's fee. They went downstairs. Two pails filled with sweepings stood at the foot of the stairs, and in the entrance lay a black dog. The dog followed them, sniffing, to the carriage. Not a soul was to be seen in the streets as they drove the long way to the station.

In one of the waiting-rooms stood Anastasia Karlovna, beside a pillar. She greeted them and asked about Nadinsky's condition. Then she handed him a passport and a filled traveling bag, they hurried out to the platform, and Nadinsky took his place in the train. After a moment he came back, walked over to Lukardis, and stretched forth his hand. An unaccountable lack of muscular response prevented Lukardis's lifting her head and turning her face towards him. He took both her hands in his, and the four hands lay together like the links of a chain. So they remained for a moment and seemed to themselves figures in a dream. Anastasia Karlovna gestured warningly. With a dragging step, Nadinsky turned back to the car and climbed in, placing himself at the window where, in the black frame and the gray of the fog, his face was a chalk-white blot. The whistle blew, and the train rolled slowly out of the station.

When Lukardis reached home she found her mother dissolved in tears. The poor woman had not dared tell her husband of Lukardis's letter, and had been at great pains to keep her disappearance from his knowledge. A strange argument ensued between daughter and mother, a scene in which the deaf and dumb mother gesticulated in her most excited and imploring manner while the girl merely shook her head and told nothing. Bit by bit the general's wife grew uneasy about Lukardis, and this uneasiness grew into dismay when the girl refused to see her fiancé, who had turned up for a few days in Moscow. Even her father's anger could not move her. She spoke no word, but looked calmly at the ground. The engagement was broken; and even more deliberately than before, Lukardis persisted in avoiding other people—friends, strangers, parents, sisters. She retired deep within herself, became a different person. The doctors having counseled travel, her mother took her first to Paris and then by the sea in Brittany. One night the general's wife came upon her daughter unexpectedly as she lay out on the flagstone terrace of her room. Hands folded behind her head, the girl was gazing with wide-open indescribably brilliant eyes, upward at the starry heavens. In her face was an expression of infinite loneliness.

Nadinsky had vanished. Several people insisted that he was living on a farm in western Canada, but Lukardis never heard his name spoken, nor heard he ever hers.

DEATH IN VENICE *

By Thomas Mann

I

On a spring afternoon of the year 19—, when our continent lay under such threatening weather for whole months, Gustav Aschenbach, or von Aschenbach as his name read officially after his fiftieth birthday, had left his apartment on the Prinzregentenstrasse in Munich and had gone for a long walk. Overwrought by the trying and precarious work of the forenoon—which had demanded a maximum wariness, prudence, penetration, and rigor of the will—the writer had not been able even after the noon meal to break the impetus of the productive mechanism within him, that *motus animi continuus* which constitutes, according to Cicero, the foundation of eloquence ; and he had not attained the healing sleep which—what with the increasing exhaustion of his strength—he needed in the middle of each day. So he had gone outdoors soon after tea, in the hopes that air and movement would restore him and prepare him for a profitable evening.

It was the beginning of May, and after cold, damp weeks a false midsummer had set in. The English Gardens, although the foliage was still fresh and sparse, were as pungent as in August, and in the parts nearer the city had been full of conveyances and promenaders. At the Aumeister, which he had reached by quieter and quieter paths, Aschenbach had surveyed for a short time the Wirtsgarten with its lively crowds and its border of cabs and carriages. From

* Translated by Kenneth Burke. Copyright, 1925, by Alfred A. Knopf, Inc.

here, as the sun was sinking, he had started home, outside the park, across the open fields; and since he felt tired and a storm was threatening from the direction of Föhring, he waited at the North Cemetery for the tram which would take him directly back to the city.

It happened that he found no one in the station or its vicinity. There was not a vehicle to be seen, either on the paved Ungererstrasse, with its solitary glistening rails stretching out towards Schwabing, or on the Föhringer Chaussee. Behind the fences of the stone-masons' establishments, where the crosses, memorial tablets, and monuments standing for sale formed a second, uninhabited burial ground, there was no sign of life; and opposite him the Byzantine structure of the Funeral Hall lay silent in the reflection of the departing day, its façade ornamented in luminous colors with Greek crosses and hieratic paintings, above which were displayed inscriptions symmetrically arranged in gold letters, and texts chosen to bear on the life beyond, such as, "They enter into the dwelling of the Lord," or, "The light of eternity shall shine upon them." And for some time, as he stood waiting, he found a grave diversion in spelling out the formulas and letting his mind's eye lose itself in their transparent mysticism, when, returning from his reveries, he noticed in the portico, above the two apocalyptic animals guarding the steps, a man whose somewhat unusual appearance gave his thoughts an entirely new direction.

Whether he had just now come out from the inside through the bronze door, or had approached and mounted from the outside unobserved, remained uncertain. Aschenbach, without applying himself especially to the matter, was inclined to believe the former. Of medium height, thin, smooth-shaven, and noticeably pug-nosed, the man belonged to the red-haired type and possessed the appropriate fresh milky complexion. Obviously, he was not of Bavarian extraction, since at least the white and straight-brimmed straw hat that covered his head gave his appearance the stamp of a foreigner, of some one who had come from a long distance. To be sure, he was wearing the customary knapsack strapped across his shoulders, and a belted suit of rough yellow wool; his left arm was resting on his thigh, and his gray storm cape was thrown across it. In his right hand he held a cane with an iron ferrule, which he had stuck diagonally into the ground, while, with his feet crossed, he was leaning his hip against the crook. His head was raised so that the Adam's-apple protruded hard and bare on a scrawny neck emerging from a loose sport-shirt. And he was staring sharply off into the distance, with colorless, red lidded eyes between which stood two strong, vertical wrin kles peculiarly suited to his short turned-up nose. Thus— and perhaps his elevated position helped to give the impres sion—his bearing had something majestic and commanding about it, something bold, or even savage. For whether he was grimacing because he was blinded by the setting sun, or whether it was a case of a permanent distortion of the physiognomy, his lips seemed too short, they were so completely pulled back from his teeth that these were exposed even to the gums, and stood out white and long.

It is quite possible that Aschenbach, in his half-distracted, half-inquisitive examination of the stranger, had been somewhat inconsiderate, for he suddenly became aware that his look was being answered, and indeed so militantly, so straight in the eye, so plainly with the intention of driving the thing through to the very end and compelling him to capitulate, that he turned away uncomfortably and began walking along by the fences, deciding casually that he would pay no further attention to the man. The next minute he had forgotten him. But perhaps the exotic element in the stranger's appearance had worked on his imagination; or a new physical or spiritual influence of some sort had come into play. He was quite astonished to note a peculiar inner expansion, a kind of roving unrest, a youthful longing after far-off places: a feeling so vivid, so new, or so long dormant and neglected, that, with his hands behind his back and his eyes on the ground, he came to a sudden stop, and examined into the nature and purport of this emotion.

It was the desire for travel, nothing more; although, to be sure, it had attacked him violently, and was heightened to a passion, even to the point of an hallucination. His yearnings crystallized; his imagination, still in ferment from his hours of work, actually pictured all the marvels and terrors of a manifold world which it was suddenly struggling to conceive. He saw a landscape, a tropical swampland under a heavy, murky sky, damp, luxuriant and enormous, a kind of prehistoric wilderness of islands, bogs, and arms of water, sluggish with mud; he saw, near him and in the distance, the hairy shafts of palms rising out of a rank lecherous thicket, out of places where the plant-life was fat, swollen, and blossoming exorbitantly; he saw strangely mis-shapen trees lowering their roots into the ground, into stagnant pools with greenish reflections; and here, between floating flowers which were milk-white and large as dishes, birds of a strange nature, high-shouldered, with crooked bills, were standing in the muck, and looking motionlessly to one side; between dense, knotted stalks of bamboo he saw the glint from the eyes of a crouching tiger—and he felt his heart knocking with fear and with puzzling desires. Then the image disappeared; and with a shake of his head Aschenbach resumed his walk along past the fences of the stone-masons' establishments.

Since the time, at least, when he could command the means to enjoy the advantages of moving about the world as he pleased, he had considered traveling simply as a hygienic precaution which must be complied with now and then despite one's feelings and one's preferences. Too busy with the tasks arranged for him by his interest in his own ego and in the problems of Europe, too burdened with the onus of production, too little prone to diversion, and in no sense an amateur of the varied amusements of the great world, he had been thoroughly satisfied with such knowledge of the earth's surface as any one can get without moving far out of his own circle; and he had never even been tempted to leave Europe. Especially now that his life was slowly on the decline, and that the artist's fear of not having finished—this uneasiness lest the clock run down before he had done his part and given himself completely—could no longer be waived aside as a mere whim, he had confined his outer existence almost exclusively to the beautiful city which had become his home and to the rough country-house which he had built in the mountains and where he spent the rainy summers.

Further, this thing which had laid hold of him so belatedly, but with such suddenness, was very readily moderated and adjusted by the force of his reason and of a discipline which he had practiced since youth. He had intended carrying his life-work forward to a certain point before removing to the country. And the thought of knocking about the world for months and neglecting his work during this time, seemed much too lax and contrary to his plans; it really could not be considered seriously. Yet he knew only too well what the reasons were for this unexpected temptation. It was the urge to escape—he admitted to himself—this yearning for the new and the remote, this appetite for freedom, for unburdening, for forgetfulness; it was a pressure away from his work, from the steady drudgery of a coldly passionate service. To be sure, he loved his work and almost loved the enervating battle that was fought daily between a proud tenacious will—so often tested—and this growing weariness which no one was to suspect and which must not betray itself in his productions by any sign of weakness or negligence. But it seemed wise not to draw the bow overtightly, and not to strangle by sheer obstinacy so strongly persistent an appetite. He thought of his work, thought of the place at which yesterday and now again today he had been forced to leave off, and which, it seemed, would yield neither to patience and coaxing nor to a definite attack. He examined it again, trying to break through or to circumvent the deadlock, but he gave up with a shudder of repugnance. There was no unusual difficulty here; what balked him were the scruples of aversion, which took the form of a fastidious insatiability. Even as a young man this insatiability had meant to him the very nature, the fullest essence, of talent; and for that reason he had restrained and chilled his emotions, since he was aware that they incline to content themselves with a happy approximate, a state of semi-completion. Were these enslaved emotions now taking their vengeance on him, by leaving him in the lurch, by refusing to forward and lubricate his art; and were they bearing off with them every enjoyment, every live interest in form and expression?

Not that he was producing anything bad; his years gave him at least this advantage, that he felt himself at all times in full and easy possession of his craftsmanship. But while the nation honored him for this, he himself was not content; and it seemed to him that his work lacked the marks of that fiery and fluctuating emotionalism which is an enormous thing in one's favor, and which, while it argues an enjoyment on the part of the author, also constitutes, more than any depth of content, the enjoyment of the amateur. He feared the summer in the country, alone in the little house with the maid who prepared his meals, and the servant who brought them to him. He feared the familiar view of the mountain peaks and the slopes which would stand about him in his boredom and his discontent. Consequently there was need of a break in some new direction. If the summer was to be endurable and productive, he must attempt something out of his usual orbit; he must relax, get a change of air, bring an element of freshness into the blood. To travel, then—that much was settled. Not far, not all the way to the tigers. But one night on the sleeper, and a rest of three or four weeks at some pleasant popular resort in the South. . . .

He thought this out while the noise of the electric tram came nearer along the Ungererstrasse; and as he boarded it, he decided to devote the evening to the study of maps and time-tables. On the platform it occurred to him to look around for the man in the straw hat, his companion during that most significant time spent waiting at the station. But his whereabouts remained uncertain, as he was not to be seen either at the place where he was formerly standing, or anywhere else in the vicinity of the station, or on the car itself.

II

The author of that lucid and powerful prose epic built around the life of Frederick of Prussia; the tenacious artist who, after long application, wove rich, varied strands of human destiny together under one single predominating theme in the fictional tapestry known as "Maya"; the creator of that stark tale which is called "The Wretch" and which pointed out for an entire oncoming generation the possibility of some moral certainty beyond pure knowledge; finally, the writer (and this sums up briefly the works of his mature period) of the impassioned treatise on "Art and the Spirit," whose capacity for mustering facts, and, further, whose fluency in their presentation, led cautious judges to place this treatise alongside Schiller's conclusions on naïve and sentimental poetry—Gustav Aschenbach, then, was the son of a higher law official, and was born in L——, a leading city in the Province of Silesia. His forbears had been officers, magistrates, government functionaries, men who had led severe, steady lives serving their king, their state. A deeper strain of spirituality had been manifest in them once, in the person of a preacher; the preceding generation had brought a brisker, more sensuous blood into the family through the author's mother, daughter of a Bohemian bandmaster. The traces of foreignness in his features came from her. A marriage of sober painstaking conscientiousness with impulses of a darker, more fiery nature had had an artist as its result, and this particular artist.

Since his whole nature was centered around acquiring a reputation, he showed himself, if not exactly precocious, at least (thanks to the firmness and pithiness of his personal-

ity, his accent) ripened and adjusted to the public at an
early age. Almost as a schoolboy he had made a name for
himself. Within ten years he had learned to face the world
through the medium of his writing-table, to discharge the
obligations of his fame in a correspondence which (since
many claims are pressed on the successful, the trustworthy)
had to be brief as well as pleasant and to the point. At forty,
wearied by the vicissitudes and the exertion of his own
work, he had to manage a daily mail which bore the post-
marks of countries in all parts of the world.

Equally removed from the banal and the eccentric, his
talents were so constituted as to gain both the confidence of
the general public and the stable admiration and sympathy
of the critical. Thus even as a young man continually devoted to the pursuit of craftsmanship—and that of no ordinary kind—he had never known the careless freedom of
youth. When, around thirty-five years of age, he had been
taken ill in Vienna, one sharp observer said of him in company: "You see, Aschenbach has always lived like this,"
and the speaker contracted the fingers of his left hand into a
fist: "never like this," and he let his open hand droop comfortably from the arm of his chair. That hit the mark; and
the heroic, the ethical about it all was that he was not of a
strong constitution, and though he was pledged by his nature to these steady efforts, he was not really born to them.

Considerations of ill health had kept him from attending
school as a boy, and had compelled him to receive instructions at home. He had grown up alone, without comrades—
and he was forced to realize soon enough that he belonged
to a race which often lacked, not talent, but that physical
substructure which talent relies on for its fullest fruition: a
race accustomed to giving its best early, and seldom extend-
ing its faculties over the years. But his favorite phrase was
"carrying through"; in his novel on Frederick he saw the
pure apotheosis of this command, which struck him as the
essential concept of the virtuous in action and passion. Also,
he wished earnestly to grow old, since he had always main-

tained that the only artistry which can be called truly great, comprehensive—yes, even truly admirable—is that which is permitted to bear fruits characteristic of each stage in human development.

Since he must carry the responsibilities of his talent on frail shoulders, and wanted to go a long way, the primary requirement was discipline—and fortunately discipline was his direct inheritance from his father's side. By forty, fifty, or at an earlier age when others are still slashing about with enthusiasm, and are contentedly putting off to some later date the execution of plans on a large scale, he would start the day early, dashing cold water over his chest and back, and then, with a couple of tall wax candles in silver candlesticks at the head of his manuscript, he would pay out to his art, in two or three eager, scrupulous morning hours, the strength which he had accumulated in sleep. It was pardonable, indeed it was a direct tribute to the effectiveness of his moral scheme, that the uninitiated took his "Maya" world, and the massive epic machinery upon which the life of the hero Frederick was unrolled, as evidence of long breath and sustaining power. While actually they had been built up layer by layer, in small daily allotments, through hundreds and hundreds of single inspirations. And if they were so excellent in both composition and texture, it was solely because their creator had held out for years under the strain of one single work, with a steadiness of will and a tenacity comparable to that which conquered his native province; and because, finally, he had turned over his most vital and valuable hours to the problem of minute revision.

In order that a significant work of the mind may exert immediately some broad and deep effect, a secret relationship, or even conformity, must exist between the personal destiny of the author and the common destiny of his contemporaries. People do not know why they raise a work of art to fame. Far from being connoisseurs, they believe that they see in it hundreds of virtues which justify so much interest; but the true reason for their applause is an unconscious sympathy. Aschenbach had once stated quite plainly in some remote place that nearly everything great which comes into being does so in spite of something—in spite of sorrow or suffering, poverty, destitution, physical weakness, depravity, passion, or a thousand other handicaps. But that was not merely an observation; it was a discovery, the formula of his life and reputation, the key to his work. And what wonder, then, that it was also the distinguishing moral trait, the dominating gesture, of his most characteristic figures?

Years before, one shrewd analyst had written of the new hero-type to which this author gave preference, and which kept turning up in variations of one sort or another: he called it the conception of "an intellectual and youthful masculinity" which "stands motionless, haughty, ashamed, with jaw set, while swords and spear-points beset the body." That was beautiful and ingenious; and it was exact, although it may have seemed to suggest too much passivity. For to be poised against fatality, to meet adverse conditions gracefully, is more than simple endurance; it is an act of aggression, a positive triumph—and the figure of Sebastian is the most beautiful figure, if not of art as a whole, at least of the art of literature. Looking into this fictional world, one saw: a delicate self-mastery by which any inner deterioration, any biological decay was kept concealed from the eyes of the world; a crude, vicious sensuality capable of fanning its rising passions into pure flame, yes, even of mounting to dominance in the realm of beauty; a pallid weakness which draws from the glowing depths of the soul the strength to bow whole arrogant peoples before the foot of the cross, or before the feet of weakness itself; a charming manner maintained in his cold, strict service to form; a false, precarious mode of living, and the keenly enervating melancholy and artifice of the born deceiver—to observe such trials as this was enough to make one question whether there really was any heroism other than weakness. And, in any case, what heroism could be more in keeping with the times? Gustav

Aschenbach was the one poet among the many workers on the verge of exhaustion: the over-burdened, the used-up, the clingers-on, in short all those moralists of production who, delicately built and destitute of means, can rely for a time at least on will-power and the shrewd husbandry of their resources to secure the effects of greatness. There are many such: they are the heroes of the period. And they all found themselves in his works; here they were indeed, upheld, intensified, applauded; they were grateful to him, they acclaimed him.

In his time he had been young and raw; and, misled by his age, he had blundered in public. He had stumbled, had exposed himself; both in writing and in talk he had offended against caution and tact. But he had acquired the dignity which, as he insisted, is the innate goad and craving of every great talent; in fact, it could be said that his entire development had been a conscious undeviating progression away from the embarrassments of skepticism and irony, and towards dignity.

The general masses are satisfied by vigor and tangibility of treatment rather than by any close intellectual processes; but youth, with its passion for the absolute, can be arrested only by the problematical. And Aschenbach had been absolute, problematical, as only a youth could be. He had been a slave to the intellect, had played havoc with knowledge, had ground up his seed crops, had divulged secrets, had discredited talent, had betrayed art—yes, while his modelings were entertaining the faithful votaries, filling them with enthusiasm, making their lives more keen, this youthful artist was taking the breath away from the generation then in its twenties by his cynicisms on the questionable nature of art, and of artistry itself.

But it seems that nothing blunts the edge of a noble, robust mind more quickly and more thoroughly than the sharp and bitter corrosion of knowledge; and certainly the moody radicalism of the youth, no matter how conscientious, was shallow in comparison with his firm determination as an

older man and a master to deny knowledge, to reject it, to
pass it with raised head, in so far as it is capable of crippling,
discouraging, or degrading to the slightest degree, our will,
acts, feelings, or even passions. How else could the famous
story of "The Wretch" be understood than as an outburst
of repugnance against the disreputable psychologism of the
times: embodied in the figure of that soft and stupid half-
clown who pilfers a destiny for himself by guiding his wife
(from powerlessness, from lasciviousness, from ethical
frailty) into the arms of an adolescent, and believes that he
may through profundity commit vileness? The verbal pressure with which he here cast out the outcast announced the
return from every moral skepticism, from all fellow-feeling
with the engulfed: it was the counter-move to the laxity of
the sympathetic principle that to understand all is to forgive
all—and the thing that was here well begun, even nearly
completed, was that "miracle of reborn ingenuousness"
which was taken up a little later in one of the author's dia-
logues expressly and not without a certain discreet emphasis.
Strange coincidences! Was it as a result of this rebirth, this
new dignity and sternness, that his feeling for beauty—a
discriminating purity, simplicity, and evenness of attack
which henceforth gave his productions such an obvious,
even such a deliberate stamp of mastery and classicism—
showed an almost excessive strengthening about this time?
But ethical resoluteness in the exclusion of science, of eman-
cipatory and restrictive knowledge—does this not in turn
signify a simplification, a reduction morally of the world to
too limited terms, and thus also a strengthened capacity for
the forbidden, the evil, the morally impossible? And does
not form have two aspects? Is it not moral and unmoral at
once—moral in that it is the result and expression of discipline, but unmoral, and even immoral, in that by nature it
contains an indifference to morality, is calculated, in fact,
to make morality bend beneath its proud and unencumbered
scepter?

Be that as it may. An evolution is a destiny; and why

should his evolution, which had been upheld by the general confidence of a vast public, not run through a different course from one accomplished outside the luster and the entanglements of fame? Only chronic vagabondage will find it tedious and be inclined to scoff when a great talent outgrows the libertine chrysalis-stage, learns to seize upon and express the dignity of the mind, and superimposes a formal etiquette upon a solitude which had been filled with unchastened and rigidly isolated sufferings and struggles and had brought all this to a point of power and honor among men. Further, how much sport, defiance, indulgence there is in the self-formation of a talent! Gradually something official, didactic, crept into Gustav Aschenbach's productions, his style in later life fought shy of any abruptness and boldness, any subtle and unexpected contrasts; he inclined towards the fixed and standardized, the conventionally elegant, the conservative, the formal, the formulated, nearly. And, as is traditionally said of Louis XIV, with the advancing years he came to omit every common word from his vocabulary. At about this time it happened that the educational authorities included selected pages by him in their prescribed school readers. This was deeply sympathetic to his nature, and he did not decline when a German prince who had just mounted the throne raised the author of the "Frederick" to knighthood on the occasion of his fiftieth birthday. After a few years of unrest, a few tentative stopping-places here and there, he soon chose Munich as his permanent home, and lived there in a state of middle-class respectability such as fits in with the life of the mind in certain individual instances. The marriage which, when still young, he had contracted with a girl of an educated family came to an end with her death after a short period of happiness. He was left with a daughter, now married. He had never had a son.

Gustav von Aschenbach was somewhat below average height, dark, and smooth-shaven. His head seemed a bit too large in comparison with his almost dapper figure. His hair was brushed straight back, thinning out towards the crown, but very full about the temples, and strongly marked with gray; it framed a high, ridged forehead. Gold spectacles with rimless lenses cut into the bridge of his bold, heavy nose. The mouth was big, sometimes drooping, sometimes suddenly pinched and firm. His cheeks were thin and wrinkled, his well-formed chin had a slight cleft. This head, usually bent patiently to one side, seemed to have gone through momentous experiences, and yet it was his art which had produced those effects in his face, effects which are elsewhere the result of hard and agitated living. Behind this brow the brilliant repartee of the dialogue on war between Voltaire and the king had been born; these eyes, peering steadily and wearily from behind their glasses, had seen the bloody inferno of the lazaret in the Seven Years' War. Even as it applies to the individual, art is a heightened mode of existence. It gives deeper pleasures, it consumes more quickly. It carves into its servants' faces the marks of imaginary and spiritual adventures, and though their external activities may be as quiet as a cloister, it produces a lasting voluptuousness, overrefinement, fatigue, and curiosity of the nerves such as can barely result from a life filled with illicit passions and enjoyments.

III

Various matters of a literary and social nature delayed his departure until about two weeks after that walk in Munich. Finally he gave orders to have his country-house ready for occupancy within a month; and one day between the middle and the end of May he took the night train for Trieste, where he made a stop-over of only twenty-four hours, and embarked the following morning for Pola.

What he was hunting was something foreign and unrelated to himself which would at the same time be quickly within reach; and so he stopped at an island in the Adriatic which had become well known in recent years. It lay not

far off the Istrian coast, with beautifully rugged cliffs front-
ing the open sea, and natives who dressed in variegated tatters and made strange sounds when they spoke. But rain
and a heavy atmosphere, a provincial and exclusively Austrian patronage at the hotel, and the lack of that restfully
intimate association with the sea which can be gotten only
by a soft, sandy beach, irritated him, and prevented him
from feeling that he had found the place he was looking for.
Something within was disturbing him, and drawing him he
was not sure where. He studied sailing dates, he looked
about him questioningly, and of a sudden, as a thing both
astounding and self-evident, his goal was before him. If
you wanted to reach over night the unique, the fabulously
different, where did you go? But that was plain. What was
he doing here? He had lost the trail. He had wanted to go
there. He did not delay in giving notice of his mistake in
stopping here. In the early morning mist, a week and a half
after his arrival on the island, a fast motor-boat was carrying him and his luggage back over the water to the naval
port, and he landed there just long enough to cross the gang-
plank to the damp deck of a ship which was lying under
steam ready for the voyage to Venice.

It was an old hulk flying the Italian flag, decrepit, sooty,
and mournful. In a cave-like, artificially lighted inside cabin
where Aschenbach, immediately upon boarding the ship,
was conducted by a dirty hunchbacked sailor, who smirked
politely, there was sitting behind a table, his hat cocked over
his forehead and a cigarette stump in the corner of his
mouth, a man with a goatee, and with the face of an old-style
circus director, who was taking down the particulars of
the passengers with professional grimaces and distributing
the tickets. "To Venice!" he repeated Aschenbach's request,
as he extended his arm and plunged his pen into the pasty
dregs of a precariously tilted inkwell. "To Venice, first
class! At your service, sir." And he wrote a generous scrawl,
sprinkled it with blue sand out of a box, let the sand run off
into a clay bowl, folded the paper with sallow, bony fingers,

and began writing again. "A happily chosen destination!" he chatted on. "Ah, Venice! A splendid city! A city of irresistible attractiveness for the educated on account of its history as well as its present-day charms." The smooth rapidity of his movements and the empty words accompanying them had something anæsthetic and reassuring about them, much as though he feared lest the traveler might still be vacillating in his decision to go to Venice. He handled the cash briskly, and let the change fall on the spotted table-cover with the skill of a croupier. "A pleasant journey, sir!" he said with a theatrical bow. "Gentlemen, I have the honor of serving you!' he called out immediately after, with his arm upraised, and he acted as if business were in full swing, although no one else was there to require his attention. Aschenbach returned to the deck.

With one arm on the railing, he watched the passengers on board and the idlers who loitered around the dock waiting for the ship to sail. The second-class passengers, men and women, were huddled together on the foredeck, using boxes and bundles as seats. A group of young people made up the travelers on the first deck, clerks from Pola, it seemed, who had gathered in the greatest excitement for an excursion to Italy. They made a considerable fuss about themselves and their enterprise, chattered, laughed, enjoyed their own antics self-contentedly, and, leaning over the hand-rails, shouted flippantly and mockingly at their comrades who, with portfolios under their arms, were going up and down the waterfront on business and kept threatening the picnickers with their canes. One, in a bright yellow summer suit of ultra-fashionable cut, with a red necktie, and a rakishly tilted Panama, surpassed all the others in his crowning good humor. But as soon as Aschenbach looked at him a bit more carefully, he discovered with a kind of horror that the youth was a cheat. He was old, that was unquestionable. There were wrinkles around his eyes and mouth. The faint crimson of the cheeks was paint, the hair under his brilliantly decorated straw hat was a wig; his neck was hollow and

stringy, his turned-up mustache and the imperial on his chin
were dyed; the full set of yellow teeth which he displayed
when he laughed, a cheap artificial plate; and his hands, with
signet rings on both index fingers, were those of an old man.
Fascinated with loathing, Aschenbach watched him in his
intercourse with his friends. Did they not know, did they
not observe that he was old, that he was not entitled to wear
their bright, foppish clothing, that he was not entitled to
play at being one of them? Unquestioningly, and as quite
the usual thing, it seemed, they allowed him among them,
treating him as one of their own kind and returning his
jovial nudges in the ribs without repugnance. How could
that be? Aschenbach laid his hand on his forehead and
closed his eyes; they were hot, since he had had too little
sleep. He felt as though everything were not quite the same
as usual, as though some dream-like estrangement, some
peculiar distortion of the world, were beginning to take possession of him, and perhaps this could be stopped if he hid
his face for a time and then looked around him again. Yet
at this moment he felt as though he were swimming; and
looking up with an unreasoned fear, he discovered that the
heavy, lugubrious body of the ship was separating slowly
from the walled bank. Inch by inch, with the driving and
reversing of the engine, the strip of dirty glistening water
widened between the dock and the side of the ship; and,
after cumbersome maneuvering, the steamer finally turned
its nose towards the open sea. Aschenbach crossed to the
starboard side, where the hunchback had set up a deck-chair
for him, and a steward in a spotted dress-coat asked after
his wants.

The sky was gray, the wind damp. Harbor and islands
had been left behind, and soon all land was lost in the haze.
Flakes of coal dust, bloated with moisture, fell over the
washed deck, which would not dry. After the first hour an
awning was spread, since it had begun to rain.

Bundled up in his coat, a book in his lap, the traveler
rested, and the hours passed unnoticed. It stopped raining;

the canvas awning was removed. The horizon was unbroken. The sea, empty, like an enormous disk, lay stretched under the curve of the sky. But in empty inarticulate space our senses lose also the dimensions of time, and we slip into the incommensurate. As he rested, strange shadowy figures, the old dandy, the goatee from the inside cabin, passed through his mind, with vague gestures, muddled dream-words—and ne was asleep.

About noon he was called to a meal down in the corridor-like dining-hall into which the doors opened from the sleeping-cabins; he ate near the head of a long table, at the other end of which the clerks, including the old man, had been drinking with the boisterous captain since ten o'clock. The food was poor, and he finished rapidly. He felt driven outside to look at the sky, to see if it showed signs of being brighter above Venice.

He had kept thinking that this had to occur, since the city had always received him in full blaze. But sky and sea remained dreary and leaden, at times a misty rain fell, and here he was reaching by water a different Venice than he had ever found when approaching on land. He stood by the forestays, looking in the distance, waiting for land. He thought of the heavy-hearted, enthusiastic poet for whom the domes and bell towers of his dreams had once risen out of these waters; he relived in silence some of that reverence, happiness and sorrow which had been turned then into cautious song; and easily susceptible to sensations already molded, he asked himself wearily and earnestly whether some new enchantment and distraction, some belated adventure of the emotions, might still be held in store for this idle traveler.

Then the flat coast emerged on the right; the sea was alive with fishing-smacks; the bathers' island appeared; it dropped behind to the left, the steamer slowly entered the narrow port which is named after it; and on the lagoon, facing gay ramshackle houses, it stopped completely, since it had to wait for the barque of the health department.

An hour passed before it appeared. He had arrived, and yet he had not; no one was in any hurry, no one was driven by impatience. The young men from Pola, patriotically attracted by the military bugle calls which rang over the water from the vicinity of the public gardens, had come on deck and, warmed by their Asti, they burst out with cheers for the drilling *bersagliere*. But it was repulsive to see what a state the primped-up old man had been brought to by his comradeship with youth. His old head was not able to resist its wine like the young and robust: he was painfully drunk. With glazed eyes, a cigarette between his trembling fingers, he stood in one place, swaying backwards and forwards from giddiness, and balancing himself laboriously. Since he would have fallen at the first step, he did not trust himself from the spot—yet he showed a deplorable insolence, buttonholed every one who came near him, stammered, winked and tittered, lifted his wrinkled, ornamented index finger in a stupid attempt at bantering, while he licked the corners of his mouth with his tongue in the most abominably suggestive manner. Aschenbach observed him darkly, and a feeling of numbness came over him again, as though the world were displaying a faint but irresistible tendency to distort itself into the peculiar and the grotesque: a feeling which circumstances prevented him from surrendering himself to completely, for just then the pounding activity of the engines commenced again, and the ship, resuming a voyage which had been interrupted so near its completion, passed through the San Marco canal.

So he saw it again, the most remarkable of landing-places, that blinding composition of fantastic buildings which the Republic lays out before the eyes of approaching seafarers: the soft splendor of the palace, the Bridge of Sighs, on the bank the columns with lion and saint, the advancing, showy flank of the enchanted temple, the glimpse through to the archway, and the giant clock. And as he looked on he thought that to reach Venice by land, on the railroad, was like entering a palace from the rear, and that this most unreal of cities should not be approached except as he was now doing, by ship, over the high seas.

The engine stopped, gondolas pressed in, the gangway was let down, customs officials climbed on board and discharged their duties perfunctorily; the disembarking could begin. Aschenbach made it understood that he wanted a gondola to take him and his luggage to the dock of those little steamers which ply between the city and the Lido, since he intended to locate near the sea. His plans were complied with, his wants were shouted down to the water, where the gondoliers were wrangling with one another in dialect. He was still hindered from descending; he was hindered by his trunk, which was being pulled and dragged with difficulty down the ladder-like steps. So that for some minutes he was not able to avoid the importunities of the atrocious old man, whose drunkenness gave him a sinister desire to do the foreigner parting honors. "We wish you a very agreeable visit," he bleated as he made an awkward bow. "We leave with pleasant recollections! *Au revoir, excusez,* and *bon jour,* your excellency!" His mouth watered, he pressed his eyes shut, he licked the corners of his mouth, and the dyed imperial turned up about his senile lips. "Our compliments," he mumbled, with two fingertips on his mouth, "our compliments to our sweetheart, the dearest, prettiest sweetheart . . ." And suddenly his false upper teeth fell down on his lower lip. Aschenbach was able to escape. "To our sweetheart, our handsome sweetheart," he heard the cooing, hollow, stuttering voice behind him while, supporting himself against the hand-rail, he went down the gangway.

Who would not have to suppress a fleeting shudder, a vague timidity and uneasiness, if it were a matter of boarding a Venetian gondola for the first time or after several years? The strange craft, an entirely unaltered survival from the times of balladry, with that peculiar blackness which is found elsewhere only in coffins—it suggests silent, criminal adventures in the rippling night, it suggests even more strongly death itself, the bier and the mournful funeral, and the last silent journey. And has it been observed that the seat of such a barque, this arm-chair of coffin-black veneer and dull black upholstery, is the softest, most luxuriant, most lulling seat in the world? Aschenbach noted this when he had relaxed at the feet of the gondolier, opposite his luggage, which lay neatly assembled on the prow. The rowers were still wrangling, harshly, incomprehensibly, with threatening gestures. But the strange silence of this canal city seemed to soften their voices, to disembody them, and dissipate them over the water. It was warm here in the harbor. Touched faintly by the warm breeze of the sirocco, leaning back against the limber portions of the cushions, the traveler closed his eyes in the enjoyment of a lassitude which was as unusual with him, as it was sweet. The trip would be short, he thought; if only it went on for ever! He felt himself glide with a gentle motion away from the crowd and the confusion of voices.

It became quieter and quieter around him! There was nothing to be heard but the splashing of the oar, the hollow slapping of the waves against the prow of the boat as it stood above the water black and bold and armed with its halberd-like tip, and a third sound, of speaking, of whispering—the whispering of the gondolier, who was talking to himself between his teeth, fitfully, in words that were pressed out by the exertion of his arms. Aschenbach looked up, and was slightly astonished to discover that the lagoon was widening, and he was headed for the open sea. This seemed to indicate that he ought not to rest too much, but should see to it that his wishes were carried out.

"To the steamer dock!" he repeated, turning around completely and looking into the face of the gondolier who stood behind on a raised platform and towered up between him and the dun-colored sky. He was a man of unpleasant, even brutal appearance, dressed in sailor-blue, with a yellow sash; a formless straw hat, its weave partially unraveled, was tilted insolently on his head. The set of his face, the blond curly mustache beneath a curtly turned-up nose, un-

doubtedly meant that he was not Italian. Although of somewhat frail build, so that one would not have thought him
especially well suited to his trade, he handled the oar with
great energy, throwing his entire body into each stroke.
Occasionally he drew back his lips from the exertion, and
disclosed his white teeth. Wrinkling his reddish brows, he
gazed on past his passenger, as he answered deliberately,
almost gruffly: "You are going to the Lido." Aschenbach
replied: "Of course. But I have just taken the gondola to
get me across to San Marco. I want to use the *vaporetto.*"

"You cannot use the *vaporetto,* sir."

"And why not?"

"Because the *vaporetto* will not haul luggage."

That was so; Aschenbach remembered. He was silent.
But the fellow's harsh, presumptuous manner, so unusual
towards a foreigner here, seemed unbearable. He said:
"That is my affair. Perhaps I want to put my things in
storage. You will turn back."

There was silence. The oar splashed, the water thudded
against the bow. And the talking and whispering began
again. The gondolier was talking to himself between his
teeth.

What was to be done? This man was strangely insolent,
and had an uncanny decisiveness; the traveler alone with
him on the water, saw no way of getting what he wanted.
And besides, how softly he could rest, if only he did not
become excited! Hadn't he wanted the trip to go on and on
for ever? It was wisest to let things take their course, and
the main thing was that he was comfortable. The poison of
inertia seemed to be issuing from the seat, from this low,
black-upholstered arm-chair, so gently cradled by the oar-
strokes of the imperious gondolier behind him. The notion
that he had fallen into the hands of a criminal passed dreamily across Aschenbach's mind—without the ability to summon his thoughts to an active defense. The possibility that
it was all simply a plan for cheating him seemed more ab-
horrent. A feeling of duty or pride, a kind of recollection

that one should prevent such things, gave him the strength
to arouse himself once more. He asked: "What are you asking for the trip?"

Looking down upon him, the gondolier answered: "You
will pay."

It was plain how this should be answered. Aschenbach
said mechanically: "I shall pay you nothing, absolutely
nothing, if you don't take me where I want to go."

"You want to go to the Lido."

"But not with you."

"I am rowing you well."

That is so, Aschenbach thought, and relaxed. That is so;
you are rowing me well. Even if you do have designs on
my cash, and send me down to Pluto with a blow of your
oar from behind, you will have rowed me well.

But nothing like that happened. They were even joined
by others: a boatload of musical brigands, men and women,
who sang to guitar and mandolin, riding persistently side
by side with the gondola and filling the silence over the
water with their covetous foreign poetry. A hat was held
out, and Aschenbach threw in money. Then they stopped
singing, and rowed away. And again the muttering of the
gondolier could be heard as he talked fitfully and jerkily to
himself.

So they arrived, tossed in the wake of a steamer plying
towards the city. Two municipal officers, their hands behind
their backs, their faces turned in the direction of the lagoon,
were walking back and forth on the bank. Aschenbach left
the gondola at the dock, supported by that old man who is
stationed with his grappling-hook at each one of Venice's
landing-places. And since he had no small money, he
crossed over to the hotel by the steamer wharf to get change
and pay the rower what was due him. He got what he
wanted in the lobby, he returned and found his traveling-
bags in a cart on the dock, and gondola and gondolier had
vanished.

"He got out in a hurry," said the old man with the grappling-hook. "A bad man, a man without a license, sir. He is the only gondolier who doesn't have a license. The others telephoned here."

Aschenbach shrugged his shoulders.

"The gentleman rode for nothing," the old man said, and held out his hat. Aschenbach tossed in a coin. He gave instructions to have his luggage taken to the beach hotel, and followed the cart through the avenue, the white-blossomed avenue which, lined on both sides with taverns, shops, and boarding-houses, runs across the island to the shore.

He entered the spacious hotel from the rear, by the terraced garden, and passed through the vestibule and the lobby until he reached the desk. Since he had been announced, he was received with obliging promptness. A manager, a small, frail, flatteringly polite man with a black mustache and a French style frock-coat, accompanied him to the third floor in the lift, and showed him his room, an agreeable place furnished in cherry wood. It was decorated with strong-smelling flowers, and its high windows afforded a view out across the open sea. He stepped up to one of them after the employee had left; and while his luggage was being brought up and placed in the room behind him, he looked down on the beach (it was comparatively deserted in the afternoon) and on the sunless ocean which was at flood-tide and was sending long low waves against the bank in a calm regular rhythm.

The experiences of a man who lives alone and in silence are both vaguer and more penetrating than those of people in society; his thoughts are heavier, more odd, and touched always with melancholy. Images and observations which could easily be disposed of by a glance, a smile, an exchange of opinion, will occupy him unbearably, sink deep into the silence, become full of meaning, become life, adventure, emotion. Loneliness ripens the eccentric, the daringly and estrangingly beautiful, the poetic. But loneliness also ripens the perverse, the disproportionate, the absurd, and the illicit. —So, the things he had met with on the trip, the ugly old fop with his twaddle about sweethearts, the lawbreaking gondolier who was cheated of his pay, still left the traveler uneasy. Without really providing any resistance to the mind, without offering any solid stuff to think over, they were nevertheless profoundly strange, as it seemed to him, and disturbing precisely because of this contradiction. In the meanwhile, he greeted the sea with his eyes, and felt pleasure at the knowledge that Venice was so conveniently near. Finally he turned away, bathed his face, left orders to the chambermaid for a few things he still needed done to make his comfort complete, and let himself be taken to the ground floor by the green-uniformed Swiss who operated the lift.

He took his tea on the terrace facing the ocean, then descended and followed the boardwalk for quite a way in the direction of the Hotel Excelsior. When he returned it seemed time to dress for dinner. He did this with his usual care and slowness, since he was accustomed to working over his toilet. And yet he came down a little early to the lobby, where he found a great many of the hotel guests assembled, mixing distantly and with a show of mutual indifference to one another, but all waiting for meal-time. He took a paper from the table, dropped into a leather chair, and observed the company; they differed agreeably from the guests where he had first stopped.

A wide and tolerantly inclusive horizon was spread out before him. Sounds of all the principal languages formed a subdued murmur. The accepted evening dress, a uniform of good manners, brought all human varieties into a fitting unity. There were Americans with their long wry features, large Russian families, English ladies, German children with French nurses. The Slavic element seemed to predominate. Polish was being spoken near by.

It was a group of children gathered around a little wicker table, under the protection of a teacher or governess: three young girls, apparently fifteen to seventeen, and a long-haired boy about fourteen years old. With astonishment Aschenbach noted that the boy was absolutely beautiful. His face, pale and reserved, framed with honey-colored hair, the straight sloping nose, the lovely mouth, the expression of sweet and godlike seriousness, recalled Greek sculpture of the noblest periods; and the complete purity of the form was accompanied by such a rare personal charm that, as he watched, he felt that he had never met with anything equally felicitous in nature or the plastic arts. He was further struck by the obviously intentional contrast with the principles of upbringing which showed in the sisters' attire and bearing. The three girls, the eldest of whom could be considered grown up, were dressed with a chasteness and severity bordering on disfigurement. Uniformly cloister-like costumes, of medium length, slate-colored, sober, and deliberately unbecoming in cut, with white turned-down collars as the only relief, suppressed every possible appeal of shapeliness. Their hair, brushed down flat and tight against the head, gave their faces a nun-like emptiness and lack of character. Surely this was a mother's influence, and it had not even occurred to her to apply the pedagogical strictness to the boy which she seemed to find necessary for her girls. It was clear that in his existence the first factors were gentleness and tenderness. The shears had been resolutely kept from his beautiful hair; like a Prince Charming's, it fell in curls over his forehead, his ears, and still deeper, across his neck. The English sailor suit, with its braids, stitchings, and embroideries, its puffy sleeves narrowing at the ends and fitting snugly about the fine wrists of his still childish but slender hands, gave the delicate figure something rich and luxurious. He was sitting, half profile to the observer, one foot in its black patent-leather shoe placed before the other, an elbow resting on the arm of his wicker chair, a cheek pressed against his fist, in a position of negligent good manners, entirely free of the almost subservient stiffness to which his sisters seemed accustomed. Did he have some illness? For his skin stood out as white as ivory against the golden darkness of the surrounding curls. Or was he simply a pampered favorite child, made this way by a doting and moody love?

Aschenbach inclined to believe the latter. Almost every artist is born with a rich and treacherous tendency to recognize injustices which have created beauty, and to meet aristocratic distinction with sympathy and reverence.

A waiter passed through and announced in English that the meal was ready. Gradually the guests disappeared through the glass door into the dining-hall. Stragglers crossed, coming from the entrance, or the lifts. Inside, they had already begun serving, but the young Poles were still waiting around the little wicker table; and Aschenbach, comfortably propped in his deep chair, and with this beauty before his eyes, stayed with them.

The governess, a small corpulent middle-class woman with a red face, finally gave the sign to rise. With lifted brows, she pushed back her chair and bowed, as a large woman dressed in gray and richly jeweled with pearls entered the lobby. This woman was advancing with coolness and precision; her lightly powdered hair and the lines of her dress were arranged with the simplicity which always signifies taste in those quarters where devoutness is taken as one element of dignity. She might have been the wife of some high German official. Except that her jewelry added something fantastically lavish to her appearance; indeed, it was almost priceless, and consisted of ear pendants and a very long triple chain of softly glowing pearls, as large as cherries.

The children had risen promptly. They bent over to kiss the hand of their mother who, with a distant smile on her well-preserved though somewhat tired and peaked features, looked over their heads and directed a few words to the governess in French. Then she walked to the glass door. The children followed her: the girls in the order of their age, after them the governess, the boy last. For some reason or other he turned around before crossing the sill, and since no one else was in the lobby his strange dusky eyes met those of Aschenbach, who, his newspaper on his knees, lost in thought, was gazing after the group.

What he saw had not been unusual in the slightest detail. They had not preceded the mother to the table; they had waited, greeted her with respect, and observed the customary forms on entering the room. But it had taken place so pointedly, with such an accent of training, duty, and self-respect, that Aschenbach felt peculiarly touched by it all. He delayed for a few moments, then he too crossed into the dining-room, and was assigned to his table, which, as he noted with a brief touch of regret, was very far removed from that of the Polish family.

Weary, and yet intellectually active, he entertained himself during the lengthy meal with abstract, or even transcendental things; he thought over the secret union which the lawful must enter upon with the individual for human beauty to result, from this he passed into general problems of form and art, and at the end he found that his thoughts and discoveries were like the seemingly felicitous promptings of a dream which, when the mind is sobered, are seen to be completely empty and unfit. After the meal, smoking, sitting, taking an occasional turn in the park with its smell of nightfall, he went to bed early and spent the night in a sleep deep and unbroken, but often enlivened with the apparitions of dreams.

The weather did not improve any the following day. A land breeze was blowing. Under a cloudy ashen sky, the sea lay in dull peacefulness; it seemed shriveled up, with a close, dreary horizon, and it had retreated from the beach, baring the long ribs of several sandbanks. As Aschenbach opened his window, he thought that he could detect the foul smell of the lagoon.

He felt depressed. He thought already of leaving. Once, years ago, after several weeks of spring here, this same weather had afflicted him, and impaired his health so seriously that he had to abandon Venice like a fugitive. Was not this old feverish unrest again setting in, the pressure in the temples, the heaviness of the eyelids? It would be annoying to change his residence still another time; but if the wind did not turn, he could not stay here. To be safe, he did not unpack completely. He breakfasted at nine in the buffet-room provided for this purpose between the lobby and the dining-room.

That formal silence reigned here which is the ambition of large hotels. The waiters who were serving walked about on soft soles. Nothing was audible but the tinkling of the tea-things, a word half whispered. In one corner, obliquely across from the door, and two tables removed from his own, Aschenbach observed the Polish girls with their governess. Erect and red-eyed, their ash-blond hair freshly smoothed down, dressed in stiff blue linen with little white cuffs and turned-down collars—they were sitting there, handing around a glass of marmalade. They had almost finished their breakfast. The boy was missing.

Aschenbach smiled. "Well, little Phæacian!" he thought. "You seem to be enjoying the pleasant privilege of having your sleep out." And, suddenly exhilarated, he recited to himself the line : "A frequent change of dress ; warm baths, and rest."

He breakfasted without haste. From the porter, who entered the hall holding his braided cap in his hand, he received some forwarded mail ; and while he smoked a cigarette he opened a few letters. In this way it happened that he was present at the entrance of the late sleeper who was being waited for over yonder.

He came through the glass door and crossed the room in silence to his sisters' table. His approach—the way he held the upper part of his body, and bent his knees, the movement of his white-shod feet—had an extraordinary charm; he walked very lightly, at once timid and proud, and this became still more lovely through the childish embarrassment with which, twice as he proceeded, he turned his face towards the center of the room, raising and lowering his eyes. Smiling, with something half muttered in his soft vague tongue, he took his place ; and now, as he turned his full profile to the observer, Aschenbach was again astonished, terrified even, by the really godlike beauty of this human child. To-day the boy was wearing a light blouse of blue and white striped cotton goods, with a red silk tie in front, and closed at the neck by a plain white high collar. This collar lacked the distinctiveness of the blouse, but above it the flowering head was poised with an incomparable seductiveness—the head of an Eros, in blended yellows of Parian marble, with fine serious brows, the temples and ears covered softly by the abrupt encroachment of his curls.

"Good, good!" Aschenbach thought, with that deliberate expert appraisal which artists sometimes employ as a subterfuge when they have been carried away with delight before a masterwork. And he thought further: "Really, if the sea and the beach weren't waiting for me, I should stay here as long as you stayed!" But he went then, passed through the lobby under the inspection of the servants, down the wide terrace, and straight across the boardwalk to the section of the beach reserved for the hotel guests. The barefoot old man in dungarees and straw hat who was functioning here as bathing-master assigned him to the bath-house he had rented; a table and a seat were placed on the sandy board platform, and he made himself comfortable in the lounge chair which he had drawn closer to the sea, out into the waxen yellow sand.

More than ever before, he was entertained and amused by the sights on the beach, this spectacle of carefree, civilized people getting sensuous enjoyment at the very edge of the elements. The gray flat sea was already alive with wading children, swimmers, a motley of figures lying on the sandbanks with arms bent behind their heads. Others were rowing about in little red and blue striped boats without keels; they were continually upsetting, amid laughter. Before the long stretches of bathing-houses, where people were sitting on the platforms as though on small verandas, there was a play of movement against the line of rest and inertness behind—visits and chatter, fastidious morning elegance alongside the nakedness which, boldly at ease, was enjoying the freedom which the place afforded. Farther in front, on the damp firm sand, people were parading about in white bathing-cloaks, in ample, brilliantly colored wrappers. An elaborate sand pile to the right, erected by children, had flags in the colors of all nations planted around it. Venders of shells, cakes, and fruit spread out their wares, kneeling. To the left, before one of the bathing-houses which stood at right angles to the others and to the sea, a Russian family was encamped: men with beards and large teeth, slow delicate women, a Baltic girl sitting by an easel and painting the sea amidst exclamations of despair, two ugly good-natured children, an old maid servant who wore a kerchief on her head and had the alert scraping manners of a slave. Delighted and appreciative, they were living there, patiently calling the names of the two rowdy disobedient children, using their scanty Italian to joke with the humorous old man from whom they were buying candy, kissing one another on the cheek, and not in the least concerned with any one who might be observing their community.

"Yes, I shall stay," Aschenbach thought. "Where would things be better?" And, his hands folded in his lap, he let his eyes lose themselves in the expanses of the sea, his gaze gliding, swimming, and failing in the monotone mist of the wilderness of space. He loved the ocean for deep-seated reasons: because of that yearning for rest, when the hard-pressed artist hungers to shut out the exacting multiplicities of experience and hide himself on the breast of the simple, the vast; and because of a forbidden hankering—seductive, by virtue of its being directly opposed to his obligations—after the incommunicable, the incommensurate, the eternal, the non-existent. To be at rest in the face of perfection is the hunger of every one who is aiming at excellence; and what is the non-existent but a form of perfection? But now, just as his dreams were so far out in vacancy, suddenly the horizontal fringe of the sea was broken by a human figure; and as he brought his eyes back from the unbounded, and focused them, it was the lovely boy who was there, coming from the left and passing him on the sand. He was bare-footed, ready for wading, his slender legs exposed above the knees; he walked slowly, but as lightly and proudly as though it were the customary thing for him to move about without shoes; and he was looking around him towards the line of bathing-houses opposite. But as soon as he had noticed the Russian family, occupied with their own harmony and contentment, a cloud of scorn and detestation passed over his face. His brow darkened, his mouth was compressed, he gave his lips an embittered twist to one side so that the cheek was distorted and the forehead became so heavily furrowed that the eyes seemed sunken beneath its pressure: malicious and glowering, they spoke the language of hate. He looked down, looked back once more threateningly, then with his shoulder made an abrupt gesture of disdain and dismissal, and left the enemy behind him.

A kind of pudency or confusion, something like respect and shyness, caused Aschenbach to turn away as though he had seen nothing. For the earnest-minded who have been casual observers of some passion, struggle against making use, even to themselves, of what they have seen. But he was both cheered and unstrung—which is to say, he was happy. This childish fanaticism, directed against the most good-natured possible aspect of life—it brought the divinely arbitrary into human relationships; it made a delightful natural picture which had appealed only to the eye now seem worthy of a deeper sympathy; and it gave the figure of this half-grown boy, who had already been important enough by his sheer beauty, something to offset him still further, and to make one take him more seriously than his years justified. Still looking away, Aschenbach could hear the boy's voice, the shrill, somewhat weak voice with which, in the distance now, he was trying to call hello to his playfellows busied around the sand pile. They answered him, shouting back his name, or some affectionate nickname; and Aschenbach listened with a certain curiosity, without being able to catch anything more definite than two melodic syllables like

"Adgio," or still more frequently "Adgiu," with a ringing
u-sound prolonged at the end. He was pleased with the resonance of this; he found it adequate to the subject. He repeated it silently and, satisfied, turned to his letters and
manuscripts.

His small portable writing-desk on his knees, he began
writing with his fountain pen an answer to this or that bit
of correspondence. But after the first fifteen minutes he
found it a pity to abandon the situation—the most enjoyable
he could think of—in this manner and waste it in activities
which did not interest him. He tossed the writing materials
to one side, and he faced the ocean again; soon afterwards,
diverted by the childish voices around the sand heap, he
revolved his head comfortably along the back of the chair
towards the right, to discover where that excellent little
Adgio might be and what he was doing.

He was found at a glance; the red tie on his breast was
not to be overlooked. Busied with the others in laying an
old plank across the damp moat of the sand castle, he was
nodding, and shouting instructions for this work. There
were about ten companions with him, boys and girls of his
age, and a few younger ones who were chattering with one
another in Polish, French, and in several Balkan tongues.
But it was his name which rang out most often. He was
openly in demand, sought after, admired. One boy especially,
like him a Pole, a stocky fellow who was called something
like "Jaschu," with sleek black hair and a belted linen coat,
seemed to be his closest vassal and friend. When the work
on the sand structure was finished for the time being, they
walked arm-in-arm along the beach and the boy who was
called "Jaschu" kissed the beauty.

Aschenbach was half minded to raise a warning finger. "I
advise you, Cristobulus," he thought, smiling, "to travel for
a year! For you need that much time at least to get over it."
And then he breakfasted on large ripe strawberries which
he got from a peddler. It had become very warm, although
the sun could no longer penetrate the blanket of mist in the

sky. Laziness clogged his brain, even while his senses delighted in the numbing, drugging distractions of the ocean's stillness. To guess, to puzzle out just what name it was that sounded something like "Adgio," seemed to the sober man an appropriate ambition, a thoroughly comprehensive pursuit. And with the aid of a few scrappy recollections of Polish he decided that they must mean "Tadzio," the shortened form of "Tadeusz," and sounding like "Tadziu" when it is called.

Tadzio was bathing. Aschenbach, who had lost sight of him, spied his head and the arm with which he was propelling himself, far out in the water; for the sea must have been smooth for a long distance out. But already people seemed worried about him; women's voices were calling after him from the bathing-houses, uttering this name again and again. It almost dominated the beach like a battle-cry, and with its soft consonants, its long-drawn *u*-note at the end, it had something at once sweet and wild about it: "Tadziu! Tadziu!" He turned back; beating the resistant water into a foam with his legs, he hurried, his head bent down over the waves. And to see how this living figure, graceful and clean-cut in its advance, with dripping curls, and lovely as some frail god, came up out of the depths of sky and sea, rose and separated from the elements—this spectacle aroused a sense of myth, it was like some poet's recovery of time at its beginning, of the origin of forms and the birth of gods. Aschenbach listened with closed eyes to this song ringing within him, and he thought again that it was pleasant here, and that he would like to remain.

Later Tadzio was resting from his bath; he lay in the sand, wrapped in his white robe, which was drawn under the right shoulder, his head supported on his bare arm. And even when Aschenbach was not observing him, but was reading a few pages in his book, he hardly ever forgot that this boy was lying there and that it would cost him only a slight turn of his head to the right to behold the mystery. It seemed that he was sitting here just to keep watch over his repose—busied with his own concerns, and yet constantly aware of this noble picture at his right, not far in the distance. And he was stirred by a paternal affection, the profound leaning which those who have devoted their thoughts to the creation of beauty feel towards those who possess beauty itself.

A little past noon he left the beach, returned to the hotel, and was taken up to his room. He stayed there for some time in front of the mirror, looking at his gray hair, his tired, sharp features. At this moment he thought of his reputation, and of the fact that he was often recognized on the streets and observed with respect, thanks to the sure aim and the appealing finish of his words. He called up all the exterior successes of his talent which he could think of, remembering also his elevation to the knighthood. Then he went down to the dining-hall for lunch, and ate at his little table. As he was riding up in the lift, after the meal was ended, a group of young people just coming from breakfast pressed into the swaying cage after him, and Tadzio entered too. He stood quite near to Aschenbach, for the first time so near that Aschenbach could see him, not with the aloofness of a picture, but in minute detail, in all his human particularities. The boy was addressed by some one or other, and as he was answering with an indescribably agreeable smile he stepped out again, on the second floor, walking backwards, and with his eyes lowered. "Beauty makes modest," Aschenbach thought, and he tried insistently to explain why this was so. But he had noticed that Tadzio's teeth were not all they should be; they were somewhat jagged and pale. The enamel did not look healthy; it had a peculiar brittleness and transparency, as is often the case with anæmics. "He is very frail, he is sickly," Aschenbach thought. "In all probability he will not grow old." And he refused to reckon with the feeling of gratification or reassurance which accompanied this notion.

He spent two hours in his room, and in the afternoon he rode in the *vaporetto* across the foul-smelling lagoon to

Venice. He got off at San Marco, took tea on the Piazza, and then, in accord with his schedule for the day, he went for a walk through the streets. Yet it was this walk which produced a complete reversal in his attitudes and his plans.

An offensive sultriness lay over the streets. The air was so heavy that the smells pouring out of homes, stores, and eating-houses became mixed with oil, vapors, clouds of perfumes, and still other odors—and these would not blow away, but hung in layers. Cigarette smoke remained suspended, disappearing very slowly. The crush of people along the narrow streets irritated rather than entertained the walker. The farther he went, the more he was depressed by the repulsive condition resulting from the combination of sea air and sirocco, which was at the same time both stimulating and enervating. He broke into an uncomfortable sweat. His eyes failed him, his chest became tight, he had a fever, the blood was pounding in his head. He fled from the crowded business streets across a bridge into the walks of the poor. On a quiet square, one of those forgotten and enchanting places which lie in the interior of Venice, he rested at the brink of a well, dried his forehead, and realized that he would have to leave here.

For the second and last time it had been demonstrated that this city in this kind of weather was decidedly unhealthy for him. It seemed foolish to attempt a stubborn resistance, while the prospects for a change of wind were completely uncertain. A quick decision was called for. It was not possible to go home this soon. Neither summer nor winter quarters were prepared to receive him. But this was not the only place where there were sea and beach; and elsewhere these could be found without the lagoon and its malarial mists. He remembered a little watering-place not far from Trieste which had been praised to him. Why not there? And without delay, so that this new change of location would still have time to do him some good. He pronounced this as good as settled, and stood up. At the next gondola station he took a boat back to San Marco, and was led through the dreary labyrinth of canals, under fancy marble balconies flanked with lions, around the corners of smooth walls, past the sorrowing façades of palaces which mirrored large dilapidated business-signs in the pulsing water. He had trouble arriving there, for the gondolier, who was in league with lace-makers and glass-blowers, was always trying to land him for inspections and purchases; and just as the bizarre trip through Venice would begin to cast its spell, the greedy business sense of the sunken Queen did all it could to destroy the illusion.

When he had returned to the hotel, he announced at the office before dinner that unforeseen developments necessitated his departure the following morning. He was assured of their regrets. He settled his accounts. He dined and spent the warm evening reading the newspapers in a rocking-chair on the rear terrace. Before going to bed he got his luggage all ready for departure.

He did not sleep so well as he might, since the impending break-up made him restless. When he opened the window in the morning, the sky was as overcast as ever, but the air seemed fresher, and he was already beginning to repent. Hadn't his decision been somewhat hasty and uncalled for, the result of a passing diffidence and indisposition? If he had delayed a little, if, instead of surrendering so easily, he had made some attempt to adjust himself to the air of Venice or to wait for an improvement in the weather, he would not be so rushed and inconvenienced. but could anticipate another forenoon on the beach like yesterday's. Too late. Now he would have to go on wanting what he had wanted yesterday. He dressed, and at about eight o'clock rode down to the ground-floor for breakfast.

As he entered, the buffet-room was still empty of guests. A few came in while he sat waiting for his order. With his tea-cup to his lips, he saw the Polish girls and their governess appear: rigid, with morning freshness, their eyes still red, they walked across to their table in the corner by the window. Immediately afterwards, the porter approached him, cap in hand, and warned him that it was time to go. The automobile is ready to take him and the other passengers to the Hotel Excelsior, and from here the motorboat will bring the ladies and gentlemen to the station through the company's private canal. Time is pressing.—Aschenbach found that it was doing nothing of the sort. It was still over an hour before his train left. He was irritated by this hotel custom of hustling departing guests out of the house, and indicated to the porter that he wished to finish his breakfast in peace. The man retired hesitatingly, to appear again five minutes later. It is impossible for the car to wait any longer. Then he would take a cab, and carry his trunk with him, Aschenbach replied in anger. He would use the public steamboat at the proper time, and he requested that it be left to him personally to worry about his departure. The employee bowed himself away. Pleased with the way he had warded off these importunate warnings, Aschenbach finished his meal at leisure; in fact, he even had the waiter bring him a newspaper. The time had become quite short when he finally arose. It was fitting that at the same moment Tadzio should come through the glass door.

On the way to his table he walked in the opposite direction to Aschenbach, lowering his eyes modestly before the man with the gray hair and high forehead, only to raise them again, in his delicious manner, soft and full upon him—and he had passed. "Good-by, Tadzio!" Aschenbach thought. "I did not see much of you." He did what was unusual with him, really formed the words on his lips and spoke them to himself; then he added: "God bless you!"—After this he left, distributed tips, was ushered out by the small gentle manager in the French frock-coat, and made off from the hotel on foot, as he had come, going along the white blossoming avenue which crossed the island to the steamer bridge, accompanied by the house servant carrying his hand luggage. He arrived, took his place—and then followed a painful journey through all the depths of regret.

It was the familiar trip across the lagoon, past San

Marco, up the Grand Canal. Aschenbach sat on the circular bench at the bow, his arm supported against the railing, shading his eyes with his hand. The public gardens were left behind, the Piazzetta opened up once more in princely splendor and was gone, then came the great flock of palaces, and as the channel made a turn the magnificently slung marble arch of the Rialto came into view. The traveler was watching; his emotions were in conflict. The atmosphere of the city, this slightly foul smell of sea and swamp which he had been so anxious to avoid—he breathed it now in deep, exquisitely painful draughts. Was it possible that he had not known, had not considered, just how much he was attached to all this? What had been a partial misgiving this morning, a faint doubt as to the advisability of his move, now became a distress, a positive misery, a spiritual hunger, and so bitter that it frequently brought tears to his eyes, while he told himself that he could not possibly have foreseen it. Hardest of all to bear, at times completely insufferable, was the thought that he would never see Venice again, that this was a leave-taking for ever. Since it had been shown for the second time that the city affected his health, since he was compelled for the second time to get away in all haste, from now on he would have to consider it a place impossible and forbidden to him, a place which he was not equal to, and which it would be foolish for him to visit again. Yes, he felt that if he left now, he would be shamefaced and defiant enough never to see again the beloved city which had twice caused him a physical breakdown. And of a sudden this struggle between his desires and his physical strength seemed to the aging man so grave and important, his physical defeat seemed so dishonorable, so much a challenge to hold out at any cost, that he could not understand the ready submissive-ness of the day before, when he had decided to give in with-out attempting any serious resistance.

Meanwhile the steamboat was nearing the station; pain and perplexity increased, he became distracted. In his afflic-tion, he felt that it was impossible to leave, and just as impossible to turn back. The conflict was intense as he entered the station. It was very late; there was not a moment to lose if he was to catch the train. He wanted to, and he did not want to. But time was pressing; it drove him on. He hurried to get his ticket, and looked about in the tumult of the hall for the officer on duty here from the hotel. The man appeared and announced that the large trunk had been transferred. Transferred already? Yes, thank you—to Como. To Como? And in the midst of hasty running back and forth, angry questions and confused answers, it came to light that the trunk had already been sent with other foreign baggage from the express office of the Hotel Excelsior in a completely wrong direction.

Aschenbach had difficulty in preserving the expression which was required under these circumstances. He was almost convulsed with an adventurous delight, an unbelievable hilarity. The employee rushed off to see if it were still possible to stop the trunk, and, as was to be expected, he returned with nothing accomplished. Aschenbach declared that he did not want to travel without his trunk, but had decided to go back and wait at the beach hotel for its return. Was the company's motorboat still at the station? The man assured him that it was lying at the door. With Italian volubility be persuaded the clerk at the ticket window to redeem the canceled ticket, he swore that they would act speedily, that no time or money would be spared in recovering the trunk promptly, and—so the strange thing happened that, twenty minutes after his arrival at the station, the traveler found himself again on the Grand Canal, returning to the Lido.

Here was an adventure, wonderful, abashing, and comically dreamlike, beyond belief: places which he had just bid farewell to for ever in the most abject misery—yet he had been turned and driven back by fate, and was seeing them again in the same hour! The spray from the prow, washing between gondolas and steamers with an absurd agility, shot the speedy little craft ahead to its goal, while the lone pas-

senger was hiding the nervousness and ebullience of a truant
boy under a mask of resigned anger. From time to time he
shook with laughter at this mishap which, as he told himself, could not have turned out better for a child of destiny.
There were explanations to be given, expressions of astonishment to be faced—and then, he told himself, everything
would be all right; then a misfortune would be avoided, a
grave error rectified. And all that he had thought he was
leaving behind him would be open to him again, there at
his disposal. . . . And, to cap it all, was the rapidity of the
ride deceiving him, or was the wind really coming from the
sea?

The waves beat against the walls of the narrow canal
which runs through the island to the Hotel Excelsior. An
automobile omnibus was awaiting his return there, and took
him above the rippling sea straight to the beach hotel. The
little manager with mustache and long-tailed frock-coat
came down the stairs to meet him.

He ingratiatingly regretted the episode, spoke of it as
highly painful to him and the establishment, but firmly approved of Aschenbach's decision to wait here for the baggage. Of course his room had been given up, but there was
another one, just as good, which he could occupy immediately. *"Pas de chance, Monsieur,"* the Swiss elevator boy
smiled as they were ascending. And so the fugitive was established again, in a room almost identical with the other in
its location and furnishings.

Tired out by the confusion of this strange forenoon, he
distributed the contents of his hand-bag about the room
and dropped into an arm-chair by the open window. The sea
had become a pale green, the air seemed thinner and purer;
the beach with its cabins and boats, seemed to have color,
although the sky was still gray. Aschenbach looked out, his
hands folded in his lap; he was content to be back, but shook
his head disapprovingly at his irresolution, his failure to
know his own mind. He sat here for the better part of an
hour, resting and dreaming vaguely. About noon he saw

Tadzio in a striped linen suit with a red tie, coming back from the sea across the private beach and along the board-walk to the hotel. Aschenbach recognized him from this alti-tude before he had actually set eyes on him; he was about to think some such words as "Well, Tadzio, there you are again!" but at the same moment he felt this careless greet-ing go dumb before the truth in his heart. He felt the ex-hilaration of his blood, a conflict of pain and pleasure, and he realized that it was Tadzio who had made it so difficult for him to leave.

He sat very still, entirely unobserved from this height, and looked within himself. His features were alert, his eye-brows raised, and an attentive, keenly inquisitive smile dis-tended his mouth. Then he raised his head, lifted both hands, which had hung relaxed over the arms of the chair, and in a slow twisting movement turned the palms upward—as though to suggest an opening and spreading outward of his arms. It was a spontaneous act of welcome, of calm accept-ance.

IV

Day after day now the naked god with the hot cheeks drove his fire-breathing quadriga across the expanses of the sky, and his yellow locks fluttered in the assault of the east wind. A white silk sheen stretched over the slowly sim-mering Ponto. The sand glowed. Beneath the quaking silver blue of the ether, rust-colored canvases were spread in front of the bathing-houses, and the afternoons were spent in the sharply demarcated spots of shade which they cast. But it was also delightful in the evening, when the vegetation in the park had the smell of balsam, and the stars were working through their courses above, and the soft persistent murmur of the sea came up enchantingly through the night. Such evenings contained the cheering promise that more sunny days of casual idleness would follow, dotted with countless closely interspersed possibilities of well-timed accidents.

The guest who was detained here by such an accommodating mishap did not consider the return of his property as sufficient grounds for another departure. He suffered some inconvenience for two days, and had to appear for meals in the large dining-room in his traveling-clothes. When the strayed luggage was finally deposited in his room again, he unpacked completely and filled the closet and drawers with his belongings; he had decided to remain here indefinitely, content now that he could pass the hours on the beach in a silk suit and appear for dinner at his little table again in appropriate evening dress.

The comfortable rhythm of this life had already cast its spell over him; he was soon enticed by the ease, the mild splendor, of his program. Indeed, what a place to be in, when the usual allurement of living in watering-places on southern shores was coupled with the immediate nearness of the most wonderful of all cities! Aschenbach was not a lover of pleasure. Whenever there was some call for him to take a holiday, to indulge himself, to have a good time—and this was especially true at an earlier age—restlessness and repugnance soon drove him back to his rigorous toil, the faithful sober efforts of his daily routine. Except that this place was bewitching him, relaxing his will, making him happy. In the mornings, under the shelter of his bathing-house, letting his eyes roam dreamily in the blue of the southern sea; or on a warm night as he leaned back against the cushions of the gondola carrying him under the broad starry sky home to the Lido from the Piazza di San Marco after long hours of idleness—and the brilliant lights, the melting notes of the serenade were being left behind—he often recalled his place in the mountains, the scene of his battles in the summer, where the clouds blew low across his garden, and terrifying storms put out the lamps at night, and the crows which he fed were swinging in the tops of the pine-trees. Then everything seemed just right to him, as though he were lifted into the Elysian fields, on the borders of the earth, where man enjoys the easiest life, where there is no snow or winter, nor storms and pouring rains. but where Oceanus continually sends forth gentle cooling breezes, and the days pass in a blessed inactivity, without work, without effort, devoted wholly to the sun and to the feast-days of the sun.

Aschenbach saw the boy Tadzio frequently, almost constantly. Owing to the limited range of territory and the regularity of their lives, the beauty was near him at short intervals throughout the day. He saw him, met him, everywhere: in the lower rooms of the hotel, on the cooling water trips to the city and back, in the arcades of the square, and at times when he was especially lucky ran across him on the streets. But principally, and with the most gratifying regularity, the forenoon on the beach allowed him to admire and study this rare spectacle at his leisure. Yes, it was this guaranty of happiness, this daily recurrence of good fortune, which made his stay here so precious, and gave him such pleasure in the constant procession of sunny days.

He was up as early as he used to be when under the driving pressure of work, and was on the beach before most people, when the sun was still mild and the sea lay blinding white in the dreaminess of morning. He spoke amiably to the guard of the private beach, and also spoke familiarly to the barefoot, white-bearded old man who had prepared his place for him, stretching the brown canopy and bringing the furniture of the cabin out on the platform. Then he took his seat. There would now be three or four hours in which the sun mounted and gained terrific strength, the sea a deeper and deeper blue, and he might look at Tadzio.

He saw him approaching from the left, along the edge of the sea; he saw him as he stepped out backwards from among the cabins; or he would suddenly find, with a shock of pleasure, that he had missed his coming, that he was already here in the blue and white bathing-suit which was his only garment now while on the beach, that he had already commenced his usual activities in the sun and the sand—a pleasantly trifling, idle, and unstable manner of living, a mixture of rest and play. Tadzio would saunter about, wade, dig, catch things, lie down, go for a swim, all the while being kept under surveillance by the women on the platform who made his name ring out in their falsetto voices: "Tadziu! Tadziu!" Then he would come running to them with a look of eagerness, to tell them what he had seen, what he had experienced, or to show them what he had found or caught: mussels, sea-horses, jelly-fish, and crabs that ran sideways. Aschenbach did not understand a word he said, and though it might have been the most ordinary thing in the world, it was a vague harmony in his ear. So the foreignness of the boy's speech turned it into music, a wanton sun poured its prodigal splendor down over him, and his figure was always set off against the background of an intense sea-blue.

This piquant body was so freely exhibited that his eyes soon knew every line and posture. He was continually rediscovering with new pleasure all this familiar beauty, and his astonishment at its delicate appeal to his senses was unending. The boy was called to greet a guest who was paying his respects to the ladies at the bathing-house. He came running, running wet perhaps out of the water, tossed back his curls, and as he held out his hand, resting on one leg and raising his other foot on the toes, the set of his body was delightful; it had a charming expectancy about it, a well-meaning shyness, a winsomeness which showed his aristocratic training. . . . He lay stretched full length, his bath towel slung across his shoulders, his delicately chiseled arm supported in the sand, his chin in his palm; the boy called Jaschu was squatting near him and making up to him—and nothing could be more enchanting than the smile of his eyes and lips when the leader glanced up at his inferior, his servant. . . . He stood on the edge of the sea, alone, apart from his people, quite near to Aschenbach—erect, his hands locked across the back of his neck, he swayed slowly on the balls of his feet, looked dreamily into the blueness of sea and sky, while tiny waves rolled up and bathed his feet. His honey-colored hair clung in rings about his neck and temples.

The sun made the down on his back glitter; the fine etching of the ribs, the symmetry of the chest, were emphasized by the tightness of the suit across the buttocks. His armpits were still as smooth as those of a statue; the hollows of his knees glistened, and their bluish veins made his body seem built of some clearer stuff. What rigor, what precision of thought were expressed in this erect, youthfully perfect body! Yet the pure and strenuous will which, darkly at work, could bring such godlike sculpture to the light—was not he, the artist, familiar with this? Did it not operate in him too when he, under the press of frugal passions, would free from the marble mass of speech some slender form which he had seen in the mind and which he put before his fellows as a statue and a mirror of intellectual beauty?

Statue and mirror! His eyes took in the noble form there bordered with blue; and with a rush of enthusiasm he felt that in this spectacle he was catching the beautiful itself, form as the thought of God, the one pure perfection which lives in the mind, and which, in this symbol and likeness, had been placed here quietly and simply as an object of devotion. That was drunkenness; and eagerly, without thinking, the aging artist welcomed it. His mind was in travail; all that he had learned dropped back into flux; his understanding threw up age-old thoughts which he had inherited with youth though they had never before lived with their own fire. Is it not written that the sun diverts our attention from intellectual to sensual things? Reason and understanding, it is said, become so numbed and enchanted that the soul forgets everything out of delight with its immediate circumstances, and in astonishment becomes attached to the most beautiful object shined on by the sun; indeed, only with the aid of a body is it capable then of raising itself to higher considerations. To be sure, Amor did as the instructors of mathematics who show backward children tangible representations of the pure forms—similarly the god, in order to make the spiritual visible for us, readily utilized the form and color of man's youth, and as a reminder he adorned these with the reflected splendor of beauty which, when we behold it, makes us flare up in pain and hope.

His enthusiasm suggested these things, put him in the mood for them. And from the noise of the sea and the luster of the sun he wove himself a charming picture. Here was the old plane-tree, not far from the walls of Athens—a holy, shadowy place filled with the smell of *agnus castus* blossoms and decorated with ornament and images sacred to Achelous and the Nymphs. Clear and pure, the brook at the foot of the spreading tree fell across the smooth pebbles; the cicadas were fiddling. But on the grass, which was like a pillow gently sloping to the head, two people were stretched out, in hiding from the heat of the day: an older man and a youth, one ugly and one beautiful, wisdom next to loveliness. And amid gallantries and skillfully engaging banter, Socrates was instructing Phædrus in matters of desire and virtue. He spoke to him of the hot terror which the initiate suffer when their eyes light on an image of the eternal beauty; spoke of the greed of the impious and the wicked who cannot think beauty when they see its likeness, and who are incapable of reverence; spoke of the holy distress which befalls the noble-minded when a god-like countenance, a perfect body, appears before them; they tremble and grow distracted, and hardly dare to raise their eyes, and they honor the man who possesses this beauty, yes, if they were not afraid of being thought downright madmen they would sacrifice to the beloved as to the image of a god. For beauty, my Phædrus, beauty alone is both lovely and visible at once; it is, mark me, the only form of the spiritual which we can receive through the senses. Else what would become of us if the divine, if reason and virtue and truth, should appear to us through the senses? Should we not perish and be consumed with love, as Semele once was with Zeus? Thus, beauty is the sensitive man's access to the spirit—but only a road, a means simply, little Phædrus. . . . And then this crafty suitor made the neatest remark of all; it was this, that the lover is more divine than the beloved, since the god is in the one, but not in the other—perhaps the most delicate, the most derisive thought which has ever been framed, and the one from which spring all the cunning and the profoundest pleasures of desire.

Writers are happiest with an idea which can become all emotion, and an emotion all idea. Just such a pulsating idea, such a precise emotion, belonged to the lonely man at this moment, was at his call. Nature, it ran, shivers with ecstasy when the spirit bows in homage before beauty. Suddenly he wanted to write. Eros loves idleness, they say, and he is suited only to idleness. But at this point in the crisis the affliction became a stimulus towards productivity. The incentive hardly mattered. A request, an agitation for an open statement on a certain large burning issue of culture and taste, was going about the intellectual world, and had finally caught up with the traveler here. He was familiar with the subject, it had touched his own experience; and suddenly he felt an irresistible desire to display it in the light of his own version. And he even went so far as to prefer working in Tadzio's presence, taking the scope of the boy as a standard for his writing, making his style follow the lines of this body which seemed godlike to him, and carrying his beauty over into the spiritual just as the eagle once carried the Trojan stag up into the ether. Never had his joy in words been more sweet. He had never been so aware that Eros is in the word as during those perilously precious hours when, at his crude table under the canopy, facing the idol and listening to the music of his voice, he followed Tadzio's beauty in the forming of his little tract, a page and a half of choice prose which was soon to excite the admiration of many through its clarity, its poise, and the vigorous curve of its emotion. Certainly it is better for people to know only the beautiful product as finished, and not in its conception, its conditions of origin. For knowledge of the sources from which the artist derives his inspiration would often confuse and alienate, and in this way detract from the effects of his mastery. Strange hours! Strangely enervating efforts! Rare creative intercourse between the spirit and body! When Aschenbach put away his work and started back from the beach, he felt exhausted, or in dispersion even; and it was as though his conscience were complaining after some transgression.

The following morning, as he was about to leave the hotel, he looked off from the steps and noticed that Tadzio, who was alone and was already on his way towards the sea, was just approaching the private beach. He was half tempted by the simple notion of seizing this opportunity to strike up a casual friendly acquaintanceship with the boy who had been the unconscious source of so much agitation and upheaval; he wanted to address him, and enjoy the answering look in his eyes. The boy was sauntering along, he could be overtaken; and Aschenbach quickened his pace. He reached him on the boardwalk behind the bathing-houses; was about to lay a hand on his head and shoulders; and some word or other, an amiable phrase in French, was on the tip of his tongue. But he felt that his heart, due also perhaps to his rapid stride, was beating like a hammer; and he was so short of breath that his voice would have been tight and trembling. He hesitated, he tried to get himself under control. Suddenly he became afraid that he had been walking too long so close behind the boy. He was afraid of arousing curiosity and causing him to look back questioningly. He made one more spurt, failed, surrendered, and passed with bowed head.

"Too late!" he thought immediately. Too late! Yet was it too late? This step which he had just been on the verge of taking would very possibly have put things on a sound, free and easy basis, and would have restored him to wholesome soberness. But the fact was that Aschenbach did not want soberness: his intoxication was too precious. Who can explain the stamp and the nature of the artist? Who can understand this deep instinctive welding of discipline and license? For to be unable to want wholesome soberness, is license. Aschenbach was no longer given to self-criticism.

their horns as they ran. Yet among the detritus of the more distant beach, waves were hopping forward like agile goats. He was caught in the enchantment of a sacredly distorted world full of Panic life—and he dreamed delicate legends. Often, when the sun was sinking behind Venice, he would sit on a bench in the park observing Tadzio, who was dressed in a white suit with a colored sash and was playing ball on the smooth gravel—and it was Hyacinth that he seemed to be watching. Hyacinth who was to die because two gods loved him. Yes, he felt Zephyr's aching jealousy of the rival who forgot the oracle, the bow, and the lyre, in order to play for ever with this beauty. He saw the discus, guided by a pitiless envy, strike the lovely head; he too, growing pale, caught the drooping body—and the flower, sprung from this sweet blood, bore the inscription of his unending grief.

Nothing is more unusual and strained than the relationship between people who know each other only with their eyes, who meet daily, even hourly, and yet are compelled, by force of custom or their own caprices, to say no word or make no move of acknowledgment, but to maintain the appearance of an aloof unconcern. There is a restlessness and a surcharged curiosity existing between them, the hysteria of an unsatisfied, unnaturally repressed desire for acquaintanceship and intercourse; and especially there is a kind of tense respect. For one person loves and honors another so long as he cannot judge him, and desire is an evidence of incomplete knowledge.

Some kind of familiarity had necessarily to form itself between Aschenbach and young Tadzio; and it gave the elderly man keen pleasure to see that his sympathies and interests were not left completely unanswered. For example, when the boy appeared on the beach in the morning and was going towards his family's bathing-house, what had induced him never to use the boardwalk on the far side of it any more, but to stroll along the front path, through the sand, past Aschenbach's habitual place, and often unneces-

cross.
weigh
mente
singin
of the
cial o
of the
Asche
hunted

Wh
portals
the lov
in wait
dren t
turned
sure th
the roa
and int
he foll
Venice.
flight i
back. H
bridges
minute:
toward:
possibl
drunk,
who de
foot.

In on
and sho
enbach,
they we
ried un
of a gen
gondola
when th

sarily close to him, almost touching his table, or his chair even? Did the attraction, the fascination of an overpowering emotion have such an effect upon the frail unthinking object of it? Aschenbach watched daily for Tadzio to approach; and sometimes he acted as though he were occupied when this event was taking place, and he let the boy pass unobserved. But at other times he would look up, and their glances met. They were both in deep earnest when this occurred. Nothing in the elderly man's cultivated and dignified expression betrayed any inner movement; but there was a searching look in Tadzio's eyes, a thoughtful questioning—he began to falter, looked down, then looked up again charmingly, and, when he had passed, something in his bearing seemed to indicate that it was only his breeding which kept him from turning around.

Once, however, one evening, things turned out differently. The Polish children and their governess had been missing at dinner in the large hall; Aschenbach had noted this uneasily. After the meal, disturbed by their absence, Aschenbach was walking in evening dress and straw hat in front of the hotel at the foot of the terrace, when suddenly he saw the nunlike sisters appear in the light of the arc-lamp, accompanied by their governess and with Tadzio a few steps behind. Evidently they were coming from the steamer pier after having dined for some reason in the city. It must have been cool on the water; Tadzio was wearing a dark blue sailor overcoat with gold buttons, and on his head he had a cap to match. The sun and sea air had not browned him; his skin still had the same yellow marble color as at first. It even seemed paler to-day than usual, whether from the coolness or from the blanching moonlight of the lamps. His regular eyebrows showed up more sharply, the darkness of his eyes was deeper. It is hard to say how beautiful he was; and Aschenbach was distressed, as he had often been before, by the thought that words can only evaluate sensuous beauty, but not re-give it.

He had not been prepared for this rich spectacle; it came

plice, assured him in the same tone that his wishes would be carried out, carried out faithfully.

Leaning back against the soft black cushions, he rocked and glided towards the other black-beaked craft where his passion was drawing him. At times it escaped; then he felt worried and uneasy. But his pilot, as though skilled in such commissions, was always able through sly maneuvers, speedy diagonals and shortcuts, to bring the quest into view again. The air was quiet and smelly, the sun burned down strong through the slate-colored mist. Water slapped against the wood and stone. The call of the gondolier, half warning, half greeting, was answered with a strange obedience far away in the silence of the labyrinth. White and purple umbels with the scent of almonds hung down from little elevated gardens over crumbling walls. Arabian window-casings were outlined through the murkiness. The marble steps of a church descended into the water; a beggar squatted there, protesting his misery, holding out his hat, and showing the whites of his eyes as though he were blind. An antiquarian in front of his den fawned on the passer-by and invited him to stop in the hopes of swindling him. That was Venice, the flatteringly and suspiciously beautiful—this city, half legend, half snare for strangers; in its foul air art once flourished gluttonously, and had suggested to its musicians seductive notes which cradle and lull. The adventurer felt as though his eyes were taking in this same luxury, as though his ears were being won by just such melodies. He recalled too that the city was diseased and was concealing this through greed—and he peered more eagerly after the retreating gondola.

Thus, in his infatuation, he wanted simply to pursue uninterrupted the object that aroused him, to dream of it when it was not there, and, after the fashion of lovers, to speak softly to its mere outline. Loneliness, strangeness, and the joy of a deep belated intoxication encouraged him and prompted him to accept even the remotest things without reserve or shame—with the result that as he returned late in

Aschenbach
marks on the
   Yet that s
pened that a
gave a perfo
men and two
lamp and tur
terrace where
their coffee ;
boys, waiters
tening by the
eager and p
chairs placed
formers; and
circle. Behind
kerchief, stoo
   Mandolin,
responding to
mental numbe
of the women
sweetly false
real talent ar
other of the ty
of *buffo* barit
have a gift fo
Often, with h
leave the rest
the platform,
aging laughte
front seemed
bility, and the
and more bol
   Aschenbach
and then with
which glowed
nerves took i
melodies; for

the evening from Venice, he stopped on the second floor of
the hotel before the door of the boy's room, laid his head in
utter drunkenness against the hinge of the door, and for a
long time could not drag himself away despite the danger of
being caught and embarrassed in such a mad situation.

Yet there were still moments of relief when he came
partly to his senses. "Where to!" he would think, alarmed.
"Where to!" Like every man whose natural abilities stimu-
late an aristocratic interest in his ancestry, he was accustomed to think of his forbears in connection with the accom-
plishments and successes of his life, to assure himself of
their approval, their satisfaction, their undeniable respect.
He thought of them now, entangled as he was in such an
illicit experience, caught in such exotic transgressions. He
thought of their characteristic rigidity of principle, their
scrupulous masculinity—and he smiled dejectedly. What
would they say? But then, what would they have said to his
whole life, which was almost degenerate in its departure
from theirs, this life under the bane of art—a life against
which he himself had once issued such youthful mockeries
out of loyalty to his fathers, but which at bottom had been
so much like theirs! He too had served, he too had been a
soldier and a warrior like many of them—for art was a war,
a destructive battle, and one was not equal to it for long,
these days. A life of self-conquest and of in-spite-ofs, a
rigid, sober, and unyielding life which he had formed into
the symbol of a delicate and timely heroism. He might well
call it masculine, or brave; and it almost seemed as though
the Eros mastering him were somehow peculiarly adapted
and inclined to such a life. Had not this Eros stood in high
repute among the bravest of people; was it not true that
precisely through bravery he had flourished in their cities?
Numerous war heroes of antiquity had willingly borne his
yoke, for nothing was deemed a disgrace which the god im-
posed; and acts which would have been rebuked as the sign
of cowardice if they had been done for other purposes—
prostrations, oaths, entreaties, abjectness—such things did

not bring
for them.
In this
thoughts,
his respec
turned his
ice, this
darkly wi
lawless h
Bent o
progress
the city c
table of t
alternated
dead was
and more
the plague
pletely is
There we
gerous co
sible. Ne
participat
derived a
questions
to silence,
fast in th
with the
French fi
about am
table for
negligent
alent in
answer, '
vent any
which mi
ening we

surrenders in all seriousness to appeals which, in sober moments, are either humorously allowed for or rejected with annoyance. At the clown's antics his features had twisted into a set painful smile. He sat there relaxed, although inwardly he was intensely awake; for six paces from him Tadzio was leaning against the stone hand-rail.

In the white belted coat which he often wore at meal times, he was standing in a position of spontaneous and inborn gracefulness, his left forearm on the railing, feet crossed, the right hand on a supporting hip; and he looked down at the street-singers with an expression which was hardly a smile, but only an aloof curiosity, a polite amiability. Often he would stand erect and, expanding his chest, would draw the white smock down under his leather belt with a beautiful gesture. And then too, the aging man observed with a tumult of fright and triumph how he would often turn his head over the left shoulder in the direction of his admirer, carefully and hesitatingly, or even with abruptness as though to attack by surprise. He did not meet Aschenbach's eyes, for a mean precaution compelled the transgressor to keep from staring at him: in the background of the terrace the women who guarded Tadzio were sitting, and things had reached a point where the lover had to fear he might be noticed and suspected. Yes, he had often observed with a kind of numbness how, when Tadzio was near him, on the beach, in the hotel lobby, in the Piazza San Marco, they called him back, they were set on keeping him at a distance—and this wounded him frightfully, causing his pride unknown tortures which his conscience would not permit him to evade.

Meanwhile the guitar-player had begun a solo to his own accompaniment, a street-ballad popular throughout Italy. It had several strophes, and the entire company joined each time in the refrain, all singing and playing, while he managed to give a plastic and dramatic twist to the performance. Of slight build, with thin and impoverished features, he stood on the gravel, apart from his companions, in an atti-

tude of insolent bravado, his shabby felt hat on the back of
his head so that a bunch of his red hair jutted out from under
the brim. And to the thrumming of the strings he flung his
jokes up at the terrace in a penetrating recitative; while the
veins were swelling on his forehead from the exertion of
his performance. He did not seem of Venetian stock, but
rather of the race of Neapolitan comedians, half pimp, half
entertainer, brutal and audacious, dangerous and amusing.
His song was stupid enough so far as the words went; but
in his mouth, by his gestures, the movements of his body, his
way of blinking significantly and letting the tongue play
across his lips, it acquired something ambiguous, something
vaguely repulsive. In addition to the customary civilian
dress, he was wearing a sport shirt; and his skinny neck protruded above the soft collar, baring a noticeably large and
active Adam's-apple. He was pale and snub-nosed. It was
hard to fix an age to his beardless features, which seemed
furrowed with grimaces and depravity; and the two wrinkles standing arrogantly, harshly, almost savagely between
his reddish eyebrows were strangely suited to the smirk on
his mobile lips. Yet what really prompted the lonely man to
pay him keen attention was the observation that the questionable figure seemed also to provide its own questionable
atmosphere. For each time they came to the refrain the
singer, amid buffoonery and familiar handshakes, began a
grotesque circular march which brought him immediately
beneath Aschenbach's place; and each time this happened
there blew up to the terrace from his clothes and body a
strong carbolic smell.

After the song was ended, he began collecting money.
He started with the Russians, who were evidently willing
to spend, and then came up the stairs. Up here he showed
himself just as humble as he had been bold during the performance. Cringing and bowing, he stole about among the
tables, and a smile of obsequious cunning exposed his strong
teeth, while the two wrinkles still stood ominously between
his red eyebrows. This singular character collecting money

to live on—they eyed him with a curiosity and a kind of repugnance, they tossed coins into his felt hat with the tips of their fingers, and were careful not to touch him. The elimination of the physical distance between the comedian and the audience, no matter how great the enjoyment may have been, always causes a certain uneasiness. He felt it, and tried to excuse it by groveling. He came up to Aschenbach, and along with him the smell, which no one else seemed concerned about.

"Listen!" the recluse said in an undertone, almost mechanically. "They are disinfecting Venice. Why?" The jester answered hoarsely: "On account of the police. That is a precaution, sir, with such heat, and the sirocco. The sirocco is oppressive. It is not good for the health." He spoke as though astonished that any one could ask such things and demonstrated with his open hand how oppressive the sirocco was. "Then there is no plague in Venice?" Aschenbach asked quietly, between his teeth. The clown's muscular features fell into a grimace of comical embarrassment. "A plague? What kind of plague? Perhaps our police are a plague? You like to joke! A plague! Of all things! A precautionary measure, you understand! A police regulation against the effects of the oppressive weather." He gesticulated. "Very well," Aschenbach said several times curtly and quietly; and he quickly dropped an unduly large coin into the hat. Then with his eyes he signaled the man to leave. He obeyed, smirking and bowing. But he had not reached the stairs before two hotel employees threw themselves upon him, and with their faces close to his began a whispered cross-examination. He shrugged his shoulders; he gave assurances, he swore that he had kept quiet—that was evident. He was released, and he returned to the garden; then, after a short conference with his companions, he stepped out once more for a final song of thanks and leave-taking.

It was a rousing song which the recluse never recalled having heard before, a "big number" in incomprehensible dialect, with a laugh refrain in which the troupe joined regularly at the tops of their voices. At this point both the words and the accompaniment of the instruments stopped, with nothing left but a laugh which was somehow arranged rhythmically although very naturally done—and the soloist especially showed great talent in giving it a most deceptive vitality. At the renewal of his professional distance from the audience, he recovered all his boldness again, and the artificial laugh that he directed up towards the terrace was derisive. Even before the end of the articulate portion of the strophe, he seemed to struggle against an irresistible tickling. He gulped, his voice trembled, he pressed his hand over his mouth, he contorted his shoulders; and at the proper moment the ungovernable laugh broke out of him, burst into such real cackles that it was infectious and communicated itself to the audience, so that on the terrace also an unfounded hilarity, living off itself alone, started up. But this seemed to double the singer's exuberance. He bent his knees, he slapped his thighs, he nearly split himself; he no longer laughed, he shrieked. He pointed up with his finger, as though nothing were more comic than the laughing guests there, and finally every one in the garden and on the veranda was laughing, even to the waiters, bell-boys, and house-servants in the doorways.

Aschenbach was no longer resting in his chair; he sat upright, as if attempting to defend himself, or to escape. But the laughter, the whiffs of the hospital smell, and the boy's nearness combined to put him into a trance that held his mind and his senses hopelessly captive. In the general movement and distraction he ventured to glance across at Tadzio, and as he did so he dared observe that the boy, in reply to his glance, was equally serious, much as though he had modeled his conduct and expression after those of one man, and the prevalent mood had no effect on him since this one man was not part of it. This portentous childish obedience had something so disarming and overpowering about it that the gray-haired man could hardly restrain himself from burying his face in his hands. It had also seemed to him that Tadzio's occasional stretching and quick breathing indicated a complaint, a congestion, of the lungs. "He is sickly, he will probably not grow old," he thought repeatedly with that positiveness which is often a peculiar relief to desire and passion. And along with pure solicitude he had a feeling of rakish gratification.

Meanwhile the Venetians had ended and were leaving. Applause accompanied them, and their leader did not miss the opportunity to cover his retreat with further jests. His bows, the kisses he blew, were laughed at—and so he doubled them. When his companions were already gone, he acted as though he had hurt himself by backing into a lamp-post, and he crept through the gate seemingly crippled with pain. Then he suddenly threw off the mask of comic hard luck, stood upright, hurried away jauntily, stuck out his tongue insolently at the guests on the terrace, and slipped into the darkness. The company was breaking up; Tadzio had been missing from the balustrade for some time. But, to the displeasure of the waiters, the lonely man sat for a long while over the remains of his pomegranate drink. Night advanced. Time was crumbling. In the house of his parents many years back there had been an hour glass—of a sudden he saw the fragile and expressive instrument again, as though it were standing in front of him. Fine and noiseless the rust-red sand was running through the glass neck; and since it was getting low in the upper half, a speedy little vortex had been formed there.

As early as the following day, in the afternoon, he had made new progress in his obstinate baiting of the people he met—and this time he had all possible success. He walked from the Piazza of St. Mark's into the English traveling-bureau located there; and after changing some money at the cash desk, he put on the expression of a distrustful foreigner and launched his fatal question at the attendant clerk. He was a Britisher; he wore a woolen suit, and was still young, with close-set eyes, and had that characteristic stolid reliability which is so peculiarly and strikingly appealing in the tricky, nimble-witted South. He began: "No reason for alarm, sir. A regulation without any serious significance. Such measures are often taken to anticipate the unhealthy effects of the heat and the sirocco . . ." But as he raised his blue eyes, he met the stare of the foreigner, a tired and somewhat unhappy stare focused on his lips with a touch of scorn. Then the Englishman blushed. "At least," he continued in an emotional undertone, "that is the official explanation which people here are content to accept. I will admit that there is something more behind it." And then in his frank and leisurely manner he told the truth.

For several years now Indian cholera had shown a heightened tendency to spread and migrate. Hatched in the warm swamps of the Ganges delta, rising with the noxious breath of that luxuriant, unfit primitive world and island wilderness which is shunned by humans and where the tiger crouches in the bamboo thickets, the plague had raged continuously and with unusual strength in Hindustan, had reached eastwards to China, westward to Afghanistan and Persia, and, following the chief caravan routes, had carried its terrors to Astrachan, and even to Moscow. But while Europe was trembling last the specter continue its advance from there across the country, it had been transported over the sea by Syrian merchantmen, and had turned up almost simultaneously in several Mediterranean ports, had raised its head in Toulon and Malaga, had showed its mask several times in Palermo and Naples, and seemed permanently entrenched through Calabria and Apulia. The north of the peninsula had been spared. Yet in the middle of this May in Venice the frightful vibrions were found on one and the same day in the blackish wasted bodies of a cabin boy and a woman who sold greengroceries. The cases were kept secret. But within a week there were ten, twenty, thirty more, and in various sections. A man from the Austrian provinces who had made a pleasure trip to Venice for a few days, returned to his home town and died with un-

mistakable symptoms—and that is how the first reports of
the pestilence in the lagoon city got into the German newspapers. The Venetian authorities answered that the city's
health conditions had never been better, and took the most
necessary preventive measures. But probably the food supply had been infected. Denied and glossed over, death was
eating its way along the narrow streets, and its dissemina-
tion was especially favored by the premature summer heat
which made the water of the canals lukewarm. Yes, it
seemed as though the plague had got renewed strength, as
though the tenacity and fruitfulness of its stimuli had doubled. Cases of recovery were rare. Out of a hundred attacks,
eighty were fatal, and in the most horrible manner. For the
plague moved with utter savagery, and often showed that
most dangerous form which is called "the drying." Water
from the blood vessels collected in pockets, and the blood
was unable to carry this off. Within a few hours the victim
was parched, his blood became as thick as glue, and he stifled
amid cramps and hoarse groans. Lncky for him if, as sometimes happened, the attack took the form of a light discom-
fiture followed by a profound coma from which he seldom
or never awakened. At the beginning of June the pest-house
of the Ospedale Civico had quietly filled; there was not
much room left in the two orphan asylums, and a frightfully active commerce was kept up between the wharf of
the Fondamenta Nuove and San Michele, the burial island.
But there was the fear of a general drop in prosperity. The
recently opened art exhibit in the public gardens was to be
considered, along with the heavy losses which, in case of
panic or unfavorable rumors, would threaten business, the
hotels, the entire elaborate system for exploiting foreigners
—and as these considerations evidently carried more weight
than love of truth or respect for international agreements,
the city authorities upheld obstinately their policy of silence
and denial. The chief health officer had resigned from his
post in indignation, and been promptly replaced by a more
tractable personality. The people knew this; and the corrup-

tion of their superiors, together with the predominating insecurity, the exceptional condition into which the prevalence of death had plunged the city, induced a certain demoralization of the lower classes, encouraging shady and antisocial impulses which manifested themselves in license, profligacy, and a rising crime wave. Contrary to custom, many drunkards were seen in the evenings; it was said that at night nasty mobs made the streets unsafe. Burglaries and even murders became frequent, for it had already been proved on two occasions that persons who had presumably fallen victim to the plague had in reality been dispatched with poison by their own relatives. And professional debauchery assumed abnormal obtrusive proportions such as had never been known here before, and to an extent which is usually found only in the southern parts of the country and in the Orient.

The Englishman pronounced the final verdict on these facts. "You would do well," he concluded, "to leave to-day rather than to-morrow. It cannot be much more than a couple of days before a quarantine zone is declared." "Thank you," Aschenbach said, and left the office.

The square lay sunless and stifling. Unsuspecting foreigners sat in front of the cafés or stood among the pigeons in front of the church and watched the swarms of birds flapping their wings, crowding one another, and pecking at grains of corn offered them in open palms. The recluse was feverishly excited, triumphant in his possession of the truth. But it had left him with a bad taste in his mouth, and a weird horror in his heart. As he walked up and down the flagstones of the gorgeous court, he was weighing an action which would meet the situation and would absolve him. This evening after dinner he could approach the woman with the pearls and make her a speech; he had figured it out word for word: "Permit a foreigner, madam, to give you some useful advice, a warning, which is being withheld from you through self-interest. Leave immediately with Tadzio and your daughters! Venice is full of the plague." Then he could lay a farewell hand on the head of this tool of a mock-ing divinity, turn away, and flee this morass. But he felt at the same time that he was very far from seriously desiring such a move. He would retract it, would disengage himself from it. . . . But when we are distracted we loathe most the thought of retracing our steps. He recalled a white building, ornamented with inscriptions which glistened in the evening and in whose transparent mysticism his mind's eye had lost itself—and then that strange wanderer's form which had awakened in the aging man the roving hankerings of youth after the foreign and the remote. And the thought of return, the thought of prudence and soberness, effort, mastery, dis-gusted him to such an extent that his face was distorted with an expression of physical nausea. "It must be kept silent!" he whispered heavily. And: "I will keep silent!" The con-sciousness of his share in the facts and the guilt intoxicated him, much as a little wine intoxicates a tired brain. The picture of the diseased and neglected city hovering deso-lately before him aroused vague hopes beyond the bounds of reason, but with an egregious sweetness. What was the scant happiness he had dreamed of a moment ago, compared with these expectations? What were art and virtue worth to him, over against the advantages of chaos? He kept silent, and remained in Venice.

This same night he had a frightful dream, if one can designate as a dream a bodily and mental experience which occurred to him in the deepest sleep, completely independent of him, and with a physical realness, although he never saw himself present or moving about among the incidents; but their stage rather was his soul itself, and they broke in from without, trampling down his resistance—a profound and spiritual resistance—by sheer force; and when they had passed through, they left his substance, the culture of his lifetime, crushed and annihilated behind them.

It began with anguish, anguish and desire, and a fright-ened curiosity as to what was coming. It was night, and his senses were on the watch. From far off a grumble, an uproar, was approaching, a jumble of noises. Clanking, blaring, and dull thunder, with shrill shouts and a definite whine in a long-drawn-out *u*-sound—all this was sweetly, ominously interspersed and dominated by the deep cooing of wickedly persistent flutes which charmed the bowels in a shamelessly penetrative manner. But he knew one word; it was veiled, and yet would name what was approaching: "The foreign god!" Vaporous fire began to glow; then he recognized mountains like those about his summer-house. And in the scattered light, from high up in the woods, among tree-trunks and crumbling moss-grown rocks— people, beasts, a throng, a raging mob plunged twisting and whirling downwards, and made the hill swarm with bodies, flames, tumult, and a riotous round dance. Women, tripped by overlong fur draperies which hung from their waists, were holding up tambourines and beating on them, their groaning heads flung back. Others swung sparking firebrands and bare daggers, or wore hissing snakes about the middle of their bodies, or shrieking held their breasts in their two hands. Men with horns on their foreheads, shaggy-haired, girded with hides, bent back their necks and raised their arms and thighs, clashed brass cymbals and beat furiously at kettledrums, while smooth boys prodded he-goats with wreathed sticks, climbing on their horns and falling off with shouts when they bounded. And the bacchantes wailed the word with the soft consonants and the drawn-out *u*-sound, at once sweet and savage, like nothing ever heard before. In one place it rang out as though piped into the air by stags, and it was echoed in another by many voices, in wild triumph—with it they incited one another to dance and to fling out their arms and legs, and it was never silent. But everything was pierced and dominated by the deep coaxing flute. He who was fighting against this experience—did it not coax him too with its shameless penetration, into the feast and the excesses of the extreme sacrifice? His repugnance, his fear, were keen—he was honorably set on defending himself to the very last against the barbarian, the

foe to intellectual poise and dignity. But the noise, the howling, multiplied by the resonant walls of the hills, grew, took
the upper hand, swelled to a fury of rapture. Odors oppressed the senses, the pungent smell of the bucks, the scent
of moist bodies, and a waft of stagnant water, with another
smell, something familiar, the smell of wounds and prevalent disease. At the beating of the drum his heart fluttered,
his head was spinning, he was caught in a frenzy, in a blinding deafening lewdness—and he yearned to join the ranks
of the god. The obscene symbol, huge, wooden, was uncovered and raised up; then they howled the magic word with
more abandon. Foaming at the mouth, they raged, teased
one another with ruttish gestures and caressing hands;
laughing and groaning, they stuck the goads into one another's flesh and licked the blood from their limbs. But the
dreamer now was with them, in them, and he belonged to
the foreign god. Yes, they were he himself, as they hurled
themselves biting and tearing upon the animals, got entangled in steaming rags, and fell in promiscuous unions on the
torn moss, in sacrifice to their god. And his soul tasted the
unchastity and fury of decay.

When he awakened from the affliction of this dream he
was unnerved, shattered, and hopelessly under the power
of the demon. He no longer avoided the inquisitive glances
of other people; he did not care if he was exciting their
suspicions. And as a matter of fact they were fleeing, traveling elsewhere. Numerous bathing-houses stood empty, the
occupants of the dining-hall became more and more scattered, and in the city now one rarely saw a foreigner. The
truth seemed to have leaked out; the panic, despite the ret-
icence of those whose interests were involved, seemed no
longer avoidable. But the woman with the pearls remained
with her family, either because the rumors had not yet
reached her, or because she was too proud and fearless to
heed them. Tadzio remained. And to Aschenbach, in his
infatuation, it seemed at times as though flight and death
might remove all the disturbing elements of life around

them, and he stay here alone with the boy. Yes, by the sea in the forenoon when his eyes rested heavily, irresponsibly, unwaveringly on the thing he coveted, or when, as the day was ending, he followed shamelessly after him through streets where the hideous death lurked in secret—at such times the atrocious seemed to him rich in possibilities, and laws of morality had dropped away.

Like any lover, he wanted to please; and he felt a bitter anguish lest it might not be possible. He added bright youthful details to his dress, he put on jewels, and used perfumes. During the day he often spent much time over his toilet, and came to the table strikingly dressed, excited, and in suspense. In the light of the sweet youthfulness which had done this to him, he detested his aging body. The sight of his gray hair, his sharp features, plunged him into shame and hopelessness. It induced him to attempt rejuvenating his body and appearance. He often visited the hotel barber.

Beneath the barber's apron, leaning back in the chair under the gossiper's expert hands, he winced to observe his reflection in the mirror.

"Gray," he said, making a wry face.

"A little," the man answered. "Due entirely to a slight neglect, an indifference to outward things, which is conceivable in people of importance, but it is not exactly praiseworthy. And all the less so since such persons are above prejudice in matters of nature or art. If the moral objections of certain people to the art of cosmetics were to be logically extended to the care of the teeth, they would give no slight offense. And after all, we are just as old as we feel, and under some circumstances gray hair would actually stand for more of an untruth than the despised correction. In your case, sir, you are entitled to the natural color of your hair. Will you permit me simply to return what belongs to you?"

"How is that?" Aschenbach asked.

Then the orator washed his client's hair with two kinds of water, one clear and one dark, and it was as black as in youth. Following this, he curled it with irons into soft waves, stepped back, and eyed his work.

"All that is left now," he said, "would be to freshen up the skin a little."

And like some one who cannot finish, cannot satisfy himself, he passed with quickening energy from one manipulation to another. Aschenbach rested comfortably, incapable of resistance, or rather his hopes aroused by what was taking place. In the glass he saw his brows arch more evenly and decisively. His eyes became longer; their brilliance was heightened by a light touching-up of the lids. A little lower, where the skin had been a leatherish brown, he saw a delicate crimson tint grow beneath a deft application of color. His lips, bloodless a little while past, became full, and as red as raspberries. The furrows in the cheeks and about the mouth, the wrinkles of the eyes, disappeared beneath lotions and cream. With a knocking heart he beheld a blossoming youth. Finally the beauty specialist declared himself content, after the manner of such people, by obsequiously thanking the man he had been serving. "A trifling assistance," he said, as he applied one parting touch. "Now the gentleman can fall in love unhesitatingly." He walked away, fascinated; he was happy, as in a dream, timid and bewildered. His necktie was red, his broad-brimmed straw hat was trimmed with a variegated band.

A tepid storm wind had risen. It was raining sparsely and at intervals, but the air was damp, thick, and filled with the smell of things rotting. All around him he heard a fluttering, pattering, and swishing; and under the fever of his cosmetics it seemed to him as though evil wind-spirits were haunting the place, impure sea-birds which rooted and gnawed at the food of the condemned and befouled it with their droppings. For the sultriness destroyed his appetite, and the fancy suggested itself that the foods were poisoned with contaminating substances. Tracking the boy one afternoon, Aschenbach had plunged deep into the tangled center of the diseased city. He was becoming uncertain of where

he was, since the alleys, waterways, bridges, and little
squares of the labyrinth were all so much alike, and he was
no longer even sure of directions. He was absorbed with
the problem of keeping the pursued figure in sight. And,
driven to disgraceful subterfuges, flattening himself against
walls, hiding behind the backs of other people, for a long
time he did not notice the weariness, the exhaustion, with
which emotion and the continual suspense had taxed his
mind and his body. Tadzio walked behind his companions.
He always allowed the governess and the nunlike sisters to
precede him in the narrow places; and, loitering behind
alone, he would turn his head occasionally to look over his
shoulder and make sure by a glance of his peculiarly dark-
gray eyes that his admirer was following. He saw him, and
did not betray him. Drunk with the knowledge of this, lured
forward by those eyes, led meekly by his passion, the lover
stole after his unseemly hope—but finally he was cheated
and lost sight of him. The Poles had crossed a short arching
bridge; the height of the curve hid them from the pursuer,
and when he himself had arrived there he no longer saw
them. He hunted for them vainly in three directions, straight
ahead and to either side along the narrow dirty wharf. In
the end he was so tired and unnerved that he had to give
up the search.

His head was on fire, his body was covered with a sticky
sweat, his knees trembled. He could no longer endure the
thirst that was torturing him, and he looked around for
some immediate relief. From a little vegetable store he
bought some fruit—strawberries, soft and overly ripe—
and he ate them as he walked. A very charming, forsaken
little square opened up before him. He recognized it; here
he had made his frustrated plans for flight weeks ago. He
let himself sink down on the steps of the cistern in the middle of the square, and laid his head against the stone cylin-
der. It was quiet; grass was growing up through the pave-
ment; refuse was scattered about. Among the weather-
beaten, unusually tall houses surrounding him there was one

like a palace, with little lion-covered balconies, and Gothic windows with blank emptiness behind them. On the ground floor of another house was a drug store. Warm gusts of wind occasionally carried the smell of carbolic acid.

He sat there, he, the master, the artist of dignity, the author of "The Wretch," a work which had, in such accurate symbols, denounced vagabondage and the depths of misery, had denied all sympathy with the engulfed, and had cast out the outcast; the man who had arrived and, victor over his own knowledge, had outgrown all irony and acclimatized himself to the obligations of public confidence; whose reputation was official, whose name had been knighted, and on whose style boys were urged to pattern themselves—he sat there. His eyelids were shut; only now and then a mocking uneasy side-glance slipped out from beneath them. And his loose lips, set off by the cosmetics, formed isolated words of the strange dream-logic created by his half-slumbering brain.

"For beauty, Phædrus, mark me, beauty alone is both divine and visible at once; and thus it is the road of the sensuous; it is, little Phædrus, the road of the artist to the spiritual. But do you now believe, my dear, that they can ever attain wisdom and true human dignity for whom the road to the spiritual leads through the senses? Or do you believe rather (I leave the choice to you) that this is a pleasant but perilous road, a really wrong and sinful road, which necessarily leads astray? For you must know that we poets cannot take the road of beauty without having Eros join us and set himself up as our leader. Indeed, we may even be heroes after our fashion, and hardened warriors, though we be like women, for passion is our exaltation, and our desire must remain love—that is our pleasure and our disgrace. You now see, do you not, that we poets cannot be wise and dignified? That we necessarily go astray, necessarily remain lascivious, and adventurers in emotion? The mastery of our style is all lies and foolishness, our renown and honor are a farce, the confidence of the masses in us is highly ridiculous, and the training of the public and of youth through art is a precarious undertaking which should be forbidden. For how, indeed, could he be a fit instructor who is born with a natural leaning towards the precipice? We might well disavow it and reach after dignity, but wherever we turn it attracts us. Let us, say, renounce the dissolvent of knowledge, since knowledge, Phædrus, has no dignity or strength. It is aware, it understands and pardons, but without reserve and form. It feels sympathy with the precipice, it *is* the precipice. This, then, we abandon with firmness, and from now on our efforts matter only by their yield of beauty, or, in other words, simplicity, greatness, and new rigor, form, and a second type of openness. But form and openness, Phædrus, lead to intoxication and to desire, lead the noble perhaps into sinister revels of emotion which his own beautiful rigor rejects as infamous, lead to the precipice—yes, they too lead to the precipice. They lead us poets there, I say, since we cannot force ourselves, since we can merely let ourselves out. And now I am going, Phædrus. You stay here; and when you no longer see me, then you go too."

A few days later, as Gustav von Aschenbach was not feeling well, he left the beach hotel at a later hour in the morning than usual. He had to fight against certain attacks of vertigo which were only partially physical and were accompanied by a pronounced malaise, a feeling of bafflement and hopelessness—while he was not certain whether this had to do with conditions outside him or with his own nature. In the lobby he noticed a large pile of luggage ready for shipment; he asked the doorkeeper who it was that was leaving, and heard in answer the Polish title which he had learned secretly. He accepted this without any alteration of his sunken features, with that curt elevation of the head by which one acknowledges something he does not need to know. Then he asked: "When?" The answer was: "After lunch." He nodded, and went to the beach.

It was not very inviting. Rippling patches of rain retreated across the wide flat water separating the beach from the first long sand-bank. An air of autumn, of things past their prime, seemed to lie over the pleasure spot which had once been so alive with color and was now almost abandoned. The sand was no longer kept clean. A camera, seemingly without an owner, stood on its tripod by the edge of the sea; and a black cloth thrown over it was flapping noisily in the wind.

Tadzio, with the three or four companions still left, was moving about to the right in front of his family's cabin. And midway between the sea and the row of bathing-houses, lying back in his chair with a robe over his knees, Aschenbach looked at him once more. The game, which was not being supervised since the women were probably occupied with preparations for the journey, seemed to have no rules, and it was degenerating. The stocky boy with the sleek black hair who was called Jaschu had been angered and blinded by sand flung in his face. He forced Tadzio into a wrestling match which quickly ended in the fall of the beauty, who was weaker. But as though, in the hour of parting, the servile feelings of the inferior had turned to merciless brutality and were trying to get vengeance for a long period of slavery, the victor did not let go of the boy underneath, but knelt on his back and pressed his face so persistently into the sand that Tadzio, already breathless from the struggle, was in danger of strangling. His attempts to shake off the weight were fitful; for moments they stopped entirely and were resumed again as mere twitchings. Enraged, Aschenbach was about to spring to the rescue, when the torturer finally released his victim. Tadzio, very pale, raised himself halfway and sat motionless for several minutes, resting on one arm with rumpled hair and glowering eyes. Then he stood up completely, and moved slowly away. They called him, cheerfully at first, then anxiously and imploringly; he did not listen. The swarthy boy, who seemed to regret his excesses immediately afterwards, caught up with him and tried to placate him. A movement of the shoulder put him at his distance. Tadzio went down obliquely to the water. He was barefoot, and wore his striped linen suit with the red bow.

He lingered on the edge of the water with his head down, drawing figures in the wet sand with one toe; then he went into the shallows, which did not cover his knees in the deepest place, crossed them leisurely, and arrived at the sand-bank. He stood there a moment, his face turned to the open sea; soon after, he began stepping slowly to the left along the narrow stretch of exposed ground. Separated from the mainland by the expanse of water, separated from his companions by a proud moodiness, he moved along, a strongly isolated and unrelated figure with fluttering hair—placed out there in the sea, the wind, against the vague mists. He stopped once more to look around. And suddenly, as though at some recollection, some impulse, with one hand on his hip he turned the upper part of his body in a beautiful twist which began from the base—and he looked over his shoulder towards the shore. The watcher sat there, as he had sat once before when for the first time those twilight-gray eyes had turned at the doorway and met his own. His head, against the back of the chair, had slowly followed the movements of the boy walking yonder. Now, simultaneously with this glance it rose and sank on his breast, so that his eyes looked out from underneath, while his face took on the loose, inwardly relaxed expression of deep sleep. But it seemed to him as though the pale and lovely lure out there were smiling to him, nodding to him; as though, removing his hand from his hip, he were signaling to come out, were vaguely guiding towards egregious promises. And, as often before, he stood up to follow him.

Some minutes passed before any one hurried to the aid of the man who had collapsed into one corner of his chair. He was brought to his room. And on the same day a respectfully shocked world received the news of his death.

AMOK *

By Stefan Zweig

In March 1912, when a big mail-boat was unloading at Naples, there was an accident about which extremely inaccurate reports appeared in the newspapers. I myself saw nothing of the affair, for (in common with many of the passengers), wishing to escape the noise and discomfort of coaling, I had gone to spend the evening ashore. As it happens, however, I am in a position to know what really occurred, and to explain the cause. So many years have now elapsed since the incidents about to be related, that there is no reason why I should not break the silence I have hitherto maintained.

I had been traveling in the Federated Malay States. Recalled home by cable on urgent private affairs, I joined the *Wotan* at Singapore, and had to put up with very poor accommodation. My cabin was a hole of a place squeezed into a corner close to the engine-room, small, hot, and dark. The fusty, stagnant air reeked of oil. I had to keep the electric fan running, with the result that a fetid draft crawled over my face reminding me of the fluttering of a crazy bat. From beneath came the persistent rattle and groans of the engines, which sounded like a coal-porter tramping and wheezing as he climbed an unending flight of iron stairs; from above came the no less persistent tread of feet upon the promenade deck. As soon as I had had my cabin luggage properly stowed away, I fled from the place to the upper deck, where with delight I inhaled deep breaths of the balmy south wind.

* Translated by Eden and Cedar Paul. Copyright, 1931, by The Viking Press, Inc.

But on this crowded ship the promenade deck, too, was full of bustle and disquiet. It was thronged with passengers, nervously irritable in their enforced idleness and unavoidable proximity, chattering without pause as they prowled to and fro. The light laughter of the women who reclined in deck-chairs, the twists and turns of those who were taking a constitutional on the encumbered deck, the general hubbub, were uncongenial. In Malaysia, and before that in Burma and Siam, I had been visiting an unfamiliar world. My mind was filled with new impressions, with lively images which chased one another in rapid succession. I wanted to contemplate them at leisure, to sort and arrange them, to digest and assimilate; but in this noisy boulevard, humming with life of a very different kind, there was no chance of finding the necessary repose. If I tried to read, the lines in the printed page ran together before my tired eyes when the shadows of the passers-by flickered over the white page. I could never be alone with myself and my thoughts in this thickly peopled alley.

For three days I did my utmost to possess my soul in patience, resigned to my fellow-passengers, staring at the sea. The sea was always the same, blue and void, except that at nightfall for a brief space it became resplendent with a play of varied colors. As for the people, I had grown sick of their faces before the three days were up. I knew every detail of them all. I was surfeited with them, and equally surfeited with the giggling of the women and with the windy argumentativeness of some Dutch officers coming home on leave. I took refuge in the saloon; though from this haven, too, I was speedily driven away because a group of English girls from Shanghai spent their time between meals hammering out waltzes on the piano. There was nothing for it but my cabin. I turned in after luncheon, having drugged myself with a couple of bottles of beer, resolved to escape dinner and the dance that was to follow, hoping to sleep the clock round and more, and thus to spend the better part of a day in oblivion.

When I awoke it was dark, and stuffier than ever in the little coffin. I had switched off the fan, and was dripping with sweat. I felt heavy after my prolonged slumber, and some minutes slipped by before I fully realized where I was. It must certainly be past midnight, for there was no music to be heard, and the tramp-tramp of feet overhead had ceased. The only sound was that of the machinery, the beating heart of the leviathan, who wheezed and groaned as he bore his living freight onward through the darkness.

I groped my way to the deck, where there was not a soul to be seen. Looking first at the smoking funnels and the ghostlike spars, I then turned my eyes upward and saw that the sky was clear; dark velvet, sprinkled with stars. It looked as if a curtain had been drawn across a vast source of light, and as if the stars were tiny rents in the curtain, through which that indescribable radiance poured. Never had I seen such a sky.

The night was refreshingly cool, as so often at this hour on a moving ship even at the equator. I breathed the fragrant air, charged with the aroma of distant isles. For the first time since I had come on board I was seized with a longing to dream, conjoined with another desire, more sensuous, to surrender my body—womanlike—to the night's soft embrace. I wanted to lie down somewhere, and gaze at the white hieroglyphs in the starry expanse. But the long chairs were all stacked and inaccessible. Nowhere on the empty deck was there a place for a dreamer to rest.

I made for the forecastle, stumbling over ropes and past iron windlasses to the bow, where I leaned over the rail watching the stem as it rose and fell, rhythmically, cutting its way through the phosphorescent waters. Did I stand there for an hour, or only for a few minutes? Who can tell? Rocked in that giant cradle, I took no note of the passing of time. All I was conscious of was a gentle lassitude, which was wellnigh voluptuous. I wanted to sleep, to dream; yet I was loath to quit this wizard's world, to return to my 'tween-decks coffin. Moving a pace or two, I felt with one foot a coil of rope. I sat down, and closing my eyes, abandoned myself to the drowsy intoxication of the night. Soon the frontiers of consciousness became obscured; I was not sure whether the sound I heard was that of my own breathing or that of the mechanical heart of the ship; I gave myself up more and more completely, more and more passively, to the environing charm of this midnight world.

* * *

A dry cough near at hand recalled me to my senses with a start. Opening eyes that were now attuned to the darkness, I saw close beside me the faint gleam of a pair of spectacles, and a few inches below this a fitful glow which obviously came from a pipe. Before I sat down I had been intent on the stars and the sea, and had thus overlooked this neighbor, who must have been sitting here motionless all the while. Still a little hazy as to my whereabouts, but feeling as if somehow I was an intruder, I murmured apologetically in my native German: "Excuse me!" The answer came promptly, "Not at all!" in the same language, and with an unmistakably German intonation.

It was strange and eerie, this darkling juxtaposition to an unseen and unknown person. I had the sensation that he was staring vainly at me just as I was staring vainly at him. Neither of us could see more than a dim silhouette, black against a dusky background. I could just hear his breathing and the faint gurgle of his pipe.

The silence became unbearable. I should have liked to get up and go away, but was restrained by the conviction that to do this without a word would be unpardonably rude. In my embarrassment I took out a cigarette and struck a match. For a second or two there was light, and we could see one another. What I saw was the face of a stranger, a man I had never yet seen in the dining saloon or on the promenade deck; a face which (was it only because the lineaments were caricatured in that momentary illumination?) seemed extraordinarily sinister and suggestive of a hobgoblin. Before I had been able to note details accurately, the darkness closed in again, so that once more all that was visible was the fitful glow from the pipe, and above it the occasional glint of the glasses. Neither of us spoke. The silence was sultry and oppressive, like tropical heat.

At length I could bear it no longer. Standing up, I said a civil "Good night."

"Good night!" came the answer, in a harsh and raucous voice.

As I stumbled aft amid the encumbrances on the foredeck, I heard footsteps behind me, hasty and uncertain. My neighbor on the coil of rope was following me with unsteady gait. He did not come quite close, but through the darkness I could sense his anxiety and uneasiness.

He was speaking hurriedly.

"You'll forgive me if I ask you a favor. I . . . I," he hesitated, "I . . . I have private, extremely private reasons for keeping to myself on board. . . . In mourning. . . . That's why I have made no acquaintances during the voyage. You excepted, of course. . . . What I want is . . . I mean I should be very greatly obliged if you would refrain from telling any one that you have seen me here. It is, let me repeat, strictly private grounds that prevent my joining in the life of the ship, and it would be most distressing to me were you to let fall a word about my frequenting this forecastle alone at night. I . . ."

He paused, and I was prompt in assuring him that his wishes should be respected. I was but a casual traveler, I said, and had no friends on board. We shook hands. I went back to my cabin to sleep out the night. But my slumbers were uneasy, for I had troublous dreams.

I kept my promise to say nothing to any one about my strange encounter, though the temptation to indiscretion was considerable. On a sea voyage the veriest trifle is an event—a sail on the horizon, a shoal of porpoises, a new flirtation, a practical joke. Besides, I was full of curiosity about this remarkable fellow-passenger. I scanned the list of bookings in search of a name which might fit him; and I looked at this person and that, wondering if they knew anything about him. All day I suffered from nervous impatience, waiting for nightfall when I hoped I might meet him again. Psychological enigmas have invariably fascinated me. An encounter with an inscrutable character makes me thrill with longing to pluck the heart out of the mystery, the urge of this desire being hardly less vehement than that of a man's desire to possess a woman. The day seemed insufferably long. I went to bed early, certain that an internal alarm would awaken me in the small hours.

Thus it was. I awoke at about the same time as on the previous night. Looking at my watch, whose figures and hands stood out luminous from the dial, I saw that the hour had just gone two. Quickly I made for the deck.

In the tropics the weather is less changeable than in our northern climes. The night was as before: dark, clear, and lit with brilliant stars. But in myself there was a difference. I no longer felt dreamy and easeful, was no longer agreeably lulled by the gentle swaying of the ship. An intangible something confused and disturbed me, drew me irresistibly to the foredeck. I wanted to know whether the mysterious stranger would again be sitting there, solitary, on the coil of rope. Reluctant and yet eager, I yielded to the impulse. As I neared the place, I caught sight of what looked like a red and glowing eye—his pipe. He was there!

Involuntarily I stopped short, and was about to retreat, when the dark figure rose, took two steps forward, and, coming close to me, said in an apologetic and lifeless voice:

"Sorry! I'm sure you were coming back to your old place, and it seems to me that you were about to turn away because you saw me. Won't you sit down? I'm just off."

I hastened to rejoin that I was only on the point of withdrawing because I was afraid of disturbing him, and that I hoped he would stay.

"You won't disturb me!" he said with some bitterness. "Far from it; I am glad not to be alone once in a while. For days upon days I have hardly spoken to a soul; years, it seems; and I find it almost more than I can bear to have to bottle everything up in myself. I can't sit in the cabin any longer, the place is like a prison-cell; and yet I can't stand the passengers either, for they chatter and laugh all day. Their perpetual frivoling drives me frantic. The silly noise they make finds its way into my cabin, so that I have to stop my ears. Of course, they don't know I can hear them, or how they exasperate me. Not that they'd care if they did, for they're only a pack of foreigners."

He suddenly pulled himself up, saying: "But I know I must be boring you. I didn't mean to be so loquacious."

He bowed, and moved to depart, but I pressed him to stay.

"You are not boring me in the least. Far from it, for I too am glad to have a quiet talk up here under the stars. Won't you have a cigarette?"

As he lighted it, I again got a glimpse of his face, the face which was now that of an acquaintance. In the momentary glare, before he threw away the match, he looked earnestly, searchingly at me, appealingly it almost seemed, as his spectacled eyes fixed themselves on mine.

I felt a thrill akin to horror. This man, so it seemed to me, had a tale to tell, was on fire to tell it, but some inward hindrance held him back. Only by silence, a silence that invited confidence, could I help him to throw off his restraint.

We sat down on the coil of rope, half facing one another, leaning against the top rail. His nervousness was betrayed by the shaking of the hand which held the cigarette. We smoked, and still I said never a word. At length he broke the silence.

"Are you tired?"

"Not an atom!"

"I should rather like to ask you something." He hesitated. "It would be more straightforward to say I want to tell you something. I know how ridiculous it is of me to begin babbling like this to the first comer; but, mentally speaking, I'm in a tight place. I've got to the point where I simply must

tell some one, or else go clean off my head. You'll understand why, as soon as I've told you. Of course, you can do
nothing to help me, but keeping my trouble to myself is
making me very ill, and you know what fools sick folk are
—or what fools they seem to healthy people."

I interrupted him, and begged him not to distress himself
with fancies of that sort, but to go ahead with his story.
"Naturally there would be no meaning in my giving you
unlimited promises of help, when I don't know the situation.
Still, I can at least assure you of my willingness to give you
what help I may. That's one's plain duty, isn't it, to show that
one's ready to pull a fellow-mortal out of a hole? One can
try to help, at least."

"Duty to offer help? Duty to try, at least? Duty to show
that one's ready to pull a fellow-mortal out of a hole?"

Thus did he repeat what I had said, staccato, in a tone of
unwonted bitterness flavored with mockery, whose significance was to become plain to me later. For the moment,
there was something in his scanning iteration of my words
which made me wonder whether he was mad, or drunk.

As if guessing my thoughts, he went on in a more ordinary
voice: "You'll perhaps think me queer in the head, or that
I've been imbibing too freely in my loneliness. That's not
what's the matter, and I'm sane enough—so far! What set
me off was one word you used, and the connection in which
you happened to use it, the word 'duty.' It touched me on the
raw, and I'm raw all over, for the strange thing is that
what torments me all the time is a question of duty, duty,
duty."

He pulled himself up with a jerk. Without further cir-
cumlocution, he began to explain himself clearly.

"I'm a doctor, you must know. That's a vital point in my
story. Now in medical practice one often has to deal with
cases in which duty is not so plain as you might think.
Fateful cases; you can call them borderline cases, if you
like. In these cases there's not just one obvious duty; there
are conflicting duties: one duty of the ordinary kind, which

runs counter to a duty to the State, and perhaps on the other side runs counter to a duty to science. Help pull a fellow-mortal out of a hole? Of course one should. That's what one's there for. But such maxims are purely theoretical. In a practical instance, how far is help to go? Here you turn up, a nocturnal visitant, and, though you've never seen me before, and I've no claim on you, I ask you not to tell any one you've seen me. Well, you hold your tongue, because you feel it your duty to help me in the way I ask. Then you turn up again, and I beg you to let me talk to you because silence is eating my heart out. You are good enough to listen. After all, that's easy enough. I haven't asked you anything very difficult. But suppose I were to say: 'Catch hold of me and throw me overboard!' You would quickly reach the limit of your complaisance, wouldn't you? You would no longer regard it as a 'duty to help,' I suppose! There must be a limit somewhere. This duty of which you speak, surely it comes to an end before the point is reached at which one's own life is gravely imperiled, or one's own responsibility to accepted public institutions is affected? Or perhaps this duty to help has no limits at all, where a doctor is concerned? Should a doctor be a universal savior, simply because he has a diploma couched in Latin? Has he for that reason to fling away his life when some one happens along and implores him to be helpful and kindhearted? There is a limit to one's duty, and one reaches it when one is at the end of one's tether!"

He went off at a tangent once more.

"I'm sorry to show so much excitement. It's not because I'm drunk. I'm not drunk—yet. True, I'm drinking heavily here on board; and I've got drunk now and again of late, for my life has been so damnably lonely in the East. Just think, for seven years I've been living almost exclusively among natives and animals; and in such conditions one naturally forgets how to talk sanely and calmly. When, at last, one gets a chance of talking to a man of one's own people, one's tongue runs away with one. Where was I? I

was going to put a question to you, was going to place a
problem before you, to ask you whether it was really incumbent on one to help, no matter in what circumstances, as an
angel from heaven might help. . . . But I'm afraid it will be
rather a long business. You're really not tired?"

"Not the least bit in the world!"

He was groping behind him in the darkness. I heard
something clink, and could make out the forms of a couple
of bottles. He poured from one of them into a glass, and
handed it to me—a large peg of neat whisky.

"Won't you have a drink?"

To keep him company, I sipped, while he, for lack of
another glass, took a bountiful swig from the bottle. There
was a moment's silence, during which came five strokes on
the ship's bell. It was half-past two in the morning.

*   *   *

"Well, I want to put a case before you. Suppose there was
a doctor practicing in a little town—in the country, really.
A doctor who . . ."

He broke off, hesitated a while, and then made a fresh
start.

"No, that won't do. I must tell you the whole thing exactly as it happened, and as it happened to myself. A direct
narrative from first to last. Otherwise you'll never be able
to understand. There must be no false shame, no concealment. When people come to consult me, they have to strip to
the buff, have to show me their excreta. If I am to help them,
they must make no bones about informing me as to the
most private matters. It will be of no use for me to tell you
of something that happened to some one else, to a mythical
Doctor Somebody, somewhere and somewhen. I shall strip
naked, as if I were your patient. Anyway, I have forgotten
all decency in that horrible place where I have been living,
in that hideous solitude, in a land which eats the soul out of
one's body and sucks the marrow out of one's bones."

I must have made some slight movement of protest, for he went off on a side issue.

"Ah, I can see you are an enthusiast for the East, an admirer of the temples and the palm trees, filled full with the romance of the regions where you have been traveling for your pleasure, to while away a month or two. No doubt the tropics are charming to one who hurries or saunters through them by rail, in a motor car, or in a rickshaw. I felt the same when I first came out here seven years ago. I was full of dreams about what I was going to do: learn the native tongue; read the Sacred Books in the original; study tropical diseases; do original scientific work; master the psychology of the indigenes (thus do we phrase it in our European jargon) ; become a missionary of civilization. . . .

"But life out there is like living in a hot-house with invisible walls. It saps the energies. You get fever, though you swallow quinine by the teaspoonful; and fever takes all the guts out of you, you become limp and lazy, as soft as a jellyfish. A European is cut adrift from his moorings if he has to leave the big towns and is sent to one of those accursed settlements in a jungle or a swamp. Sooner or later he will lose his poise. Some take to drink; others learn opium-smoking from the Chinese; others find relief in brutality, sadism, or what not—they all go off the rails. How one longs for home! To walk along a street with proper buildings in it! To sit in a solidly constructed room with glass windows, and among white men and women. So it goes on year after year, until at length the time for home leave comes round—and a man finds he has grown too inert even to take his furlough. What would be the use? He knows he has been forgotten, and that, if he did go home, there would be no welcome awaiting him or (worse still) his coming might be utterly ignored. So he stays where he is, in a mangrove swamp, or in a steaming forest. It was a sad day for me when I sold myself into servitude on the equator.

"Besides, forgoing my home leave was not quite so voluntary an affair as I have implied. I had studied medicine in

Germany, where I was born, and, soon after I was qualified, I got a good post at the Leipzig Clinic. If you were to look up the files of the medical papers of that date, you would find that a new method of treatment I advocated for one of the commoner diseases made some little stir, so that I had been a good deal talked about for so young a man.

"Then came a love affair which ruined my chances. It was with a woman whose acquaintance I made at the hospital. She'd been living with a man she'd driven so crazy that he tried to shoot himself and failed to make a clean job of it. Soon I was as crazy as he. She had a sort of cold pride about her which I found irresistible. Women that are domineering and rather impudent can always do anything they like with me, but this woman reduced me to pulp. I did whatever she wanted and in the end (it seems hard to tell you, though the story's an old one now, dating from eight years ago) for her sake I stole some money from the hospital safe. The thing came out, of course, and there was the devil to pay. An uncle of mine made the loss good, but there was no more career for me in Leipzig.

"Just at this time I heard that the Dutch Government was short of doctors in the colonial service, would take Germans and was actually offering a premium. That told me there must be a catch in it somewhere, and I knew well enough that in these tropical plantations tombstones grow as luxuriantly as the vegetation. But when one is young one is always ready to believe that fever and death will strike some other fellow down and give one's self the go-by.

"After all, I hadn't much choice. I made my way to Rotterdam, signed on for ten years, and got a fine, thick wad of banknotes. I sent half of them to my uncle. A girl of the town got the rest—the half of the premium and any other money I could raise—all because she was so like the young woman to whom I owed my downfall. Without money, without even a watch, without illusions, I steamed away from Europe, and was by no means sad at heart when the vessel cleared the port. I sat on deck much as you are sitting now;

ready to take delight in the East, in the palm trees under new skies; dreaming of the wonderful forests, of solitude, and of peace.

"I soon had my fill of solitude. They did not station me in Batavia or in Surabaya, in one of the big towns where there are human beings with white skins, a club and a golf-course, books and newspapers. They sent me to—well, never mind the name! A god-forgotten place up country, a day's journey from the nearest town. The 'society' consisted of two or three dull-witted and sun-dried officials and one or two half-castes. The settlement was encircled by interminable forests, plantations, jungles, and swamps.

"Still, it was tolerable at first. There was the charm of novelty. I studied hard for a time. Then the Vice-Resident was making a tour of inspection through the district, and had a motor smash. Compound fracture of the leg, no other doctor within hail, an operation needed, followed by a good recovery—and a considerable amount of kudos for me, since the patient was a big gun. I did some anthropological work, on the poisons and weapons used by the primitives. Until the freshness had worn off, I found a hundred and one things which helped to keep me alive.

"This lasted just as long as the vigor I had brought with me from Europe. Then the climate got hold of me. The other white men in the settlement bored me to death. I shunned their company, began to drink rather heavily, and to browse on my own weary thoughts. After all, I had only to stick it for another two years. Then I could retire on a pension, and start life afresh in Europe. Nothing to do but wait till the time was up. And there I should still be waiting, but for the unexpected happening I am going to tell you about."

* * *

The voice in the darkness ceased. So still was the night that once more I could hear the sound of the ship's stem clearing the water, and the distant pulsing of the machinery.

I should have been glad to light a cigarette, but I was afraid I might startle the narrator by any sudden movement and by the unexpected glare.

For a time the silence was unbroken. Had he changed his mind, and decided it would be indiscreet to tell me any more? Had he dropped off into a doze?

While I was thus meditating, six bells struck. It was three in the morning. He stirred, and I heard a faint click as he picked up the whisky bottle. He was priming himself again. Then he resumed, with a fresh access of tense passion.

"Well, so things went with me. Month after month, I had been sitting inactive in that detestable spot, as motionless as a spider in the center of its web. The rainy season was over. For weeks I had been listening to the downpour on the roof, and not a soul had come near me—no European, that is to say. I had been alone in the house with my native servants and my whisky. Being even more homesick than usual, when I read in a novel about lighted streets and white women, my fingers would begin to tremble. You are only what we call a globe-trotter; you don't know the country as those who live there know it. A white man is seized at times by what might be accounted one of the tropical diseases, a nostalgia so acute as to drive him almost into delirium. Well, in some such paroxysm I was poring over an atlas, dreaming of journeys possible and impossible. At this moment two of my servants came, open-mouthed with astonishment, to say that a lady had called to see me—a white lady.

"I, too, was amazed. I had heard no sound of carriage or of car. What the devil was a white woman doing in this wilderness?

"I was sitting in the upstairs veranda of my two-storied house, and not dressed for white company. In the minute or two that were needed for me to make myself presentable, I was able to pull myself together a little; but I was still nervous, uneasy, filled with disagreeable forebodings, when at length I went downstairs. Who on earth could it be? I was friendless. Why should a white woman come to visit me in the wilds?

"The lady was sitting in the ante-room, and behind her chair was standing a China boy, obviously her servant. As she jumped up to greet me, I saw that her face was hidden by a thick motor-veil. She began to speak before I could say a word.

"'Good morning, Doctor,' she said in English. 'You'll excuse my dropping in like this without an appointment, won't you?' She spoke rather rapidly, almost as if repeating a speech which had been mentally rehearsed. 'When we were driving through the settlement, and had to stop the car for a moment, I remembered that you lived here.' This was puzzling! If she had come in a car, why hadn't she driven up to the house? 'I've heard so much about you—what a wonder you worked when the Vice-Resident had that accident. I saw him the other day playing golf as well as ever. Your name is in every one's mouth down there, and we'd all gladly give away our grumpy old senior surgeon and his two assistants if we could but get you in exchange. Besides, why do you never come to headquarters? You live up here like a yogi!'

"She ran on and on, without giving me a chance to get in a word edgewise. Manifestly her loquacity was the outcome of nervousness, and it made me nervous in my turn. 'Why does she go on chattering like this?' I wondered. 'Why doesn't she tell me who she is? Why doesn't she take off her veil? Has she got fever? Is she a madwoman?' I grew more and more distraught, feeling like a fool as I stood there mumchance, while she overwhelmed me with her babble. At length the stream ran dry, so that I was able to invite her upstairs. She made a sign to the boy to stay where he was, and swept up the stairway in front of me.

"'Pleasant quarters here,' she exclaimed, letting her gaze roam over my sitting-room. 'Ah, what lovely books. How I should like to read them all!' She strolled to the bookcase and began to con the titles. For the first time since she had said good morning to me, she was silent for a space.

" 'May I offer you a cup of tea?' I inquired.

"She answered without turning round.

" 'No, thank you, Doctor. I've only a few minutes to spare. Hullo, there's Flaubert's *Éducation sentimentale*. What a book! So you read French, too. Wonderful people, you Germans—they teach you so many languages at school. It must be splendid to be able to speak them as you do. The Vice-Resident swears he would never allow any one but you to use a knife on him. That senior surgeon of ours, all he's fit for is bridge. But you—well, it came into my head to-day that I should like to consult you, and, as I was driving through the settlement, I thought to myself, "There's no time like the present!" But'—all this she said without looking at me, for she kept her face towards the books—'I expect you're frightfully busy. Perhaps I'd better call another day?'

" 'Are you going to show your cards at last?' I wondered. Of course I gave no sign of this, but assured her that I was at her service, now or later, as she preferred.

" 'Oh, well, since I'm here!' She turned half round towards me, but did not look up, continuing to flutter the pages of a book she had taken from the shelf. 'It's nothing serious. The sort of troubles women often have. Giddiness, fainting-fits, nausea. This morning in the car, when we were rounding a curve, I suddenly lost my senses completely. The boy had to hold me up, or I should have slipped on to the floor. He got me some water, and then I felt better. I suppose the chauffeur must have been driving too fast. Don't you think so, Doctor?'

" 'I can't answer that offhand. Have you had many such fainting-fits?'

" 'No. Not until recently, that is. During the last few weeks, pretty often. And I've been feeling so sick in the mornings.'

"She was back at the bookcase, had taken down another

volume, and was fluttering the pages as before. Why did she behave so strangely? Why didn't she lift her veil and look me in the face? Purposely I made no answer. It pleased me to let her wait. If she could behave queerly, so could I! At length she went on, in her nonchalant, detached way.

"'You agree, don't you, Doctor? It can't be anything serious. Not one of those horrid tropical diseases, surely? Nothing dangerous.'

"'I must see if you have any fever. Let me feel your pulse.'

"I moved towards her, but she evaded me.

"'No, Doctor, I'm sure I have no fever. I've taken my temperature every day since . . . since I began to be troubled with this faintness. Never above normal. And my digestion's all right, too.'

"I hesitated for a little. The visitor's strange manner had aroused my suspicions. Obviously she wanted to get something out of me. She had not driven a couple of hundred miles into this remote corner in order to discuss Flaubert! I kept her waiting for a minute or two before saying: 'Excuse me, but may I ask you a few plain questions?'

"'Of course, of course. One comes to a doctor for that,' she said lightly. But she had turned her back on me again, and was fiddling with the books.

"'Have you had any children?'

"'Yes, one, a boy.'

"'Well, did you have the same sort of symptoms then, in the early months, when you were pregnant?'

"'Yes.'

"The answer was decisive, blunt, and no longer in the tone of mere prattle which had characterized her previous utterances.

"'Well, isn't it possible that that's what's the matter with you now?'

"'Yes.'

"Again the response was sharp and decisive.

" 'You'd better come into my consulting room. An examination will settle the question in a moment.'

"At length she turned to face me squarely, and I could almost feel her eyes piercing me through her veil.

" 'No need for that, Doctor. I haven't a shadow of doubt as to my condition.' "

*   *   *

A pause.

I heard the narrator take another dose of his favorite stimulant. Then he resumed:

"Think the matter over for yourself. I had been rotting away there in my loneliness, and then this woman turned up from nowhere, the first white woman I had seen for years —and I felt as if something evil, something dangerous, had come into my room. Her iron determination made my flesh creep. She had come, it seemed, for idle chatter; and then without warning she voiced a demand as if she were throwing a knife at me. For what she wanted of me was plain enough. That was not the first time women had come to me with such a request. But they had come imploringly, had with tears besought me to help them in their trouble. Here, however, was a woman of exceptional, of virile determination. From the outset I had felt that she was stronger than I, that she could probably mold me to her will. Yet if there were evil in the room, it was in me likewise, in me the man. Bitterness had risen in me, a revolt against her. I had sensed in her an enemy.

"For a time I maintained an obstinate silence. I felt that she was eyeing me from behind her veil, that she was challenging me; that she wanted to force me to speak. But I was not ready to comply. When I did answer, I spoke beside the point, as if unconsciously mimicking her discursive and indifferent manner. I pretended that I had not understood her; tried to compel her to be candid. I was unwilling to meet her halfway. I wanted her to implore me, as the others had done—wanted it for the very reason that she had approached me so imperiously, and precisely because I knew myself to be a weakling in face of such arrogance as hers.

"Consequently, I talked all round the subject, saying that her symptoms were of trifling importance, that such faint-ing-fits were common form in early pregnancy, and that, far from being ominous, they generally meant that things would go well. I quoted cases I had seen and cases I had read of; I treated the whole affair as a bagatelle; I talked and talked, waiting for her to interrupt me. For I knew she would have to cut me short.

"She did so with a wave of the hand, as if sweeping my words of reassurance into the void.

" 'That's not what worries me, Doctor. I'm not so well as I was the time before. My heart troubles me.'

" 'Heart trouble, you say?' I rejoined, feigning an anxiety I did not feel. 'Well, I'd better go into that at once.' I made a movement as if to reach for my stethoscope.

"Once more she was recalcitrant. She spoke command-ingly, almost like a drill-sergeant.

" 'You may take my word for it that I have heart trouble. I don't want to waste my time and yours with examinations that are quite unnecessary. Besides, I think you might show a little more confidence in what I tell you. I have trusted you to the full!'

"This was a declaration of war. She had thrown down the glove, and I did not hesitate to lift it.

" 'Trust implies frankness, perfect frankness. Please speak to me straightforwardly. But, above all, take off your veil and sit down. Let the books alone and put your cards on the table. One doesn't keep a veil on when one comes to consult a medical man.'

"In her turn she accepted the challenge. Sitting down in front of me, she lifted her veil. The face thus disclosed was the sort of face I had dreaded; it was controlled and inscru-table; one of those exceptionally beautiful English faces which age cannot wither; but this lovely woman was still quite young, this woman with gray eyes that seemed so full of self-confident repose, and yet to hint at depths of passion.

Her lips were firmly set, an~~d~~
wished to keep to herself. For :
another; she imperiously and y
almost cruelly cold, so that in t'

"Her knuckles rattled agai~~n~~ ~~t~~ray nothing she
shake off her nervousness. Sudden~~ly~~ gazed at one

" 'Doctor, do you or do you not k~~now~~ with a look
you?' my eyes.

" 'I can make a shrewd guess, I fancy! ~~cou~~ld not
plainly. You want to put an end to your present ~~~~
You want me to free you from the fainting-fits, the ~~n~~
and so on—by removing the cause. Is that it?'

" 'Yes.'

"The word was as decisive as the fall of the knife in a
guillotine.

" 'Are you aware that such things are dangerous—to both
the persons concerned?'

" 'Yes.'

" 'That the operation is illegal?'

" 'I know that there are circumstances in which it is not
prohibited; nay, in which it is regarded as essential.'

" 'Yes, when there are good medical grounds for undertaking it.'

" 'Well, you can find such grounds. You are a doctor.'

"She looked at me without a quiver, as if issuing an order;
and I, the weakling, trembled in my amazement at the
elemental power of her resolve. Yet I still resisted. I would
not let her see that she was too strong for me. 'Not so fast,'
I thought. 'Make difficulties! Compel her to sue!'

" 'A doctor cannot always find sufficient reasons. Still, I
don't mind having a consultation with one of my colleagues. . . .'

" 'I don't want one of your colleagues. It is you I have
come to consult.'

" 'Why me, may I ask?'

"She regarded me coldly, and said:

" 'I don't mind telling you that! I came to you because

f-the-way place, because you have never
use of your known ability, and because'
the first time, 'because . . . you are not
va much longer—especially if you have a
ney in hand to go home with.'

ran through me. This mercantile calculation
flesh creep. No tears, no beseeching. She had taken
asure, had reckoned up my price, and had sought me
in full confidence that she could mold me to her will. In
truth I was almost overpowered; but her attitude towards
me filled me with gall, and I constrained myself to reply with
a chilly, almost sarcastic inflection:

" 'This large sum of money you speak of, you offer it me
for . . . ?'

" 'For your help now, to be followed by your immediate
departure from the Dutch Indies.'

" 'Surely you must know that that would cost me my
pension?'

" 'The fee I propose would more than compensate you.'

" 'You are good enough to use plain terms, but I should
like you to be even more explicit. What fee were you thinking of?'

" 'One hundred thousand gulden, in a draft on Amster-
dam.'

"I trembled, both with anger and surprise. She had reckoned it all out, had calculated my price, and offered me this
preposterous fee upon the condition that I should break my
contract with the Dutch Government; she had bought me
before seeing me; she had counted on my compliance. I felt
like slapping her face, so angered was I by this contumelious
treatment. But when I rose up in my wrath (she, too, was
standing once more), the sight of that proud, cold mouth
of hers which would not beg a favor, the flash of her arrogant eyes, aroused the brute in me, and of a sudden I burned
with desire. Something in my expression must have betrayed my feeling, for she raised her eyebrows as one does
when a beggar is importunate. In that instant we hated one

another, and were aware of our mutual detestation. She hated me because she had to make use of me, and I hated her because she demanded my help instead of imploring it. In this moment of silence we were for the first time speaking frankly to one another. As if a venomous serpent had bitten me, a terrible thought entered my mind, and I said to her . . . I said to her . . .

"But I go too fast, and you will misunderstand me. I must first of all explain to you whence this crazy notion came."

* * *

He paused. More whisky. His voice was stronger when he resumed.

"I'm not trying to make excuses for myself. But I don't want you to misunderstand me. I suppose I've never been what is called a 'good' man, and yet I think I've always been ready to help people whenever I could. In the rotten sort of life I had to live out there, my one pleasure was to use the knowledge I had scraped together, and thus to give poor sick wretches new hopes of health. That's a creative pleasure, you know; makes a man feel as if, for once, he were a god. It was pure delight to me when a brown-skinned Javanese was brought in, foot swollen to the size of his head from snake-bite, shrieking with terror lest the only thing that would save him might be an amputation—and I was able to save both life and leg. I have driven hours into the jungle to help a native woman laid up with fever. At Leipzig, in the clinic, I was ready enough, sometimes, to help women in just the same plight as my lady here. But in those cases, at least, one felt that one's patient had come to one in bitter need, asking to be rescued from death or from despair. It was the feeling of another's need that made me ready to help.

"But this particular woman—how can I make you understand? She had irritated me from the first moment when she dropped in with the pretense that she was on a casual excursion. Her arrogance had set my back up. Her manner had aroused the slumbering demon, the Caliban that lies hidden in us all. I was furious that she should come to me with her fine-lady airs, with her assumption of dispassionateness in what was really a life-or-death matter. Besides, a woman does not get in the family way from playing golf, or some such trifle. I pictured to myself with exasperating plainness that this imperious creature, so cold, so aloof—for whom I was to be a mere instrument, and, apart from that, of no more significance to her than the dirt beneath her feet —must, only two or three months before, have been passionate enough when clasped in the arms of the father of this unborn child she now wished to destroy. Such was the thought which obsessed me. She had approached me with supercilious contempt; but I would make her mine with all the virile masterfulness and impetus and ardor of that unknown man. This is what I want you to grasp. Never before had I tried to take advantage of my position as doctor. If I did so now, it was not from lust, not from an animal longing for sexual possession. I assure you it was not. I was moved by the craving to master her pride, to prove myself a dominant male, and thus to assert the supremacy of my ego over hers.

"I have already told you that arrogant, seemingly cold women have always exercised a peculiar power over me. Superadded to this, on the present occasion, was the fact that for seven years I had not had a white woman in my arms, had never encountered resistance in my wooing. Native girls are timorous little creatures who tremble with respectful ecstasy when a 'white lord,' a 'tuan,' deigns to take possession of them. They are overflowing with humility, always ready to give themselves for the asking— with a servility that robs voluptuousness of its tang. The Arab girls are different, I believe, and perhaps even the Chinese and the Malays; but I had been living among the Javanese. You can understand, then, how thrilled I was by this woman, so haughty and fierce and reserved; so brim-

ful of mystery, and gravid with the fruit of a recent passion. You can realize what it meant to me that such a
woman should walk boldly into the cage of such a man as I
—a veritable beast, lonely, starved, cut off from human
fellowship. I tell you all this that you may understand what
follows. Those were the thoughts that coursed through my
brain, those were the impulses that stirred me, when, simu-
lating indifference, I said coolly:

" 'One hundred thousand gulden? No, I won't do it for
that.'

"She looked at me, paling a little. No doubt she felt intui-
tively that the obstacle was not a matter of money. All she
said, however, was:

" 'What fee do you ask, then?'

" 'Let us be frank with one another,' I rejoined. 'I am no
trader. You must not look upon me as the poverty-stricken
apothecary in *Romeo and Juliet* who vends poison for the
"worse poison," gold. You will never get what you want
from me if you regard me as a mere man of business.'

" 'You won't do it, then?'

" 'Not for money.'

"For a moment there was silence. The room was so still
that I could hear her breathing.

" 'What else can you want?'

"I answered hotly.

" 'I want, first of all, that you should approach me, not as
a trader, but as a man. That when you need help you should
come to me, not with a parade of your gold "that's poison
to men's souls," but with a prayer to me, the human being,
that I should help you, the human being. I am not only a
doctor. "Hours of Consultation" are not the only hours I
have to dispose of. There are other hours as well—and you
may have chanced upon me in one of those other hours.'

"A brief silence followed. Then she pursed up her lips,
and said:

" 'So you would do it if I were to implore you?'

" 'I did not say so. You are still trying to bargain, and

will only plead if you have my implied promise. Plead first,
and then I will answer you.'

"She tossed her head defiantly, like a spirited horse.

"'I will not plead for your help. I would rather die.'

"I saw red, and answered furiously.

"'If you will not sue, I will demand. I think there is no
need of words. You know already what I want. When you
have given it, I will help you.'

"She stared at me for a moment. Then (how can I make
you realize the horror of it?) the tension of her features
relaxed and she burst out laughing. She laughed with a contempt which at once ground me to powder and intoxicated
me to madness. It came like an explosion of incredible violence, this disdainful laughter; and its effect on me was
such that I wanted to abase myself before her, longed to kiss
her feet. The energy of her scorn blasted me like lightning
—and in that instant she turned and made for the door.

"Involuntarily I pursued her to mumble excuses, to pray
forgiveness, so crushed was I in spirit. But she faced me
before leaving, to say, to command:

"'Do not dare to follow me, or try to find out who I am.
If you do, you will repent it.'

"In a flash she was gone."

*   *   *

Further hesitation. Another silence. Then the voice issued from the darkness once more.

"She vanished through the doorway, and I stood rooted
to the spot. I was, as it were, hypnotized by her prohibition.
I heard her going downstairs; I heard the house-door close;
I heard everything. I longed to follow her. Why? I don't
know whether it was to call her back, to strike her, to
strangle her. Anyhow, I wanted to follow her—and could
not. It was as if her fierce answer had paralyzed me. I know
this will sound absurd; such, however, was the fact. Minutes
passed—five, ten, it may be—before I could stir.

"But as soon as I made the first movement, the spell was

broken. I rushed down the stairs. There was only one road by which she could have gone, first to the settlement, and thence back to civilization. I hastened to the shed to get my bicycle, only to find that I had forgotten the key. Without waiting to fetch it I dragged the frail bamboo door from its hinges and seized the wheel. Next moment I was pedaling madly down the road in pursuit. I must catch her up; I must overtake her before she could get to her car; I must speak to her.

"The dusty track unrolled itself in front of me, and the distance I had to ride before I caught sight of her showed me how long I must have stood entranced after she left. There she was at last, where the road curved round the forest just before entering the settlement. She was walking quickly; behind her strode the China boy. She must have become aware of my pursuit the instant I saw her, for she stopped to speak to the boy and then went on alone, while he stood waiting. Why did she go on alone? Did she want to speak to me where no one could listen? I put on a spurt, when suddenly the boy, as I was about to pass him, leapt in front of me. I swerved to avoid him, ran up the bank, and fell.

"I was on my feet again in an instant, cursing the boy, and I raised my fist to deal him a blow, but he evaded it. Not bothering about him any more, I picked up my bicycle and was about to remount when the rascal sprang forward and seized the handle-bar, saying in pidgin-English:

" 'Master stoppee here.'

"You haven't lived in the tropics. You can hardly realize the intolerable impudence of such an action on the part of a native, and a servant at that. A yellow beast of a China boy actually presumed to catch hold of my bicycle and to tell me, a white 'tuan,' to stay where I was! My natural answer was to give him one between the eyes. He staggered, but maintained his grip on the cycle. His slit-like, slanting eyes were full of slavish fear, but for all that he was stout of heart, and would not let go.

" 'Master stoppee here !' he repeated.

"It was lucky I had not brought my automatic pistol. Had I had it with me, I should infallibly have shot him then and there.

" 'Let go, you dog !' I shouted.

"He stared at me, panic-stricken, but would not obey. In a fury, and feeling sure that further delay would enable her to escape me, I gave him a knock-out blow on the chin, which crumpled him up in the road.

"Now the cycle was free; but, when I tried to mount, I found that the front wheel had been buckled in the fall and would not turn. After a vain attempt to straighten the wheel, I flung the machine in the dust beside the China boy (who, bleeding from my violence, was coming to his senses) and ran along the road into the settlement.

"Yes, I ran; and here again, you, who have not lived in the tropics, will find it hard to realize all that this implies. For a white man, a European, thus to forget his dignity, and to run before a lot of staring natives, is to make himself a laughing-stock. Well, I was past thinking of my dignity. I ran like a madman in front of the huts, where the inmates gaped to see the settlement doctor, the white lord, running like a rickshaw coolie.

"I was dripping with sweat when I reached the settlement.

" 'Where's the car ?' I shouted breathless.

" 'Just gone, Tuan,' came the answer.

"They were staring at me in astonishment. I must have looked like a lunatic, wet and dirty, as I shouted out my question the moment I was within hail. Glancing down the road I saw, no longer the car, but the dust raised by its passing. She had made good her escape. Her device of leaving the boy to hinder me had been successful.

"Yet, after all, her flight availed her nothing. In the tropics the names and the doings of the scattered members of the ruling European caste are known to all. From this outlook, Java is but a big village where gossip is rife. While she had been visiting me, her chauffeur had spent an idle hour in the settlement headquarters. Within a few minutes I knew everything; knew her name, and that she lived in the provincial capital more than a hundred and fifty miles away. She was (as, indeed, I knew already) an English-woman. Her husband was a Dutch merchant, fabulously rich. He had been away five months, on a business journey to America, and was expected back in a few days. Then husband and wife were to pay a visit to England.

"Her husband had been five months away. It had been obvious to me that she could not be more than three months pregnant."

* * *

"Till now it has been easy enough for me to explain everything to you clearly, for up to this point my motives were plain to myself. As a doctor, a trained observer, I could readily diagnose my own condition. But from now on I was like a man in delirium. I had completely lost self-control. I knew how preposterous were my actions, and yet I went on doing them. Have you ever heard of 'running amuck'?"

"Yes, I think so. It's some sort of drunken frenzy among the Malays, isn't it?"

"More than drunkenness. More than frenzy. It's a condition which makes a man behave like a rabid dog, trans-forms him into a homicidal maniac. It's a strange and ter-rible mental disorder. I've seen cases of it and studied them carefully while in the East, without ever being able to clear up its true nature. It's partly an outcome of the climate, of the sultry, damp, oppressive atmosphere, which strains the nerves until at last they snap. Of course a Malay who runs amuck has generally been in trouble of some sort—jealousy, gambling losses, or what not. The man will be sitting quietly, as if there were nothing wrong—just as I was sitting in my room before she came to see me.

"Suddenly he will spring to his feet, seize his kris, dash

into the street, and run headlong, no matter where. He stabs any who happen to find themselves in his path, and the shedding of blood infuriates him more and more. He foams at the mouth, shouts as he runs, tears on and on, brandishing his blood-stained dagger. Every one knows that nothing but death will stop the madman; they scurry out of his way, shouting 'Amok, Amok,' to warn others. Thus he runs, killing, killing, killing, until he is shot down like the mad dog that he is.

"It is because I have seen Malays running amuck that I know so well what was my condition during those days, those days still so recent, those days about which I am going to tell you. Like such a Malay, I ran my furious course in pursuit of that Englishwoman, looking neither to the right nor to the left, obsessed with the one thought of seeing her again. I can scarcely remember all I did in the hurried moments before I actually set out on her trail. Within a minute or two of learning her name and where she lived, I had borrowed a bicycle and was racing back to my own quarters. I flung a spare suit or two into a valise, stuffed a bundle of notes into my pocket, and rode off to the nearest railway station. I did not report to the district officer; I made no arrangements about a substitute; I left the house just as it was, paying no heed to the servants who gathered round me asking for instructions. Within an hour from the time when that woman had first called to see me, I had broken with the past and was running amuck into the void.

"In truth I gained nothing by my haste, as I should have known had I been able to think. It was late afternoon when I got to the railway station, and in the Javanese mountains the trains do not run after dark for fear of wash-outs. After a sleepless night in the dak-bungalow and a day's journey by rail, at six in the evening I reached the town where she lived, feeling sure that, by car, she would have got there long before me. Within ten minutes I was at her door. 'What could have been more senseless?' you will say. I know, I know; but one who is running amuck runs amuck; he does not look where he is going.

"I sent in my card. The servant (not the China boy—I suppose he had not turned up yet) came back to say that his mistress was not well enough to see any one.

"I stumbled into the street. For an hour or more I hung around the house, in the forlorn hope that perhaps she would relent and would send out for me. Then I took a room at a neighboring hotel and had a couple of bottles of whisky sent upstairs. With these and a stiff dose of veronal I at length managed to drug myself into unconsciousness—a heavy sleep that was the only interlude in the race from life to death."

* * *

Eight bells struck. It was four in the morning. The sudden noise startled the narrator, and he broke off abruptly. In a little while, however, collecting himself, he went on with his story.

"It is hard to describe the hours that followed. I think I must have had fever. Anyhow I was in a state of irritability bordering on madness. I was running amuck. It was on Tuesday evening that I got to the coast town, and, as I learned next morning, her husband was expected on Saturday. There were three clear days during which I might help her out of her trouble. I knew there wasn't a moment to waste—and she wouldn't see me! My longing to help, and my longing (still greater, if possible) to excuse myself for my insane demand, intensified the disorder of my nerves. Every second was precious. The whole thing hung by a hair, and I had behaved so outrageously that she would not let me come near her. Imagine that you are running after some one to warn him against an assassin, and that he takes you for the would-be assassin, so that he flees from you towards destruction. All that she could see in me was the frenzied pursuer who had humiliated her with a base proposal and now wanted to renew it.

"That was the absurdity of the whole thing. My one wish was to help her, and she would not see me. I would have committed any crime to help her, but she did not know.

"Next morning when I called, the China boy was standing at the door. I suppose that he had got back by the same train as myself. He must have been on the look-out; for the instant I appeared he whisked out of sight—though not before I had seen the bruises on his face. Perhaps he had only hurried in to announce my coming. That is one of the things that maddens me now, to think that she may have realized that, after all, I wanted to help, and may have been ready to receive me. But the sight of him reminded me of my shame, so that I turned back from the door without venturing to send in my name. I went away; went away in torment, when she, perhaps, in no less torment, was awaiting me.

"I did not know how to pass the weary hours in this unfamiliar town. At length it occurred to me to call on the Vice-Resident, the man whose leg I had set to rights up country after he had had a motor smash. He was at home, and was, of course, delighted to see me. Did I tell you that I can speak Dutch as fluently as any Dutchman? I was at school in Holland for a couple of years. That was one reason why I chose the Dutch colonial service when I had to clear out of Leipzig.

"There must have been something queer about my manner, though. My grateful patient, for all his civility, eyed me askance, as if he divined that I was running amuck! I told him I had come to ask for a transfer. I couldn't live in the wilds any longer. I wanted an instant remove to the provincial capital. He looked at me questionably, and in a noncommittal way—much as a medical man looks at a patient.

" 'A nervous break-down, Doctor?' he inquired. 'I understand that only too well. We can arrange matters for you, but you'll have to wait for a little while; three or four weeks, let us say, while we're finding some one to relieve you at your present post.'

" 'Three or four weeks!' I exclaimed. 'I can't wait a sin-gle day!'

"Again that questioning look.

" 'I'm afraid you'll have to put up with it, Doctor. We mustn't leave your station unattended. Still, I promise you I'll set matters in train this very day.'

"I stood there biting my lips and realizing for the first time how completely I had sold myself into slavery. It was in my mind to defy him and his regulations; but he was tactful, he was indebted to me, and he did not want an open breach. Forestalling my determination to reply angrily, he went on:

" 'You've been living like a hermit, you know, and that's enough to put any one's nerves on edge. We've all been wondering why you never asked for leave, why you never came to see us down here. Some cheerful company, now and then, would have done you all the good in the world. This evening, by the way, there's a reception at Government House. Won't you join me? The whole colony will be there, including a good many people who have often asked about you, and have wanted very much to make your acquaint-ance.'

"At this I pricked up my ears. 'Asked about me?' 'Wanted to make my acquaintance?' Was she one of them? The thought was like wine to me. I remembered my manners, thanked him for his invitation, and promised to come early.

"I did go early, too early! Spurred on by impatience, I was the first to appear in the great drawing-room at the Residency. There I had to sit cooling my heels and listening to the soft tread of the bare-footed native servants who went to and fro about their business and (so it seemed to my morbid imagination) were sniggering at me behind my back. For a quarter of an hour I was the only guest amid a silence which, when the servants had finished their prep-arations, became so profound that I could hear the ticking of my watch in my pocket.

"Then the other guests began to arrive, some government

officials with their wives, and the Vice-Resident put in an appearance. He welcomed me most graciously, and entered into a long conversation, in which (I think) I was able to keep my end up all right—until, of a sudden, my nervousness returned, and I began to falter.

"She had entered the room, and it was a good thing that at this moment the Vice-Resident wound up his talk with me and began a conversation with some one else, for otherwise I believe I should simply have turned my back on the man. She was dressed in yellow silk, which set off her ivory shoulders admirably, and was talking brightly amid a group. Yet I, who knew her secret trouble, could read (or fancied I could read) care beneath her smile. I moved nearer, but she did not or would not see me. That smile of hers maddened me once more, for I knew it to be feigned. 'To-day is Wednesday,' I thought. 'On Saturday her husband will be back. How can she smile so unconcernedly? How can she toy with her fan, instead of breaking it with a convulsive clutch?'

"I, a stranger, was trembling in face of what awaited her. I, a stranger, had for two days been suffering with her suffering. What could her smile be but a mask to hide the storm that raged within?

"From the next room came the sound of music. Dancing was to begin. A middle-aged officer claimed her as his partner. Excusing herself to those with whom she had been conversing, she took his arm and walked with him towards the ballroom. This brought her close to me, and she could not fail to see me. For a moment she was startled, and then (before I could make up my mind whether or not to claim acquaintance) she nodded in a friendly way, said 'Good evening, Doctor,' and passed on.

"No one could have guessed what lay hidden behind that casual glance. Indeed, I myself was puzzled. Why had she openly recognized me? Was she making an advance, an offer of reconciliation? Was she still on the defensive? Had she merely been taken by surprise? How could I tell? All I knew was that I had been stirred to the depths.

"I watched her as she waltzed, a smile of enjoyment playing about her lips, and I knew that all the while she must be thinking, not of the dance, but of the one thing of which I was thinking, of the dread secret which she and I alone shared. The thought intensified (if possible) my anxiety, my longing, and my bewilderment. I don't know if any one else was observing me, but I am sure that my eager scrutiny of her must have been in manifest contrast to her ostensible unconcern. I simply could not look at any one but her, for I was watching all the time to see whether she would not, were it but for a moment, let the mask fall. The fixity of my stare must have been disagreeable to her. As she came back on her partner's arm, she flashed a look at me, dictatorial, angry, as if bidding me to exercise a little more self-control.

"But I, as I have explained to you, was running amuck. I knew well enough what her glance meant! 'Don't attract attention to me like this. Keep yourself in hand.' She was asking me to show some discretion in this place of public assembly. I felt assured, now, that if I went quietly home she would receive me should I call on the morrow; that all she wanted of me was that I should behave decorously; that she was (with good reason) afraid of my making a scene. Yes, I understood what she wanted; but I was running amuck, and I had to speak to her there and then. I moved over to the group amid which she was talking. They were all strangers to me; yet I rudely shouldered my way in among them. There I stood my ground listening to her, though I trembled like a whipped cur whenever her eyes rested coldly on mine. I was obviously unwelcome. No one said a word to me, and it must have been plain that she resented my intrusion.

"I cannot tell how long I should have gone on standing there. To all eternity, perhaps. I was spellbound. To her, however, the strain became unbearable. Suddenly she broke off, and, with a charming and convincing assumption of indifference, said: 'Well, I'm rather tired, so I shall turn in early. I'll ask you to excuse me. Good night!'

"She gave a friendly nod which included me with the others, and turned away. I watched her smooth, white, well-shaped back above her yellow silk gown, and at first (so dazed was I) I scarcely realized that I was to see her no more that evening, that I was to have no word with her on that last evening to which I had looked forward as the evening of salvation. I stood stock-still until I grasped this. Then ... then ...

"I must put the whole picture before you, if I am to make you understand what an idiot I made of myself. The big drawing-room at the Residency was now almost empty, though blazing with light. Most of the guests were dancing in the ballroom, while the older men who had lost taste for pairing off in this way had settled down to cards elsewhere. There were but a few scattered groups talking here and there. Across this huge hall she walked, with that dignity and grace which enthralled me, nodding farewell to one and to another as she passed. By the time I had fully taken in the situation, she was at the other end of the room and about to leave it. At that instant, becoming aware that she would escape me, I started to run after her, yes, to run, my pumps clattering as I sped across the polished floor. Of course every one stared at me, and I was overwhelmed with shame—yet I could not stop. I caught her up as she reached the door, and she turned on me, her eyes blazing, her nostrils quivering with scorn.

"But she had the self-command which in me was so lamentably lacking, and in an instant she had mastered her anger and burst out laughing. With ready wit, speaking loudly so that all could hear, she said :

" 'Ah, Doctor, so you've just remembered that prescription for my little boy, after all ! You men of science are apt to be forgetful now and again, aren't you?'

"Two men standing near by grinned good-humoredly. I understood, admired the skill with which she was glossing over my clownishness, and had the sense to take her hint.

Pulling out my pocketbook, in which there were some prescription blanks, I tore one off and handed it to her with a
muttered apology. Taking the paper from me with a smile
and a 'Good night!' she departed.

"She had saved the situation; but I felt that, as far as my
position with her was concerned, the case was hopeless, that
she loathed me for my insensate folly, hated me more than
death; that again and again and again (however often I
might come) she would drive me from her door like a dog.

"I stumbled across the room, people staring at me. No
doubt there was something strange about my appearance.
Making my way to the buffet, I drank four glasses of brandy
in brief succession. My nerves were worn to rags, and nothing but this overdose of stimulant would have kept me
going. I slipped away by a side door, furtively, as if I had
been a burglar. Not for a kingdom would I have crossed
the great hall again, have exposed myself to mocking eyes.
What did I do next? I can hardly remember. Wandering
from one saloon to another, I tried to drink myself into oblivion; but nothing could dull my senses. Still I heard the
laugh which had first driven me crazy, and the feigned
laughter with which she had covered up my boorishness
that evening. Walking on the quays, I looked down into the
water, and regretted bitterly that I had not brought my
pistol with me, so that I could blow out my brains and drop
into the quiet pool. My mind became fixed on this automatic,
and I resolved to make an end of myself. I wearily went
back to the hotel.

"If I refrained from shooting myself in the small hours,
it was not, believe me, from cowardice. Nothing I should
have liked better than to press the trigger, in the conviction
that thus I could put an end to the torment of my thoughts.
After all, I was obsessed by the idea of duty, that accursed
notion of duty. It maddened me to think that she might still
have need of me, to know that she really did need me. Here
was Thursday morning. In two days her husband would be

back. I was sure this proud woman would never live to face the shame that must ensue upon discovery. I tramped up and down my room for hours, turning these thoughts over in my mind, cursing the impatience, the blunders, that had made it impossible for me to help her. How was I to approach her now? How was I to convince her that all I asked was to be allowed to serve her? She would not see me, she would not see me. In fancy I heard her fierce laughter, and watched her nostrils twitching with contempt. Up and down, up and down the ten feet of my narrow room, till the tropic day had dawned, and, speedily, the morning sun was glaring into the veranda. As you know, in the tropics every one is up and about by six.

"Flinging myself into a chair, I seized some letter-paper and began to write to her, anything, everything, a cringing letter, in which I implored her forgiveness, proclaimed myself a madman and a villain, besought her to trust me, to put herself in my hands after all. I swore that I would disappear thereafter, from the town, the colony, the world, if she wanted me to. Let her only forgive me and trust me, allow me to help her in this supreme moment.

"I covered twenty pages. It must have been a fantastic letter, like one penned in a lunatic asylum, or by a man in the delirium of fever. When I had finished, I was dripping with sweat, and the room whirled round me as I rose to my feet. Gulping down a glass of water, I tried to read through what I had written, but the words swam before my eyes. I reached for an envelope, and then it occurred to me to add something that might move her. Snatching up the pen once more, I scrawled across the back of the last page: 'Shall await a word of forgiveness here at the hotel. If I don't hear from you before nightfall, I shall shoot myself.'

"Closing the letter, I shouted for one of the boys and told him to have the chit delivered instantly. There was nothing more for me to do but to await an answer."

* * *

As if to mark this interval, it was some minutes before he spoke again. When he did so, the words came with a renewed impetus.

"Christianity has lost its meaning for me. The old myths of heaven and hell no longer influence me. But if there were a hell, I should dread it little, for there could be no hell worse than those hours I spent in the hotel. A little room, baking in the noonday heat. You know these hotel rooms in the tropics—only a bed and a table and a chair. Nothing on the table but a watch and an automatic. Sitting on the chair in front of the table a man staring at the watch and the pistol —a man who ate nothing, drank nothing, did not even smoke, but sat without stirring as he looked at the dial of his watch and saw the second hand making its unending circuit. That was how I spent the day, waiting, waiting, waiting. And yet, for all that I was motionless, I was still like the Malay running amuck, or like a rabid dog, pursuing my frenzied course to destruction.

"Well, I won't make any further attempt to describe those hours. Enough to say that I don't understand how any one can live through such a time and keep reasonably sane.

"At twenty-two minutes past three (my eyes were still glued to the watch) there came a knock at the door. A native youngster with a folded scrap of paper—no envelope. I snatched it from him, and he was gone before I had time to tear open the note. Then, to begin with, I could not read the brief message. Here was her reply at last, and the words ran together before my eyes! They conveyed no meaning to me. I had to dip my head in cold water and calm my agitation before my senses cleared and I could grasp the meaning of the penciled English.

" 'Too late! Still, you'd better stay at the hotel. Perhaps I shall have to send for you in the end.'

"There was no signature on the crumpled page, a blank half-sheet torn from a prospectus or something of the kind. The writing was unsteady, perhaps from agitation, perhaps because it had been written in a moving carriage. How could

I tell? All I knew was that anxiety, haste, horror, seemed to cling to it; that it gripped me profoundly; and yet that I was glad, for at least she had written to me. I was to keep alive, for she might need me, she might let me help her after all. I lost myself in the maddest conjectures and hopes. I read the curt words again and again; I kissed them repeatedly; I grew calmer, and passed into a state betwixt sleep and waking when time no longer had any meaning—coma-vigil is what we doctors call it.

"This must have lasted for hours. Dusk was at hand when I came to myself with a start, so it was certainly near six o'clock. Had there been another knock? I listened intently. Then it was unmistakable—a knocking, gentle yet insistent. Unsteadily (for I felt giddy and faint) I sprang to the door. There in the passage stood the China boy. It was still light enough to show me, not only the traces of my rough handling, not only black eyes and a bruised chin, but that his yellow face was ashen pale.

" 'Master, come quickly.' That was all.

"I ran downstairs, the boy at my heels. A gharry was waiting, and we jumped in.

" 'What has happened?' I asked, as the man drove off, without further orders.

"The boy looked at me, his lips twitched, but he said never a word. I repeated my questions; still he was silent. I felt angry enough to strike him once more; yet I was touched by his devotion to his mistress, and so I kept myself in hand. If he wouldn't speak, he wouldn't; that was all.

"The gharryman was flogging his ponies, driving so furiously that people had to jump out of the way to avoid being run over. The streets were thronged, for we had left the European settlement, and were on our way through the Javanese and Malay town into the Chinese quarter. Here the gharry drew up in a narrow alley, in front of a tumble-down house. It was a sordid place, a little shop in front, lighted by a tallow candle; the attached dwelling was an unsavory hotel—one of those opium-dens, brothels, thieves' kitchens, or receivers' stores, such as are run by the worser sort of Chinese in all the big cities of the East.

"The boy knocked at the door. It opened for an inch or two, and a tedious parley ensued. Impatiently I, too, jumped out of the gharry, put my shoulder to the door, forced it open—an elderly Chinese woman fled before me with a shriek. I dashed along a passage, the boy after me, to another door. Opening this, I found myself in a dim interior, reeking of brandy and of blood. Some one was groaning. I could make out nothing in the gloom, but I groped my way towards the sound."

Another pause. When he spoke again, it was with sobs almost as much as with words.

"I groped my way towards the sound—and there she was, lying on a strip of dirty matting, twisted with pain, sighing and groaning. I could not see her face, so dark was the room. Stretching out my hand, I found hers, which was burning hot. She was in a high fever. I shuddered as I realized what had happened. She had come to this foul den in quest of the service I had refused, had sought out a Chinese midwife, hoping in this way to find the secrecy she no longer trusted me to observe. Rather than place herself in my care, she had come to the old witch I had seen in the passage, had had herself mauled by a bungler—because I had behaved like a madman, had so grievously affronted her that she thought it better to take any risks rather than to let me give the aid which, to begin with, I had only been willing to grant on monstrous terms.

"I shouted for light, and that detestable beldame brought a stinking and smoky kerosene lamp. I should have liked to strangle her—but what good would that have done? She put the lamp down on the table; and now, in its yellow glare, I could see the poor, martyred body.

"Then, of a sudden, the fumes were lifted from my brain. No longer half crazed, I forgot my anger, and even for the time forgot the evil mood that had brought us to this pass. Once more I was the doctor, the man of skill and knowledge to whom there had come an urgent call to use them for the best advantage of a suffering fellow-mortal. I forgot my wretched self; and, with reawakened intelligence, I was ready to do battle with the forces of destruction.

"I passed my hands over the nude body which so recently I had lusted for. Now it had become the body of my patient, and was nothing more. I saw in it only the seat of a life at grips with death, only the form of one writhing in torment. Her blood on my hands was not horrible to me, now that I was again the expert upon whose coolness everything turned. I saw, as an expert, the greatness of her danger. . . .

"I saw, indeed, that all was lost, short of a miracle. She had been so mishandled that her life-blood was rapidly draining away. And what was there, in this filthy hovel, which I could make use of in the hope of stanching the flow? Everything I looked at, everything I touched, was besoiled. Not even a clean basin and clean water!

" 'We must have you removed to hospital instantly,' I said. Thereupon, torture of mind superadded to torture of body, she writhed protestingly.

" 'No,' she whispered, 'no, no. I would rather die. No one must know. No one must know. Take me home, home!'

"I understood. Her reputation was more to her than her life. I understood, and I obeyed. The boy fetched a litter. We lifted her on to it, and then carried her, half dead, home through the night. Ignoring the terrified questions and exclamations of the servants, we took her to her room. Then began the struggle; the prolonged and futile struggle with death."

* * *

He clutched my arm, so that it was hard not to shout from surprise and pain. His face was so close that I could see the white gleam of teeth and the pale sheen of spectacle-glasses in the starlight. He spoke with such intensity, with such fierce wrath, that his voice assailed me like something betwixt a hiss and a shriek.

"You, a stranger I have never glimpsed in the daylight, you who are (I suppose) touring the world at your ease, do you know what it is to see some one die? Have you ever sat by any one in the death agony, seen the body twisting in the last wrestle and the blue fingernails clawing at vacancy; heard the rattle in the throat; watched the inexpressible horror in the eyes of the dying? Have you ever had that terrible experience—you, an idler, a globe-trotter, who can talk so glibly about one's duty to help?

"I have seen it often enough as a doctor, have studied death as a clinical happening. Once only have I experienced it in the full sense of the term. Once only have I lived with another and died with another. Once only, during that ghastly vigil a few nights ago when I sat cudgeling my brains for some way of stopping the flow of blood, some means of cooling the fever which was consuming her before my eyes, some method of staving off imminent death.

"Do you understand what it is to be a doctor, thoroughly trained in the science and practice of medicine, and (as you sagely remark) one whose first duty is to help—and to sit powerless by the bedside of the dying; knowing, for all one's knowledge, only one thing—that one can give no help? To feel the pulse as it flickers and fades? My hands were tied! I could not take her to the hospital, where something might have been done to give her a chance. I could not summon aid. I could only sit and watch her die, mumbling meaningless invocations like an old applewoman at church, and next minute clenching my fists in impotent wrath against a nonexistent deity.

"Can you understand? Can you understand? What I cannot understand is how one survives such hours, why one does not die with the dying, how one can get up next morning and clean one's teeth and put on one's necktie; how one can go on living in the ordinary way after feeling what I had felt, for the first time, that one I would give anything and everything to save was slipping away, somewhither, beyond recall.

"There was an additional torment. As I sat beside the bed (I had given her an injection of morphine to ease the pain, and she lay quiet now, with cheeks ashen pale), I felt the unceasing tension of a fixed gaze boring into my back. The China boy was sitting cross-legged on the floor, murmuring prayers in his own tongue. Whenever I glanced at him, he raised his eyes imploringly to mine, like a hound dumbly beseeching aid. He lifted his hands as if in supplication to a god—lifted them to me, the impotent weakling who knew that all was vain, that I was of no more use in that room than an insect running across the floor.

"It added to my torture, this petitioning of his, this fanatical conviction that my skill would enable me to save the woman whose life was ebbing as he looked on and prayed. I could have screamed at him and have trampled him under foot, so much did his eager expectancy hurt me; and yet I felt that he and I were bound together by our fondness for the dying woman and by the dread secret we shared.

"Like an animal at watch, he sat huddled up behind me; but the instant I wanted anything he was alert, eager to fetch it, hoping I had thought of something that might help even now. He would have given his own blood to save her life. I am sure of it. So would I. But what was the use of thinking of transfusion (even if I had had the instruments) when there were no means of arresting the flow of blood? It would only have prolonged her agony. But this China boy would have died for her, as would I. Such was the power she had. And I had not even the power to save her from bleeding to death!

"Towards daybreak she regained consciousness, awoke from the drugged sleep. She opened her eyes, which were no longer proud and cold. The heat of fever glowed in them as she looked round the room. Catching sight of me, she was puzzled for a moment, and needed an effort to recall who this stranger was. Then she remembered. She regarded me at first with enmity, waving her arms feebly as if to repel me, and showing by her movements that she would have fled from me had she but had the strength. Then, collecting her thoughts, she looked at me more calmly. Her breathing was labored; she tried to speak; she wanted to sit up, but was too weak. Begging her to desist, I leaned closer to her, so that I should be able to hear her lightest whisper. She regarded me piteously, her lips moved, and faint indeed was the whisper that came from them:

"'No one will find out? No one?'

"'No one,' I responded, with heartfelt conviction. 'No one shall ever know.'

"Her eyes were still uneasy. With a great effort she managed to breathe the words:

"'Swear that no one shall know. Swear it.'

"I raised my hand solemnly and murmured: 'I pledge you my word.'

"She looked at me, weak though she was, cordially, gratefully. Yes, despite all the harm I had done, she was grateful to me at the last, she smiled her thanks. A little later she tried to speak again, but was not equal to the exertion. Then she lay peacefully, with her eyes closed. Before daylight shone clearly into the room, all was over."

* * *

A long silence. He had overcome the frenzy which had prompted him to seize me by the arm, and had sunk back exhausted. The stars were paling when three bells struck. A fresh though gentle breeze was blowing as herald of the dawn that comes so quickly in the tropics. Soon I could see him plainly. He had taken off his cap, so that his face was exposed. It was pinched with misery. He scanned me through his spectacles with some interest, to see what sort of a man was this stranger to whom he had been pouring out his heart. Then he went on with his story, speaking with a scornful intonation.

"For her, all was over; but not for me. I was alone with the corpse, in a strange house; in a town where (as in all such places) gossip runs like wildfire, and I had pledged my

word that her secret should be kept! Consider the situation.
Here was a woman moving in the best society of the colony,
and, to all seeming, in perfect health. She had danced the
evening before last at Government House. Now she was
dead, and the only doctor who knew anything about the matter, the man who had sat by her while she died, was a chance
visitor to the town, summoned to her bedside by one of the
servants. This doctor and this servant had brought her home
in a litter under cover of darkness and had kept every one
else out of the way. Not until morning did they call the other
servants, to tell them their mistress was dead. The news
would be all over the town within an hour or two, and how
was I, the doctor from an up-country station, to account for
the sudden death, for what I had done and for what I had
failed to do? Why hadn't I sent for one of my colleagues
to share the responsibility? Why?...Why?...Why?

"I knew what lay before me. My only helper was the
China boy; but he, at any rate, was a devoted assistant, who
realized that there was still a fight to be fought.

"I had said to him: 'You understand, don't you? Your
mistress's last wish was that no one shall know what has
happened.'

"'Savvee plenty, Master,' he answered simply; and I
knew that I could trust him.

"He washed the blood stains from the floor, set all to
rights as quickly as possible, and his fortitude sustained
mine.

"Never before have I had so much concentrated energy,
nor shall I ever have it again. When one has lost everything
but a last remnant, one fights for that last remnant with des-
perate courage, with fierce resolution. The remnant for
which I was fighting was her legacy to me, her secret. I was
calm and self-assured in my reception of every one who
came, telling them the tale I had decided upon to account
for the death. After all, people are used to sudden, grave,
and fatal illness in the tropics; and the laity cannot openly
question a doctor's authoritative statements. I explained that

the China boy, whom she had sent to fetch the doctor when
she was taken ill, had chanced to meet me. But while talking thus to all and sundry with apparent composure, I was
awaiting the one man who really mattered, the senior surgeon, who would have to inspect the body before burial could
take place. It was Thursday morning, and on Saturday the
husband was coming back. Speedy burial is the rule in this
part of the world; but the senior surgeon, not I, would have
to sign the necessary certificates.

"At nine he was announced. I had sent for him, of course.
He was my superior in rank, and he bore me a grudge because of the local reputation I had acquired in the little matter of the Vice-Resident's broken leg. This was the doctor
of whom she had spoken so contemptuously, as good only
for bridge. According to official routine my wish for a transfer would pass through his hands. No doubt the Vice-Resident had already mentioned it to him.

"The instant we met that morning, I guessed his enmity,
but this only steeled me to my task.

"As soon as I came into the ante-room where he was
waiting, he began the attack:

" 'When did Madame Blank die?'

" 'At six this morning.'

" 'When did she send for you?'

" 'At nightfall yesterday.'

" 'Did you know that I was her regular professional attendant?'

" 'Yes.'

" 'Why didn't you send for me, then?'

" 'There wasn't time—and, besides, Madame Blank had
put herself in my hands exclusively. In fact, she expressly
forbade me to call in any other doctor.'

"He stared at me. His face flushed. Suppressing an angry
retort, he said with assumed indifference:

" 'Well, even though you could get on without me so long
as she was alive, you have fulfilled your official duty in send-

ing for me now, and I must fulfill mine by verifying the death and ascertaining the cause.'

"I made no answer, and let him lead the way to the death-chamber. As soon as we were there, and before he could touch the body, I said :

" 'It is not a question of ascertaining the cause of death, but of inventing a cause. Madame Blank sent for me to save her, if I could, from the consequences of an abortion, clumsily performed by a Chinese midwife. To save her life was impossible, but I pledged my word to save her reputation. I want you to help me.'

"He looked his surprise.

" 'You actually want me, the senior surgeon of this province, to join you in concealing a crime?'

" 'Yes, that is what I want you to do.'

" 'In fact,' he said with a sneer, 'I am to help in the hushing-up of a crime you have committed.'

" 'I have given you to understand that, as far as Madame Blank is concerned, all I have done is to try to save her from the consequences of her own indiscretion and some one else's crime (if you want to insist on the word). Had I been the culprit, I should not be alive at this hour. She has herself paid the extreme penalty, and the miserable bungler who procured the abortion really does not matter one way or the other. You cannot punish the criminal without tarnishing the dead woman's reputation, and that I will not suffer.'

" 'You will not suffer it? You talk to me as if you were my official chief, instead of my being yours. You dare to order me about. I had already surmised there must be something queer when you were summoned from your nook in the backwoods. A fine beginning you've made of it with your attempt to interlope here. Well, all that remains for me is to make my own investigation, and I can assure you that I shall report exactly what I find. I'm not going to put my name to a false certificate ; you needn't think so !'

"I was imperturbable.

" 'You'll have to, this once. If you don't you'll never leave the room alive.'

"I put my hand in my pocket. The pistol was not there (I had left it in my room at the hotel), but the bluff worked. He drew back in alarm; whereupon I made a step forward and said, with a calculated mingling of threat and conciliation :

" 'Look here ! I shall be sorry to go to extremes, but you'd better understand that I don't value either my life or yours at a single stiver. I'm so far through that there's only one thing in the world left for me to care about, and that's the keeping of my promise to this dead woman that the manner of her death shall remain secret. I give you my word that if you sign a certificate to the effect that she died of— what shall we say ?—a sudden access of malignant tropical fever with hyperpyrexia, leading to heart failure—that will sound plausible enough—if you do this, I will leave the Indies within a week. I will, if you like, put a bullet through my head as soon as she is buried and I can be sure that no one (you understand, no one) can make any further examination. That should satisfy you. In fact, it must satisfy you.'

"My voice, my whole aspect, must have been menacing, for he was cowed. Whenever I advanced a little, he retreated, showing that uncontrollable fear with which people flee from a man brandishing a blood-stained kris, a man who is running amuck. He wilted visibly, and changed his tone. He was no longer the adamantine official, standing invincibly upon punctilio.

"Still, with a last vestige of resistance, he murmured :

" 'Never in my life have I signed a false certificate. Perhaps there would be no question raised if I were to word the document as you suggest. It is perfectly clear to me, however, that I ought not to do anything of the kind.'

" 'Of course you "ought not," judging by conventional standards,' I rejoined, wishing to help him to save his face. 'But this is a special case. When you know that the disclosure of the truth can only bring grievous suffering to a living man and blast the reputation of a dead woman, why hesitate?'

"He nodded. We sat down together at the table. Amicable enough now to all seeming, we concocted the certificate which was the basis of the account of the matter published in next day's newspaper. Then he stood up and looked at me searchingly:

" 'You'll sail for Europe by the next boat, won't you?'

" 'Of course! I've pledged you my word.'

"He continued to stare at me. I saw that he wanted to be strict and businesslike, and that the task was hard. It was as much in the endeavor to hide his embarrassment as from any wish to convey information that he said:

" 'Blank was going home with his wife immediately after his arrival from Yokohama. I expect the poor fellow will want to take his wife's body back to her people in England. He's a wealthy man, you know, and the rich can indulge these fancies. I shall order the coffin instantly, and have it lined with sheet lead so that it can be sealed. That will get over immediate difficulties, and he will know that in this sweltering heat there was no possibility of awaiting his appearance on the scene. Even if he thinks we've been precipitate, he won't venture to say so. We're officials, and he's only a merchant after all, though he could buy us both up and never miss the money. Besides, we're acting as we do to save him needless pain.'

"My enemy of a few minutes back was now my acknowledged confederate. Well, he knew he was soon going to be rid of me for ever; and he had to justify himself to himself. But what he did next was utterly unexpected. He shook me warmly by the hand!

" 'I hope you'll soon be all right again,' he said.

"What on earth did he mean? Was I ill? Was I mad? I opened the door for him ceremoniously, and bade him farewell. Therewith my energies ran down. The room swam round me, and I collapsed beside her bed, as the frenzied

Malay collapses when he has run his murderous course and
is at last shot down.

"I don't know how long I lay on the floor. At length there
was a rustling noise, a movement in the room. I looked up.
There stood the China boy, regarding me uneasily.

" 'Some one have come. Wanchee see Mississee,' he said.

" 'You mustn't let any one in.'

" 'But, Master . . .'

"He hesitated, looked at me timidly, and tried in vain
to speak. The poor wretch was obviously suffering.

" 'Who is it?'

"He trembled like a dog in fear of a blow. He did not utter any name. A sense of delicacy rare in a native servant restrained him. He said simply:

" 'B'long that man!'

"He did not need to be explicit. I knew instantly whom
he meant. At the word I was all eagerness to see this unknown, whose very existence I had forgotten. For, strange
as it may seem to you, after the first disclosure she had made
to me and her rejection of my infamous proposal, I had completely put him out of my mind. Amid the hurry and anxiety
and stress of what had happened since, it had actually slipped
my memory that there was another man concerned in the
affair, the man this woman had loved, the man to whom she
had passionately given what she had refused to give me.
The day before, I should have hated him, should have longed
to tear him to pieces. Now I was eager to see him because I
loved him—yes, loved the man whom she had loved.

"With a bound I was in the ante-room. A young, very
young, fair-haired officer was standing there, awkward and
shy. He was pale and slender, looking little more than a boy,
and yet touchingly anxious to appear man-like, calm, and
composed. His hand was trembling as he raised it in salute.
I could have put my arms round him and hugged him, so
perfectly did he fulfill my ideal of the man I should have
wished to be this woman's lover—not a self-confident se-

ducer, but a tender stripling to whom she had thought fit to give herself.

"He stood before me, abashed. My sudden apparition, my eager scrutiny, increased his embarrassment. His face puckered slightly, and it was plain that he was on the verge of tears.

" 'I don't want to push in,' he said at length, 'but I should like so much to see Madame Blank once more.'

"Scarcely aware of what I was doing, I put an arm round the young fellow's shoulders and guided him towards the door. He looked at me with astonishment, but with gratitude as well. At this instant we had an indubitable sense of fellowship. We went together to the bedside. She lay there; all but the head, shoulders, and arms hidden by the white linen. Feeling that my closeness must be distasteful to him, I withdrew to a distance. Suddenly he collapsed, as I had done; sank to his knees, and, no longer ashamed to show his emotion, burst into tears.

"What could I say? Nothing!

"What could I do? I raised him to his feet and led him to the sofa. There we sat side by side; and, to soothe him, I gently stroked his soft, blond hair. He took my hand in his and pressed it affectionately. Then he said:

" 'Tell me the whole truth, Doctor. She didn't kill herself, did she?'

" 'No,' I answered.

" 'Then is any one else to blame for her death?'

" 'No,' I said once more, although from within was welling up the answer: 'I, I, I—and you. The two of us. We are to blame. We two—and her unhappy pride.'

"But I kept the words unuttered, and was content to say yet again:

" 'No! No one was to blame. It was her doom.'

" 'I can't realize it,' he groaned. 'It seems incredible. The night before last she was at the ball; she nodded to me and smiled. How could it happen? How did she come to die so unexpectedly, so swiftly?'

"I told him a string of falsehoods. Even from her lover I must keep the secret. We spent that day and the next and the next together in brotherly converse, both aware (though we did not give the knowledge voice) that our lives were intertwined by our relationship to the dead woman. Again and again I found it hard to keep my own counsel, but I did so. He never learned that she had been with child by him; that she had come to me to have the fruit of their love destroyed; and that, after my refusal, she had taken the step which had ended her own life as well. Yet we talked of nothing but her during those days when I was hidden in his quarters. I had forgotten to tell you that! They were searching for me. Her husband had arrived after the coffin had been closed. He was suspicious—all sorts of rumors were afoot—and he wanted my account of the matter at first hand. But I simply couldn't endure the thought of meeting him, the man through whom I knew she had suffered; so I hid myself, and during four days I never left the house. Her lover took a passage for me under a false name, and late at night I went on board the boat bound for Singapore. I left everything, all my possessions, the work I had done in the last seven years. My house stood open to any one who chose to enter it. No doubt the authorities have already erased my name from the list of their officials as 'absent without leave.' But I could not go on living in that house, that town, that world, where everything reminded me of her. If I fled like a thief in the night it was to escape her, to forget her.

"Vain was the attempt! When I came on board at midnight, my friend with me to see me off, a great, oblong, brass-bound chest was being hoisted on board by the crane. It was her coffin, her coffin! It had followed me, just as I had followed her down from the hills to the coast. I could make no sign, I had to look on unheeding, for her husband was there, too. He was on his way to England. Perhaps he means to have the coffin opened when he gets there; to have a post-mortem made; to find out . . . Anyhow, he has taken her back to him, has snatched her away from us; she belongs to him now, not to us. At Singapore, where I transshipped to this German mail-boat, the coffin was transshipped as well; and he is here, too, the husband. But I am still watching over her, and shall watch over her to the end. He shall never learn her secret. I shall defend her to the last against the man to escape whom she went to her death. He shall learn nothing, nothing. Her secret belongs to me, and to no one else in the world.

"Do you understand? Do you understand why I keep out of the other passengers' way, why I cannot bear to hear them laugh and chatter, to watch their foolish flirtations—when I know that deep down in the hold, among the tea-chests and the cases of brazil nuts, her body lies? I can't get near it, for the hatches are closed; but I feel its nearness by day and by night, when the passengers are tramping up and down the promenade deck or dancing merrily in the saloon. It is stupid of me, I know. The sea ebbs and flows above millions of corpses, and the dead are rotting beneath every spot where one sets foot on land. All the same, I cannot bear it. I cannot bear it when they dance and laugh in this ship which is taking her body home. I know what she expects of me. There is still something left for me to do. Her secret is not yet safe; and, until it is safe, my pledge to her will be unfulfilled."

* * *

From midships there came splashing and scraping noises. The sailors were swabbing the decks. He stared at the sound, and jumped to his feet.

"I must be going," he murmured.

He was a distressing sight, with his careworn expression, and his eyes reddened by weeping and by drink. He had suddenly become distant in his manner. Obviously he was regretting his loquacity, was ashamed of himself for having opened his heart to me as he had done. Wishing to be friendly, however, I said:

"Won't you let me pay you a visit in your cabin this afternoon?"

A smile—mocking, harsh, cynical—twisted his lips; and when he answered, after a momentary hesitation, it was with appropriate emphasis.

"Ah, yes, 'it's one's duty to help.' That's your favorite maxim, isn't it? Your use of it a few hours ago, when you caught me in a weak moment, has loosened my tongue finely! Thank you for your good intentions, but I'd rather be left to myself. Don't imagine, either, that I feel any better for having turned myself inside out before you and for having shown you my very entrails. My life has been torn to shreds, and no one can patch it together again. I have gained nothing by working in the Dutch colonial service for seven years. My pension has gone phut, and I am returning to Germany a pauper—like a dog that slinks behind a coffin. A man cannot run amuck without paying for it. In the end, he is shot down; and I hope that for me the end will come soon. I'm obliged to you for proposing to call, but I've the best of companions to prevent my feeling lonely in my cabin—plenty of bottles of excellent whisky. They're a great consolation. Then there's another old friend, and my only regret is that I didn't make use of it soon instead of late. My automatic, I mean, which will in the end be better for my soul than any amount of open confession. So I won't trouble you to call, if you don't mind. Among the 'rights of man' there is a right which no one can take away, the right to croak when and where and how one pleases, without a 'helping hand.'"

He looked at me scornfully and with a challenging air, but I knew that at bottom his feeling was one of shame, infinite shame. Saying no word of farewell, he turned on his heel, and slouched off in the direction of the cabins. I never saw him again, though I visited the fore-deck several times after midnight. So completely did he vanish that I might have thought myself the victim of hallucination had I not noticed among the other passengers a man wearing a crape armlet, a Dutchman, I was told, whose wife had recently died of tropical fever. He walked apart, holding converse with no one, and was melancholy of mien. Watching him, I was distressed by the feeling that I was aware of his secret trouble. When my path crossed his, I turned my face away, lest he should divine from my expression that I knew more about his fate than he did himself.

* * *

In Naples harbor occurred the accident which was explicable to me in the light of the stranger's tale. Most of the passengers were, as I have said, ashore at the time. I had been to the opera, and had then supped in one of the brightly lit cafés in the Via Roma. As I was being rowed back to the steamer, I noticed that there was a commotion going on round the gangway, boats moving to and fro, and men in them holding torches and acetylene lamps as they scanned the water. On deck there were several carabinieri, talking in low tones. I asked one of the deck-hands what was the matter. He answered evasively, so that it was obvious he had been told to be discreet. Next morning, too, when we were steaming towards Genoa, I found it impossible to glean any information. But at Genoa, in an Italian newspaper, I read a high-flown account of what had happened that night at Naples.

Under cover of darkness, it appeared, to avoid disquieting the passengers, a coffin from the Dutch Indies was being lowered into a boat. It contained the body of a lady; and her husband (who was taking it home for burial) was already waiting in the boat. Something heavy had, when the coffin was halfway down the ship's side, dropped on it from the upper deck, carrying it away, so that it fell with a crash into the boat, which instantly capsized. The coffin, being lined with lead, sank. Fortunately there had been no loss of life, for no one had been struck by the falling coffin, and the widower together with the other persons in the boat had been rescued, though not without difficulty.

What had caused the accident? One story, said the re-

porter, was that a lunatic had jumped overboard, and in his
fall had wrenched the coffin from its lashings. Perhaps the
story of the falling body had been invented to cover up the
remissness of those responsible for lowering the coffin, who
had used tackle that was too weak, so that the lead-weighted
box had broken away of itself. Anyhow, the officers were
extremely reticent.

In another part of the paper was a brief notice to the
effect that the body of an unknown man, apparently about
thirty-five years of age, had been picked up in Naples harbor. There was a bullet-wound in the head. No one connected
this with the accident which occurred when the coffin was
being lowered.

Before my own eyes, however, as I read the brief para-
graphs, there loomed from the printed page the ghostly
countenance of the unhappy man whose story I have here
set down.

THE PARCEL [*]

By Arnold Zweig

"Pray don't trouble, my dear Doctor," said Claudia in her deep soft voice, as he eagerly offered to fetch her things from the cloak-room. "James will have seen to that already" ; and, in fact, as she spoke, a youthful footman in livery—yellowish gray coat, white breeches, and top-boots—appeared with his mistress's pink evening cloak and a thin shawl. Doctor Rohme stood helplessly among the chattering groups in the foyer. Beyond the æsthetic excitement of the evening, he still felt the resolve that had brought him there, like the note of a taut harp string, ringing in his mind, though as yet it was a resolve and nothing more ; and as Claudia stood for the footman to arrange the cloak about her with a deftness that betrayed long practice, he brooded with set lips and vacant dreamy eyes, under the hostile looks of the audience now struggling for their coats and wraps, upon the wave of weary depression that had fallen upon him yesterday, and now once more swept over him as the sea flings a swirling wave against a cliff. When he noticed the announcement of that night's performance of Goethe's *Götz,* he picked up the play and began to read it, at first idly and then with growing dismay, for Weislingen's vacillation had struck him like a blow in the face. A choking feeling of disgust and contempt rose in his throat, at the thought that for three weeks he had known that he must reach some definite understanding in his relations with this girl, whom he loved to adoration, without finding the courage to bring matters to a decision. Her calm and friendly attitude

[*] From "Claudia" by Arnold Zweig. Copyright 1930, by The Viking Press, Inc.

towards him seemed to show that she did not in the least know how impossible it all was. His sense of order would not let him rest; he felt he was degrading himself and her, so he prescribed himself the torment of this performance, and the specific had worked. He would end it all that very evening, open his soul to her, at the risk of being dismissed for ever and thrust out into the darkness and the cold. That was what he must do, and he would do it.

Claudia's face seemed altered as she smiled at him over the white silk about her throat; she slipped her hand without a word under her companion's arm, and let him appear to lead her to the door, though it was really she who guided him. James had already beckoned to the chauffeur, and the familiar blue car stood, panting like a great beast, among the crowds that surged into the streets. He felt her guidance with a sharp thrill of shame, which he at once saw was futile, and would have preferred to go away, but could not; and when she disappeared into the dark vehicle without a word that would have given him excuse for departure, he had to get in after her. The chauffeur started almost before he sat down; so he sank back on to the leather cushions, looking suspiciously for a smile on that mobile mouth that would have made him unhappy. But the lovely pale face remained unchanged in its expression of gentle kindliness as she smoothed her frock and turned her bright gaze to his, and he felt his purpose quail under the spell of those perilous great black eyes that so glowed with understanding. For a few moments the faint hiss and throb of the speeding car stirred the stillness of their thoughts, that still lingered with enjoyment over the play they had just left. The curtain had fallen, but they could still hear the clash of brandished weapons and hear the ring of that crisp and soldierly prose. *Götz von Berlichingen* had been played as though to give two great actors the opportunity to prove their art upon the creations of the youthful Goethe: the forceful talent of the older man made a vigorous living figure of the bluff Knight, while the younger with countless nervous subtle touches tried to present the unstable Weislingen as a man of to-day, and his abrupt uncertain gestures appealed strongly to an audience whose minds were not dissimilar to his. The balance between the two characters was presented in a fashion that thrilled and delighted the audience, and at the end their enthusiasm burst forth in a torrent of applause that swept on to the stage.

While these now vague recollections were hovering in his mind, he tortured himself to discover some means, some way, in which, without shocking her by blurting out his position—how well he could imagine her raised eyebrows and contemptuous curled lips!—he might make his mind clear to her, and say, in effect: "This is what I am like— now decide." But it was not easy and the words would not come.

At last Claudia said in a light conventional tone: "An interesting performance, Herr Doctor, don't you think?"

To Rohme, it was as though that murmurous silence were a living entity that her words had shattered; he collected himself and answered, in a high voice with a touch of hoarseness that concealed his intonation, and a slightly formal air:

"Most interesting, indeed. Old-fashioned and yet modern, one might say. I wonder whether Goethe saw his Weislingen like that?"

She smiled faintly. "So you are thinking of Weislingen? It is Götz that is in my mind. . . . But I will ask the same question: I wonder whether he saw Götz like that?"

He took off his glasses and polished them with a white handkerchief as he observed slowly:

"I rather doubt, Fräulein Claudia, whether Götz is the center of interest just now. I'm sure the people who were sitting round us this evening will be talking much more about Weislingen, just as you caught me doing. He is one of them—of us. The Götz we saw was a possible embodiment of Goethe's idea of him, but as to Weislingen—I am at least doubtful. Goethe's age would certainly have regarded a man so easily swayed and so . . ." he hesitated for an instant and brought out his succeeding word in an emphatic tone ... "unmanly, as a pitiable object. This kind of Weislingen is reserved for us. ..." He concluded with peculiar bitterness.

Claudia Eggeling thought that she could grasp all that was implied by his tone; she had not failed to notice her old friend's intense interest in Weislingen's character during the performance of the play. But as she wanted to postpone a discussion that was not at all unwelcome to her, until their relation had become easier and more manageable, she said lightly:

"Well, we must talk about that later; I don't agree with you. You condemn poor Weislingen, I see."

"Condemn him? Nothing was further from my mind. ..."

"Well, you disapprove of him. But how do you reconcile the unmanly man with your philosophy, my learned friend?"

She hoped a touch of banter might enliven his answers, but in vain; he answered just as gloomily as before.

"Perfectly well. ... One can imagine a type, Man, possessing all the characteristics that constitute manhood, can't one?—and possessing them in the highest degree. The individual falls short of this type, and in specially unfortunate cases, so far short that manhood is no longer there. And yet he still walks about on two legs."

The car suddenly swept into a broad avenue. After bumping wildly for a minute or two on the slightly uneven paving, the wheels seemed to leave the asphalt surface altogether and shoot through a whirl of white and red lights. And the faint hum of traffic, and the glitter of the great highway flooded that little rushing room and made the faces of the two stand out, pale and sharp, in a kind of intenser actuality.

Claudia forgot her resolve, and took up the theme once more with her usual reluctance to abandon an idea: "I wish," she said, "you would describe the type to me a little." And she wondered whether he would describe his own character.

"So you agreed with me," he said, shading his eyes against

the speeding lights. "We need not go further than Götz, for Götz is very much a man. I need not mention every quality that distinguishes a man—such as kindness, simplicity, courage, and so on. Weislingen, too, can be kind—but from weakness. Fundamentally man is a creative, productive creature. . . ."

"And woman?" she asked.

"Conceives, transmutes, and gives forth: brings, in fact, to birth. But the man sows the seed. He has the power of vision, he creates because he sees the world anew. . . . Weislingen sees what is to be, and understands it—he has intelligence. But he never builds a bridge from one point to another, he only sees the result. Götz never realizes that there are difficulties. . . . Götz takes things piecemeal, as warring elements that need a unity, and yet has more respect for them than Weislingen who blindly surrenders to a circumstance or a situation and is continually lost."

Claudia felt suddenly baffled. At first he seemed to be talking about himself, disparagingly. Was he not, preëminently, intelligent—like Herod and Kandaules, typically manly characters, and much more akin to him than Götz, who was his opposite? Then it flashed across her mind that there was a ring of deeper purpose in his hesitating speech, and she had been listening not so much to what he said but to his tone, which was strangely moving and suggested a burdened soul finding its deliverance. However, he had rather overweighted the conversation, so she decided to turn the subject. What she wanted to say was: "You are being deliberately unfair to yourself"; but she took refuge in a generality and said:

"I think this type of yours is unjust to our present society. However, we can talk about that later on; at present all I know is that I'm vulgar enough to be terribly hungry, and Mamma made it quite clear that there would be some bread and butter for you, if you would give us your company so late."

He listened eagerly; it was, indeed, a torture to him to

talk just then of what he felt so deeply. He let his mind dwell on what she had just said. What joy!—one more hour in her company. Then a stab of uneasiness went through him: could he be sure they were expecting him as a welcome guest, or did his enjoyment of that lovely house blind him to the fact that his was the pitiable rôle of an intrusive visitor?

"Your mother is very kind," he said gently, "... but I don't know ... I had tried to make up my mind not to come to your house so often...."

A bitter loathing of himself and a burst of fury against his unlucky tongue exploded within him. He ought to have put and said this quite differently—now it rang quite false.

From time to time the klaxon gave forth a loud deep roar, full of the power and purpose of a mighty beast, that is certain of its way and will not harm those weaker than itself. Shrill rasping answers came from other cars as they shot across the road ahead, or came up behind, plunging from darkness into darkness. On either side of them was blackness, against which stood out a few lamps, trees, and foliage; they had almost imperceptibly left the City and were speeding along the asphalt highway that seemed to undulate before them under the flooding glare of the headlights, as they neared the villas and gardens. Claudia turned her face once more to her companion:

"Do we bore you?" she asked in an astonished tone, but with an air of unbelief that softened it. She understood him pretty well, and by way of reply, she thought to herself with not a little satisfaction: How charmingly gauche such a clever man can be! If only he wouldn't torment himself so....

He passed his hand over his forehead and said: "You know that is unfair, Fräulein Claudia. But I am so often at your house now, and stay so long ..." he began to speak at last with rather less constraint ... "that I don't understand how you and your mother ... After all I am not a very presentable sort of person . . . and you're so considerate of me. . . ."

He was cut short by a ripple of laughter, the dear delightful laughter of a girl, to which she gave herself more gladly as it was just what was wanted to relieve the situation. She could not have him shamed, or, even faintly, humiliated. She shook her head quickly.

"Considerate, my dear Doctor Rohme? And what for? You have never broken a vase, or spilt your tea or your wine on the table cloth at our house. Don't you want us to be glad to see you? Really. . . ."

"But I might do one of those things at any moment, indeed I'm quite surprised I haven't," he said with a smile. Her cheerfulness did him good, and shifted the conversation into a lighter and less highly charged atmosphere.

"Ah, don't be always thinking of what might happen. You think too much about yourself in that way, you know—you must be careful," and she assumed a maternal tone that went through him with an almost physical sweetness. Good God, how he loved her—far too much. But perhaps it was true that they did find him quite a tolerable guest. There was something like joy in his voice as he asked:

"Did your mother really expect me?"

"She certainly did, and I ventured to expect you too. Didn't I invite you to our box? I could not suspect that you would make up your mind to neglect us or me."

She knew quite well that he would understand her jesting tone; he did, and helped her to lighten the conversation. He shook his head smilingly, and a long wisp of reddish hair fell down over his broad white forehead, now freckled by the summer sunshine; he smoothed his thick fair mustache, took up her tone of persiflage which he turned against himself.

"Well, I must confess you were too strong for me. While I was dressing, I proved to myself with algebraic exactitude, that what I was doing was foolish because I did not intend to come to your box."

"That was very wrong of you, Doctor Rohme," she said reprovingly. She appeared to be calmly listening, but she was, in fact, watching him with some care. He was clearly in a state of nervous tension.

"As I finally found myself at the theater," he continued, "and even at the box-office, I tried to buy a seat, but they were all sold out." He explained that he had made up his mind not to read so much. It did him no good, and did not help him, for he had, in the end, to think everything out for himself.

"Ah." She smiled; her lovely gray eyes were strangely expressionless that day.

"There was only standing-room, and boxes. Neither was any good: I did not want to stand, and I could not take a box—it would have been almost an insult."

"Certainly it would," she interjected. "I should never have forgiven you."

She realized she must be careful, but she could not help looking at him again. Could she imagine that he was no longer there? She struggled; of course! Hardly fair, certainly. Meanwhile, she heard him say:

"So I decided to go home."

"Oh!" said she indignantly.

Lights began to flash through the windows; they were near their destination. Then the glasses of his spectacles clouded and she could no longer see his eyes. It was almost discourteous to sit there without a word, absorbed in his thoughts. Perhaps he was pondering on her own inattention. . . . If he only knew! However, he soon went on. . . .

"And then I discovered as I walked up and down the foyer once or twice that for some days I had inwardly made up my mind to spend this evening at the theater and . . . with you, and I felt the force of that tyrannical resolve. Besides the place was crowded with people coming in, not a soul was going out. So I let myself be carried on and found myself outside your box just as I was finally deciding that I had better go home. If I had had to open the door myself, I should probably have found it impossible and retreated to the street; but at that instant an attendant opened it—and you gave me a whispered greeting, for the piece had of course begun. But you gave me your hand, Fräulein Claudia."

She would not let his words sink far into her mind, and she merely replied:

"And why not? You weren't disturbing any one. Boxes are so agreeable because one can do as one likes. Theaters and concerts are only possible when one can listen in peace. But I think we have arrived. At last!" And she gave a sigh of satisfaction. In a room there was space to move about and use one's voice, and the four familiar walls made companionship and conversation easy.... The car swept in a grinding curve through the iron gates and stopped at the front door of the villa. The footman opened the door; the air was cool, and their breath was faintly visible.

Doctor Rohme walked up and down alone in the lovely drawing-room, and pondered—a black conventional figure with broad black necktie and white shirt-front. He knew every piece of furniture and every picture, although his enthusiasm for the latest pictures was somewhat artificial. His restless pacing feet sank silently into the thick blue carpet. He thought of Claudia. His lips moved excitedly as though he were speaking silently to himself. He loved her—that he could no longer doubt. When he was with her, she filled his heart, and then at least he ceased to think of her. Indeed he often had to rouse himself from his absorption, but she had always been so kind. At first he had put it all down to the house, the lovely rooms, where he came to tea with the two of them, and then with one of them alone; and then to the delightful mother; but at last he had discovered that it was the daughter who attracted him and held him fast. Well, he knew his duty: he would go, and go at once. For what would come of it? He could not marry her. He was a young university teacher, making very little money, with a certain reputation in academic circles for a polemical and drastic treatise on the "Will," and no more; and she, Claudia Eg-

geling, was generally reputed to be excessively rich. A for-
tune-hunter, eh? Of course, it was utterly impossible ...
there was nothing for it but to go, irrevocably, and at once.
For how could he explain his reasons? Should he begin:
"Claudia, I love you, but ..." There now—he broke off in
desperation, he was thinking of himself as he had always
done. Presumably she had to give some sort of consent before a man could marry her. How fatuous and stupid he
was!

He stopped before the mirror to confirm the fact that it
was absurd and hopeless for him, Walter Rohme, to look
for a wife. Not merely because he was red-haired, with a
complexion like a copper kettle, and freckled into the bargain—his appearance was merely comic; and he glared with
impotent fury at the object in the mirror that he so longed
to be able to destroy—the commonplace familiar image of a
broad-shouldered man, with thick bushy eyebrows and
mustache, rather like the conventional representations of a
pirate—an impression that was on second glance destroyed
by the blinking gray eyes behind the thick glasses of the
fragile gold spectacles, the pale and hesitating lips beneath
the mustache, the high thin voice, the rounded chin, and
pensive forehead. Indeed this counterpart might well pro-
voke to laughter when he reminded himself that all his
gestures were clumsy and ill-turned, emphatic and yet meaningless, and would never be otherwise. Never in his life
had he been so disgusted with his appearance. ... Claudia
had indeed warmly maintained not long before that she
cared little for a man's appearance, that Adonis and Ab-
salom had probably been stupid—still, he must go. She
hardly knew him, quick-witted as she was. Indeed how
should she, deeply as he now knew her? For only sorrow
gives men vision and unlocks the soul. He walked at her
side, unknown and eternally a stranger. For he could not
talk about himself, and when he tried, shame and self-hatred
thrust a distorting mask upon his face. She could not have
guessed whom he was condemning when he proclaimed

Berlichingen as the type of manhood—how could she? And if she did not know him, he ought not to stay with her, and if she saw him as he was, their relation was equally at an end. Had she even an idea how unreliable he often was, and that in the affairs of daily life he was often guided by the last piece of advice he had been given, she would of course very soon control him, and in everything his will would soon be hers. Inevitably: and the certain result would be that she would first find him ridiculous, and then contemptible. She called him her friend, it was true; they read agreeable philosophic books together, they went to concerts together now and then, she played to him, and they went to the theater or to the Opera as they had done this evening—but that proved nothing. No, Claudia was a determined young woman, she rode, she knew her own mind and thought at once of Götz. What was it she had said not long ago when her mother was late? "I am punctual myself and I demand punctuality in others." It was true, she had a horror of undependable people.... The blood throbbed in his throat and he clenched his hands; he was condemned, and despair seized and shook him.

Thus, in his honest fashion, he tormented his soul with this monstrous psychology.

"You must excuse Mother, my dear Doctor, she has already gone to bed," said Claudia's voice behind him. During the few minutes he had been waiting, she had put on a favorite frock of his, a loose brown house-frock edged with gray-green at the neck and sleeves. This was the image of his dreams, this slim soft being with her quiet movements and her clear quick eyes, in whose irises the brown hue of her dress shone and was transfigured, while the pupils were black with the deep glowing blackness of her hair. Her nose was bold yet delicately molded; Roman she was from head to heel, with the liquid voice of a warbling bird. Yes, this was the woman whom he loved, and must give up.

"You will have to put up with me," she went on.

Then he decided upon a sudden and abrupt departure:

he would say nothing, rush from the house, and settle the affair in a letter—that would be the easiest way.

"I think it would be better if I went now, Fräulein Claudia," he said, and tried to steady his voice so that it should not betray his misery: "It's time now. . . ."

The girl walked quietly to the threshold of the dining-room, turned with her fingers upon the door handle, and observed:

"I think it would be better if you stayed and had some supper with me. There are only eggs, I'm afraid. We always have them when we go to the theater."

She opened the door and went in; he hesitated, shrugged his shoulders helplessly, and followed.

Under a strong light from the white ceiling, the black paneling and the black wood of the furniture looked somewhat formal, but the gay grass-green of the carpet, chair-seats, and curtains softened the gravity of the beautiful room and made it look sedately cheerful. It was a pleasant place in which to sit and eat. The table at which they sat opposite each other was covered with a fine white linen cloth and laid with dishes of inviting bread and rolls, various sorts of red and reddish sausages, glasses for beer and tea, silver cutlery, goblet-shaped egg-cups of thin porcelain, and plates, large and small, of the same fine white china. At this bright delightful table they sat down opposite each other—Claudia Eggeling and Doctor Rohme, she unconstrained and cheerful, bending slightly forward as she ate, a gay and animated figure in her faintly rustling silk frock, he still stiff and starched and angular, black with a white shirt-front, high collar, and red shock of hair that somehow recalled a wood-pecker's crest. . . . They both ate assiduously; it was late—though time had no existence in that shining room—and they were hungry, and even if Claudia had wanted to start a conversation she would have had to rouse her companion. His expressionless fixed vacant gaze betrayed but too clearly that only his bodily self was present, his spirit was ranging over fields unknown. . . . Claudia smiled a little roguish smile, because in the meantime she could indulge herself by gazing at him to her heart's content. She thought him still at the play or somewhere in the world of Goethe; but how startled she would have been if she could have heard her companion's thoughts! He had not gone far, indeed he was in that very room, wandering slowly and gloomily round those two seated figures.

"Why do I feel so mean and full of faults when I am with you, Claudia? Why do you sit there so clear and confident while I humble myself before you? Because I have reached up to you from the lowly place where I was born, entered an air in which my soul can breathe, and because my intellect is greater than yours though it is housed in the body of a slave; because in every problem I see many possible solutions, because I will not let some element within me make a blind choice, because I reflect, and am in the meantime overborne? Because I cannot help smiling, a little contemptuously, I think, at decisions and deeds; because these people so full of pompous energy and so wanting in intelligence are grotesque in their crudity. . . . They have more strength and more success—but since when do success and strength count for anything in the region of the spirit? No, my little Claudia, though they conquer me and laugh, I am the higher type, weaker, subtler, and more spiritual, and what gives your class power over me, what allows Götz to triumph over Weislingen, is no more than the brute force of nature."

But this outburst of pride died down as the meal proceeded, and as he watched her hands, moving so nimbly and gracefully to serve him, the convulsions of a soul thus damned to solitude passed into a peaceful melancholy; nothing remained of it but a soft sad look behind those glittering glasses. This pleasant life would soon be over. Perhaps this was the last time—and he shuddered at his empty rooms which he once looked on as a refuge. They now meant banishment.

While they ate, only a few brief words passed between

them, a little joke, a request for bread, the offer of a dish. But when their first hunger was stayed, the conversation grew more personal. Claudia now decided to open the subject that she had hitherto avoided. While she chose some of the cold sausage from the dish at her side, she observed:

"Well, you found your way to our box at last—but do you often change your mind so many times as that?"

He sighed gently.

"Ah, Fräulein Claudia, I have given up counting these absurd moral defeats. It is not worth the trouble. Have I ever told you the story of the parcel I once sent from Freiburg?"

He started with astonishment as the words fell quite unexpectedly from his lips. How on earth had this foolish and forgotten story suddenly occurred to him? Perhaps it was the prompting of a subconscious search beneath the surface of his mind that had produced so apt an instance of his folly. But he greeted it with grim exultation. It was none the less welcome and timely: by it she would know him, and all would be at an end.

"Never; you must tell it me. Shall I like it? Tea or beer?"

What was all this about a parcel? His demeanor that evening had been eloquent of tension and excitement. She must find out what his trouble was; she felt so much at ease with him that he must not be allowed to torment himself for nothing.

"Tea, please; not too strong, thank you. It's a very foolish and tedious story, and I can't tell it properly, but I'll try. After that I'm sure you won't want to hear anything more of me." And he gloomily enjoyed the double meaning that only he could understand.

"Ah well, we shall see, Doctor," she said gayly.

How small and white her hands were. She wore no ring. And this was the woman he was to lose! A surge of self-pity threatened to overwhelm his resolve, but he beat it down. He felt his fate upon him, and he began bravely.

"Well then, I had been living for a time in Freiburg. It

rained a great deal and I thought I would move elsewhere.
I packed all my things into trunks and cases to be sent on
by a firm of forwarding agents, Sabelberger & Co., who
seemed efficient people and accepted liability." He stopped,
as he noticed her lips were slightly parted as though she
were about to speak, and he was glad to stop.

"Had you all your books at that time?" She was just
peeling an egg, and her fingers moved with the light grace
of dancing children—he could do nothing but watch them.
. . . He recovered himself with a start, and answered:

"Indeed I had, do you suppose I could have endured it
otherwise? Besides it is not very long ago. The books were
in a large case, carefully packed as you may imagine. But I
could not get them all in, and as I reflected that the case
would take some time to reach me, I chose my favorite books
and made a parcel of them, a good stout parcel, stiffened
with cardboard and securely tied with string. It contained
the *Critique of Pure Reason* in a large volume bound in
leather, a first edition of Schopenhauer, a *Meditationes* of
1650, a handsome edition in vellum"—he smiled slyly—"you
know, Descartes—three or four old French editions of
Montaigne and others, a volume of Shakespeare in English,
and so on. Books that I really valued."

What if he stopped and changed the subject before it
was too late? No, that would be cowardly.

"Did they include the La Rochefoucauld you lent me?"

"Yes, that was there. So I took the parcel under my arm
(it seemed very heavy), and carried it to the post office on
a Saturday afternoon. The official I saw had red and dirty
hands but a good heart, for he weighed the package sym-
pathetically and advised me to make it a little lighter, for it
weighed twenty-five pounds and would cost a lot of money
to send by post. He suggested that I might send it by express
instead. So I took back the parcel, thanked him, and went
off to the express-office."

"So you took his advice?" She asked the question with an
almost dream-like air, for she said to herself meanwhile:

If he is so careful of his beloved books, a . . . person that he loved would be very safe with him. . . . And she blushed in confusion.

"I did. As I now knew I was carrying a weight of twenty-five pounds my burden seemed all the heavier. The office was at the railway station about twelve minutes away from the post office. I was received rather hastily, as on Saturday afternoon about half-past five the men are already contemplating their well-earned Sunday rest. The man said he would see that the parcel went off, but did I know what it would cost? And he told me, for railwaymen are kindly fellows. It was twice the postal rate. 'Ah,' said I thoughtfully. 'Yes,' said he, 'that is what it will cost'; and he suggested I might just as well save my money and send it by post or by ordinary freight. For which purpose I had only to cross over to the freight station."

He was in for it now and must go on, however much he longed to stop.

"So you went to the post office again?" she asked with a little laugh. How meticulous men were sometimes; but it was just that which made him so deliciously ingenuous.

"No, I thought I would send it by freight, Fräulein Claudia. I went to the freight station. It was some distance outside the town as such places usually are. I shifted my five and twenty pounds from one arm to the other, but it still weighed just the same. Ah, now you're laughing at me," he said, and laughed too. Perhaps it would be all right after all. And he prayed, to what power he could not tell, that it might be so.

"But didn't it occur to you to pay some one to carry it?"

He looked very boyish when he laughed.

"Yes, as a matter of fact it did, in a vague sort of way, but in the first place there wasn't any one about, and secondly, the two of us and the parcel would have looked so silly marching through the streets. So at last I reached the freight station."

"And there I hope your poor soul found peace?"

The dreadful truth, that his hopes and his half-serious tone had covered up, now stood forth dark and menacing; he gave himself up for lost.

"Yes, Claudia, in a certain sense at least. Well, there I was, and all around me was a complicated system of sheds, and inclines, and vast sliding doors. But all shut. It was, indeed, a quarter past six; I could hear the Cathedral bell ringing for vespers. I walked along an interminable wall, and turned a corner, for I reflected that a place like this is never entirely deserted. Not a dog barked, at which I was relieved, for dogs make me nervous. At last I heard the sound of knocking and tramping feet, and I came upon a few men in railwaymen's caps, lazily pushing some cases about, and in charge of them a man who did not look at all professional, wearing a short jacket and a traveling cap, a sort of jockey's cap. To him I addressed myself. Ah, said he, with immense affability, I need only leave the stuff there, and he would look after it, and see it went off on Monday without fail. I thanked him warmly, left my precious volumes, which he had described as 'stuff,' in his charge, and went home."

His rather thin high voice sounded even hoarser than usual. Claudia noticed it.

"So all was well," she said, smiling. "Will you have some more tea?"

"Yes, I thought so too. Just one more cup, if I may, and that must be the last. I felt quite cheerful; shortly afterwards the sun set, the air was delightfully cool, and I seem to remember whistling as I walked back home."

He stopped for a moment, and turned his hungry eyes away from her face. They had finished supper some while before. What a pity, he thought, as he surveyed the table, now strewn with used plates and dishes, that our needs are fated to leave ugliness behind them. How pretty the little table looked before they started with all its shining white linen and porcelain—and what an uninviting sight it was now. . . . Claudia stood up.

"One moment, my friend, I propose an adjournment; this table disturbs me. Let us take our cups and smoke a cigarette in the next room."

His delight at finding that she felt as he did left him without a word to say; he merely picked up his cup and followed her slowly and cautiously into the red drawing-room. And as they went backwards and forwards once or twice to fetch what they needed, these casual acts seemed to awaken in him the phantom of a hope. They had something in common, perhaps more than they knew—why should he not make plain to her that in those days he had lived the life of the mind, and had been quite blank and indifferent to the world outside? Why should he merely accuse himself, why shouldn't he excuse and explain himself as well? Why shouldn't he confess that for her sake he would act, and act without compunction or delay? No! he must not. When she had seen him as he was, then she could decide. He need not be certain she would reject him; but hope had nearly gone.

Between them was a small table on which stood a lamp with an orange-colored shade; they sat down in two deep arm-chairs, and round them the room and all that it contained seemed vague and far away in the red half-light. A tall clock ticked with admonitory persistence.

"Please—you prefer cigars," said Claudia, already blowing white fragrant cigarette smoke from between her lips.

"I really oughtn't to smoke.... Thank you, I have a match. Where was I?... If you really want me to go on. As I warned you, it is a tedious story."

If she had had enough and turned the subject, then he could in honor break off the matter and stage the farewell scene for another day. All he wanted now was to enjoy this hour, and watch the lovely creature smoking, her face flecked with golden light behind the veil of smoke.

"Not in the least, go on; though I don't see that there can be any more to tell. The story's over, and you are going cheerfully home."

Yes, the story was indeed over, utterly and absolutely over, and the very word seemed to quiver in his mind.

"Very well then. I was whistling, and suddenly I stopped —it was the *Tannhäuser March,* I remember—and I shuddered at a thought that had come into my mind. I suddenly realized how careless I had been. The man had given me no receipt, no paper to show that he had received a parcel from Doctor Rohme. And he bore no recognizable sign of being a railway official. After all, the fact of being in charge of a few men in railway-caps, or rather of watching them while they worked, was no proof of respectability. The fellow had only to open the parcel to scatter my beautiful books among all the dealers in the town the very next day, and I did not even know his name; all I could say about him was that he had worn a short jacket and a jockey-cap, which was not much. I had already gone some distance, but I stopped and tried to decide to go back——"

"Which would have been a very sensible thing to do," put in Claudia reprovingly.

"Then I remembered that the men in railway-men's caps who had been working in such an such a place at a quarter past six could certainly be traced. They were witnesses, three reliable witnesses. That would be enough. They would, if necessary, have to swear that I had given a large round parcel into the charge of jockey-cap. Comforted at last, I again pursued my way home, for I was tired and hungry." And he smiled faintly as the memories of the past came over him.

"But you would not have got your books back through them either," she said, in a matter-of-fact tone. It was now too late, she noticed, for the talk that she had put off once before; well, to-morrow would do.

"Probably not, or at any rate not easily. But I reckoned on the man in the short jacket thinking of them too. They constituted a moral quantity. But the adjective gave a new turn to my thoughts. Moral? But money was stronger than morality. Poor people prefer money to morality; workmen are poor people; consequently . . ." He had to stop for a moment. While he was speaking, he became aware that from thenceforward he was condemned to monologue and silence; and he caught his breath. He looked at her; she thought he wanted her to speak, and she innocently drew the inference, while she reflected that his eyes were very kind. "Consequently, he would pay them to say nothing." (And his forehead was finely shaped as well as intelligent.)

"Of course," he cried, with rather exaggerated emphasis, "they could be bribed. Jockey-cap would get a respectable sum for my books, he could afford to sacrifice a few marks and my witnesses would be as silent as the grave, as the phrase goes. The probability of this so impressed me that I stopped, overcame my hunger and weariness, and tramped back again. Shortly after a quarter to seven I reached the place where I had handed over my package. Not a soul to be seen. I wandered through all the warehouses. Not a sign of any one. I shouted, but in vain. At last, at a quarter past seven, full of disgust and misery at my carelessness, twice as tired and hungry as before, I turned to go home. At eight o'clock I reached the town. I thought of consulting my landlord's mother, or the police, but I was ashamed to, and besides I was sick of the whole business."

She found herself wondering faintly why he was telling her all this; it was not very amusing. But she was ashamed of her thought and made up for it by saying with obvious sympathy:

"I quite understand."

He silently flicked the ash from his cigar, and went on, more rapidly as the story hurried to the precipice that must engulf it, and as he spoke, his eyes rested on her hands that were lying quietly on the table.

"That night I slept badly. Next morning I got up at six o'clock, though it was Sunday, and even on week-days I used not to get up before ten, as I was staying in Freiburg for a rest after an illness. Well, I got up at six, and went to the freight station. Naturally I did not find a soul. I repeated this futile journey at ten, half-past eleven, and four, each time with the same result. I had ceased to think; I was simply obsessed with the idea of getting back my own."

Again he was silent and inspected his cigar which was near its end. She was watching him with a reflective and faintly mocking expression: he was really making a great deal of fuss about all this.

"Well?" she said at last. He started.

"I have nearly finished," he said, and looked down once more from her face to the carpet. "My train went at shortly after nine on Monday. On Monday at half-past six I was standing in the office of the freight station, and of course I saw my parcel as soon as I came in. It lay in its proper place; the man had done what was necessary, and it was ready to send off."

He stopped and did not look up.

"Then all was well," she said indifferently, for she felt he was waiting for a word. He propped his head on his hand and looked down at the table.

"And what do you think I did then?"

"You made your excuses and went to the railway station feeling much relieved in mind," she answered without hesitation.

"Well, I didn't. I took back the parcel, saying it was urgent, and carried it to the post office."

Claudia seemed to stiffen as she sat, and sank back slowly in her chair.

"You carried it to the post office?" she said in amazement, and nearly burst into mocking laughter, but restrained herself.

"Yes, to a different post office. I didn't like to go to the first one, you see." And he nodded several times without lifting his head from his hand or raising his eyes from the table, smiled sadly, and once more said "Yes."

Claudia's eyes were eloquent of the fear that sank slowly into her soul like a bucket into a well, and mockery and shocked contempt wrote a wry line round her mouth. She was angry, and in her heart flung him a question that she did not utter : Why had he told her such a futile story? She stared at him with hard eyes and saw nothing. The great clock ticked unceasingly; Doctor Rohme sat with bent head looking at the reddish reflection of the lamp on the table-cover. There sat the hero of this exploit, she thought angrily. Why didn't he defend himself? Where was all his cleverness and charm? He, who had so often led her to believe that he could preserve her life from ugliness, and let nothing vex or disquiet her, why was he displaying himself to-day as so feckless and so weak? There he sat, with bent head, like a man condemned, and did not stir. . . .

And then she knew. A sudden flash illuminated everything; she saw him as he was, clear and undisguised. Her joy rose up within her like a bucket from a sunlit fountain, brimming with golden water. She felt a warmth and soft pressure at her heart and knew that it was joy. Slowly she lifted her hand and stretched it towards him across the table, until her delicate finger-tips touched the back of his hands. He started out of his dead despair, looked uncomprehendingly into her happy eyes, caught his breath in a choking gasp as he understood, and kissed her hand with a long burning kiss of deliverance.

"You must go now," she said, and got up: "Thank you for your story, I liked it very much."

Her eyes still shone, and he still held her hand; for he was saved.

"Come to tea to-morrow, and we will talk about Weislingen, and play some music, or do whatever you like."

There was a deep thrill in her voice that he had never heard before, and he pressed the beloved hand.

"I will," he said.

was angry, and in her heart flung him a question that she did not utter: Why had he told her such a futile story? She stared at him with hard eyes and saw nothing. The great clock ticked unceasingly; Doctor Rolure sat with bent head looking at the reddish reflection of the lamp on the table-cover. There sat the hero of this exploit, she thought angrily. Why didn't he defend himself? There was all his cleverness and charm? He, who had so often led her to believe that he could preserve her life from ugliness, and let nothing vex or disquiet her, why was he displaying himself to-day as so feckless and so weak? There he sat, with bent head, like a man condemned, and did not stir.

And then she knew. A sudden flash illuminated everything; she saw him as he was, clear and undisguised. Her joy rose up within her like a bucket from a sunlit fountain, brimming with golden water. She felt a warmth and soft pressure at her heart and knew that it was joy. Slowly she lifted her hand and stretched it towards him across the table, until her delicate finger-tips touched the back of his hands. He started out of his dead despair, looked uncompre-hendingly into her happy eyes, caught his breath in a choking gasp as he understood, and kissed her hand with a long burning kiss of deliverance.

"You must go now," she said, and got up: "Thank you for your story, I liked it very much."

Her eyes still shone, and he still held her hand; for he was saved.

"Come to tea to-morrow, and we will talk about Weis-lingen, and play some music; we do whatever you like."

There was a deep thrill in her voice that he had never heard before, and he pressed the beloved hand.

"I will," he said.

Modern Library of the World's Best Books

COMPLETE LIST OF TITLES IN

THE MODERN LIBRARY

For convenience in ordering use number at right of title

MODERN LIBRARY GIANTS

A series of full-sized library editions of books that formerly were available only in cumbersome and expensive sets.

THE MODERN LIBRARY GIANTS REPRESENT A SELECTION OF THE WORLD'S GREATEST BOOKS

Many are illustrated and some of them are over 1200 pages long.

G1. TOLSTOY, LEO. War and Peace.

G2. BOSWELL, JAMES. Life of Samuel Johnson.

G3. HUGO, VICTOR. Les Miserables.

G4. THE COMPLETE POEMS OF KEATS AND SHELLEY.

G5. PLUTARCH'S LIVES (The Dryden Translation).

G6.
G7. } GIBBON, EDWARD. The Decline and Fall of the Roman
G8. } Empire (Complete in three volumes)

G9. YOUNG, G. F. The Medici (Illustrated).

G10. TWELVE FAMOUS RESTORATION PLAYS (1660-1820) (Congreve, Wycherley, Gay, Goldsmith, Sheridan, etc.)

G11. THE ESSAYS OF MONTAIGNE (The E. J. Trechmann Translation).

G12. THE MOST POPULAR NOVELS OF SIR WALTER SCOTT (Quentin Durward, Ivanhoe and Kenilworth).

G13. CARLYLE, THOMAS. The French Revolution (Illustrated).

G14. BULFINCH'S MYTHOLOGY (Illustrated).

G15. CERVANTES. Don Quixote (Illustrated).

G16. WOLFE, THOMAS. Look Homeward, Angel.

G17. THE POEMS AND PLAYS OF ROBERT BROWNING.

G18. ELEVEN PLAYS OF HENRIK IBSEN.

G19. THE COMPLETE WORKS OF HOMER.

G20. THE LIFE AND WRITINGS OF ABRAHAM LINCOLN.

G21. SIXTEEN FAMOUS AMERICAN PLAYS.

G22. CLAUSEWITZ, KARL VON. On War.

G23. TOLSTOY, LEO. Anna Karenina.

G24. LAMB, CHARLES. The Complete Works and Letters of Charles Lamb.

G25. THE COMPLETE PLAYS OF GILBERT AND SULLIVAN.

G26. MARX, KARL. Capital.

G27. DARWIN, CHARLES. The Origin of Species and The Descent of Man.

G28. THE COMPLETE WORKS OF LEWIS CARROLL.

G29. PRESCOTT, WILLIAM H. The Conquest of Mexico and The Conquest of Peru.

G30. MYERS, GUSTAVUS. History of the Great American Fortunes.